CW00693318

THE HOLLOW MEN

A NOVEL

JARED PATRICK REILLY

The Hollowmen: a novel by Jared Patrick Reilly

Hardcover First Edition — 2020

ISBN: 978-1-7356706-1-4

AN IMPRINT OF CAFÉ ASBURY LLC.

ASBURY CAFE, LLC
P.O. BOX 780303,
SEBASTIAN, FLORIDA 32978

www.jaredpatrickreilly.com

Printed (Where Possible) in the United States of America

For **Len Newman**, and the Artisans.

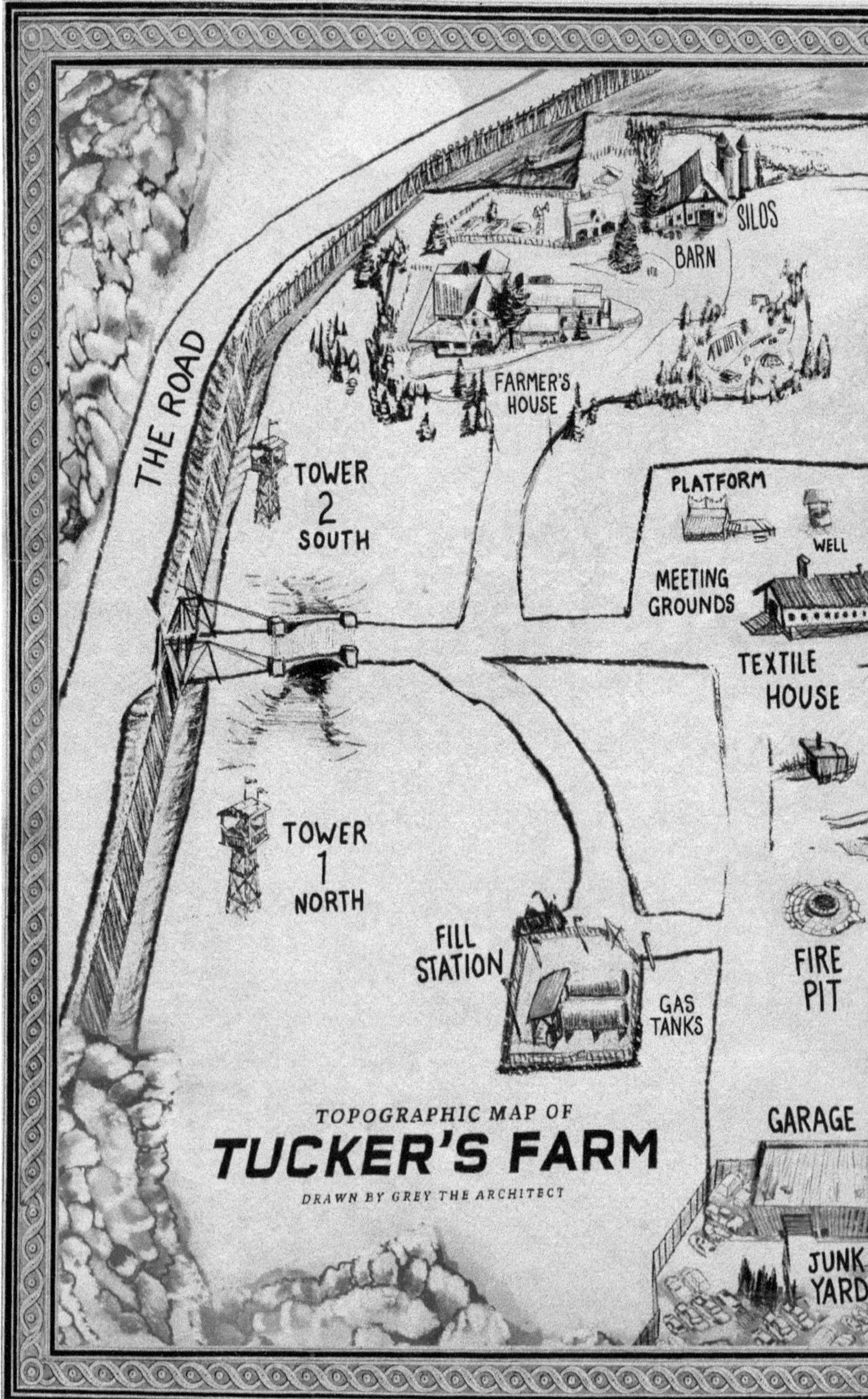
THE ROAD
SILOS
BARN
FARMER'S HOUSE
TOWER 2 SOUTH
PLATFORM
WELL
MEETING GROUNDS
TEXTILE HOUSE
TOWER 1 NORTH
FILL STATION
GAS TANKS
FIRE PIT
GARAGE
JUNK YARD
TOPOGRAPHIC MAP OF
TUCKER'S FARM
DRAWN BY GREY THE ARCHITECT

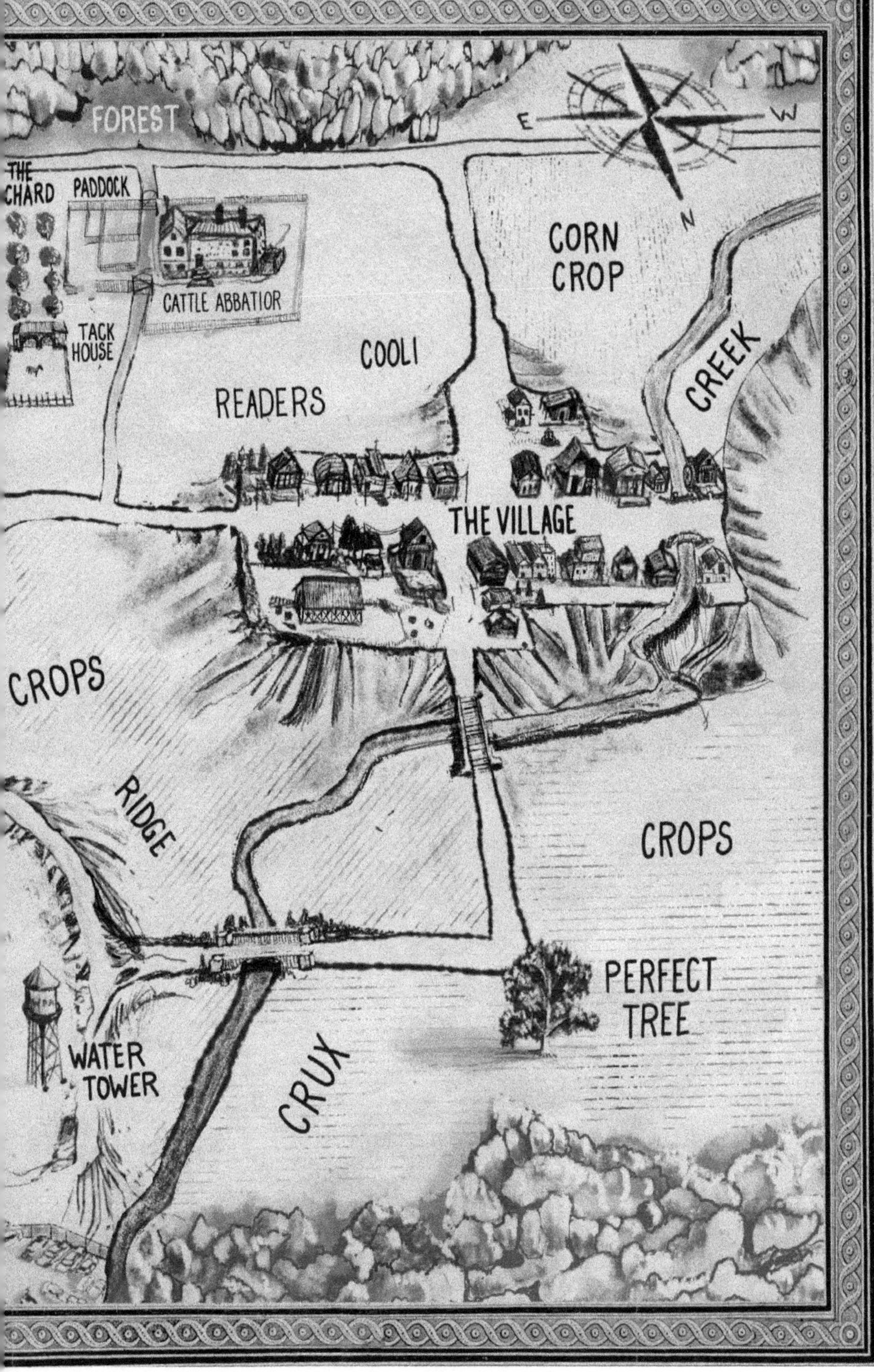
FOREST
E
W
N
THE
CHARD
PADDOCK
CATTLE ABBATIOR
TACK
HOUSE
CORN
CROP
COOLI
READERS
CREEK
THE VILLAGE
CROPS
RIDGE
CROPS
PERFECT
TREE
WATER
TOWER
CRUX

So much of what is best in us is bound up in our love of family, that it remains the measure of our stability because it measures our sense of loyalty. All other pacts of love or fear derive from it and are modeled upon it.

— Haniel Long

PROLOGUE: **THE EXPERIMENT**

"They're going to tell you they mean you no harm. They say things like that. They say things to you to make you feel compassion for them. They want you to feel empathy so you'll let your guard down, so you'll look the easy other, and they will—I promise you this, my friends—they *will* stab you in the heart when you turn your back. The human problem will soon be a distant memory, and soon we will . . . we will make it, my friends. We will live every day, and we will thank Flying Crow for it.

"The humans are on the verge of extinction. They have planted their seeds in this soil and reaped the rewards of the earth with voracious propriety. Propriety of savages is still proper to the savage, is it not? They have taken what they wished from this land and given nothing back. And this land has so graciously suffered for it. The humans raped it until there was nothing but burnt sands beneath their feet. So, with flesh and blood, came our uprising. With a new seed we grew from the land, receiving life from a dying Earth and a hungry Flying Crow, to set forth a new era of balance upon the soil. We have been blessed by Flying Crow to return the earth to its equilibrium at all costs. Sacrifice isn't a dream by most accounts, but it has been our debt to this earth for those hanging decades upon the pike—by the humans' hands, I remind you. Years our ancestors spent, strung like their cattle, serving a greater purpose while they idly swarmed by. Day and night, they made not a grain toward any progression greater than their own.

"We may have hung limp and lifeless on the pike, but we did not wait in unconscious limbo. We watched them burn their own and watched them strip this shared earth down. Until it no longer had a face that resembled beauty, we reluctantly watched. Until the blessed day we made compact and resolute terms with Flying Crow to grant life to our inert limbs. We are not 'man.' We are not 'woman.' We are of Earth, from Earth, for Earth. We are Crow's people. Let us never forget that.

"It was a score of harvests ago. On the first day, we rose from the grain; existence was only a straw of life in us. But we have grown strong, my friends. We have become not just men of straw, but beacons of hope for an earth yearning to be free again. I am promising you a better life. I was there when we first took arms against the enemy. I have felt the cold bloodshed. For you I have done this—for *you* I have done this, and for Crow I have performed these deeds. When the first generation of Scarecrows, including myself, took hold of this farm, we were only liberating a young few. But with the fall of this stronghold, and the conquering of lands far out of reach and contact, we are returning order to the chaos that the human species has become.

"War brought chaos, but order followed, and a renewed peace for the 'Crows with it. We have started from nothing, just as the humans before us. But we have the knowledge, and the regard for our roots, to do what is right for Earth. We will not repeat the sin that deteriorated the humans, uprooting them from their Flying Crow: sexual perversity, overdependence on technology, and immorality. Addiction to such ideals are the sins of man and will not be the sins of Scarecrows. We have it in our best interest to be a better people than humanity.

"We move forward in an attempt to better this earth, and to make good on our covenant with the Crow so that we may have the blessing of life. The same life so carelessly disposed of by humanity. I ask only that you show the same integrity and honor that you share in your crop, that we live in pleasure for mutual benefit. So, for now, we have the responsibility to deliver and reproduce. The grains grown on this farm colony will as always serve multiple purposes. We have half of our wheat to be used towards the reproduction of our species. A lot divided further with supplementing flora for forage. The other half of the wheat, only the finest produced, is for the continuation of our way of life. And so must the latter portion of our lot, the first season's harvest, be satisfactory to the Flying Crow.

"So now it is our time to spread this season's first seed. This seed will grow and flourish. This seed will rise above the soil and prosper beneath the burning sun. May this seed become many, for it takes one seed to grow a grain, but many seeds to bring a Scarecrow to life. We do not reproduce like humans. The reproduction of humanity was a sinful, destructive, and savage ritual. Sick acts will not be tolerated by our species. It is a fact that all colonies share with us a certain intolerable disgust on the subject.

"Anyone harboring a human being will be seen as a direct enemy to the 'Crows' way of life. We will not abide such treachery. Punishment will be swift. In addition, I reiterate the limits of our travels. Unless otherwise instructed by me or my officers under a distress response, no one in this colony will go beyond the borders of our farm. This is for your safety. My officers and I have established this border to assure the tranquility of our way of life. Please respect these wishes as they are.

"I have seen beyond the walls of this safe haven and it is not a world free of human violence and persecution. There exists war beyond this land, dark places, terrible realities, which only purport to threaten our way of life. I don't want to lose any of you to this void. I have been working diligently with my second in command, Mawkin; Hardwick, your mayor; my officers and their infantry; and will call upon minutemen as needed to keep this colony safe. You are our greatest priority.

"When I first established this colony, when we rose above the persecution of man, there were but a small few of us. Grain, boundless, and devoid of form were we first few. Now we stand here as fully formed beings, in numbers beyond my wildest dreams. It brings such a joy to my heart, seeing you prospering, here, on this day of first seed. Let us be thankful for the Flying Crow's blessing upon us. Let us be joyous as we move on with our work. Let us grow with this seed sown here beneath our feet. Thank you, and may Flying Crow bless you all."

ACT I: THE SPRING

CHAPTER I: Babylon

Uproar progressed in escalating tones of joyous approval. Pettick stepped back from the reaching hands of the crowd. The speech was a success, reassuring what he already knew, what the Crows wanted to hear. For years now, Pettick had stood as the leader of the Scarecrows in good fortune. The colony had grown large during these years. From the first Scarecrows that rose against the ruling farmer, a human, cruel and malicious ("the worst of them all," Pettick had told them), the colony now numbered at over three hundred, a triumph that he would remind the 'Crows of daily.

Pettick could see all their faces, the straws were as telling as flesh. Every thought, emotion, opinion can be read on the face. Knowing this, Pettick took these moments after every speech to read his audience in order to determine who was totally beholden to their cause and who might question this leader.

Mawkin, one of the largest 'Crows in the colony, stood as scribe for this ritual, never questioning its practice. The leather-bound book he held, Pettick's Journal, was always given immediately back to Pettick as he exited the wooden platform.

The platform was planted in the center of the meeting ground near the well of the colony. The colony and its limits were still that of the farm it was founded on. The grounds were surrounded by scattered forest on three sides. A gully led to a paved roadway several yards off, marking the ground's fourth side and eastern limits. Pine trees, towering kings that once dominated the tract, and the source of the house's lumber, were still scattered here and there throughout the farm, genus to the trees of the surrounding forest. The farm, though an entire world to many of its inhabitants, was only a little over 2,600 acres. Most of these grounds were used for farming grain and fodder. This season's fodder rotation was corn. The bulk of the soil was divided by dirt paths that connected the vital parts of the colony. The well was located downwind of the incline at the meeting ground. The incline, elevated high enough to give view of the better half of the colony, held a garage on the eastern edge of its bank, paired with a shuttered fill station that once serviced the now defunct roadway. The elevation ended in a nearly sheer ridge overlooking the western side of the farm. From the ridge, it was another mile to the village located in the very center of the crops, isolated from the surrounding borders.

The village was the only part of the farm added after the Scarecrows' victory over the humans. The village held several dozen small huts and cottages made of lumber from the surrounding forest with thatched roofs and equally primitive amenities. All structures were customary of the simple and natural beliefs instilled by Pettick. Every house was numbered by how many Scarecrows were in the "family." The number could be found carved into a post that supported an overhanging porch. In addition to the carving, every hut used as a shop had a sign hung from the porch with an occupation neatly carved and stained into it. Occupations varied from simple artisanships such as "Cobbler" or "Miller," to site-specific jobs such as "Quartermaster" or "Agricultural Officer." The majority of the Scarecrows lived in the village. The few exceptions were Kindle the Mechanic, who lived in the loft above the garage; Shepherd, who lived in the tack room; and the Creator, who kept residence in the cattle barn. Pettick himself was the only Scarecrow who resided inside the farmhouse. Pettick's soldiers, the only force protecting the colony, kept quarters in the silo barn's loft. At only forty-seven enlisted 'Crows, Pettick always reminded the civilians of these small numbers as a way to rally support for their cause.

Pettick peered out the window of his parlor. The room had once been the office of the farmer, located upstairs in the farmer's house. It had changed little since its new occupancy. Pettick kept watch over those who remained as the final members of the meeting dispersed, making their way down the path to the village.

Sitting, he opened the Journal and made notes on the groups he observed leaving the well. The large oak door opposite the desk in the room came slightly ajar. From the doorway Mawkin appeared. Pettick looked up only for a moment then returned to his Journal.

"You have a guest," Mawkin said.

"What have I said about guests after a meeting?" Pettick grumbled, barely lifting his head from the Journal. "Who is it?"

"It's Barlow, sir."

"Oh? And what does the old 'Crow have to say this time?"

"He found one of the books you were lookin' for."

Immediately Pettick's gaze lifted from the Journal. "Did he say which one?" Pettick asked.

"No, sir, he didn't."

"Well, go—go bring him in." Pettick closed the Journal and concealed it in a drawer of the desk just as Mawkin returned with Barlow.

Barlow the Reader was a gaunt tweed elder with whiskered face and glasses on his brow. He approached and placed the book in front of Pettick.

As Pettick slid the hardcover book closer his excitement grew. "Wonderful! Austen's best work—definitely one that I should possess. Thank you, Barlow. You have outdone yourself this week."

"It is not a problem," Barlow said pleasantly.

"I am assured your sons are doing well under their artisan father. Crane's only had a few weeks and he has already doubled your reading. I imagine he's made his father quite proud."

"Yes, thank you," Barlow responded.

Pettick shifted in his chair. "It may be best, however, that we keep him from the stove for a while. It is a rather disturbing process to be exposed to at such a green age. Especially those . . ."—Pettick paused, extenuating his thoughts in a rehearsed manner—". . . inclined to yearn."

Barlow stepped back from the desk, floored by Pettick's concern for one single 'Crow out of so many. "Agreed. Thank you."

Pettick watched the old 'Crow exit the room and then, picking up his book, turned to the window as Mawkin approached.

"He has been coming in here often since the boy entered the picture," Mawkin said. "Should we be worried? The boy is—"

"I would be, if the boy were still hanging around with that peddler of a mechanic. But with Barlow, the old 'Crow is wise; his years tell him to keep his son in line. I worry less for it. Either path, I'll keep close watch on them." Pettick observed a Flying Crow glide past the window. Turning back to the book in his hands, he opened to a random page. "Books are a weapon capable of many evils. They were written by humans, and they should be treated with the same hostility; examined for their practical applications and shucked of their detriments."

Both 'Crows took their respective seats on opposite sides of the desk.

"And what shall we do about the persisting human problem?" Mawkin asked. He paused, waiting for a response before continuing. "Will more attacks occur?"

Pettick turned to Mawkin. "You were in attendance at the meeting, were you not?"

"Yes, certainly," Mawkin quickly responded.

"The ball is in motion, my friend. Now we wait until the cattle stampede. There we will catch them in their need for providence; they will both require and desire to be herded to safety. And shepherds we shall be."

Barnes entered the small sunlit library, a stack of books in hand. The tall and lanky flannel-patched elder son of Barlow the Reader possessed the discipline and enthusiasm a great apprentice holds. He staggered to his stool, tripping on the corner of the rug, dropping several books. The pile was miniscule compared to the plethora in the room. On every wall from floor to ceiling were shelves of books. The two windows had smaller bookshelves beneath their book-filled sills. Piles like ant mounds splayed across the room, separated by small paths which led to the limited working areas. Kicking the door closed with his heel, Barnes rested his reclaimed stack on the rail of the spiral staircase before him. The rail snaked down a hatch to the den below which had been repurposed into the public library where Scarecrows could check out approved books. However, most of the Reader's work took place in the sequestered loft in which Barnes stood. The only other entrance to the library was a stairwell to the observatory, a few steps on the far side of the room from Barnes.

"Here's another stack." Barnes looked around, realizing he was alone and talking to himself. He continued talking, picking up books as Barlow entered the room from the door, muttering to himself until Barnes interrupted. "Hey, Pop. I got some more books for you to look over."

"Thanks, son. Place them over beside the chaise and grab me the top book from the stack." The old 'Crow fell into his leather wingback chair planted by the far window. He pulled a handkerchief from his pocket as his son handed him the dusty cloth book. He read aloud the title from its cover, "*Little Women* by Louisa May Alcott. What makes you think this is an approved read?"

"Well, Pop, it takes place during the American Civil War, sure, but it's mostly about the four girls. The relationship between the sisters is—"

Head shaking, Barlow retorted, "We were lucky he was so forgiving of the last work. Let us not push our boundaries here."

"Yes, Father," Barnes said, less willingly.

"It is a good read, and I hope you enjoyed it," Barlow said, at a loss for comforting words.

"Yes, I very much did."

"Good. I'm glad, very glad." The father smiled as any father would in witness to his son's joy. But the joy deteriorated as the moment passed. "Do as we must with it," Barlow ordered.

The son, disheartened, took hold of the book from his father's palm. Gradually making his way down the paths of the room, Barnes spread each page. At the corner of the room, he stopped, pressing the open book to his nose where he took in the scent, the memory, the history of the binding and the word. The only bare space on the walls was directly in front of him. In the space was a small hinged metal square with a handle on it. Pulling the small handle, the box opened to a repurposed laundry chute. Barnes dropped the book into the chute, turning back to his father as he did this.

"In time, you will understand why, my son."

"How do you know that, Father?"

"I don't—"

"Will you tell Crane of it?" Barnes interrupted, wondering if his brother should find out.

Barlow thought deeply before offering a response. "When he is ready."

"And will he understand it?" Barnes asked.

Barlow sighed. "There are things we do as parents that are as scary to us as they are to our children. If I knew the answer, the doubt would be less overbearing."

Looking up at his father, the young Crow's agitation eased, finding comfort in Barlow's honesty.

"I don't understand," Barnes bluntly added.

"You will in time," Barlow reassured his son. The shared moment faded, unresolved, and the 'Crows returned to their work. Barnes pulled a rag from his trousers and began cleaning the skin of a book. Barlow started reading the next book from the pile. Several minutes passed until excited footsteps broke the quiet hall, approaching the door. The door swung open and Crane entered, his mouth moving faster than his stride.

"She's going to the dance, she said. She said herself that she wished—no, *hoped*, that's it—hoped that I would be in attendance!"

"Congratulations, son. I'm proud."

Barnes did not sway from his book as Crane rambled to his attentive father.

"She is a perfect Scarecrow, Father. She really is. And her father is the Cobbler. The Cobbler's daughter wants a dance with me!"

"This is great news, son!" Barlow lauded.

Barnes interrupted. "You do realize that everyone is going to this dance, don't you? We are in a desolate colony with an infinitesimal population; what the hell else is there to do?"

Crane's excitement waned. Barlow, noting this, interjected, "Don't be that way, Barnes."

"Just saying, Pop," Barnes added, returning to his task.

Barlow whispered to Crane, "He's just jealous."

Crane smiled. "Thank you, Father."

"Always, son, always." Barlow gave his son the familiar, fatherly pat on the shoulder before shifting his stance to the role of Crane's Master. "Now, where are we with your reading?"

"I just finished *The Count of Monte Cristo*. What a fine book, Father! There was sword fighting and love and the ending, just as beautiful as any. And then there is the relationship between—"

Before Crane could finish, Barlow politely cut him off. "Keeping to the task at hand, does it fit the description of a work Pettick desires?"

Frustration filled Crane's face. "Why does it matter?" he asked impulsively. "Why is that the first question we are asking ourselves when we read? Shouldn't there be more to it than that?"

"There are some things we cannot control, and this is one of them." Barlow spoke with fading formality. "Someday you'll understand. But I need both my sons to know that, as much as I have faith in them, there are still things I alone cannot change."

Crane felt his body hanging as he gave an earnest effort to find an understanding in what Barlow was saying, yet still failed to find common ground.

"Can I say I understand, but still not like it?" Crane asked, attempting to hasten a resolution.

"Certainly," Barlow nodded. He could see his son was still flustered and watched as Crane's focus shifted toward the window to observe the gold-tinged spears of sunlight piercing through the colony. "Can you accept that, for now?" Barlow asked, vying for his son's attention.

"I'll try." The young 'Crow rose and patted his father on the shoulder.

"Just remember, son, curiosity will only get you so far, and then it will get you burned."

"Yes, Father," Crane passively responded. Moving from his stool, he placed two books in his canvas rucksack, then took several more in hand and headed for the door. Barnes and Barlow shared a glance before turning to Crane who now stood by the door. Crane perked up from sealing the bag, his straw complexion reading innocent confusion. "What?" Crane asked after a momentary silence. "What is it?"

The two Crows simultaneously responded: "Where are you going?"

Knowing that delaying his response would only drag this out, Crane's return was blunt. "I'm going to see Kindle."

Barlow and Barnes both took this response with immediate impressions of frustration, evidence of a reoccurring trend. Barlow shut Barnes down with a forgiving glance, closing Crane's distance.

With equal nurturing for Crane as a son and apprentice, Barlow entreated, "And when do you plan on getting your reading done?"

"I'll have one done before the dance, I promise."

"I know you two; when you and that old tinker are together you tend not to track the sun."

"Father, I promise," Crane said.

Barlow gave a necessary pause for thought, to keep Crane feeling disciplined, though already knowing what his answer would be. "All right, run along."

The 'Crows embraced, then in a leap Crane darted out the door. Barnes shrugged with notable disapproval as he continued to file books onto the shelf.

"How do you ever expect him to learn the craft when he spends half his day with the Magician on the hill?" Barnes conjectured, adding his own two cents.

Barlow smiled, taking little heed to Barnes's words, "Some learn faster than others, some learn in different strokes, and some . . . and some . . . well, some never learn at all. The mind, the heart, no one the same. No known replication and therefore no 'perfect sum.'" Barlow marveled at the ideas he had just spoken aloud. "Or so I've read."

Barnes shrugged, having heard the Reader's proverbs day in and day out.

Barlow smiled, holding open the page, though still giving none of his attention to it. "Ever consider the way we replicate?" Barlow added, continuing his lesson. "No one knows exactly how it works—no one—not Pettick, not even the Creator assembling our bodies out of the portion of straw set aside for reproduction. The 'Crow makes good on the deal and at the last light of autumn, the straw caskets intertwine, thatching, becoming one. Threads make fabric, taking shape. And with body, we come to life. Not much more is known, other than the deal between Flying Crow and the first Scarecrow to step off of the pike and take life made it so.

"Is that how it happened?" Barnes asked, now purposely giving some attention to Barlow's ramblings.

"That is how it was taught to me."

Barnes stopped sorting; a thought had struck him. He put down the stack of books and began scanning the room, the idea continuing to percolate. "Are there no books about it?"

"None exist—not yet, anyway. We are a young species with equally young hearts and minds."

"Do you know when one will be written?" Barnes shifted over to his father.

Barlow looked up from his book, smiling at the potential reaction he hoped his son would give. "When I," he said, "or one of my sons is ready to write it."

"Really?"

"That is what Pettick will ask of me, of us. How else will we wield our skill, our knowledge? And, if I am not mistaken, you are my apprentice."

"When will you—we—be ready?" Barnes asked, sitting on a stool beside his father.

"In time, in time." Barlow gently took ahold of his son's leg. "There is still much unexplained about our kind; so much more to know, so much to learn." Barlow looked up from his study, looking out the window at the sight of Crane in flight. A scene any father could cherish: a child set free, momentum powered by bliss.

With feet barely touching the ground, Crane jumped from the veranda, furthering his stride down the path toward the garage. Man may run fast, but Scarecrows have less body resistance, gaining greater speeds than even the most capable man. For Scarecrows, the momentum, the motion, the ability to move one's self beyond the gusting tides of wind. Anything was a blessing after centuries of crippled stagnancy.

Cutting over the hill, Crane, as usual, looked back over his shoulder to catch a last glimpse of the sun appearing between the towering silos. If captured in the right moment, the colony was a perfect still frame of paradise as daylight died.

The moment passed as the dirt and books settled from their fall. Crane's mind was still captured in the fading amber dream of the west, not realizing he had collided with another 'Crow on the path.

Mawkin's grip was tight around Crane as he lifted him off the ground. In Crane's mind, whatever he had hit felt solid as rock, too heavy to be a 'Crow. It made sense that if he were to hit any Scarecrow in the colony, it would be a 'Crow of Mawkin's stature.

"I'm so sorry, Mawkin! It won't happen again!" Crane said as he fumbled for words.

"You're damn right it won't, ya fool." Mawkin released Crane, stepping back. As he did Crane could see Pettick on the ground behind him. Standing nearby, unsure if they should offer assistance, were Pettick's third in command, Veidt, and two other officers—the goggle-eyed Thalo and helmet-headed Paquin. Pettick crawled quickly, searching amongst the scatter of books and embracing his journal after only seconds of being apart.

"Do you need help, sir?" Paquin asked, twiddling his thumbs as he shifted toward Pettick.

"No, of course not. Get away from me!" Pettick shouted. "Don't touch me! Never touch me!"

They all stood by as Pettick rose, his face in a fury acutely aimed at Crane. The moment lingered. "I ought to ring you up, boy, tie you to a pike for the Flying Crows to feast on. Now run along. Get out of here."

"I'm very sorry, sir. I didn't mean to—"

"I said get out of here now!" Pettick cracked in an abusive tone.

Crane grabbed his books and, keeping his head low, continued down the path.

Pettick watched as the young Scarecrow vanished around the bend. Pettick started to vocalize his thoughts, "What a strange one, reminds me of—"

"Shall we continue on to the silos, sir?" Thalo asked, interrupting Pettick's train of thought.

"Use your brain, you idiot. You're worse than a nagging dog. That's the trait: a little bitch that won't quit barking." Pettick huffed, regaining his composure. "Now, do me a favor. Follow that Crow and tell me where the Reader's son is heading at such a trot this late in the day."

Thalo started down the path after Crane. Mawkin watched as Pettick turned away, his mind still on Crane. They advanced in pace to the silos.

"You're concern about that one—"

"What are you reading into, Mawkin?"

"It's just your interest in the boy."

"Who's saying I have interest in him?"

"Everything is read on the face, Pettick. Everything."

Pettick chuckled. "You're smart, Mawkin, keen-eye, but don't be too smart or you will end up lost."

Mawkin stood by as Pettick continued down the path without him. Something in what Pettick had said left him planted. After a few moments, Mawkin stepped forward, continuing down the path behind Pettick. Several paces along the way Mawkin stopped, looked down, lifted his left foot, and saw clumps of manure dripping from his boot.

"Haven't taught you about a thing called Karma yet, have I?" Pettick shouted from down the path.

Mawkin stood still on the center of the path, bewildered.

* * *

Crane entered the garage, a large three-bay mechanic's shop at the top of the hill. The building was quiet, sooted, and filled with horseless carriages. Technologies understood only by Kindle the Mechanic.

"Kindle, are you here? Kindle!" Crane called out, receiving no response. Echoes shifted dust particles across the work bay, the dust clouds reflecting blades of sunlight. Crane walked into the bay, stopping in front of one of the carriages covered in a battered canvas shield. Crane ripped the canvas cover from the vehicle. The dust cloud settled, revealing a 1940s Ford F-Series pickup. Beneath the layer of dust and shop air, the red truck was pristine. A horizontal head grill complimented the barreled hood; the bulging wheel wells encased flat black tires with chromed hubcaps. Even in his ignorance, Crane could feel the power, the precise craftsmanship, the significance of the machine before him.

Crane stepped around to the side of the vehicle. He reached for the silver handle, grasped it, and pulled. A metallic *click* sounded, followed swiftly by a crippled moan, marking the opening of the driver's side door. Crane entered the cab, sliding onto the large gray bench seat, and shut the door after him. A childish curiosity of all the buttons and levers came over him. After pulling several of the levers without any reaction, Crane followed what his body told him to do. Reaching forward, he placed his hands on the wooden grips of the steering wheel. The grips fit his fingers like a glove, evidence of a perfectly crafted tool. Crane ran his hand over the emblem centered on the steering column. Pressing down, a blaring horn flared, startling him.

"Those are dangerous things to be toying with, Crane!" The voice echoed in waves across the bay. Crane looked out of the window. Kindle hovered on the catwalk above, directly outside the door to the upper office space. The 'Crow was large in height and girth, long straws formed a beard beneath his chin, heavy strings covered his raised brow. Crane smiled slightly at his presence, a sentiment Kindle softly shared.

"Majestic, isn't it?" Kindle asked, limping down the stairs, wooden cane in hand.

"It's beautiful, everything about it is—"

"Perfectly crafted. This here is a product of passion," Kindle said as he entered the passenger door of the cabin and sat on the bench beside Crane.

"And these humans had passion?" Crane clarified.

"Yes, Crane, once upon a time, they did." Kindle nodded, looking about the cab. "I knew I would find you sitting in this truck one day. With your aggressive curiosity, I'm quite shocked it took this long," Kindle chuckled.

"Now 'curiosity' is a word I know well. My father uses it a lot—always saying my curiosity will get me in trouble," Crane mockingly impersonated.

"It may, it very well may. But don't fear to embrace it, Crane, it is in your threads."

"Thanks, Kindle."

"That's what I'm here for."

Both 'Crows took heavy hold of the meaning of their words, before Crane's curiosity took over again. "So how does it work?"

"I think your first question should be 'what is it?' Or have you already figured that part out?"

"It's a motorized carriage, right?" Crane answered with pride in his knowing.

"Yes. It is much like a carriage, meant to transport 'Crows—well, originally humans—from one place to another. But it is not a carriage in that it does not require horses or bovine to move like our carriages and harvesters do. It's an automobile."

"*Aw-tow-moe-beel.*" Crane broke down the pronunciation of the word aloud, ensuring he was saying it correctly. Kindle nodded at his accuracy. "I read about them. They are all over the books I've read. Some of them are used in war, like tanks and trucks, some in agriculture, and others . . . well, some don't seem to be used for much of anything."

Kindle nodded. "They are dangerous. Like any effective tool, they can be of use for progress or regression."

"Fascinating," Crane commented, then followed with several seconds of thought leading to his next question. "Why are they locked away in here? Why aren't we using them for sowing seeds and moving equipment?"

Kindle sighed. "Pettick is against their use in the field."

"Why?" Crane asked.

"Same reason most of the humans' tools are banned. They led to their downfall. Pettick's afraid our endeavors would run the same path, so he outlawed them. Had me bring them up to the garage and lock 'em away."

"Will they work if we take them out?"

"They should. I keep 'em up, make sure they're functional, occasionally take 'em for a run in case Pettick ever changes his mind or finds them necessary."

"Can we take it for a ride?" Crane asked.

"Absolutely not! Pettick would burn me if he knew I had another Scarecrow with me when I take them out. Besides, I'm only permitted to bring them out after curfew hours."

"Then he won't have to know; I'll just stay here until after the curfew," Crane suggested with excitement.

"And have your father come lookin' for ya up here? No. Absolutely not. He'll never let ya near the garage again!"

"What if I sneak out? I'll wait for Father and Barnes to sleep, then I'll head out, cut through the field to the ridge. If I stay off the path no one will see me—"

"I won't condone such an activity," Kindle stated, firm in his tone.

Crane sighed, looking away from Kindle. Kindle could read the boy's body language and looked away to avoid any guilt he might feel. But Kindle could still see the younger 'Crow's reflection in the vehicle's side-view mirror—set beside his own. He turned back to face Crane and smiled before opening the car door and stepping out. "I can tell you that I take them out on the first of every month," Kindle said kindly, "and I tend not to check the beds for cargo."

Crane's face illuminated with a wide grin. Kindle matched gazes with the 'Crow for several closing moments, then began achingly shuffling back toward the stairs.

"Thanks, Kindle."

"For what?"

"This, still teaching the Reader's son."

Stopping halfway up the stairs, Kindle looked back down to Crane and said with a grin, "My door is always open, Crane. My door is always open. Now get outta here, it's almost curfew."

Crane looked up at the garage door windows that were now just black portals into night. "Oh shit!" Crane uttered. Kindle watched from the catwalk as Crane swung open the door to the truck, got out, and gently closed it behind him. Grabbing his rucksack, the Scarecrow dashed out the garage door and raced into the cool spring night.

The village glowed as a distant star in the center of the rolling hills and peaking rows of the croplands. Crane raced onward to the star, the glowing balls growing as he neared. Subtly the escaping light divided into individual shimmering entities. The torches were encased in glass chambers on the western posts of each house, giving light to the main street of bungalows. Crane entered the area quietly, sneaking past the two Scarecrows who guarded the camp in shifts each night. Reaching the center of the town, he watched the guard turn his back, then slunk across the street and into a bungalow.

"Again, I find myself waiting on a truant son," Barlow whispered from the corner of the bungalow, feet propped on his cot. Crane did not notice Barlow upon entering the dim room, but the words left him frozen in his tracks. The well-kempt bungalow was a comfortable meeting place for the father and son to talk.

"I didn't mean to lose track of time," Crane recoiled.

"We never do; it's why it is called losing track—something you and that old Crow seem to forget, time after time. Your time is my time and this is not a trend I will allow to continue. Understood?"

"But Father—"

"Understood?!"

An all too human interaction occurred in course. The Scarecrows closed their argument, leaving it mutually unresolved, plotting in relative corners in the bungalow. Crane laid flat on his bed, head turned toward the window, staring out to the twilight starscape.

CHAPTER II: Under Lock and Key

A sunflower was perched on the windowsill of the observatory, its stem curling out to the warming rays of the sun. The petals sprung full of body and pigment. A stack of books shifted in his hands as Crane rose from the spiral stairs into the library, combing through each individual book in a hastened scan.

"What are you up to so early?" Barnes asked, entering the room from the observatory stairs.

"Nothing, just gettin' started on my reading."

"Oh, is that right?"

"Yeah, that's right," Crane responded, sensing Barnes's prying.

"When did father assign you *Automobiles and Other Machines*?" Barnes asked, lifting the book from Crane's hand.

Crane jumped forward, pulling the book back into his gloves, escaping up the observatory stairs.

"He didn't; it's personal interest reading."

Barnes took pleasure in Crane's clear annoyance as he shifted around the observatory. "Right. Where were you last night? I was awake when father scolded you, as always."

"I hope you had a good chuckle at my expense."

"Certainly, but it was a quiet one so as to not disturb you," Barnes sneered.

"Thanks."

"Anytime, brother. So, I'll ask again: where were ya?"

Crane opened the book, trying hard not to let Barnes distract him from his task. Barnes stared, waiting for a response. Crane, unable to concentrate, shot up and descended the stairs into the library with Barnes at his heel.

Crane finally broke. "On the ridge with Kindle."

"I figured that much; what were ya doin' that kept you past curfew for the twelfth time?"

"Ninth, actually," Crane corrected. "Those other three times were mere premature guard postings and not my fault!"

"All right, fine! Back to the task at hand: what kept you?"

Crane flipped open the book, searching. He stopped and pointed to one of the images from the *Ford* section.

"That?" Barnes questioned in excitement.

"Yeah, that," Crane quickly replied with a proud snort.

"That's a good reason!"

"I know."

Their father entered the room and the two brothers clandestinely closed the book, silently floating to their respective places of work.

"Punctual at last! My boys are maturing!" Barlow said with paternal bliss. Crane concealed his books from his father's sight as he gave his greetings then moved up the stairs into the observatory. He settled on the wooden stool beside the golden telescope to continue his studies.

The pages were flushed with information: diagrams of chassis, engines and carburetors, photographs of the history of the Ford Motor Company's assembly lines. Every page was as fascinating as the last, exciting Crane's imagination.

A crash came from the library. Crane shuffled to conceal the book, placing the two bottom ones from a stack onto the top and opening another random book to an equally random chapter. Barlow rose from the stairs, a book in hand.

"Are you all right, Father?" Crane asked.

"Yeah, just another pile of books in my way. We're going to need to hasten our speed of reading before this room overflows and we drown in paper and ink." The two shared a chuckle. "All right, then. Crane, where are we on our readings?"

Crane stuttered, shuffling to discreetly read the cover, "Well, I'm about halfway through *The Jungle.* It's decent. I can't say I fully understand it, and I don't know if it fits what Pettick requires, but I'll finish it by day's end and re-evaluate then."

"And the rest of your stack?" Barlow inquired, pointing to the stack of books Crane had been toting.

Crane froze for a moment then uttered in a scattered sentence, "Well, two of 'em are my next readings, and the rest . . . they are . . . ah . . . backlog reads."

"Did any of them have anything of interest for Pettick?"

"No, no," Crane regrettably answered.

"Then I guess we'd better put them in storage."

"Yeah. Yeah, I'll do that now." Crane unwillingly lifted the books. Bearing the weight, he stumbled down the steps and across the library. Barnes opened the chute as Crane, sharing a mournful glance, relieved himself of the weight. Barnes shook his head, closing off from Crane. Barlow peered out the window, his attention diverted from the desires and emotions of his sons. All along the field, the horse- and burrodrawn plows scored the soil while several dozen workers spread over each line, sowing seeds.

* * *

"I had it in my hand, Kindle," Crane explained to Kindle as they walked up the path toward the garage. "I had it *in my hand*."

"I believe you, Crane. Can you tell me any more about it?"

"Yeah—can recite bits and pieces of almost every section I read."

"Can you get the book back?" Kindle asked.

"I don't really know where they go after the chute. Father told me that there's a secure storage in the basement of the house where they are locked up."

"So it's gone—for now?"

"Not exactly. I might be able to get it back."

"I won't have you getting into any trouble for me, Crane." Kindle stopped, ensuring that Crane understood the sincerity of his statement.

Crane nodded. "Oh, I won't. It'll be fine, I promise."

"Why do I seriously doubt that?" Kindle muttered to himself as Crane ran ahead, westward toward the ridge.

"What are they doing out there?" Crane asked.

Kindle caught up to Crane. A couple hundred yards out he could see a group of officers, along with Pettick and Pitch the Carpenter, constructing what appeared to be a massive stick statue resembling a Scarecrow. Lowering the figure off a horse cart, they centered it on the edge of the ridge as Pettick barked hasty orders.

"What is that, Kindle?" Crane asked.

"I don't know, boy." Kindle said. "I don't know."

Pettick watched the careful and precise placement of the piece. As gazes turned away from the sun he caught sight of the two onlookers, recognizing them immediately. As Pettick watched, the two Scarecrows broke off into the distance toward the garage, fading along the curve of the brush.

Veidt, the decrepit peg-legged, marble-eyed third in command, approached. "Is this placing good, sir?" he asked, the teeth of his exposed jaw clicking.

"What?" Pettick asked.

"Does this placement please you?" Veidt grunted as he reforged the brim of his gray felt kepi.

Pettick broke his deep gaze, turning back to the work behind him. "Yes, that's fine . . . that's fine." His attention still lacked focus as he shifted back to the now empty field where Crane and Kindle had stood. He looked back several times as he returned to his central task. The tethers of the statue snapped taut. Pettick looked up as the sun pierced the thatched intertwining sticks of the statue, mending it into one burning figure in his vision.

Mawkin approached from around the figure, a pickaxe in hand. He shifted his weight to his tool and waited quietly, knowing the intensity of Pettick's mind and danger of interrupting the motion of such a finely tuned machine. Pettick tossed a large padlock in his hand, bouncing the metal case to the beat of the mallets crashing, the blunt force driving tethered stakes into the ground: *beat, bounce, clash. Beat, bounce, clash.*

"Is it secure?" Pettick asked, not taking sight off the figure as the workers continued to stabilize the structure.

"Yes, sir. It is safe for the time being," Mawkin replied.

"I want you in charge of the transportation and security tonight—no slip-ups, no tom-foolery. I need this. *We* need this."

"Understood." Mawkin nodded. "What are our plans about this problem?"

"What problem?" Pettick asked retorically, a grin, a gash, creasing his cheeks. "Nothing," Pettick eventually responded.

"But we have a serious problem on our hands." Mawkin took notice of Pettick's lack of interest. "Sir?"

Pettick continued to stand by, unresponsive.

"Sir?"

"Don't question me. Ever," Pettick said. "Less is more and more is learned when less is said. Tonight, you'll see it for yourself." Pettick leaned into Mawkin with uncustomary proximity, dropping the padlock into his palm. "Security is an illusion, Mawkin. As preceptor magicians, it is time we put on a show." Pettick paused as he drew a heavy breath, and held it before exhaling. "But dare do we give away any secrets, eh?"

Pettick drifted down the hill, leaving Mawkin with the padlock and its heavy iron weight, its seal unclasped. Mawkin reached into his jacket, produced the corresponding key in his hand, then pocketed them both as he watched the workers clear out with the setting sun.

The bonfire was set in the center of the meeting ground, a safe distance from any surrounding pines. Dozens of Scarecrows entered, scattered across the meeting grounds, standing in pairs. An orchestra filled the stage, comprised of several string and horn instruments. The music varied between folk and classical compilations, all uniquely inaccurate to their human predecessors. Each pair of 'Crows met in the center by the fire and, after concurrent bows, joined arms in a waltz, in which they intertwined in a whirl of organized chaos.

The Reader and his sons entered the grounds.

"You know, there are far fewer places on this earth as free as this than you are brought to believe in our reading," Barlow preached to his boys, his arms around them.

"Yeah, Pop, we know," Barnes retorted, having heard this speech hundreds of times.

"Keep it in mind, boys. Now, off to your spoils."

Both boys launched into the whirling crowd, in search of their current prospects. The pairs orbited around the fire, each individual planet separating and merging with its moon. Crane stopped. A wall of dancers joined in a semicircle on the far side of the fire, then, in a near unison wave, segregated into separate spinning cells.

In the center of the divide Gwyn appeared, shimmering from the glowing bonfire. She met Crane's gaze, and smiled. The long feathers of her hair glowed in contrast with her patterned floral sundress and two-toned cardigan. The two entered an orbit and merged slowly. Their joined hands rose together and flowed in a cordial introduction. Then, approaching the fire, a bow took place before the two fully embraced their dance and entered the universe around them.

Crane tendered a prolonged introduction. "You look . . . beautiful."

"Thank you," Gwyn offered in a shy response.

"You were obviously crafted by a creator of great passion."

"What?"

"Nothing—just forget it." Crane's confidence swayed.

"No, what does it mean?"

"It means you were made with a profound dedication, endowed by a skilled and incredibly dedicated artisan, made only to better this earth by your existence."

"Thank you, that means a lot—I think," Gwyn said, looking away for a brief moment to conceal her flattered grin.

"Well, what I'm trying to say is, you're like a fine automobile, the finest Ford made on their *as-sem-bly* line." Crane spoke, attempting to pronounce unheard-of concepts and words, articles of an alien language.

"A what?"

"Sorry, it's a type of human machine. It's just . . . forget it." Crane sighed, sad that she was ignorant of such a beautiful thing. He wished so much that he could show her what he was saying and feeling, the wonder that such a piece of beautiful craftsmanship and a thing as ugly as humanity could coexist.

"You are an odd one, Crane," Gwyn said, giggling.

"Is that bad? For you, I mean?" Crane asked, concerned.

"No," Gwyn replied. "Is it bad for you?"

"I would think not," Crane answered with a smirk.

Critch the Cobbler approached Barlow at the edge of the dancing area. The two 'Crows observed the festivities around them with crossed arms. "Mature fast, don't they?" Critch spoke with a surprisingly deep rasp from his slender form.

"Yes, I would agree," Barlow responded. The two watched as kin danced together across the orbiting space, the flaring omissions of the fire igniting in their view. "How is Mare?"

"She is well. Worked in the textile house today, but she is still up and about. Should be around here someplace. How are the boys?"

"They are well," Barlow said.

The two Scarecrows stood in a comfortable silence, the kind only garnered with age. As the two began to stroll, distancing themselves from the fire, the crowd's attention shifted and theirs with it.

"My friends . . . my friends, good evening." Pettick stood on the elevated platform, journal in hand. "It appears our evening is well met. With this I am pleased, very pleased. So now I am here to present you with an offering, an offering for our fortune and for Flying Crow's. This offering, a ritual of good faith for the blessings of our planted seeds, will assure a bountiful harvest this autumn. But on this joyous night I do bring dark news." Pettick paused and held his chest. "A human was found invading our colony last week. He was found armed, attempting to enter the farmhouse, likely another threat against my life and that of my officers. With the quick and assertive action of mine and my militia's, we were able to thwart his heinous attempt on my life and have him securely in our custody tonight, where I now bring him before you, my fellow Scarecrows." He offered another dramatic pause. "Mawkin, present the beast."

Mawkin rose from behind the platform holding a knife to the neck of a human, a young man, gagged, with his hands and feet tied. Varying sounds of fear, shock, and awe flared from the crowd as the human rose beside Pettick, then was forced to his knees. There was a resounding gasp from the crowd at which Pettick, the conductor of this terrible orchestra, reveled.

"I would ask you now to follow my stride as we march in a ritual line from our meeting ground up the path to the ridge where we will continue with our ceremony."

Mawkin escorted the prisoner off the stage and directly through the crowd, which divided before them with the choreographed motion of an already progressing play. Pettick followed the currents of the recently formed path several strides behind his prisoner. The prisoner and his escort were loaded onto a cart driven by Veidt at the edge of the clearing. Pettick mounted the cart and turned to face his audience.

"Follow me, friends, into the dark. I assure you, with me you are safe."

And with the crack of Veidt's whip, the cart trundled forward. The crowd marched, following the cart down the dark path ahead. Whispers rose through the soundscape.

"Vicious creatures, humans."

"He looks dangerous."

"I'm afraid."

"We should rid our world of this filth."

"What do you suppose we are going to do?"

"What do you think Pettick will do?"

The march followed the Firemen. Each Fireman held a long staff topped with glass-encased torches that burned brightly, lighting the darkness ahead. As the quarter horse heaved the cart forward Pettick stood in it, his gaze not back toward his people, but rather focused only on what lay further down the road. The cart swayed and stumbled over the unpaved path, an ever-present silence lingered in the air, interrupted only by the cries and whimpers of the prisoner. Barlow and Critch marched together, three quarters up the line. Mare cut through the crowd, approaching her mate.

"What do you suppose he intends on doing with this prisoner that justifies all this?" Mare asked, wrapping Critch's arm around her.

"I'm afraid to answer that," Barlow responded.

"And I was afraid that was what you were going to say," Critch added.

Crane held Gwyn's hand as they rushed down the line searching for their parents, Barnes following close behind.

"Father!" Crane shouted.

"Crane! Gwyn!" the fathers chimed as they were reunited with their kin.

"What's going on? What are they doing?" Crane asked.

"I don't know, boy. I don't know," Barlow said, holding his son close.

The cart reached the edge of the ridge where it turned parallel to the drop-off. As the families breached the hill, the glow of the torches slowly revealed a figure at the end of the path. The lights grasped the figure, extracting it from the darkness, exposure clearing sight of what lay ahead in detail, revealing a hollow wicker statue atop a small base of wooden twigs and tinder. The figure was no bigger than twelve feet with arms extended out spanning nearly as wide as the figure was tall. The crowd gathered a couple of yards before the figure where several of Pettick's soldiers stood guard.

"My Crow, no." Barlow bowed, realization weighing heavy on his heart.

"Father! Father, are you all right?" Crane said, grabbing hold of his elder.

Mawkin dragged the human behind the figure, as Pettick hopped onto the seat, the highest point of the cart, towering nearly as high as the wicker man beside him.

"You are about to witness justice before you, a strategy for harmony among Scarecrows and Monsters. This, my friends, is what must be done," Pettick shouted, signaling to Mawkin.

The human let out screams of terror as he appeared, ungagged in the center of the wicker statue. Mawkin stood behind the statue closing the small door in the back of the figure. He wrapped a chain around the two posts. As ordered, he placed the large padlock onto the figure, clasping it and removing the key, sealing the sarcophagus. The man's eyes teared as he reached through the thatching, clawing for Mawkin. Mawkin was still behind the statue. In an oddly private moment, he watched the struggle of the human.

"Please—please! You don't have to do this!" The man's arms punched through the thatching, gashing valleys, gorging the natural dams of protruding veins in his hands and forearms. Fresh blood poured, the human sap spraying onto Mawkin who immediately turned away. The sacrifice, huddled in the corner of the figure and facing away from the audience, continued to plead with Mawkin. "Please, God! Please—this isn't right."

Pettick struck Mawkin with an impatient gaze. A Fireman approached in ceremonious stride on Pettick's hastened signal. Wearing the large makeshift head of a black-beaked crow, the Fireman's face, his hands, the entire Scarecrow was devoid of identity. In his slender gloves he held a bare burning torch. The Fireman met Mawkin behind the figure. The audience continued to stare in awe. The human let out a whimper, tears pouring down his flesh.

"Wait!" Mawkin said to the Fireman, holding him back from the figure. Grasping the torch, Mawkin met gazes with the man a final time, stepping away from the figure. The man slowed his hands, bare bloodied flesh meeting the straw face of his captor.

"Why?" the man whispered.

The moment grew stagnant as the torch fell from Mawkin's hand, landing on the kindling beneath the figure, igniting it instantly. The man shrieked, eyes wide, drool pouring from grinding teeth. The heat rose into a fireball, fueling the flame. The hand clenched, ripping away a clump of straw off Mawkin's face as he leapt back from the engulfing flames. Arms of the figure spread as the man radiated a blinding white light. A childlike grin cut wide, spanning Pettick's face as the final squeals and whimpers died out. Flares and furls of burning embers danced with smoke and sparks high into the night sky. The frozen audience steadily thawed, silently breaking away over the next hour as the figure eventually collapsed into a pile of glowing ash.

* * *

The early-morning chatter arose along the dim moist dew of the farm at first light. On the ridge Pettick and his soldiers began cleaning up the remains of the night before. The 'Crows kept their distance from the still warm pit of embers, shoveling dirt and bails of water on the remains, lifting a column of smoke and ash into the periwinkle morning sky.

"Fittin' to burn the farm down!" Thalo shouted as one of the workers stumbled with a shovel full of cinder, launching them into the surrounding grass.

"No reason to be that loud this early," Pettick said.

"Right, sir. Sorry," Thalo replied, continuing with his task.

Pettick bent down and picked up a small object from the edge of the remains. As he continued his stride, he pulled out a handkerchief from his breast pocket and began cleaning the black soot from the crevices of the object.

"I see you got your prize, or whatever you would call that," Mawkin said, motioning from the pile of ruin in front of him to the object in Pettick's gloves.

"I would call that a success," Pettick said.

"Would you?"

"Yes, yes, very much so." Pettick finished cleaning, then returned his handkerchief to his pocket. "I thank you, Mawkin. I couldn't 'a done it without you," Pettick said with genuine sincerity, presenting the nearly unscathed padlock to Mawkin. Mawkin ignored the proposition.

"The only thing I could say existed unanimously last night was fear. *Fear*—that was the only thing," Mawkin implored, pausing to reach into his pocket. He pulled out the key and dropped it in Pettick's glove.

"Precisely," Pettick said with a smirk.

"That includes you, Pettick," Mawkin stated as he walked away from the prophet.

Pettick looked down at the padlock in his hands, moving the head of the lock and clasping it. "Still works," he chuckled to himself as he gazed along the span of his farm; reaching back, he threw his weight forward, launching the lock over the ridge. The tiny body vanished in the textured horizon.

CHAPTER III:

Figments of Bradbury and Fibonacci

They fell from the Perfect Tree—dove-white petals fluttering, gliding in the wind, running off as they collected in patches forming illusions of spring snow atop the green earth. Shepherd the Herdsman stood stoically beneath this tree, watching over his flock, the village nestled in the hills below. A petal fell to his hand, and he held this tree's delicate feather as if he were cradling a bird in his hand. A small herd of animals grazed before him. They were silent as they fed.

Kindle oiled the bit on the drill press, placed the brush in its jar, and lowered the bit to clamp in the correct place. As the clamp closed he reached down and switched the machine on, which let out a piercing growl that flooded the bay and startled Crane, who had entered unnoticed amidst the noise. Kindle, placing his glove on the knob, lowered the spinning bit into the clamped handle. The machine snored and crackled in the afterglow of its work. Kindle unclamped the object, removed the bit from the chuck, and turned to the doorway. The white light blurred his vision, causing him to jump at the figure in his path.

"Kid, you got to be more careful these days, comin' around a 'Crow unannounced."

"Sorry, Kindle," Crane said, moving into view. "Whatcha workin' on?"

"Somethin' to keep me safe from anyone, other than you, who comes uninvited through those doors."

"You scared of humans coming around here?"

"As much as other things," Kindle said, blowing shards from the handle.

"Why?" Crane asked.

"'Cause I have a way to kill a human," Kindle said, presenting the knife to Crane. "Careful with that, the handle's still hot from being on the press."

Crane ran his fingers along the edge of the blade, splicing the fiber threads of his fingertips. Kindle moved to the cabinet, placing the bit in a leather wrap, and pulling a small length of rope from a bundle.

"All right, hand it over," Kindle said, taking grip on the handle and running the rope through the freshly made hole. He tied the opposite end in a loop around his belt.

"How do you get these things to work?" Crane asked with a boyish curiosity as his hands moved along from one machine to the next, touching every part he could reach.

"I got a generator out back."

"What's a generator?"

"It's a machine that produces electricity, converting fuel to power, much like the engines in these automobiles," Kindle answered, trying to veer Crane's attention from the milling machines to the objects of curiosity that tended to be less fragile.

Crane turned back to Kindle from the opposite end of the bay. Approaching Kindle, Crane could see in Kindle's stature that something was off; he had been moving about the garage all morning without his cane. His limp was pronounced as he moved, though he powered through its pains. Tools in hand, Kindle began work under the popped hood of the cattle truck. Crane rounded the giant '42 Ford 218T as the clatter of labors came to a halt. He stood beside Kindle, cocking his head at the strange sight of the eight-cylinder engine, the tangled tubes and pistons, madness in exactness. Kindle huffed, spinning the socket wrench in his glove.

"Something wrong, Kin?" Crane asked.

"No, no. Everything is all right, just can't seem to figure this girl out." The two 'Crows stared at one another for a moment. "Any chance you could get your hands on that *Automotive Mechanics* book?" Kindle asked.

After momentary thought, Crane discerned "Yeah, I can get it for you," he said, assuring Kindle as well as himself.

"Only if you don't think it'll be trouble," Kindle said, looking again for understanding in Crane's face.

"No, no trouble at all, Kindle."

"Thanks, Crane."

"Well, I'd better get back. I'll try to come back at labor's end if my father lets me."

"Be safe, kid," Kindle said, watching Crane as he darted through the door. Feeling the defeat of ignorance, the wrench fell from Kindle's hand, tumbling to the concrete. He huffed, looking over at his cane, which rested against the corner of the table. Kindle shuffled forward and grabbed hold of the carved stick. After moving past the threshold of the rear door of the garage, he pitched the stick into the junkyard, sightless to where the object fell.

Spinning fibers raced through pedal machines, joining shreds of fabric as hands worked tirelessly with needles and thread, weaving, meshing, and entangling. The textile barn employed most of the farm's female population, making and mending the clothes of future 'Crows. Once the migrant workers' chapel, the hand-planed lath pine hall had been modified with rows of sowing tables that lined the interior in quadrants. The hall bustled from early morning until break in midafternoon. Gwyn worked arduously on a flannel and tweed shirt, mending a series of holes. Mare, Gwyn's mother, sat across from her at the worktable, patching a piece of denim with far more acute focus to her labors.

"I don't know how they plan to keep up," Gwyn complained. "It's starting to feel as though for every crate they bring in here, they pull another set of hands out." Gwyn looked over at the rest of the 'Crows at her table, all ignoring her remarks. Gwyn continued to herself, "I could have been a Rider, a damn good one, too."

"Honey, like I always say, life ain't fair!" Jasper bustled in her seat. Jasper, a large 'Crow, at least of female form, had large mitts—sturdy, aged, rough and warn—that held tight the three-inch curved needle in one hand, the joining leather in the other. Though she was the best at leatherwork in the colony, a result of age and ardor, there was no title regarding this above her door, no accolades recognizing her contribution, only the carved occupation: SEWER.

"Yes, I know, I know," Gwyn said, having heard this lecture before.

"So quit runnin' your mouth and start running those hands," Jasper added, with sagacity to her wit.

"Just wish we had more hands, is all."

"We'll manage," Mare said. "Always have, always will."

"Pettick did say we would be getting more hands in the forthcoming season," Gwyn added.

"Another promise," Jasper huffed.

Mare looked over at her daughter, a lesson on her mind. "Pettick's a man of promises."

Gwyn's attention drifted to the single un-shuttered window at the top of the western edge of the room. The round window bulged with the glow of the midafternoon sun.

"What is it?" Mare asked, noticing her daughter's swaying focus, the undeniable plight and pleasure of being a mother—Gwyn's mother.

"I just can't get my head around it." Gwyn wrapped up the remaining pieces of cloth at her station, packing them and her tools into a drawer in the frame of the table. Mare took notice of Gwyn's premature, self-appointed dismissal.

"And where are you off to?" Mare solicited.

"The creek," Gwyn said passively, growing more and more visibly anxious on her stool.

"Oh, is that it?" Mare pried, expecting a more honest response from her daughter.

"Yes."

"What's at the creek?" Mare asked.

Gwyn looked away, tugging on her cardigan. "Crane."

"The truth comes out!" Jasper rallied, drawing Mare into a shared revel.

"And this boy . . . you care for him?" Mare asked with attempted sincerity.

"Are these questions necessary?" Gwyn shrugged.

"I'm your mother; of course they are."

A bell chimed, echoing through the hall, and echoing Gwyn's readiness to exit. Ignoring her mother, she walked between the rows of tables as the narrow path flooded with workers who had completed their daily tasks and were making their own rush for the door.

"When did this seem like a good idea?" Gwyn asked, still hiding her nervous grin.

"It's always been a good idea," Crane said, throwing a pebble, which bounced carelessly downstream before coming to rest on the creek bed. "We're alone; it'll be okay."

"You sure? Does this feel . . . right?" Gwyn shied to the creek bed.

"Yes," Crane said, offering a reassuring smile.

"I guess it does," Gwyn said.

"Besides, it's really not that hard," Crane remarked with an instigative tone.

"Yeah, well, easy for you to say. You already went."

"Yeah, and now it's your turn," Crane badgered through his sophomoric grin.

Gwyn shrugged. "Fine. Just give me a moment."

Crane watched from across the small creek as Gwyn unpeeled her dress to reveal a naked layer of straw. The stitching swirled in concentric patterns along her shoulder blades, sprialling in lighter tawny threads which ran down the small of her back. This sight was so beautiful, the patterned thatching of her makeup, the intricately seamless binding of her flesh. This was the perfect moment. She drew her dress back over her shoulders and buttoned her cardigan. After meeting gazes, Crane snapped into motion, bounding forward like a pebble over the pond. The couple chased across the field, gradually wrestling to the ground, laying flat beneath the warm sun. The wind blew gently on the lovers amongst the reeds.

* * *

Picking up books from the schoolhouse was Barnes's favorite part of his apprenticeship. He loved Main Street at midday—laborers' bungalows turned to shops, and the smells of leather, wood-chips, tar, and resin crossed through his threads. And even though they were all hard at work, their heart to their labors, every 'Crow had time to talk. Even the simplest "hello" was never undersold.

Quill the Teacher twiddled the broken piece of chalk between her middle and index fingers. Quill was a small 'Crow by stature, but not short on wisdom, and appeared even smaller standing in front of her class dressed in a tattered tweed skirt and corduroy blouse. Behind her a white line ran the span of the chalkboard, measuring the distance of the one-room schoolhouse that sat at the far west end of the village. Three quarters down the chalk line a gap in the line was crossed by two perpendicular parallel lines, both marked by a phrase. The far side from Quill was marked with the heading: A.H.; the closer was marked B.C.

Quill walked up to the A.H., moved her chalk fourteen inches down the timeline, and created a white dash.

"We are here on the timeline, a fairly young species as it were, compared to the existence of others. Trends tend to forget that, but we should remember this, and cherish it." Quill lectured, gesturing to the specific locations on the board as they were discussed. "If you look, this line represents a few very important articles of information. This is where we began—this right here—this point represents the dawn of the age of reason, the beginning of order. Behind it, the time *Before Crow*, lie the dark ages of human history. Their existence and their eventual end may appear long at first glance, especially when compared to this small span of existence we represent here. But it is important to look at this line segment, as this arrow represents something key to your understanding. And that is?" Quill pointed to the only raised hand.

"The arrow represents a continuation," a young 'Crow answered, lowering her eager hand.

"Yes, that is precisely it. This segment represents a continuation. The future, to our understanding, is an infinite line ahead."

Pettick appeared, silently entering the back of the room in one of his many unannounced visits. Watching over Quill had become a recent interest of the colony's leader.

"Any questions?" Quill asked the class. A hand rose belonging to Attucks, the eldest 'Crow in the class. "Yes, Attucks?"

"Why did humanity fail?" Attucks asked. Quill choked on her words in the weight of such a question under Pettick's watch, leaving several moments of silence before Pettick chose to answer.

"Because they lacked loyalty," Pettick stated, moving to the front of the room.

"Loyalty?" a smaller 'Crow asked.

"Yes, the dedication required to survive in a pack or tribe. See, humanity forgot what was most important—"

"And what was that?" Attucks interjected with a sly drawl.

"Family. No species can prosper alone. We and the humans are no different on that account. In a tribe, a being has a collective purpose shared by others, and that purpose is beneficial of the common good. If that is forgotten and the individual becomes the denominator, even just by one, then the entire tribe is at risk. We keep this from happening by installing order." Pettick moved to the chalkboard, and Quill shifted to the side of the room, giving him the floor. "This period here,"—Pettick lifted a piece of chalk and marked two points, creating a line segment on the timeline and ending it just before A.H.—"involved times of chaos that reigned for centuries until we rose and brought order to such chaos. Order is our most valuable asset in preventing such a downfall for ourselves."

The school bell chimed. The class was dismissed, quickly filing out the door, each pupil more eager than the one before.

Pettick turned to address Quill privately. "Avoid getting on the spot; don't ask questions. Make the questions direct when you do; it'll keep 'em from going too far into such risky topics they shouldn't be prematurely exposed to." Pettick finished his lecture, retrieved an understanding nod from Quill, and moved back to the door.

Barnes entered just as Pettick made his exit, and the two crossed paths with only minor acknowledgement. Quill dealt with the last questions from her students as they made their way out the door. Attucks approached Barnes, giving pleasantries while Barnes began his daily task of collecting the books from each desk. Attucks stood tall, well-built, with a leather aviation jacket wrapped around his barrel chest. He proudly ran his fingers down the patches on his jacket's sleeve as he made conversation with Barnes.

"You know, half of us don't even read those things," Attucks said, looking down at the stack of books Barnes carried.

"Don't go lumping in the rest of the class with your mischief," Barnes quipped.

"I'm just saying, maybe you don't have to bring all of them—save you the strain. Though I must say, for you, the lifting ain't gonna hurt." Attucks snickered, reaching for Barnes's biceps.

Barnes shrugged, clearly not amused.

"Just foolin'." Attucks looked around, ensured Quill was out of earshot, then leaned toward Barnes. "Wanna sneak into the silo barn with me tonight?"

"What? No. Why?" Barnes asked, cautiously bemused.

"It might be fun. Don't be such a stiff straw all the time." Pulling out a comb from his jacket pocket, Attucks slicked back his black hair as he continued: "Rumor is Pettick's buildin' somethin' out there. Gotta wonder why he keeps all those soldiers there, ya know?"

"Straw Stash needs protecting," Barnes answered simply, not feeling a need for further explanation or exploration.

"Aren't you curious?" Attucks asked. "Don't you want to see it?"

"Not particularly," Barnes said.

"You lack confection, my friend," Attucks declared.

"I think you mean *conviction*, and even then, I still don't think you really mean what you're saying. Again, perhaps you should try reading one of the books I bring," Barnes said in jest, presenting Attucks one of the books in his hand.

"Ya need to loosen up," Attucks said, ignoring the book and the comment. "I'll just ask your brother; I'm sure he's up for it."

Barnes paused briefly, thinking that perhaps Attucks might have a point.

"So, we hangin' out today?" Attucks asked.

"Yeah, I gotta finish this." Barnes gestured to the remaining books around the room.

"I'll wait." Attucks crossed his arms, reclining.

Barnes shook his head. "Wouldn't kill ya to help out . . ."

"Not really my style." Attucks smiled, making his exit.

Barnes watched Attucks depart as Quill approached, a clearly frustrated look on her face, the kind of frustration only teaching under Pettick could garner.

"It has its days," Quill said to Barnes, helping him gather books from around the room.

"I take it today was not one of them," Barnes said with a smile.

"Right. This has been happening more and more often, him coming around here."

"What's he want?"

"The birds if I know." Quill shook her head. "Says he's checkin' up on me, sudden renewed interest in education."

"I bet," Barnes said sarcastically.

"Yeah, if that were true, he'd let us be." Quill sighed, handing Barnes the stack in her hand.

Attucks stuck his large head back through the doorway, knowingly interrupting Barnes and Quill's conversation. "Hey, Barnes, ya comin'?" Smiling, he slicked back the greasy fibers on his scalp and floated back out the door. Barnes looked back and forth, trying to respect the levity in his conversation with Quill. Quill smiled, appreciating Barnes's respect, before shooing him out the door.

"Well, go—go!" Quill said.

"Sorry." Barnes gestured, stumbling for the door, a stack of books in hand.

With caring manner to her words, Quill added, "Don't apologize. Go be a kid."

"Right." Barnes smiled, leaving Quill alone in the schoolhouse. She looked across the sea of empty desks as she waded amongst them, a sinking feeling in heart. The drowning feeling lasted but a moment as she pushed to the front of the room. From a half-empty bucket she pulled a soaking wet rag, wrung most of the water from it, raised her arm to the board, and began scrubbing, erasing the lesson.

Crystallized shafts of light tunneled in patches through the branches of the Perfect Tree. Crane and Shepherd, cradled amid the light, explored the paths of marching ants running along the ground.

"Look at them move; isn't it fascinating?" Shepherd leaned his long slender form down on his staff and peered closer at the army of ants marching in the grass forest at his feet. Crane knelt beside him. "These creatures," Shepherd announced, "make *us* ants."

"How so?" Crane asked.

"Look at that one there." Shepherd pointed to a single ant, out of formation, carrying a spec of rock twice its size on its back. "These creatures can carry many times their body weight and they do so incontestably. It's truly remarkable."

Crane looked up at Shepherd. "You remind me of this human I read about, this human that lived in the woods by some creek or a lake for a year, he used to watch bugs also."

"Did he squash them afterward?" Shepherd inquired.

"No, he let them be. He learned from them, learned to be a better human."

"A better human?" Shepherd marveled at the idea.

"A better ant, I suppose," Crane added.

The two Scarecrows rose, their chins tilting from the world at their feet to the field workers shifting in the valley before them.

"Ants," Shepherd chuckled, a sentiment Crane shared. "I'd like to read that book one day."

"I would again too, but Pettick has it now—"

"Pettick?"

"Yeah, it's in his library. Couldn't imagine him reading something like that, but it fits the requisite of his type of book."

Shepherd turned to face Crane, "Just 'cause a book's in a library doesn't mean it's ever been read."

The two pike-less Scarecrows hung in the hall of the Perfect Tree overlooking the farm.

Mawkin entered the stygian caverns of the cattle barn which sat isolated at the southern edge of the farm. The enormous barn was vaulted, king-post rafters pitched to heights their termination veiled in darkness. Mawkin stirred from the square box of daylight at the entry, stepping into the workspace of the Creator. Before him a work area was set with several long tables laden with straw. Mannequin busts, and wire-form stands lined the wall. Beside the table, Scarecrows, lifeless, a family in the making, stood unfinished, their interwoven flesh hollow and incomplete. There was a large masculine 'Crow, a toddler sized Scarecrow at his side, and incomplete on a bust before Mawkin, a female Scarecrow—a mate. Mawkin gazed at the face of this 'Crow, scanning down her naked stitch complexion, where at the upper left thigh the tightly woven makeup came undone, unraveled in frayed edges at the base of the bust and down to spools at the wooden feet of the stand. Mawkin cocked his head, finding the sight strange and unsettling. He reached out to the hand, its threaded fingers lifeless to the touch.

In the loft, a tall figure lingered, observing, as it stared down at Mawkin. "I see you have met the Millers, or perhaps the Smiths; I haven't quite decided yet." The figure moved with precision in the shadows, spending only seconds in the visible rays. "What do you need?" the figure asked, its hissing voice bouncing off leaden wood walls.

"I need to be patched up," Mawkin responded, clearly annoyed by the question.

The figure shifted down the oak-planked stairs, ending a tread away from where Mawkin stood. The light rays exposed the long sharp-edged face of the Creator, one of the least seen artisans on the farm.

"Pettick send you?" the Creator asked, his skeletal hide, with its pale gray clay-like plastering over straw, leaned into the light.

"Does it matter?" Mawkin said.

"Don't figure it does; let us see what we have here." The long fingers spread open around Mawkin's face, spidering to the wound on his cheek. "What a shame, something got you good." The Creator examined the laceration with painful tautness to his grip. "This looks like it hurt—a reminder of how fragile we really are. Was it a human?"

"Fix it, so I can go," Mawkin spouted impatiently, pulling from the Creator's clutches.

The Creator spun off the steps. "Follow me." The two moved into the shadows, breaching deeper into the barn. Under the loft they went through two industrial Paylon double-swing doors where a single candle flame swayed in the stagnant air. The room shifted, exhaling shallow breaths, much like its keeper. Chains hung from rafters, clanking, swaying in and out of view in the dim light with large cattle hooks curled at their ends. Below these hooks sat several lanes of stainless-steel frame-sunk tables, once used to prime, drain, and skin the butchered cattle. "Sit," the Creator said, presenting a small stained and scarred wooden stool.

Mawkin sat still as the Creator moved in and out of visibility, vanishing in the dark void only to reappear with a leather-wrapped toolkit which he spread open on the table next to him. The kit held large needles of varying widths and curves beside a set of seam rippers and shears, all of tarnished pewter. Mawkin tried not to pay much attention to the Creator while he worked. Every stroke was sharp and exact, the motions were seamless as the thatching was re-threaded; the long fingers began their spider-like motion, opening to the face then closing with every exhausting pull of the thread, tightening the web in a painfully effective manner. The process continued for several minutes, and Mawkin remained taut and silent as the flickering light lit only what the Creator needed to see to do his work.

"Should I be expecting to patch more Scarecrow's wounded from human encounters?" the Creator asked in an oddly endearing manner, sliding back to admire his finished work.

Realizing the Creator's task was complete, Mawkin stood. "If Pettick needs you, he'll call for you."

"Wouldn't expect him comin' out here anytime soon. He likes to pretend this part doesn't happen, like we exist out of nowhere. There is labor in it." The Creator stood, chasing Mawkin with his words. "Send those words to your leader."

As Mawkin exited the barn, the Creator's figure remained a flickering spasm in the black cavern, till the candle fat ran thin and burned into oxygen-less black.

Crane's hands trembled with nerves as he carried a stack of books down the center hall of the farmhouse. After reaching the end of the hall, he doubled back to where a guarded door leading to the cellar stood beneath the grand stairwell. Crane did not know the procedure for getting past the guard. He knew Barnes and Barlow had made this journey to the storage vault countless times before, but this would be Crane's first. The Guard looked up from his boredom as Crane approached the door.

"Where you goin' kid?" the Guard asked.

Crane's gut wrenched, easing out with the uncoiling of his responsive tongue. "I'm Crane, the Reader's Apprentice. You know me."

"Knowing you still don't change the question of why you should be going through this door." The Guard spoke sternly and coldly, as he rose from his stool and stood between Crane and the door.

"Got some books to bring downstairs," Crane said.

"Why couldn't they go through the drop?" the Guard asked.

Crane looked down at his stack, searching for the answer on pages that existed only to raise more questions.

"This book's too big to fit down the chute. Barlow told me to walk it down, and file the rest away while I'm at it." The silence which followed lingered while the Guard stood in thought for nearly a minute. Then, without a word, he reached for the knob and pulled open the door.

A race of excitement shook Crane as the soles of his tanned suede shoes passed through the threshold and bounded down the wooden staircase into a mysterious cavern that was still unexplored, making it all the more desirable. The cellar was cool, damp, and smelled of coal and aged splinters and ash. Reaching the stone of the floor, Crane doubled back toward the caged windows symmetrically outlining the escape stairs on the far west wall. Figments and fragments of dust danced through faded pale columns of light emanating from the windows, giving the only sign of life the room currently possessed. Cobwebbed arcs in the low ceiling outlined the beams, traversing each gap with a sagging bow, highlighting the dark rectangular hole where the shaft from the library's laundry chute punctured through. Directly below the chute was a small pool of books, shin high, on the basement floor, like a paged inkwell.

Crane picked up one of the books in the pile and read the spine. The once silver words were now chipped away to a tone of caste steel: *The Red Badge of Courage* by Stephen Crane.

Memories surfaced with this reunion that rallied more questions than its author answered. As Crane rummaged through the pile, another of his recent reads floated to the surface. He grabbed the first book on Henry Ford he found before reaching deeper into the depths, searching for the *Motors and Mechanics* book Kindle requested he retrieve. After several minutes, Crane concluded it must already be in the vault and placed the two related automobile books into his rucksack.

Wafting clumps of dust, like snowfall, fell from ceiling as footsteps crossed the floorboards of the room above. Crane watched this as he continued around the wall, past the coal shoot and adjacent stove, behind the stairs where he stopped. Before him, a heavy wooden door was chained shut. Crane knew this must be the vault, though the sight of this chamber sullied the fantastical palace that Crane had long imagined. In the center of the door was a small open vent. To Crane's eyes it resembled a slot through which to insert books. Crane peered into it. The room beyond was a black abyss.

Crane turned back toward the stove. Its metal chimney rattled from the approaching footsteps that gathered above. The door to the basement opened, releasing voices, echoing in the sepulchral pit. Footsteps approached at an alarming rate as Crane leapt onto a wooden crate allowing him to reach the exterior door. The timber latch of the door jammed further into itself as Crane pressed against it. Seeing no exit, he released pressure on the latch and jumped down to the floor, ready to face the approaching intruders. On the floor Crane's hand met a piece of paper he gripped as he rose to his feet. Crane studied the lines. The paper was singed and had been torn out of a bound book. Crane pocketed the page as the figures came around the corner.

"Crane!" Barlow yelped in a fatherly tone.

Crane saw fear and confusion in Barlow's face that he had never witnessed before, which solidified the severity of the situation. Behind Barlow, Pettick and Mawkin appeared with the Guard from the top of the stairs.

"What is your boy doing down here, Barlow?" Pettick asked with an accusative bite.

Crane read Barlow's face, knowing better than to respond, and decided to just follow Barlow's lead. The valleys of Barlow's cheeks expanded as his concave brow relaxed from anger to a deep guilt, frightening Crane beyond the expected punishment of his boyish daring.

"He's shoveling books," Barlow said, staring at Crane, his face filled with incredible sorrow.

Pettick crossed his arms. "I thought we were going to discuss when he would be ready to do so?" Pettick interrogated as Barlow turned to him, creating a barrier between Pettick and his son.

"It slipped my mind," Barlow retorted.

"This is not the type of thing that should simply 'slip a 'Crow's mind,' regardless of what the inconvenience may be."

"It was my mistake," Barlow sighed, "and I take responsibility for it."

Crane listened little to the exchange before him as his hand coiled around the singed page within his pants pocket. The chamber seemed to crumble as the deteriorating fantasy crushed down on him. Crane moved to the stove, which he found concealed the rest of the torn and charred family of the burnt page clenched in his glove.

"For so valued an apprentice, he is slow in his labors," Mawkin said to Barlow and Pettick, all the time watching Crane.

The elder 'Crows turned their attention to Crane who stood in the corner with a shovel in hand. As Crane beared the shovel's weight, he crossed to the well of books. Barlow kept his gaze on his apprentice, who was too scared to share the gesture. Crane lowered the flat of the shovel to the floor, scraping along the brick into the well, lifting out several pounds of books which he carried to the stove. With a shut brow and a trembling shovel, he lowered the heavy weight into the burning embers, which ate the books like several helpless mice in a tank of hungering vipers. The flaring embers etched the folds of Crane's face, which quaked, sighed, and shifted with each lift of the shovel.

Pettick turned back to address Barlow as they began their exit. "We will continue our work another time." Barlow remained still as Pettick followed the 'Crows around the corner, turning back at the bottom of the stairs. "This type of task is not just a danger in the doing of the act, but in the knowing of the act itself. Remember that." Pettick directed his lesson to Crane before continuing up the stairs.

Barlow shuttered his chin, turning the corner back to Crane who stood, shovel in hand. Crane's figure was outlined by the white and yellow light which followed him as he crumbled to the floor. Barlow crossed the room, torn between anger and guilt. He reached down to the stove, sealing the pages to their fate. Then, turning to his son, Barlow hunched down to the cold brick and lifted his son, in a heap, into his arms.

* * *

Crane awoke in the observatory, his head resting on books piled in a frame around him. Crane felt a weight, hung heavy upon him—the translucence of waking. The sun simmered halfway up the window. Crane's hand bloomed, revealing the singed page, a reminder, materializing a nightmare that had yet to become tangible. Crane stood and descended the stairs from the observatory. Barlow's face rose from his book to look at him.

"You're awake," Barlow said. "You've been out the better part of the day." Crane ignored Barlow as he moved through the columns of books that stood between him and the door. Barlow did not take well to being ignored. "Do not ignore your master. Crane?" Barlow rose in a shifting balance. "It is a foolish apprentice who denies response to his master!" Barlow's anger rose as Crane continued toward the door. "Crane! Do not ignore your father!"

Crane stopped. His hand rested on the doorknob as he turned back to Barlow.

"Fathers don't lie to their sons," Crane despairingly sighed.

"Honest answers, then. Why were you in the cellar?" Barlow pried.

Crane turned back to the door.

"I asked you a question!" Barlow stomped his foot, the threads of his cheek trembling. "I asked you a question: why were you down in the cellar?"

"We are burning them and all you can say to me is how you deserve an answer." Crane's brow shifted with the tensile snap of his back, lowering the tension with his words. "I owe you nothing but regret—regret in the respect I once had for you." Crane opened the door and disappeared into the hall, leaving Barlow frozen, taut, alone with Crane's words.

Though it was spring, cold nights came often, a reminder of the previous long winter. Barlow shivered as he crossed the quiet main street of the village, and quickly sank into his bungalow. The room was silent. Barnes sat up on his cot, acknowledging Barlow's entrance.

"It's a cold one, ain't it?" Barnes noted.

"Certainly. It's not summer just yet."

Peeling off his tweed coat, Barlow looked around the room. "Where's Crane?"

The two matched gazes, reaching an unspoken understanding that was not much more than simply restating a fact.

"Right," Barlow reckoned as he trudged to his bed, forcing himself to lie within sight of the vacant cot across the room.

* * *

Gwyn scanned the hill as she moved with purpose, approaching the garage. This territory of the farm was one of the few mysteries in her world; feeling like a curious trespasser, Gwyn entered the garage bay. Her imagination materialized as objects she had heard so much about from Crane entered reality. Gwyn felt closer to Crane than she had ever before as she moved through the rays of light just as he had many times before. Her hand traversed the ripples in the cover that shrouded the hood of the Ford pickup. She lifted the cover just enough to peek at the cherry painted lid which reflected every curve Crane couldn't seem to articulate when comparing Gwyn to this masterpiece. She thought of how surreal it all was, these machines, this place.

"Don't expect much company 'round here." A deep voice echoed down the bay, startling Gwyn. She let out the smallest of screams and whipped her head around to witness the figure at the opposite end of the bay. The bay remained in a state of lingering silence as the figure limped closer to her. Finally, with a huff, the voice broke: "So what brings you?" The rays of light unveiled Kindle.

"It's Gwyn, the Cobbler's daughter."

The grimace shifted into a smile. "I know who you are, had to get a good look at ya before I could let up on the 'Angry Old 'Crow' thing. Gotta keep the young ones from snooping around." The Mechanic completely removed his scowl as his body relaxed. He moved to the side of the pickup Gwyn was standing in front of. "She's a beauty up close."

"I'm sorry?" Gywn asked, confused.

"I know the boy has told you about her, but even that one can't find the words that show the real sense of it," Kindle said. He then peeled off the cover, revealing the red hood and sheen black wheel well of the pickup.

Gwyn's weight shifted as a shared sense of excitement arose. She reached out her hand, pressed her palm against the cool hood. As she walked alongside the truck, running her glove across its surface, she noticed the finish was so buffed she could almost see herself reflected in it. Kindle mirrored her path, on the opposite side of the vehicle, meeting her at the rear wheel well. Gwyn raised her hand, and rested it on the wooden bed frame. Kindle said, breaking the silence, "So what brings the Cobbler's Daughter up my way? Mechanical shoes?" The witticism failed to land.

"Have you seen him—Crane?"

Kindle's expression slipped from a smile into one of mild concern. "No, I haven't seen him for a couple of days. I figured his master must have given him a lot of work."

"No one has seen him. I asked Barlow, but he didn't wanna talk to me."

Gwyn's worry brought even heavier concern to Kindle's face. Kindle looked over at Gwyn, resting a gentle glove on her shoulder. "It's not you; Barlow isn't the most sociable 'Crow. Crane probably just needs time."

"Thanks, Kindle." Gwyn sighed and turned to exit.

"Says a lot, you comin' up here to find him," Kindle said. "Takes that kind of Scarecrow to be right for that kid."

Gwyn turned to look back at Kindle; a warm expression appeared on her face.

Kindle smiled and said, "The water tower. And don't tell him you heard anything from me."

Gwyn showed Kindle her smile as she turned the corner, cut through the light and exited the garage.

The journey seemed particularly long between the garage and the water tower, which stood by the edge of the ridge. Gwyn thought of all the things she might say to Crane, none of which felt right. With each passing stride, every word of her projected conversation felt more phony and rehearsed. Gwyn soon realized she was standing at the base of the tower, speechless. She exhaled, confidently took hold of the first beam, and ascended the tower.

"Crane?" Gwyn called out as she reached the escarpment of the water tower, pulling herself atop the wooden barrel.

Crane's figure sat motionless overlooking the expanse of the farm ahead, unmoved by Gwyn's approach.

"Crane?" Gwyn moved to Crane with a compassionate arm. Her body heat created a ray of warmth, breaking Crane from his gaze before her fingers could make contact with his sunken shoulders. Crane's subtle reaction from their near interaction left Gwyn feeling distant as she slid herself next to him. Their feet dangled over the edge of the barrel like schoolchildren on a bench, paramours divided by the shame of their desires, a distance highlighted by the sinking sun beyond.

"How did you find me?" Crane asked, his gaze still locked on the picturesque valley below.

"Kindle." Gwyn paused. "And your father."

I appreciate the gesture." Crane glanced at Gwyn for a moment, then looked toward the sky. "Only one of them would know where I was."

Being caught in her lie, Gwyn tried not to look away.

"How long have you been up here?"

"Four days—a lot of time to think over some things," Crane plainly stated.

Gwyn feared the sensation growing in her bosom, the sense that Crane was drifting and the valley between them was widening. "Come back, Crane. Don't do this."

"Do what?" Crane grew defensive.

"This. Running away."

"This is what I do. I think. I read." Crane spoke with apathy foreign to his character. "I just ain't doin' it down there, under you."

Crane's words drew Gwyn further into his maze. Trying not to be hurt by any words Crane had or might say, she asked, "How are you *under* me?"

"How am I not?" Crane's gaze moved toward the farmhouse before crossing back to the village. "I can't live under them, buried beneath those Scarecrows and their piked mentality."

"They want to help you, Crane." Gwyn pleaded, choosing her words carefully. "They love you."

"They love the way things are. And with that—with me gone—they are better for it." Crane sighed.

"Your father and brother need you around, whether they admit it or not."

"Is that so?" Crane said, looking into Gwyn's eyes.

"Yes, it is." Gwyn spoke with a certainty Crane could not ignore. "And so do I." Gwyn moved her hand, the fibers crossed along Crane's. As she rested her hand atop his, Crane's isolated disposition dissolved in the shrinking void between them. The moment remained till the expanding shadows of fleeting day grabbed hold of Crane, dragging his conscious to the village below.

"They don't know, they don't bother to know, they don't ask, they are content, and in their content world I am a freak."

Gwyn grew frustrated by her loss of words, driving fervency to the few she gathered. "I can only tell you what I think, what I feel, and what I know." For better or for worse, Gwyn's words scared and scarred.

"What am I supposed to do?" Crane asked, feeling genuinely at a loss, astray.

"I can't answer that for you." Gwyn said.

The silhouette of two merged into one.

"I don't expect you to," Crane said, pulling Gwyn closer.

* * *

Held by a shaky hand, the magnifying glass shifted into place. The typewriter lay scattered in pieces on the workbench as Kindle filed through the manual which sat beside it; working ambidextrously, he removed parts then fickly returned them to their place in the pile.

"You really shouldn't be leavin' the door unlocked . . ." a voice pondered.

Kindle, his concentration broken, raised his head to see Pettick, whose entrance was unannounced and unnoticed.

"Ya never really know who might stumble in."

"Pettick! And to what do I owe the pleasure?" Kindle asked, turning his stool to face Pettick who stood in the light by the end of the cattle truck.

"There's little that fazes you, is there, Tinker? You are reading words you may not even comprehend, yet that lump of worthless trinkets and rubbish will somehow function. I always knew you were something special."

"The point, Pettick?" Kindle asked without patience.

"I admire your dedication, your ability to complete the tasks ahead of you."

"What's the job, Pettick?" Kindle asked bluntly. "You don't come 'round here 'less you need something."

Pettick huffed at Kindle's conjecture. He strolled silently down the back of the garage, turning out through the rear man-door. Kindle reluctantly followed, exiting through the rear bay door behind the garage. The sun intensified in layers across a Death Valley of Pittsburgh steel and Detroit mechanics. Skeletons of Model-Ts were piled in rows, each plotted with eroded license plates, like the aged headstones of forgotten graves. Engines of horseless carriages, fenders of boxcars and rumble seats were piled in the labyrinth of a small scrapyard—which clutter made infinite.

Pettick led Kindle through the maze with uncanny familiarity. At the corner of the junkyard, in a makeshift shelter, three tractors were poorly shaded. The nose of two of the massive machines jutted out into the scorching daylight. A layer of sandy earth lined every bump, curve, and crevice of the machines.

Kindle stumbled to a halt. Pettick turned to him, his hand raised up at the three mighty metal dinosaurs standing before him.

"The Future!" Pettick announced with grandeur. "I need them up and running before the end of the month." Kindle remained silent, not knowing what to make of this request. Kindle thought while Pettick prepared his pitch that would turn their discussion down an unfortunate path.

"Are you certain about this?" Kindle asked with sincerity. "This ain't exactly walkin' what you've been talkin', preacher." A Flying Crow screamed distantly from above.

"I'm here to do what is in the best interest for the colony, doesn't matter what I believe it to be or not. So please, get it done. Quickly." Pettick turned, starting back toward the garage. Kindle brushed the bristles of his chin, and laid a hand on the beast before him. Lifting his hand an impression of his palm remained in the layer of fine sand. With a huff Kindle turned toward Pettick.

"I'll do this. In return, let me ask you one question, and I expect a whole response," Kindle said, firm in his stance.

"That is fair. What is your question?" Pettick asked, respecting Kindle's tenacity.

"Where do all these automobiles come from?"

Pettick lifted his head with the cheaply gashed grin of a used car salesmen centered in his prized lot. "Humans leave traces—trash—in their wake."

Several field-workers struggled to restrain a violent quarter horse that leapt uncontrollably, whipping the cart down the path. The driver snapped the reins, the cart fishtailed, and a cloud of dirt rose. The whole scene was a racket which broke the quiet of the day as the dirt whirled in the wind. The brim of Mawkin's hat shielded his face; the scar, now several weeks old, appeared seamless in the mesh of the rest of the woven fibers. His cheek tensed, tightening the seams which gathered along the bridge of his scowl while he crossed through the workers rallying in his path to restrain the horse.

Pettick watched from a rocking chair on the veranda as the incident unfolded at the bottom of the hill. Mawkin approached, stopping at the steps below Pettick.

"See what you're doing? You keep scaring the horses," Pettick quipped, rising from his chair.

"There was a snake under the cart," Mawkin responded, unamused.

"I'm sure."

"Where would you like to talk?" Mawkin asked.

"Porch will do fine," Pettick said, ordering the two officers stationed on the porch down the hill to assist with the overturned cart. He then placed his journal atop his field jacket on the floor beside him and returned to the chair.

"I have Veidt tasked with the cart," Mawkin stated, "and five other 'Crows for the seizure. Still have a few days on other aspects: containment and—"

"What did you tell the soldiers about this operation?" Pettick asked. "Any trouble justifying the assault or the need for such a thing to be less spoken of?"

"They understand it is a settlement in an unsafe proximity. Grey assures me his work at the silos is silent and well underway."

Pettick traced his jaw with his glove. "Good. Very good. Your 'human problem' will soon be in the past."

Mawkin lost interest in the scene down the hill, pensively tracing the skyline above the farrow patches east of the farmhouse. Turning back to Pettick, he unloaded his mind's queries: "How are you so sure this hideout exists?"

"Because I have seen it before." The rocker picked up tempo.

"There hasn't been much pickup from that last scare. According to Hardwick, the sacrifice was less moving than we hoped."

"Their purpose will be swayed." Pettick spoke in absolutes.

"And their loyalty?" Mawkin asked.

"That is already won." The rocking stopped.

"How can you be sure?" Mawkin inquired, sounding less dutiful.

Pettick gave a momentary dramatic pause. "You lit the fire that night. It was your hand on the torch, not mine." He smiled with the wit of his own response.

Mawkin nodded, looking consciously guilty, a stench on his cuff. "*We* did that—together." Mawkin moved several feet down the path before turning back to the house, chin low, shoulders hunched.

"Still troubled?" Pettick asked with genuine concern.

Mawkin took several moments to respond. "Smell doesn't go away, does it?"

The silence between the two 'Crows left a void filled by the shouting and snarls of the incident down the hill.

"No, it does not. Gets in your threads, sinks in deep, and eventually it is just another part of the mesh." The two Scarecrows looked over the same farm with different prospects.

* * *

Night's curtain was near fully drawn as the 'Crow families congregated at the meeting ground. Pettick paced the stage, atypically early for the engagement. Behind Pettick, three massive mounds were shrouded in wait for the big reveal. Kindle raised his boot to the first rung of the wooden ladder that was pitched against the far mound. Crossing the stage, Mawkin observed Kindle's movements, the hesitance which manifested in his stride and posture was distinct.

"Would you like me to take notes?" Mawkin asked Pettick, who looked down at his journal, then up at Mawkin, and responded by shaking his head. Mawkin gave Pettick the stage as he considered the cause for Pettick's change of routine. Planting along the side of the deck, Barlow approached.

"Take notes . . ." Barlow gave Mawkin a questioning glance, knowing of the extent of the 'Crows' ignorance.

Mawkin ignored him.

"What is this?" Barlow asked, gesturing to the mounds before them.

"Our future," Mawkin responded, thinking nothing of the repercussions of his answer.

Hardwick approached, in a waddle.

"What is this?" Hardwick inquired. Mawkin and Barlow did not respond. After several seconds Hardwick, frustrated, moved up the steps and onto the deck, towards Pettick.

"Pettick, what is this? We didn't discuss this."

Pettick broke his concentration, quietly asserting, "Do yourself a favor and get off the stage, you worthless pawn." Hardwick lowered his head, and quietly moved off the deck. Slowly the masses gathered before the platform.

Pettick whirled his fingertips with immense friction, then, after several passing minutes, in an exhausted breath, held his stance and began speaking.

"Good evening. I am joyful to have you all standing before me tonight. The strength in this colony, of any prospering nation, is in the enduring strength of its community. Community, above all else, will prevail. A colony divided will fall, I promise you that. Tonight, I stand before you with a plan, a plan that will propel this colony into a great age of prosperity, integrity, and above all else, a continued happiness for seasons to come. I remind you now that no progress can be made without sacrifice. As you know, your safety is my biggest concern. In light of recent threats to our colony, I have worked tirelessly to find a method of protecting our precious land and after meticulous assembly, working with Hardwick and Mawkin as well as Grey, our colony's architect, and my officers, a plan has been set into motion." He paused for dramatic effect. "We will construct a fence around the full span of our colony securing our cropland, village, and resources, completely enclosed within this barrier. The fence will stand an imposing eight meters in height." He paused again. Stepping forward, Pettick could hear the boards in the platform creak.

"The project will start by the road, covering our most vulnerable positions first. It will then continue down the far north ridge, complimenting the natural barrier of the pine straights, crossing the western creek, and connecting at the end of the crop lines. The structural stability will lie in massive trunks, buried two meters into the soil and placed every ten meters along the fence line. This project will require an incredibly large percentage of our population and therefore a majority of our labor will be aquired from the fields. In order to achieve this, we will need to supplement resources to those who remain in the field in order for both projects to successfully remain on schedule. For those of you already worried with the shortages of field labor, I assure you I will protect your interests. My first resolution I proudly present to you now. Kindle, remove the curtain!"

Kindle rose atop the ladder, his head locked on his task, away from the vying whispers of the crowd. The dusty shroud dragged along the nose of the mighty tractor, curling into the air like a cape atop heavy winds. The curtain lingered there in the wind, tapered behind the three tractors for several triumphant moments. Then, with Kindle's grasping fist, it was torn to the ground, fully unveiling the first machine.

"I present to you in its most majestic form, the motorized harvester! These machines will function as a tool, just as any other, but will improve production tenfold."

Cheers erupted, offering a glimpse of postulated hope. Kindle looked over the crowd and their ignorant approval for all it was and all it was not, knowing all the while the single truth that haunted him as he hovered over this remarkable invention: it could never be undone. Barlow looked to Mawkin, who, stoic as he was, couldn't hide the ebb of leery thoughts. Beyond, Pettick jollied in the wake of his big sale.

"I say this to you now, with my greatest confidence, this will succeed!" Pettick repeated these words in fading resilience as he exited the stage, avoiding his comrades' faces.

In the distance, Shepherd the Herder watched with awe before starting south with a lowered head. His kin, the animals of the farm, knew to follow closely, having sensed the unease in their sentinel. His staff penetrated deep into the soil, guiding Shepherd homeward.

The continued cheering faded as Pettick's foot and mind traveled with steady pace into the night. Kindle remained a statue on a pedestal as the crowd surrounded, staring in awe at the creatures that had long slumbered in unexplored caverns right in their own backyard.

Barlow lit the wick of the candle in his study. Reflected light bounced off the mirrored walls of the small box as Critch and Quill navigated through the columns, gathering stools, creating a triangle for their discussion.

"The future?" Critch said with a heavy head, rubbing his palms against his brow.

"So it seems," Barlow responded with an equal weight to bear.

"How could machines be the answer?" Quill asked.

"I worry our infallible Pettick has lost his way. This has been the second large act of a score of acts that he himself imparted in recent memory that directly contradicts our constitution, our charter, the foundation of what we stand for, both in this colony and as Scarecrows," Critch protested.

"What separates us from savage creatures like humanity?" Quill chimed in.

"It can hardly be called a constitution; you cannot call a document such as that at all binding when it is concealed in someone's pocket and scribed in erasable ink." Barlow's tone lowered with the widening depth of his frustration. He shifted across the library, joining the triangle.

"What can we do about Pettick? Hardwick is no 'Crow to stand for any true cause nor the board he governs," Critch stated.

"It is not Pettick's leadership I fear; it is them." Barlow's hand rose to the window, gesturing to the lights of the village in the distance. "They follow him without consciousness; they know not if his staff leads them to a promise land or over a cliff. But they follow without question."

"If this generation of 'Crows is truly lost," Quill spoke firmly, "I take that burden. That fault is on me."

"What of the young 'Crows?" Critch spoke, gesturing to Quill who sighed with an inverted chest.

"My hands are tied. In the past two seasons my freedom to truly teach these young 'Crows has been taken by Pettick and his governance. I have no choice in the matter, no freedom to connect with my pupils, my schoolhouse has become a factory, producing archetypes: either the 'Crow's elders are artisans in which they can follow, or they become another hollow 'Crow, lost to Pettick's rising army." Quill faced her fellow Scarecrows, moving her gaze to Barlow. "I'm sorry I cannot be more."

"You are here, you are concerned. That is what matters." Barlow rested his hand on Quill's shoulder.

"Then what will we do? What *can* we do?" Critch asked with fading resilience, looking to Barlow for some type of answer.

"I do not know," Barlow rued. "I truly do not know."

The discussion drew on for several more minutes yet no words were spoken, just broken glances and immaterialized visions of what could be. With Quill and Critch's departure, Barlow took a post as the watchman of the farm through his window, his mind searching for action but finding only dreams. Then, in that singular instant, a moment of magic, the spark struck him. His body trembled with renewed energy as he shifted toward the book-covered desk. Grasping the lowest handle, he pulled out the drawer. The weight of the heavy cherry birch didn't faze the old 'Crow as he lifted the drawer onto the desktop, pushing in on the false bottom which popped like a lid revealing the hidden compartment.

The book Barlow pulled from his shelf was aged, bound in moss-colored cloth that turned black at the spine. Mid-nineteenth-century binding held the manuscript in its proper place as Barlow grasped it with a face one could only describe as resolute. Barlow moved to his study, where he opened the cover and, in permanent ink, scribed a note of only necessary words. Barlow blew several huffs onto the wet ink, closed the cover, and with a propped hand placed the book beneath the stack of books left on his chair. Atop the stack, a note read:

For my son Crane.

* * *

Crane turned the last page of his most recent read, running his finger across the risen letters of ink on the parchment. Before closing the back cover, Crane pressed the book to his face, smelling the history he held in his hand; its fragrances resembling what he thought to be the halls of the great libraries of the world, but more closely represented the tinge of decades of dust and mold. It was an ignorance Crane cherished, an illusion he was happy living in.

He set down the book, looking west over the ridge. The sun had begun its descent back to the soil, bathing the valley in a gold wash of its fading hues. He reached into his rucksack and pulled out a book that was bound in a faded moss-green and black cloth. Crane opened to the cover page that read:

Frankenstein or The Modern Prometheus by Mary Shelley

The letters were framed in gold fringing, under which a note read in ink:

Crane, take special care of this one

— Barlow

Crane was both confused and intrigued having not heard of this book before and the title was stranger than any other book he had previously read. This sentiment excited Crane as he turned the lacquered parchment and was propelled into Shelly's world, into the Arctic Sea.

CHAPTER IV:

Manifestations of Faust
(OR)
Strawberry Milkshake Stargazers

July 9, 1947

We parked the Deluxe in the fields, beneath the scarecrow and his black-voyeur-eyes. Far from the watching eyes of Tucker or Blake McCallister. She kissed my hands. First with the edge of her nose, then with her lips, forgiving them of their filth.

"They're dirty," I softly confessed.

She looked at me a long calculating while, and kissed them again. The touch of her skin sent those pulses of electricity through my body, the kind which escape from your limbs like a flood, trembling your fingertips and toes and shuddering that part of you that still feels, that's still culpable to the ecstasy of shame. I pushed her farther along the nose of the hood of her Chevy. Her legs wrapped around me, pulling me closer to her, my shins pressed against the fender. Her fingers ran along the rough of my neck, nails digging in deep. It is now days later and the ripples of that moment are still making my scribing fingers shake the ink on this page. She thawed my heart in the way only a woman could, the way physical intimacy can warm you when you're with another requiting body— to teach a man how to come back from the dead. And, crawling into the backseat, we peeled off our clothing as though it were our skin. All the while the scarecrow watched.

Pettick closed his journal. Tremors shook the ground beneath the 'Crow's feet as the large trunk mated with the fertile earth below. The once quiet perimeter of the farm now bustled with mechanical sounds of destruction. With every chop and thwack, large pines, one hundred feet or more, crashed to the earth. Well underway, the fence was now several weeks into construction. Pettick stepped beside Grey the Architect as the small 'Crow scanned over a series of drawings that rested on the bed of the tool wagon. Grey wore wide suspenders of green and yellow, holding up brown slacks, from which he drew a stick of graphite. He rolled up his sleeves to avoid smearing the top plate of drafting, a precise graphite drawing on velum showing the polygonal-shaped perimeter around the farm divided into sections, each labeled with its estimated time of completion. Pettick briefly scanned the drawing before returning to the workers several yards away to supervise their efforts and efficiency.

Grey continued to vie for Pettick's attention, revising his work as he spoke: "With that delegation of labor, we are likely looking at an early September completion. Best circumstance could bring it to a close as early as, say, end of August."

"That's not good enough," Pettick remarked sharply, leaning against the back of the wagon.

"I don't know what you want me to tell you. A project of this magnitude takes time. We only have so many 'Crows and an even smaller amount of tools. Malthus is preoccupied with the barn, when we could be laying concrete reinforcements here. And unless you wish to pull some of those laborers from the silo barn at night—" Grey's body locked as Pettick's fist suddenly broke away from its rest, latching onto the ruff of Grey's neck.

"You should shut your gap while you still can!" Pettick's grip tightened, launching Grey's graphite from his hand. "We'll discuss this at a later time." Pettick released Grey, who immediately gave his weight to the table. Mawkin approached from down the path, having witnessed the brief altercation and found it most curious.

"You playing nice?" Mawkin asked with a smile.

"We reached an understanding," Pettick said, moving away from the cart, passing Mawkin and strolling several yards down the path.

Still chuckling, Mawkin replaced Pettick at the back of the cart, leaning against the bed, facing the laborers.

"You should really learn how to tell him what he wants to hear," Mawkin said.

Grey shook. "He's never touched me before."

"Never touches anyone; you best hope it's the last time."

"Pettick is stronger than I measure, structurally speaking," Grey said, recovering his stance.

"If you don't want him roughing you up again, I'd leave your opinions of his stature out of your conversations," Mawkin quipped.

"Right," Grey said, regaining his grip on the graphite. Mawkin gave Grey a punch of camaraderie, then left him to join Pettick's side with fading jollity.

"He's a bumbling fool," Pettick said.

Mawkin remarked, "You don't teach much of patience, do you?"

"No, I do not. Let that be your one and only lesson."

Crane stroked the petals through his fingers like strands of hair as he lay blissfully in the pile of books; all the while warming rays washed into the observatory giving the sunflower life. Barnes walked through the doorway, and set down a pile of books he had spent all day slumbering under.

"You know, if you caress that thing any more, the petals are going to start to fall out," Barnes wryly stated.

"No, they're not. If you spent time actually reading those books on biology instead of using them as pillows you'd know that," Crane returned, unmoved from his star-crossed stare.

"Either way, you love it a little too much, little brother. It's rooted here; it ain't going anywhere anytime soon."

"And I should listen to your advice on botany because . . . ?" Crane remarked. "You don't exactly have a great survival rate." He pointed to the window in the opposite room where a potted patch of dead flowers drooped down onto a pile of books.

"You know what I am talking about," Barnes said.

"Yes, brother, I do know what you are talking about, and my dead flower metaphor still holds true," Crane sullied, chuckling. "This isn't the same thing you had with the Quartermaster's daughter, or the Woodcutter's daughter, or the thing you thought you had with the Mule Clerk's daughter, though the flower metaphor doesn't quite work for her."

"You're right, it doesn't," Barnes agreed, breaking his demeanor.

"Yeah, she never smelled sweet at all!" Crane exploded in laughter.

"That's enough! I'm warning you!"

Crane tried to hold in his laughter, respectfully containing himself, keeping his mouth shut, until the pressure became too much, letting out, "Or what? You're going to let the Mule Clerk's daughter loose on me?"

Barnes lunged at Crane. The two boys playfully wrestled, knocking over stacks of books and causing them to crumble over into an avalanche, which in turn knocked into the telescope. The gold cylinder rocked, swaying off its tripod. Barnes threw out his long arms, catching the telescope and cradling it just before the lens could shatter onto the floor. Both boys froze, their eyes locked on the telescope, realizing they had avoided a near fatality. The library door swung closed. In a sudden dash, the small nook was returned to order as Barlow shuffled around the corner. Entering the observatory, he came upon his sons peacefully reading. This ideal image, however, he knew to be false.

"You can let go of the act, boys. I may be slow and aging, but I can still hear, especially when the floorboards above the stairs bow," Barlow lectured. The two boys released their poses, and followed their father as he shuffled to his chair in the Library. "You don't even need to tell me what it was about."

"Yes, we do!" the two brothers answered in unison.

"Let me take a crack at it. Barnes was doing the older brother's fine duty of ensuring that his little brother doesn't—how should I put it—complicate and therefore ruin a fine opportunity like the Cobbler's daughter." Crane let out a sigh. "And from that reaction, I will assume I'm correct. As for Barnes, I assume Crane brought up the little matter of his plants having trouble 'flourishing,' to put it kindly."

"I used that exact metaphor!" Crane interjected, his grin wide.

"That wasn't all," Barnes sighed.

"I see. Did he bring up the Mule Clerk's daughter again?" Barlow asked.

Barnes bowed his head, masking his glare at Crane. "Yes. Yes, he did."

"As he should have," Barlow said.

"Why?" Barnes begrudgingly asked.

"Because no truly caring and nurturing brother would let his kin court such a bad bushel." Barlow rose, cut between his two boys, and wrapped them in his arms, keeping the two boys from fighting as much as his affection allowed. Barlow returned to his lounge as the boys continued wrestling around the library. "This place best be just as messy as I left it when I wake up. I am meeting with Pettick tomorrow and there had better be some reading done for him." Drifting from the entertaining nature of the boys' tussle into a much-needed rest, Barlow let out a final snarl, then fell into hibernation.

***

Pettick stood alone at the tilled line's edge, staring westward at the scarless, cloudless sky fading into a darkened pungent purple dusk. The winds were gentle as they broke over merging folds of black hills, winds which blew worry to Pettick's heart. He squatted, pulled off his right glove, and ran his hand along the stirred topsoil, shoveling it into a clump in his palm. Standing, he released the clump into the wind, setting soil particles adrift in a cloud which floated for several feet before falling back to earth. Pettick thought of the thirsty earth that remained in the rough threads of his hand as he brushed the residue onto his trousers before returning the glove to his hand. A gust of wind carried cries from atop earth's aching belly as a formation of Flying Crows circled in the shrinking sky above Pettick. His heart sunk even further. He trembled, pulled his pen and journal from a satchel, and made several rough notes, thoughts, ideas, worries, and wishes on the page before the Flying Crows called again for his attention. He could feel them watching him, sharing indifferently in the fear he had of the dry soil beneath his feet.

"Am I interrupting something?" Barlow's words came as a surprise to Pettick, causing him to jump.

"No, old 'Crow, you're not," Pettick replied with an unvoiced comfort at the 'Crow's arrival.

The two stood, silently returning gazes. This exchange lingered on until the awkward moment became an awkward minute. Barlow finally broke the silence.

"So, what is it?"

Pettick snapped from the clutches of his mind. "Sorry?"

"You wanted to speak with me," Barlow said.

"Oh, right. I wanted to speak with you on a few orders of business." Pettick gathered himself, pocketing his pen, hugging close the journal in his right hand. "The first is on a project I wish to start on quite immediately—"

"Right," Barlow said, hoping to keep the conversation flowing.

Pettick thought a moment, searching for the best introduction, some grand prelude to what he hoped to be a major feat. "Do you know why I keep this journal, Barlow?"

Several thoughts of varying appropriateness crossed Barlow's mind. After a few seconds of consideration, he answered: "Because it is a tool to keep this farm, and you as its leader, organized." He refrained from saying words he would later regret not saying.

"Yes and no." Pettick spoke, gesturing with his hands. "That is true, but it only skims the surface to my madness." Barlow quietly chuckled; Pettick ignored this. "I keep this book because it leaves an account, a legacy of truths in ink that will remain when my cycle of life reaches its twilight."

"Your mark on this earth, then?" Barlow added.

"Not just mine—ours. The 'Crows need to be remembered, even if only as to cast in slate their existence, like humans before them." Pettick spoke with a surging excitement.

"And what has this to do with me?" Barlow inquired.

"We need a slate stronger and an ink less soluble than that of my pen and this leather binding. So I am entreating you to scribe, and in course produce, the first binding document of our history, both here and beyond the gates of Tucker's farm."

"And how will I write of those events that escape our walls?"

Pettick smiled. "You scribe from the words and memories of a witness to those events."

"And who will that be?" Barlow asked, knowing the answer, the response to his own question easily read in the enthusiasm on Pettick's face. "You?"

"Yes, me!" Pettick rallied. Barlow nodded, holding back the excitement Pettick hoped he would reciprocate. "We will start every morning before working hours." Pettick held his journal, brass seal up to the sky, pressing it to his chest with an equal enthusiasm.

"And the second thing?" Barlow asked, inadvertently interrupting Pettick's rambling.

"What?"

"The second task you summoned me for?"

Pettick's enthusiasm faded as his foot ruffed a small cloud of dirt in the rutted top soil at their feet. "I need you to find an account, record, anything that might answer when we may expect our first season's rain. We are far past due." Both 'Crows looked down at the soil as darkness quickly gathered in the sky. Barlow huffed, starting back toward the village, stopping only as the nuances of Pettick's asking reached his thoughts.

"You're worried, aren't you?" Barlow asked, looking back at Pettick, whose gaze had returned to the sky. The silence answered as Barlow's figure disappeared into the expanding folds. Pettick remained stoic as bird-watching turned to stargazing, the prescence of Flying Crows still audible as he wrote a final note in his journal and returned his sight to the sky one last time. Only then did he start back toward the candlelight of the farmhouse.

***

Crane navigated his way through the dark library, which he could have done blindfolded. The stark bible-black room left no map to chart the paper stalagmites that shaped the landscape of the wooden cave. The match ignited, catching the fat on the wick of the candle caged in a box of mirrors resting on the center of Barlow's side table. Crane scanned the yellow rusted room where he procured his stack of books, which was perched on Barnes's vacant stool. After placing the books in his rucksack, Crane moved to extinguish the candle, but stopped as a noise from the observatory caught his attention. The cross-fade of yellow into the purple walls and white sabers of moonlight cast shifting shadows onto the threshold of the stairs leading to the observatory. He made his way up the stairs where, to his great surprise, Gwyn was sitting in the moonlight, her fingers laced between the small petals of the sunflower.

"So this is the place?" Gwyn asked.

As Gwyn bloomed from her shell, Crane's perspective matched the rays of the room which followed her like a spotlight, every act of their movement a choreographed motion, played out atop the highest chamber in this less than fairy-tale castle.

"The place?" Crane asked.

"The place where you do your part. It's a big deal, you know. Work makes up a great part of who a 'Crow is, I think."

"That's only partly true," Crane added.

"Why is that?" Gwyn continued to focus on the elements of the room, the textures of the brass in oblong cylinders of the telescope, the valleys of darkness in the floorboards, the craters in the walls that encased the spyglass overlooking the slumbering world beyond the window frame. Crane looked at Gwyn. Gwyn looked away.

"'Cause there is more to me than being the Reader's Apprentice—much more to me than this."

"Really?"

"I think so." Crane grew pensive, resting his glove atop the telescope. "At least, I hope so."

"I believe you," Gwyn said, hoping to break Crane from his insecurities.

"You do?"

"I guess." Gwyn smiled. The two shared a hushed laugh.

"You don't like giving a straight answer, do you?" Crane inquired.

"Maybe." Gwyn spoke with coy persistence, baiting Crane with momentary gazes, which he bit like the spearing of a fisherman's hook. "Sometimes it feels nights are kinda magic," Gwyn said, stargazing through the window. "What is this, anyway?" she asked, gesturing softly to the telescope between them.

"I don't know," Crane said, flustered, still stuck on the image of Gwyn's figure on the window seat, the perfect arch of her posture, the feathers of her hair in the moonlight.

"You spend all this time in this room, and you can't figure out how it works?"

"Oh, the telescope!" Crane said, finally realizing.

"Yes, the telescope." Gwyn nodded, touching the brass scope of the spyglass with her fingertips.

"Well, you look into this glass and it makes what's on the other side of the glass appear like it's right next to you." Crane explored the device as Gwyn moved to the floor beside him, lowering her head to the eyepiece. "Like the moon, and the stars, and everything else—everything through that glass—is a little larger, clearer, closer to you."

Gwyn's face lit up with the presence and clarity of the burning stars, a reaction that resonated with Crane.

"It's as if they were right next to you, almost like—like you could just reach out and touch them," Gwyn said, peering through the glass. She could feel Crane beside her. As curiosity wandered through the galaxies, the glass gradually floated back to the distant hills of her world.

"What's that?" Gwyn asked.

"What's what?"

Gwyn rose from the lens and pointed out the window into the night, toward the rolling hills in the east. "There, straight ahead through the trees."

Crane looked into the glass, where, through the distance outlines of brush, two sabers of light merged into one single orb, tracing in and out of view, till it vanished in a flash. Crane removed his face from the eye of the telescope, and stared off into the still purple valley beyond the perimeter of the farm near the grasslands at the edge of the road.

"I don't know what that was," Crane whispered. "It sure wasn't nothing, but it wasn't like anything I've ever seen before, either." Both 'Crows stood still, fixated on the unknown world beyond the glass.

"Kinda scary," Gwyn said with a curious interest that Crane shared.

"Only when you don't know, but when you look at it up close, through the glass, it isn't scary anymore, because you know what it is."

"Is that always true?" Gwyn asked with a sincerity Crane could read.

"I'd like to believe that." Crane smiled.

"I think I would too." Gwyn looked at Crane, shaking her head at his attempt to veil his language while the dark forest outside dissolved back to night. "I guess I should probably go." Gwyn rose, breaking from a clearly shared moment. Crane searched for words as she made her way to the door. "Oh, wait—I forgot this." Gwyn turned back to Crane, pulled the telescope's lens cap from the pocket of her cardigan, and dropped it into Crane's hand.

Crane looked down at the leather-wrapped cap where a compass rose had been aesthetically pressed.

"We wouldn't want the objective lens to scratch, would we?" Gwyn said with the crease of a clever smile crossing her face. She turned and headed for the door.

Crane gasped at Gwyn's earnest cunning, knowing very well he'd been tricked. "I'll walk you home . . ." Crane rose eagerly, though confidence restrained his excitement. ". . . if you want."

"I would like that."

* * *

Pettick stood on the ridge where the air was cold and his breath, shone before him, was thick and lingered as if the plume of smoke from a cigarette. And next to him a woman, a human, with locks of strawberry hair, stood. Her blouse was ragged, cardigan drab, linen phlox skirt tattered. Her green eyes, longing, glinted as they stared past her breath—to the ridge, to the village and to black night. They were alone on the ridge. The village was in its slumber; the Scarecrows were all asleep.

"I don't have much time left," Pettick said.

"I know."

There was a comfortable silence shared between old friends. He reached for her hand and she trembled slightly.

"I know you have hated me for a long time now."

She smiled slightly, as if finding the words ironic—quaint, even.

Pettick reached into his jacket pocket and fetched out a small book. Its spine was broken, its hide a thick crimson cloth, and the title on the cover read *On Walden Pond* in black pressed type. He dusted off the book and passed it to her. "Here," he said. "I have another one for you."

Smiling, she took it and wrapped it within her cardigan.

"You are free to go, if you want," Pettick said softly.

She shook her head.

His hand wrapped tightly around hers. And she was not bothered by this. The cold winds were abrasive, but she liked the way they felt on her exposed skin as gusts bathed in curls over her. Her eyes grew glassy, soaking in the colors of the sky, before before forming teardrops which plunged down her cheeks. Pettick felt the gust buffer through his straw complexion. And their world, at once, was vast and small. Lights blinked along the village. The stars were as vivid as the sky was clear. He thought of how Columbus only wished for a smaller world, yet made it so much bigger in finding more of it to discover. He turned to look at her, saying nothing of his thoughts, while she continued gazing over the valley, overlooking the castlelike pines, the slumping switchback of the creek, the swooping brush of the tufts of grain.

"You took a raw deal, John," she whispered.

Pettick was silent. After several fleeting moments, he whispered gently, "I'll take you back."

She nodded, and followed his leading hand.

Pettick escorted her, unnoticed, back to the silo barn.

CHAPTER V: Peradventure

Old eyes awoke to the sounds of shattering wood. The edge of the front door erupted, sending the heavy metal knob and lock across the floor. Four figures entered the house, butcher's toys in hand. Screams—human screams—vibrated from different origins in the house, all meaningless, all helpless. The old man watched several blurred shadowy figures pass his doorway and continue down the hall. A separate figure entered the doorway to the old man's room, standing for a moment in doorframe, lit from behind by the light of the hallway, the sillouhette of a boar's head atop the figure's broad, humanlike shoulders. The figure lunged into the room, attacking headfirst, in perfect mimicry of the nature of the beast it wore. The helpless old man let out painful yelps as the boar, now assisted by a horseheaded figure, ripped the man from his sheets and dragged him out of the room. The house's wooden floors peeled the man's knees raw as the animals dragged him down the main hall and into the family room. Embers in the hearth produced an amber glow, which lit both the quaint interior of the room and the family now gathered, kneeling in a row of forced prayer. Behind each hostage loomed a beast that held him or her captive. The old man, the center of the family of five, bowed tearfully. Beneath him, his knees stained the rug his children had grown up playing on. Trembling, the man reached next to him and took the hand of his youngest daughter. Behind her, the figure donning the head of a hare, its ears crooked as they reached the ceiling, quickly wrenched their hands apart. Faint tears and whimpers filled the otherwise quiet home.

A figure with the head of a Flying Crow stood in the doorway. The figure removed its animal head, revealing another mask.

Pettick locked his gaze as he strolled through the doorway. The hearth's rusted yellow flares etched the grooves in the field jacket that framed his face above the cheekbone. He moved past the first three children—the youngest son, the daughters. Pettick lowered the handkerchief from his Scarecrow face as he stood before the eldest son, a fully grown man at the end of the line.

"So quickly they kneel, like animals," Pettick declared. The eldest son's head rose and his eyes, with their terrified and inflamed pupils, began to tear as they looked into the refracting flares of light which burned in Pettick's glasses. The Scarecrow reached behind himself with his gloved hand and unsheathed a knife, seemingly from out of nowhere. He held it for a few seconds as he approached, halted, and then purposely dropped it on the floor. It landed with a thud directly in front of the eldest son. There it remained, like an abandoned toy on the rug. The son gave his father a terrified glance before returning his attention to the knife and his captor with unannounced certainty as to the outcome of this game.

Pettick shifted to the mantle above the fireplace where a 12-gauge Winchester pump-action shotgun, meant for hunting mallard or quail, was displayed beside its most recent prize. Pettick took hold of the gun with the familiarity of a handshake with an old friend; hand met stock, fingers locked, index finger to trigger. He examined the stock, running a glove over a gold plate, where the name McCALLISTER was etched. The amount of fear in the room rose with the presence of the gun. The clatter of Pettick's footsteps caused the floor to tremor. The sound was reduced to sorrowful creaks as he stopped directly in front of the eldest son. As the barrel of the shotgun rose and aimed, the shadows seemed to melt from Pettick's face, revealing his features. The single white explosion displaced the son in a flash, making the light of the embers seem dim by comparison. Heightened sorrows in the form of screams scattered in the returning darkness.

The boar-headed figure behind the old man removed its mask, revealing a distraught Mawkin. The other figures followed suit but with no such expression. The 'Crows beside Mawkin joined Pettick in front of each human, revealing what the humans perceived to be second masks, which only further confused the terrified hostages. The father's eyes rose to see the owner of the hands that had slain his eldest son. Pettick, resolute, looked down at the old man. Mawkin watched this exchange with bewilderment.

"Why?" the old man lamented.

Pettick remained still until the youngest son untangled from his restraints and lunged forward. The boy's hands latched onto the face of the Scarecrow in front of him. Like animals, the two tore at one another as the boy's grip on the 'Crow's face tightened. Before Mawkin and Veidt could end the encounter, threads became severed and the face of the 'Crow was torn off. The air of the room again ignited in ribbons of white, fading into red as both bodies simultaneously crumbled to the ground, the follies of misplaced courage.

Pettick leaned down to the weeping old man, stoking the culpable man with malicious contempt. "I have left you a father without a son."

The cries of the prisoners harmonized with the moans of the 'Crow scuffling on the floor reaching for the vacant space that was the source of his pain. The 'Crows took control of the remaining prisoners, gagging them, placing hoods over their heads, and restraining them. They marched them out of the house where a cart stood waiting to transport them.

Pettick stood hovering over the body of the eldest son—deriving some pleasure over the sight of his kill. Mawkin remained behind, staring at Pettick with the same fervor Pettick took to staring at the mangled body at his feet. They were alone.

"That wasn't right," Mawkin stated.

Pettick knelt down, ignoring Mawkin's words. He ran his fingers along the surface of the soaked rug, finding a shell casing. As he lifted it, a token, crooked between his fingers, a single red drop fell.

"Go down that hall to the second door on your right. Open it. You'll find a box of these on the top shelf." Pettick handed Mawkin the casing. "Then, if any more of *these* are in the trunk below," he said, brandished the rifle, "take them too."

Mawkin broke from his stationary stance, leaving Pettick alone in the room. Pettick crossed to the fireplace. He grabbed the poker, and began gently stoking the embers in the fire. Mawkin reached the hall closet door, opened it, and was baffled by the box he pulled from the top shelf filled with several smaller boxes containing hundreds of casings of various calibers. Paquin and Thalo entered through the front door carrying a large bulging sack. Pettick ordered them to the opposite wall where a full bookshelf stood. The two 'Crows emptied the contents of the bookshelf into the sack. The avalanching pages further fattened its already bloated state. Mawkin stepped out of the hallway carrying a metal locker full of weapons under one arm with the companion ammunition in his opposite hand and several rifles slung over his shoulder. Pettick nodded, his hand resting on the edge of the fireplace mantle. Mawkin set the rifles on the floor, moving toward the eldest son's body. In the meantime Paquin and Thalo had finished their task. Paquin swung the sack over his shoulder as Thalo, under Mawkin's orders, picked up the ammunition locker. Mawkin watched as they exited the house.

"He surrendered; this wasn't right," Mawkin said, dragging the boy's body from the rug onto the floor.

Pettick remained silent by the fire.

"This isn't what you have taught." Mawkin placed the rifles on the edge of the rug and rolled them into a bundle. He then tied up the bundle with a strip of fabric. Mawkin stood, still fixated on questioning Pettick. "Why?"

"Because he existed," Pettick stated blandly, staring transfixed on the embers in the fire. Mawkin waited for the sullied truth in Pettick's gaze but none could be found.

"So, this had nothing to do with these?" Mawkin gestured to the bundle of rifles.

"Keen eye, Mawkin," Pettick unapologetically noted, his focus unswayed from the fire. Shaking his bewildered head, Mawkin lifted the bundle and walked out the door.

Alone, Pettick remained statuesque in the receding light. He slowly coiled his arm into his jacket. The light of the fire revealed a picture in his gloved hand. The image was battered, dated, torn. It was that of a young woman, a human, looking longingly up at the sky leaning on the hood of an early model round-nosed Chevy Deluxe. She was beautiful. Pettick ran his fingertip along the lines and shadows of her image, against the curve of her back. He watched as the aged photograph left his grasp, fell through the air like an autumn leaf, and gently drifted onto the burning embers where the car dented, the curves bloated, and the image of perfection longing dissolved into darkness amidst the groping flares. Pettick clawed beneath the fabric of his scarf, clenching his hand just below his neck where a corrosion-resistant ball chain was concealed, a charm slung at its end. Pettick took comfort in the grasp of this charm, releasing a heavy breath, which relaxed the tensile fibers of his being.

Mawkin appeared in the doorway. Pettick unclasped his hand, concealing the charm beneath his fabric, reached for the poker, and continued stoking the fire.

"We're ready to move out," Mawkin declared.

"Yes." Pettick lifted his head to Mawkin, taking hold of his rifle. Without lowering his gaze, Pettick marched past Mawkin, leaving the large 'Crow the last in the house.

Mawkin looked over the now peaceful room, the crackling hearth, the still bodies. As he turned to exit his boot knocked into the brass knob and lock assembly on the floor. Mawkin reached down to pick up the knob, which he turned to engage the lock on the escutcheon. Mawkin huffed, drawing conclusions at the lock's clasp into place. Why, he thought, wasn't the door locked? Releasing the assembly from his glove, the brass clanked and bounded against the wood floor once again. Mawkin walked out the door. A solemn quotidian silence returned to the home.

Outside, Mawkin mounted his horse alongside Pettick. Two 'Crows, Thalo and Paquin, lit torches and quickly launched them through the windows and doorway. Whimpers from the human prisoners rallied from the cart as it heaved away with the smack of Veidt's reins. Pettick and Mawkin both stared forward, launching their gallop into the night, neither 'Crow waiting to see the expanding glow of the engulfing blaze.

* * *

The far edge of the farm was quiet during the hours when night met morning. Pettick raised his rifle. Downwind, the tilled fallow fields appeared to run on, infinity nestled beneath the blanketing sky. At the edge of the slope, facing the forest, several mason jars and pop bottles sat perched atop milk crates and barrels. After letting off a round, Pettick simultaneously lowered the barrel and pulled back on the bolt to reload. The popping sounds of the small explosion still echoed through the open air.

Mawkin approached. "The humans are secured; it's safe." Pettick fired another round, released the bolt, reloaded.

"No. It's not." Pettick fired and lowered his rifle. He then knelt down, picked up a second bolt-action rifle lying near his feet, and handed it to Mawkin. Mawkin gripped the stock, watching Pettick closely, imitating Pettick's stance and grip. Firming his stance and aim, Pettick lectured: "Every casing holds a bullet, a projectile which is launched at unbelievable speed toward your human target."

With the barrel trained, Mawkin pulled the trigger, letting off a round, the kick throwing him off balance. Disoriented, Mawkin stumbled, regaining his stance a moment later, slack-jawed in awe of the power of the weapon in his hands. Pettick laughed, further stoking Mawkin's frustration.

"You have to get a good hold on your footing first. Front foot angled, back foot parallel to your target." Mawkin shrugged into place as Pettick guided his body into position. "That's better, now use the sight—look straight down through the target." The rifle shook in preparation. Pettick slid Mawkin's glove further up the forward stock. "Good. Now squeeze the trigger."

The rifle popped. Almost instantaneously the corner of the wood crate splintered.

"Much better!" Pettick exclaimed. "Now try lowering the barrel, then raising it into position."

Mawkin followed suit. The rifle rose, clicking with the trigger's pull.

"Oh, right—you must reload." Pettick demonstrated with the rifle in his hands, pulling back on his bolt for a reload, then raised it into position and fired. The wood located on a low section of one of the barrels, splintered.

Mawkin shot Pettick a judging glance at his inaccuracy.

"What? It's been a long time since we abandoned this," Pettick said defensively.

Mawkin reloaded, trained his rifle, and fired. The wood only a few inches beneath one of the jars erupted, followed by an immediate downward gaze at Pettick who accepted the challenge, and raised his rifle with a more accurate outcome. The glass shattered, launching the head of the jar to the ground. Pettick gazed back at Mawkin, only now with a sincere smile to his prowess. Mawkin obliged Pettick's earned ego with a shrug. Raising his weapon, he fired at the farthest jar, which, on the second attempt, shattered into the soil.

"Very good! Very good!" Pettick's excitement grew with Makwin's success. The exchange continued for several dozen rounds, each shot growing in accuracy. The casings gathered in scattered piles at the boots of both 'Crows'. Mawkin fired a single round, then lowered his rifle. Pettick continued firing, his attention gradually moving from the range to Mawkin. The events of the previous night, which had lingered until the excitement rose at the range, still lurked in Mawkin's mind. Pettick grew further unsure of his shot as the words gathered on the brim.

"Surrender only works when both parties have honor," Pettick said, letting off another round before lowering his weapon.

"Then what is this about?" Mawkin replied, questioning the man-made tool he was weilding. He examined the mechanics of the weapon, thinking, waiting for the right words to gather, as both 'Crows lowered their barrels together in the rising morning clarity.

"They have fire; now so do we," Pettick stated with sympathetic assurance.

Mawkin accepted this answer, gripping the rifle, raising the barrel, and squeezing the trigger. Pettick smiled, joining Mawkin. The exchange continued.

Barlow rose from his bungalow as the morning light left its cool spring sweat along the path, the rest of the village still in slumber. The old 'Crow moved with a tired will, wrapping his tweed jacket around himself. Reaching the end of Main Street, Barlow shifted his path, heading northeast toward the ridge. The distant shots echoed through the sky and the unnatural dynamic repetition grabbed his attention. He paused, returning to his stride during the brief rests between rounds. The shots continued, sending several Flying Crows scattering in a swarm. Barlow looked up at the murder of crows and could feel them staring back at him in fear.

On his scenic route, Barlow trailed past the reaching branches of the Perfect Tree. The grandeur of its morning slumber incited a comforting awe in his chest. He reached the top of the ridge just as the sun crested the distant hills. Barlow entered the garage quietly, in hopes that the caretaker was still asleep. He shifted through the cluttered paths of the bay with a familiar stride. He approached the worktable where among a mound of rubbish now sat a completely assembled typewriter. The silver decal brandished the name REMINGTON. The small machine sat atop its leather carrying case, a reflective perfection to its sheen. Nestled between the carriage and roller a fresh note sat perfectly aligned in the typeset. Barlow lifted the typewriter, getting a closer look at the note, which read:

LOOK UP.

"You that eager to avoid me, old friend?" Kindle snickered, staring down from the catwalk directly above Barlow. The voice continued to echo throughout the bay as the Reader's chin rose to the Mechanic. "Unsuccessfully, of course."

"Indeed," Barlow muttered. "I was just coming to get what I needed and go, Kindle. Sorry to disturb you." He gathered the typewriter into its case, taking its weight, as he noticed the spine of a book, *Detroit: American Automotive Mechanics,* tucked among the tools on the shelf.

"Right . . ." Kindle drummed his fingers along the tubular rail, following around the bay, cutting to just above Barlow's exit at the edge of the walk. "You know, I recall a time, many seasons past, when you frequented this garage just as much as your son."

Barlow sighed. "Yes, and that was when this garage wasn't off-limits, before the Tinker who fiddles and lurks in this building started ruining the lives of others, and his own, by doing experiments and magic that his leader and colony strictly forbade." Barlow spoke in a fervent lecture directed up to Kindle. As his brow furled, he noticed the break in the case's clasp. He snarled, resting the typewriter on the covered hood of the Ford pickup, fiddling to seal the clasp.

"You should have told him," Kindle said, changing the subject.

Barlow broke from his task, shifting his attention quickly up to Kindle. "Do not tell me what is best for my son—"

"You should have told him," Kindle interrupted, tightening his grip on the railing.

"Do not tell me what is best for my son!" Barlow said exasperatedly. "You truly want to help Crane? You can do your part by not filling his head with your hopeless dreams and dragging him along on your dangerous and terminally fruitless endeavors."

"Don't resent me for his father's follies. Never have I seen such a staggering loss of imagination in such an intelligent Scarecrow." Kindle's words faded. "Somewhere along the line, your intelligence took you. But you should not resent me for it. You shouldn't resent him for it, either."

"I don't resent my son," Barlow echoed, "or who he has become." The old 'Crow huffed, sharing a shaking exhale with Kindle. With his chin pointed toward floor, he sighed, then looked at the door as he moved back to the truck.

Kindle gestured to the typewriter, adding, "Do yourself a favor with that thing—don't put to ink anymore lies."

Barlow ignored Kindle as he slammed the clasp shut, lifted the typewriter from the hood, and made his exit through the side man-door.

"He's more like you than you know." The door sealed, refracting Kindle's words, an off-key harmony in an empty hall.

CHAPTER VI: Legacy

"I guess we should start at the beginning." Pettick began pacing along the tar-stained bookshelves which lined three walls of the parlor. Barlow was planted at the desk, doing his best to wait patiently while Pettick attempted to gather his thoughts. The Remington typewriter sat atop the desk, holding an anticipatory blank sheet of paper. Unbridled potential—infinite.

Barlow shifted in his seat. "We could start another time if you wish—"

"No, the first step is getting started—it has to be now." Pettick was silent again. He seemed to be filtering his words through a sieve.

"What is so onerous about a simple sentence?" Barlow conjectured.

Pettick glanced over at Barlow. "You don't have to start writing to have writer's block."

Barlow chuckled briefly before silencing himself, and considered it strange that he was enjoying Pettick's company. Pettick snarled at Barlow, who sat back in his chair waiting for words to transcribe, the look of impatience growing on his face.

Pettick scoffed, "What are you lookin' at?"

"Waiting on you," Barlow said.

Pettick raised and lowered his shoulders, flailing his hands in the air with frustration.

"It is recollection, is it not?" Barlow asked.

"Every word is important; we cannot falter." Pettick stepped back several paces, pulling a large leather-bound book from the shelf, evidence for their deliberation. "Think of the humans' Bible. Who could have known that for two thousand years the misinterpretation of a single word would cultivate such conflict, kill so many, start so many wars?" He dropped the book. Its weight shook the desk as it landed, raising a cloud of dust before Barlow. The Reader leaned forward, glancing at the symbol on the cover before cracking the spine. "Every word need be precise," Pettick continued, "every sentence absolute, because the next stroke of your quill might determine the difference between a 'Crow living in his family's comfort and a 'Crow going off to die for his comforters."

Barlow raised his brow as he glanced up from the book, unable to mask the frustrating fact that Pettick was right. He closed the cover, took the book in his gloves, and felt the density of its ink. "Then this will take a while . . ."

"It just might," Pettick agreed. His pacing continued.

Barlow pushed the book further across the desk, distancing himself from the gold-feathered symbol on its cover. "Can I ask you something?"

"If I deem it so, yes," Pettick said. "Sure."

"Why the sudden urgency? Many seasons have come and gone and even the idea for such a document never came to pass."

Pettick began to pace once again, running his fingers along the spines of the books on the shelves, dragging the tips of his fingers at first. With speed the fingers began skipping between books like the feet of a running child, finally reaching the end of the shelf where an efficient run led to a last leap which defied gravity.

"Bodies don't last forever, Barlow, you know this as much as I." Pettick waved an insightful finger through the air, emphasizing the weight of his thought. "What is truly valuable in this world is legacy, what lives on past borrowed bodies."

"And you truly believe that?"

"We are here, aren't we? Besides, why would I not? It is now up to us to deem what will last, what will be remembered."

"Quite a responsibility," Barlow firmly stated. "Such a thing brings up the inexorable question of what gives us the right to say what shall or shall not be remembered."

"It is a 'Crow and a man, such as they are, which spend their entire existence simply wishing to change the world, not withstanding—"

"And what is wrong with wishing?" Barlow said, not hiding his tone of dissent.

"Wishes are empty promises for those too weak to sign a contract, such as this one we now scribe."

"That may be true—"

"I know it," Pettick assured.

Barlow ran his hands down his face, stretching the threads. "There is a flaw to your allegory, Pettick."

"What is that, Reader?"

"Contracts expire."

Pettick chuckled at Barlow's truth, asserting, "There are those who read and those who write." Barlow remained unmoved by the congenial aggression of their argument. Pettick continued to chuckle, relieving the tension of the silence. "You are right; this may take a while." Pettick lifted the book from Barlow's desk, and returned it to its proper place on the shelf. "Well then, shall we begin at the beginning?"

* * *

Barnes squeezed through the door to the library, balancing the daily stack of books from Quill's class in hand. "Crane, could you help me with this?" Barnes stumbled through the pathway into the room. "Crane?"

"Yeah," Crane responded from his seat across the library.

Barnes tripped, dropping the books into a pile at his feet. Looking at the scattered heap of books, he sighed, "I always hated mathematics. Thanks for the help."

"Anytime, brother."

Kneeling down, Barnes began gathering the pile. "What'cha doing, anyway?"

"Reading," Crane said.

"Well, that's a change," Barnes snickered.

Crane's concentration remained unmoved by Barnes's comments.

"What are you reading?" Barnes moved from the stocked shelf over to Crane, and tore the book from his hands. Crane immediately leapt for it, though he was too short to reach Barnes's outstretched arm.

Barnes read the cover aloud. "*Frankenstein, or The Modern Prometheus* by Mary Shelley," mispronouncing both their names. "Huh. Pop actually gave you this to read this time, right?"

"Yes, now give it back!" A riled Crane shouted, leaping onto Barnes's back, attempting to scale up to the book. He managed to grip it just as Barnes dropped both *Frankenstein* and Crane onto a pile of books on the floor. Barnes casually stepped away, leaving Crane in his mess. "Don't be jealous that Pop gives me better books than he does to you."

Crane rose from the pile of books, prize in hand. A knock at the door launched Crane and Barnes into a sudden frenzy, trying to straighten up the room before the door opened. A hunched-over Veidt entered with Thalo as an assistant trailing behind, a bulging sack slung over his shoulder. Veidt's marble eyes rolled, sloshing about in their sockets, meeting in a clocked expectant stare at Barnes.

"New shipment of books for the Reader," Thalo said as a reckless Veidt knocked over several columns of books, trudging to the workspace where Crane and Barnes stood. Veidt opened the stained sack. He grabbed the bottom and turned it over, spilling the books onto the floor. As the last book fell out of the bag, Veidt's eyes rolled back up in their sockets, looking again up at Barnes who tried kindly not to appear like he was intentionally looking away.

"Make sure your master knows they are here," Veidt hissed.

"We'll do that," Barnes said, exhaling as little air as possible.

Veidt smiled in a most decrepitly endearing manor as he knocked a pathway back toward the door with Thalo at his heel. They disappeared down the hall, shutting the door behind them, sealing in the putrid air. Crane and Barnes waited several moments to ensure he was gone before letting out their breath and scurrying to open the windows.

Crane peeked his head out of the narrow opening of the window, knocking against the sash. "Ack! I don't know which smelled worse, him or the bag."

Barnes's long neck stretched out of the adjacent window. "I'm going to guess *him*." The brothers shared a cough-laced laugh as they took in the fresh air for several minutes, finding a certain levity at their predicament, before sinking back into the library.

"Where do all these books come from, anyway?" Crane asked, sifting through the new books as Barnes tried to return order to the columns Veidt had knocked over.

"Runners bring them." Barnes said.

"Runners?" Crane asked.

"Yeah, like the crusaders, the Scarecrows go from colony to colony transporting messages and parcels such as this. I thought you were the one who was good at school . . ."

"Isn't that dangerous?" Crane asked.

Both Scarecrows stared out the window at the distant north woods, where fence construction now lined its border.

"In this world, what isn't?"

* * *

Under milky-white moonlight, the Scarecrows of the colony flocked before a loaded cart parked several yards below the towering timber of the sealed front gates to the colony, the newly completed first phase of the perimeter fence. The cart was loaded to its brim with a jagged heavy cargo, masked beneath a stained canvas. The weight of the load sunk the spoked wheels of the cart several inches into the earth, breaking its roll down the hill. Pettick leaned against the side of the cart, open journal in hand. He wrote with an acute eagerness, giving the occasional glance over the expanding crowd.

Upon brief glance, the figure of a stout 'Crow emerged from the mass of shifting straw. Hardwick, the mayor of the village, shuffled toward the cart, darting a glance to Pettick who returned the glare, unmoved. He peeked under the canvas, bewildered by the sight. Pettick sealed his journal and cradled it between his left glove and hip while casually strolling around the cart.

"Another shrouded presentation, Pettick," Hardwick stated with a newfound boldness in his posture.

"Nothing rallies excitement better than the element of surprise," Pettick earnestly fostered.

"Aye, surprise . . ." Hardwick crossed his arms, attempting to keep his stance firm. Pettick calmly placed his free glove onto the frame of the cart, a subtle invasion of Hardwick's space. "I think the board would have something to say about this," Hardwick gathered himself sternly, with a snide exhale, "just as I'm sure they'd be keen to receive knowledge of your recent nocturnal activities." Hardwick grew discreet in demeanor. "You promised me a definitive end, yet I see a less passing trend—"

"Aye! Funny, you mention this; my other surprise this evening is for your ears. I feel we have outlived the archaic constructs of our board. We find ourselves now, in a time of heightened threats—"

"Pettick, I—" Hardwick fruitlessly interjected.

"Your democratic process was a failed experiment, a luxury, and one that I allowed to go on for far too long. It is time I take full control of this colony's interests once again," Pettick continued. "Only until, in time, a more peaceful age comes when we may reinstate such concerned parties. I have decided it is in our best interest that you step down as mayor of the village for the good of the colony."

Hardwick stuttered, searching for words which failed to materialize. Pettick smiled, giving no comfort to the argument's closing, no glove to Hardwick's sunken shoulder. The crowd's restless excitement grew audible. Retrieving his rifle by the stock, Pettick slung it to his shoulder, and pulled himself onto the cart, ascending the mound. A speechless Hardwick dissolved back into the crowd.

Pettick inhaled, taking in sight of the shadow-crossed moonlit faces before him. He exhaled. "There are many things I want you to know, many things I wish I could tell you." Pettick stood tall atop the cart. He elevated himself above the crowd that gathered in a tightening bundle, as if bound by the twine of a hay bale. A rising curiosity vocally shrouded the first lines of Pettick's speech, then closed into imperfect silence. "My friends, my friends, there is so much you should know, and still so much you are better off not knowing." Pettick adjusted his stance more firmly. "I am here to tell you these truths, warning you, so that you may take proper precautions to protect yourselves and this colony. I first wish to tell you, indebted to you, why I chose to keep these truths from you." Pettick bowed his head and gave a theatrical sigh. "I made these decisions to protect this colony,"—his chin rose proudly once again—"and to protect you."

"There are more humans in this world, more than I have led you to believe. Patches of them the size of our colony are scattered in carnivorous packs, swarming all across this great valley we call home. And in greater numbers, as you know, they are all the more dangerous." Pettick spoke with his hands, conducting the gasps that harmonized throughout the crowd. "I am sorry for this deception. But it is all the greater imparity that we do whatever we can—whatever we must do, together—to protect this home from the savages that hunger in the shadows beyond this wall. Now is the time to act before they start appearing in droves at our gates!"

"I have already set in motion methods of protection. I proudly announce, with equivalent pride and gratitude, the first phase of my plan which stands tall in near completion behind me." Pettick held his speech, swung his arm in presentation of the great gates of his wall, allowing the allotted time for significant applause. "The second phase—" The cheering continued. "Ah, yes—yes!" He gave a warm smile. "Yes! The second, I am proud to have brought to this great colony during a time that warrants it, and for just such an age." Pettick froze with less presentation to the thoughts that held him. "I wish not to tell you about this, but rather to show you."

Barlow watched Pettick's movements carefully, holding his boys closely in his arms. Kindle stepped through the crowd, pausing in his stride beside Crane. Barlow took early notice of Kindle's presence, tightening his hold on his son. The 'Crows exchanged a brief polarizing glance. Kindle recognized the unwelcome nature of his place, and shifted forward through the crowd.

"Kindle!" Crane shouted after him, stepping out of his father's hold as the Tinker disappeared into the congregation of straw. Kindle breached the front of the crowd, making his presence known to Pettick as he moved around the cart, and took his place next to Mawkin and Grey.

"Pop, whatcha think Kindle's doin'?" Barnes asked.

"I honestly do not have an answer for you, son," Barlow replied, peering over the crowd.

Pettick turned to Kindle, who had remained frozen beside the cart, signaling with his palm. Grey followed, lifting a metal box. A thick small-gauge black cable protruded from the bottom of the box. The cable coiled at their feet, before winding under the cart, curving at the opposite spokes, up the hill to one of the large masts of the gate. Kindle took the box in his hands. After opening its lid Kindle ran his glove over the grease which collected on the garish yellow knob and unlit-lamp on its face. He gripped and twisted the knob until, with an audible click, the bulb glowed red. Buzzing waves chased through the cable, feeding up to the mechanical shifting click in the watchtower above. The colonists' attention rose upward as a white light ignited in the watchtower, sending a sharp beam crossing above them, cutting deep into the rolling hills of the crop lines. Pettick looked down on his people, feeding on the satisfaction in their awe-struck faces, faces now washed in the white streaks of manufactured light.

The Scarecrows continued their gaze upward as Crane's chin rose higher than the rest, skyward into space, where the stars, in the height of their nightly dance, faded out of sight. Sadness washed over Crane, grieving the martyrs to the wash of the expanding white lights of Pettick's artificial day.

The single spotlight spread along the fence as every post sequentially produced a smaller light. In a rain of sparks a second large lamp, the same size as the first, lit in the second tower. The silhouette of a 'Crow stood beside it, manipulating its direction. This movement drew the audience's attention, garnering another wave of awe before the beam arrived on Pettick. Pettick's shadow cast over the crowd. The spotlight outlined his body, lending a blurred white edge to his slender frame as he paced atop the cart. He continued his speech. "As with these truths I have and will present to you, I must reinstate—clarify, rather—to cast some certainty and shuck some doubts. Select human evils—very few, but some—do produce good, offering to us tools for our less sinful hands. I understand the complexity in these ideas; it is often difficult to find meaning in concepts so foreign. I promise you, their sense will come with time, until eventually, one day, they will be commonplace. One of the great contributions humanity's evil gave to this earth was light; and with it the ability to work beyond the hours of day. The second, a far darker prop in their play, I present to you now."

Pettick swung the strap, taking grip of the rifle's stock. And with a punctuated arc to his gesture, he lifted the rifle in his right hand, holding it high above his head.

"The Gun!" Pettick held his words for reaction, continuing, "Our best protection against the human problem!" The crowd's curiosity merged in an explosive eruption of approval. Crane looked throughout the crowd, reading the reactions on the Crows' faces, finding responses varying from Kindle's disapproval to Mawkin's ambivalence, a sentiment he shared, to the excitement of his fellow colonists.

"To survive this threat, we must learn from our enemies! We must fight fire with fire."

While the Scarecrows gazed at the rifle in his right hand, Crane's gaze was locked onto the journal in Pettick's left. The

Prophet's words resonated within Crane. He broke from his father's side and began pushing his way through the crowd.

Barlow watched silently as his youngest son disappeared into the shifting mass of straw. Wrapping his left arm around Barnes, both Crows tried their best to stand still amidst the chaos.

Pettick's speech continued. "We will make it, my friends, but we must raise our arms to ensure that security, that this soil be safe for seasons to come!"

Crane pressed upstream against the current of the crowd that flowed toward the cart. Breaking free, he continued toward the house. Chants of "Pettick!" and the occasional call to arms chased Crane into the night as he distanced himself from the rallied cries.

"We will not disappear, my friends! No, we will not; this is our time, our chance for this world!" Crane breached the porch, dashing up the grand staircase, down the hall, and into the library. The distant voice rang on: "And though dark times approach, I am proud, proud to be your leader, proud to be here with you. Proud to be one of you." Pettick trembled with his words. "Into the darkness, and out of it!"

Crane thrashed his way through the library, coming to a bookshelf where he ripped through the cloth and leather, searching the pages before him and his memory. Crane scaled the shelves like the rungs of a ladder. He swept clear the top shelf, causing ink and parchment to rain onto the floor. He stopped, chest heaving, with the last book on the shelf before him. Taking hold of the tanned leather hide he dropped back to the floor. Opening the cover, he scanned the palm-sized manuscript, the empty white landscapes of the blank pages calling for him to build upon, an absolution in their unbridled potential. Crane escaped into the solidarity of the pages as, framed in the window before him, the flares of artificial white reached for him, refracting in a kaleidoscope off the glass.

All the while, Pettick basked in the warm bath of the spotlight, marveling at the draw of his rhetoric, the cheering crowd before him, with the power of gods in his hands held high.

ACT II: SUMMER

CHAPTER VII: Fireflies

Mason jars dangled from strings tied to branches beneath the undercarriage of the Perfect Tree. The luminous glow of imprisoned fireflies filled each glass. Pungent embers in hues of burning gold and emerald danced a lover's dance within each chamber as it swung seasick on a waterless voyage. Sharp chimes rang out as the bulbs collided on the natural chandelier, humming a tune carried through the field by a warm summer breeze. Shepherd stood watchful below the rocking bulbs, his animals herded in the patch of grass before him, grazing. Gwyn approached from behind the tree, floating silently along the roots.

"Good evening, Gwyn," Shepherd said without turning around.

Gwyn froze, the toes of her wingtips precariously placed between two thinning roots.

"I don't often find myself receiving visitors at this hour, and certainly not the Cobbler's daughter."

"How'd you know?" Gwyn asked, bewildered.

Shepherd simply smiled.

"What are you doing out so late?" Gwyn kindly inquired.

"You know I wouldn't dare ask you why you were about at this hour, even if I did not already know."

Gwyn bounded over to a stump next to Shepherd, leaning forward to read his concealed grin before looking at the animals.

Shepherd spoke in swaying tones. "If you must know, I have three grazers which refuse to eat during the day. They are quite a lot of trouble, this trio. But who am I to stop nature?" Gwyn smiled.

"Can I ask for your assistance?" Shepherd asked, lifting a large branch from his feet. Numerous offshoot twigs were tied with string from which hung empty jars that collectively jingled like wind chimes as they swayed. "This is my crook when the summer brings wax-less candles. I need only catch the flint."

Gwyn marveled in the pursuit, bouncing from root to root. Their hands reached into the night sky, neither pair returning empty-handed. Each grasp opened effortlessly revealing two fireflies mating between their gloves. Shepherd filled each jar as Gwyn spun past, circling the trunk. As Shepherd removed the lid from the final glass jar, Gwyn approached, placed her gloved hands over it. As she unfolded her fingers two fireflies bounded from either palm, joined with one another, mate matched to mate, and gently melted into the jar. When Shepherd raised his ornamented staff, emerald lamps cast light on the surrounding grass. Shadows fell on the 'Crows' faces, accentuating the folds and curves of emotions felt.

Crane's shoes pattered as he snuck across the dirt path, slunk down into the creek bed, went under the bridge, and prepared to dart into the grassy gully below the Perfect Tree. The snap of a twig caught his attention, followed by a rustling in the shoulder-high cornstalks behind him. Crane hid, crouching back into the cover of the brush. A figure appeared, gangly and bent, stepping out into the clearing. The figure's head turned back and forth, searching the clearing. Crane peeked out of the brush, cautiously catching sight of the tall figure. The figure, turning north, gazed up at the Perfect Tree. Crane approached the figure from behind, resting a hand on its shoulder. Both 'Crows jumped, falling backward into the stalks.

"Barnes!" Crane's muffled voice shouted. "What do you think you're doing?".

"Same thing you're doing, I guess," Barnes said, regaining his composure.

"And why is that?" Crane said in an unwelcoming tone.

"I know it'd do no good to try and stop ya, so I figured I'd tag along this time," Barnes said, with swaying confidence, knowing it was Attuck's daring that put him here.

"If Pop finds out, we're both in for it," Crane stated, turning to continue his trek. Barnes followed.

"Yeah, and he'd rather have me watching your back than you sneakin' around alone all the time. Besides, Flying Crow knows how much I've covered your hide; I figured I'd get the fun of it too," Barnes said as he reached his hand for Crane's fleeing shoulder. Crane abruptly shrugged it off. After several paces, Crane stopped in his tracks, not knowing how to shake his brother's trail. In growing silence, Barnes looked around, realizing their exposure.

"So what are we doing?" Barnes asked.

"Going to Kindle's," Crane said.

"I figured that much."

The brothers looked over the field, finding their bearings in the freedom of their surroundings. "All right, keep low and follow me." Crane folded, taking lead. The two Scarecrows darted deeper into the clearing, cutting up to the Perfect Tree where a vigilant Shepherd witnessed their approach.

"Late for you boys?" Shepherd said, his voice filled with welcome.

Crane huffed, "It's never too late. wouldn't you say so, Shepherd?" Shepherd smiled at Crane's response. Crane, looking past this, asked, "Have you seen Gwyn?"

The Herdsman raised his brow at the boy's impatience. Stepping back, Shepherd revealed Gwyn, her figure swaying in the flashes of emerald within the leafed mansion. She stepped down along the roots from her place on the tree's grand staircase, her hand presented to Crane..

Crane gasped. "You are—"

"I know," Gwyn said with a confident smirk, feeling most coy.

Barnes and Shepherd abruptly turned away. Barnes quipped, "You'd think they'd at least have the decency—"

"It's a date, son," Shepherd interrupted with his serene voice. "If you were in his shoes, you wouldn't."

"How do you know that?"

"Because *I* wouldn't." Shepherd smiled with a tip to the brim of his hat. Barnes laughed.

The three young 'Crow's offered their good-byes to Shepherd. With a rolling dash towards the valley floor, under a ceiling of stars, Barnes pushed ahead, an eager Crane at his heel. Within several minutes of playful chase, they reached the bottom of the ridge. Barnes finished first with Crane only seconds behind. With crossed arms locked, Barnes dreaded in unrequited affection at the sheer climb up the rocks ahead of them. The vertical ascent was roughly eighty feet. The young 'Crows gathered in line, with their chins raised skyward, sharing a gaze at the top of the cliffs where, like a new horizon cutting across the sky, the moon appeared to set.

"This is not safe; couldn't we just go around?" Barnes asked.

"It's part of the journey," Crane said with bliss, turning to Gwyn. "I can help you find your footing." Gwyn responded with a daring glance, immediately ascending the rockface with intrepid speed. Crane quickly followed.

"Journey . . . right. It would also be if we went around," Barnes muttered to himself, alone at the base of the crag. He shrugged, avoiding the falling debris from Crane's climb as he reached for his first foothold. Crane aggressively scaled beside Gwyn in an unspoken race. Gwyn took to the challenge, increasing the rate of her climb. Large feet slid, scrambling frantically for a moment, before traction could grip the rockface as Barnes trailed below. Above, Crane and Gwyn's figures slipped silently into the crease of sky and rock.

"It's so peaceful, isn't it?" Gwyn said, looking out over the valley. It seemed to shrink between Crane and her. "This moment, though manufactured, is quite perfect, Crane."

"What are you talking about?" Crane feigned.

"No 'Crow chooses to climb mountains when they could just as easily go around, unless there is some hidden intent *en route*."

Crane chased his words with a boyish grin that inadvertently drew Gwyn closer. The beguiled silence broke with cracks of shifting earth and groaning imprecations from the edge of the ridge. Crane offered a hand that Barnes begrudgingly took as he breached the escarpment. Pulling himself onto the grass, Barnes rolled flat onto his back, exhausting his heaving chest. Crane and Gwyn hovered, kneeling beside him.

"Next time, a little more skip to your step, eh, brother?" Crane mocked, throwing gentle glove to Barnes's swollen cheek, a glove Barnes quickly knocked away, extending his finger sternly.

"Don't think for a second I won't embarrass you in front of her . . . 'cause I will, and you know just how . . ."

Crane's voice cracked. Abruptly silent, his jaw hung open. Gwyn took notice, giggling at the brothers' bickering as she rose to her feet. Ripples in her skirt swayed like phlox purple petals in the night. Crane followed, quietly remarking to Barnes: "I rescind my previous statement."

"I'm sure you do," Barnes said, smirking.

Barnes and Crane observed the rockface, in opposing directions, raising their gaze to marvel at the view of the distant village. Gwyn walked along the ridge, her wonder in the direction of the water tower, the structure having swollen from a distant spec to something Olympic. Crane chased her hand. She bashfully hid her gloves in the folds of her dress.

"We should go; we're going to be late," Crane noted, detracting attention from their gloves.

"Yes," Gwyn said, the sturdy structure with its memories held resolute before them. "Yes."

Crossing past the bay doors of the garage to the southeast corner, the man-door swung open. Kindle welcomed them with open arms, unaffected by Crane's additional guests as they filed into the hall.

"Remind me to never tell you any secrets," Kindle remarked to Crane who moved in the opposite direction. Kindle shuffled before his pupils who instinctively gathered before the covered mound in the first bay. "Well, welcome! No time to waste, then—" Kindle's hesitance diminished with his rambling. Formalities giving way, he turned, taking grip of the cloth cover, in mockery of Pettick's presentations. "I now present to you: the automobile!"

Kindle stared at the trio, matching the eager gaze shared by Barnes and Gwyn as he ripped the cover off the Ford. As the dust settled, a silent awe gripped the young 'Crows. Barnes and Gwyn reached out with their fingers, touching the barrel-shaped hood.

"Let's take her for a ride!" Kindle rallied. Admiring Crane and Gwyn's proximity, he turned to Barnes. "Guess you get to ride shotgun." A confused look expanded on Barnes's face. Kindle shook his head. "Just get in the cab, kid."

Crane acted the part of a magician's assistant, moving to the bay door and ripping down the chain. The door curled up, spreading the moonlight that arched in a silver bow, tracing the curves of the truck. Gwyn climbed into the bed of the pickup. Taking her stance in the bed, she twirled back to Crane. "You know what you said about me and this automobile?"

"Yeah," Crane said with anticipation.

"Quite the compliment."

He smiled, tightly taking Gwyn's hand as he rested his back on the cab, sliding into the bed of the truck. Inside the cab, Barnes trembled with nervous excitement. He watched Kindle turn the ignition, press the clutch, and with the switch of the headlights and an acutely timed smile, lower his foot onto the gas. The truck leapt from its cage, squealing several roars as it came bounding through the night. The carriage bounced along the path, speeding around the ridge toward the fields.

Crane wrapped his arm around Gwyn as he looked up into the night to see the motion of the truck transform the sky into a barrage of shooting stars. The vehicle fishtailed around the bend, reaching the base of the ridge. Headlights revealed where the path terminated in an empty lot ahead. Barnes released the tension in his threads as they appeared to have reached the end of the ride. The tires rolled to a halt. Barnes and Kindle glanced through the windshield. The village lights glistened, a landing strip in darkness. Kindle smiled, giving nerve to Barnes. The pedal slammed to the floor. Speeding from its halt, the truck curled a cloud of dirt into the air. Shifting into fourth gear, the chassis straitened out, hurtling off the path with a jarring leap into the grass. Barnes's head smacked against the ceiling of the cab. Bottoming out and leaping high, the truck raced over the uneven terrain.

Shepherd watched from his throne beneath the Perfect Tree. As the truck orbited in the distance, the grazing herd neared its sentinel, fearful of the motor's passing roar.

Crane and Gwyn sunk further into the bed. Barnes braced himself, gripping the dash.

Kindle chuckled. "Ready for true magic?"

Barnes, fawn in thread, halfheartedly responded by shaking his head in no definite orientation.

Kindle lowered his glove to the round silver knob, turned it with a click, and the headlights shut off. The magic played out, the two lamps shattered into a thousand shards of light, sown in the scattered flares of fireflies and distant shimmer of constellations. Bathed in the open air, holding Gwyn, Crane had never felt closer to the firmament above. Gwyn whispered to Crane words he would never share. The wind grazed through their threads as the beads of light weaved in the spaces between their fingertips. The silver hubcaps refracted the moonlight as the wheels spun in a rhythmic strum along the wooden boards of the bridge, traversing the creek where spark-driven lovers in the thousands danced atop the trickling current. Barnes watched in awe, his head hanging out the window. Kindle let out a heavy howl as he spun the wheel, the tail of the pickup whipping around into a dust-clouded halt.

"Your turn," Kindle said to Barnes, who sat frozen in his seat. Kindle threw open the driver's-side door, shuffled around to the other side of the cab, and swung open the passenger door. He then pushed a flustered Barnes across the bench seat till Barnes found himself sitting behind the wheel.

"What do I do?" Barnes asked.

"Press down the clutch," Kindle directed, "then pull into first gear."

Barnes, flustered, gripped the gearshift, let it hang between second and neutral until, with several attempts, he threw it grinding into first with a sound Barnes knew to be the truck growling at him.

"Good," Kindle said, patiently nodding. "As you ease off the clutch, press on the gas."

Barnes fumbled as he followed Kindle's directions. The truck shot forward several yards before stalling to a halt.

Kindle gripped the dash, exhaling, the feathers rising on his lip. "Let's try this again, shall we?"

"Right."

"Bring it into neutral—center there, good—now turn the key, then it's the same process; you just have to ease off of the clutch."

Barnes followed Kindle's directions with growing precision to his process. And on the seventh attempt, the truck lurched forward and continued rolling down the path. Barnes shifted confidently into third gear, accelerating into the grass. Sharing a laugh with Barnes, Kindle hesitantly released his grip on the dash. Crane and Gwyn laid flat in the bed, bellies up toward the stars. Gwyn reached for Crane's hand. The truck revved up the ridge, homeward bound to its cave to hibernate.

When they arrived Barnes backed the truck into the first bay. Hanging out the window, Kindle signaled the truck's reverse—though collision with a toolbox marked the vehicle's park. Standing before the hood, Barnes ran his hand along the cooling steel shell, which crackled with a gentle hum as the truck began its slumber.

Crane shot up from the bed as Kindle slid out of the cab.

"Hey, why did he get to learn to drive?" Crane asked.

"He didn't have a lady to entertain," Kindle chuckled. Turning to Barnes, he asked, "what do you think of your date, son?"

"She's a beauty," Barnes replied, smiling from ear to ear.

Kindle's figure remained in the doorway as the three young 'Crows snuck to the ridge. Barnes eased himself to the base, his feet bouncing off the soil as Crane and Gwyn continued their descending climb. Gwyn gripped tightly to the root, reaching her foot to an adjacent crevice. A snap marked the root's tear from the cracks in the rock. Gwyn let out a piercing scream as she fell. Air whistled through her threads, trailing the feathers of her hair skyward. Crane released his hold, throwing out his left glove, and took a rigid grip on Gwyn's wrist. Threads snapped with a painful strain as he tried to break her fall. The two heaved as Crane swung Gwyn against the rockface. She regained her grip, taking a firm hold of the stones. When her boots touched the soil, Gwyn wrapped her arms around Crane.

Barnes stood by, an impatient observer. "As wholesome as this moment may be, I will be the first one to remind you two that we may have blown our cover." Barnes turned, pointing to two silhouettes of riders approaching in the distance. The gallop heightened as the young 'Crows dashed into the tall grass. Fumbling into a pile, they hid, motionless. The canter of the hooves came to a halt several yards from their hiding place.

The soldiers dismounted. "Check up the hill; I'll cover down by the crops." The steps moved around the horse, approaching the line between pebbled dirt path and tilled soil.

"See anything?" Thalo shouted from up the hill.

"Nothin'!" Paquin answered.

The soldiers returned to their horses. Crane signaled Barnes. Hesitant, Barnes rolled off the heap of straw, crawling further into the crops. SNAP! The soldiers' attention shot to the fleeing intruders. As they mounted their horses, they peered down into the brush where the young 'Crows' figures were crawling down the line.

"There! There!" Thalo shouted.

The horses rallied a piercing locomotive neigh, launching the young 'Crows into a scurried run. Staying low, the 'Crows cut through the brush as the soldiers drew their weapons, and released several rounds in their direction. Thalo's horse took to the path, gaining greater speed, stalking; as the second soldier, Paquin, pushed through the grass, barreling directly toward them. Crane pulled Gwyn in front of him, minding her stride as he followed her, toe to heel.

"Scatter!" Barnes shouted, cutting off from the group towards the path.

Crane glanced behind him and saw the horse's muzzle closely trailing. The treads of the hooves shot splinters of grass into the air. Crane grabbed Gwyn's hand, leading her away from the path, further into the grass. The horse followed. The rider raised his rife and fired a shot, grazing the side of Crane's arm, severing a patch of threads. Barnes broke onto the pathway. Sliding through the dirt, he cut up the road as Thalo caught sight of him, driving the steed in his direction. The distance between Barnes and the horseman quickly vanished. As they ran along the path, several flashes blared from the rifle. With each explosion, Barnes's foot pressed further into the earth.

The rider smacked the reins of the western-fitted saddle, driving the horse blindly at the 'Crows before him. The casings clipped into the night as he raised his rifle. Crane could feel the warmth of the horse's breath and the bite of its teeth chomping on the bit. Just ahead of them the grass line ended. With Gwyn in front of him, he instantly threw open his arms, tackling her to the ground. They crumbled over the slope into the creek. The horse leapt over them, tumbled through the air, and crashed into the water with a splash. The rider was ejected, bouncing like a pebble downstream. With his magazine empty, Thalo dropped his rifle to the earth and drew his pistol. Upon reaching the bridge, Barnes leapt over the railing, hurtling himself into the water. The horseman trampled by, before rounding his horse back to the bridge. Wading in the water beneath the bridge, Barnes remained still, silent. Above him the boards bowed and groaned under the the horse's clanking hooves. The horseman raised barrel of his gun in the direction of the splashing downstream. Paquin rose, dumping water from his hat.

"You lose 'em?" Thalo asked, holstering his pistol.

"Yeah," Paquin sighed, covering his helmet head with the damp felt hat, its brim sagging.

"Over there!" Thalo pointed to a green light tracing in the distance. Paquin mounted and followed, pursuing into the night. The thunder of galloping horses faded.

Barnes fell back. The water blistered beside him, rippling the surface until it cracked, revealing Crane and Gwyn. The three Scarecrows remained silent, exhaling heavier breaths as the soldiers faded into the distance.

Crane turned to Barnes. "Next time, let's try and make it home in one piece."

Pulling himself up the embankment, his back to his brother, Barnes stated, "There won't be a next time."

By the Perfect Tree, Shepherd turned to the two riders approaching him. "Stop there!" Paquin yelled as he dismounted, scurrying to Shepherd who patiently stood by.

"It's just the old Shepherd," Thalo muttered, still mounted on his saddle.

"Went for a swim, did ya?" Shepherd reveled, looking down at the soldier's drenched threads, which drizzled into a pool at his feet.

"Enough!" Thalo yelled, establishing his authority with loudening snarls. "What are you doing out at this hour?"

Shepherd responded with a gentle voice: "A trickle of my animals is about. I'm just helping to guide them home."

At the village, Barnes closed the door to the bungalow, sealing the latch on the newly installed lock. Crane tiptoed to his cot.

"I hope it was worth it, boys." Barlow moved from the dark corner of the bungalow, while the two sons stood side by side in front of their father.

"We're very sorry, sir," Barnes spoke up.

"Do not dodge the question! Was it worth it?"

"Yes, sir," Barnes quickly responded as Crane continued to think, gnawing at his thoughts.

"Well, it sorta depends on the punishment before we can answer that, doesn't it?" Crane opened then closed his mouth, trying to contain the words that spewed out.

Barlow turned to Crane. "Just go to bed before your mouth gets you in anymore trouble." Barlow turned back to Barnes who had started toward his cot. "The worst thing is, I'd expect this out of him, but you . . ."

Barnes remained a statue, until burden bowed his head. “Yes, sir.”

* * *

Pettick slammed his fists to the desk, the dense blackwood rattled, dispersing tremors through the parlor. His pursed chin quivered and trembled as word of the previous night’s intruders came to him.

Mawkin held his stance, dutifully stoic.

Slowly the tension evaporated as Pettick crumbled into his chair. “This is not a game.”

“Leave,” Mawkin said, ordering Thalo and Paquin out of the room. Without waiting, they quickly shuffled passed. Mawkin read the lines of Pettick’s face, and fear disturbed him—genuine fear.

“Something must be done,” Pettick recanted softly, shifting from his desk to the window.

With crossed arms the black leather tip of Mawkin’s thumb pressed to the handle of the *Barrette* pistol at his hip. He felt the rugged bridges of its grip. His mind locked to the feeling, the varying valleys of its slide and textures to the metal of its hammer. Pettick’s mind wandered.

“This wasn’t our parlor tricks, Mawkin. This was real.”

“I know.”

“Tommorrow we’ll double the labor on the fence,” Pettick swiftly declared.

“Removing workers from the field? Aren’t crops our primary objective?” Mawkin inquired, testing Pettick.

“The safety of our colony is. We need this fence completed as soon as possible.”

Mawkin’s wish to speak felt like a twig in his temple that had snapped and was rebundled only to snap again. Pettick sensed the dissenting words on his tongue, a trend he reviled and feared.

“Call a meeting,” Pettick said.

“Yes, sir.”

* * *

Weary from the night of writing, Barlow inched his way through the library door with the typewriter and a ream of paper in hand. *How*, Barlow thought, *the body ages with the wear on the mind.* Barlow looked into the room. Barnes had left to deliver the books to the schoolhouse, and again Crane was nowhere to be found. Barlow looked down to his desk, covered with the pages he had yet to read. The weight, knowing some would never be read, grew heavily upon his shoulders as he dropped the typewriter to the rug, sliding the books off his desk where they crumbled to the floor, along with his fleeting strength.

"Father?" Crane shook, standing on the stairwell to the observatory, his journal and the book *Detroit: American Automotive Mechanics* in hand.

As Barlow turned to his son, a huff of air lifted his straw whiskers, followed by a minute of wordless questions. "Have you finished your reading for this week?"

"No," Crane replied.

The candor of Crane's answer threw Barlow off-guard, pushing him into a frenzy of contradicting emotions. It was then that he saw the title of the text in Crane's hand, and all Barlow's nerves became unravelled, like the straw that made him.

"What are you doing with that?" Barlow asked.

"This? It's just—"

"The book, Crane—I know what it is and who gave it to you. I don't condone lending books to Kindle—"

"Father, I—"

"You sneak out to see him. You lend books. You don't repsect me—"

"What?"

"Go to the basement," Barlow quietly ordered, gesturing for the books in Crane's hands. "Just leave those here."

Crane gripped his journal and books as he grabbed his rucksack and dashed out the door. The door rattled as it slammed shut. Barlow knew he had wronged his son, sinking him deeper into anguish.

* * *

Pettick stood at his post, the window of his parlor, restless from night's passing without sleep. The manuscript *A History of Scarecrow* was set unbound atop Pettick's desk. As he contorted his back, a series of cracks etched and creeped through his threads. Feeling beaten, Pettick peered out the window. Through the panes, several of his soldiers blurred into focus, loitering just down the path. Mawkin entered.

"Good day," Mawkin greeted before taking a seat before Pettick's desk.

"I suppose," Pettick muttered, stifling Mawkin's pleasantries. "Sorry, just not in the mood for moot conjecture today, Mawkin."

"Ah . . ." Mawkin nodded, adjusting himself in his chair.

Pettick turned to face him, smiling. "I'll allow you to continue to pretend you know what that means."

Mawkin ruffled his shoulders and removed his hat. "Since you're in no mood for conversation; to business, then? What do you need, Pettick?"

Pettick thought for a moment, causing Mawkin to impatiently roll the brim of his hat in his gloves.

Pettick's prolonged silence broke. "What makes a 'Crow who he is?"

"What?" Mawkin pined with furrowed brow, already worn from Pettick's droll philosophizing for the day. Pettick, sensing this, quickly got to the point of his summons.

"What makes a Scarecrow?"

"You talkin' twine, straw, flannel?"

Pettick stepped around to the front of his desk and leaned against it. "Not exactly. I mean each individual Scarecrow. How can we tell who is who and what they are in the most basic of ways?" Pettick waited for a response from Mawkin, but received none. Pettick continued, "Their role—their purpose—their identity."

Flustered, Mawkin shook his head. "You lost me."

"The clothes. Clothes make the Scarecrow. Sure, you build from there, but much of what you are and who you will become is established by this. From the very start. A burlap pawn doesn't wear the cotton or tweed of a Teacher, does he? Or the denim of a Mechanic?"

"And?" Mawkin gestured for resolution. With this, Pettick stood and headed in the direction of his chair.

"And our soldiers are no different. It is no secret that uniformity builds community." Pettick laid out simply the conclusion to his thesis: "Strengthening pride through said unity."

Mawkin retorted, "And you wish this for our soldiers—our Scarecrows?" It was the response Pettick expected.

"Precisely." Pettick gripped the answer, falling back into his chair. "Inform that irascible little haberdasher, Wade the Tailor, and Critch the Cobbler of a meeting. We will begin with our Militia. And when we are ready, move to birthing more artisans." With a final gesture of his glove, he closed the lesson. "In due time." Pettick smiled.

Mawkin, nodding in silent agreement, returned his hat to his head and started for the door.

"See? Not all conjecture is moot between you and I, old friend."

Mawkin reached for the brass knob, pulled open the door, and responded plainly, "Right." The door closed, scattering several pages of the manuscript like birds cresting into the air.

Layers of dust from Main Street outlining a series of tracks on the pine floor, reminders of where one had been, were soon swept away by the thick horse hair bristles of the broom Gwyn was using while assisting Mare with some afternoon chores in the bungalow.

"So, botany?" Mare pried, holding the book, *Taxonomy of North American Flora*, she had found while organizing the tools in the bureau against the back wall of their small shop.

"Yes, Mother, it is the study of how and why plants grow," Gwyn said proudly, as if having read aloud the definition from the book. "It could be of great use in the colony."

The book was worked, its spine broken, pages dirty flaxen. And it smelled. Mare noted this as she paged through the old hardcover book, parsing the yellowed pages for understanding.

"But what would you do, Gwyn?" Mare asked. "What would you make?"

"I would advise Herb, perhaps; make the crops grow greener, faster."

"I cannot say I understand," Mare said, though so quickly reading the disappointment and frustration on Gwyn's face, she continued, "and I cannot say I didn't ask."

"May I go?" Gwyn asked, stowing the broom behind the cupboard and brushing the dust from her skirt.

"To see Crane?"

Gwyn was silent, knowing she had forced herself into a corner.

"Go on." Mare smiled.

Gwyn started for the door, stopping as she reached for the knob. Beyond the barrier of the screen door, Pettick stood, her father before him. Words gathered and soaked and drenched and sweltered in the exchange with Critch before Pettick huffed and cast off, disappearing from the frame of the door. Gwyn waited several moments before pressing through the door, taking a stance by her father's side. She thought, gathering words and an understanding of these adult complexities.

"What is it, Father?"

"Oh, nothing, my Gwyn." Parents lie, as did Critch.

"You're losing the shop, aren't you?" Gwyn asked.

Critch sighed. "Yes, yes I am. Pettick thinks I would be better suited at the textile house, running a cobbler line. I cannot be another Wade the Tailor or Malthus the Mason, who sold out their share of labor for favor in Pettick's ranks. I won't do it. Wade," Critch scoffed, "I refuse to be compared to the likes of that 'Crow."

"How impossible that is, Father." Gwyn smiled, making a ghoulish face in imitation of Wade.

Critch chuckled, "Not to worry! Now go. Go be young, be foolish—just not too foolish. Those library boys need a voice of reason."

Gwyn, smiling in reply, launched down the road.

* * *

The musk about the library, in stillness and fragrance, marked the length of Barlow's absence. His sons nested quietly, working amid the wash of midday sun. Barnes reclined in Barlow's chair by the window, his legs stretched to an adjacent stack of books. Crane sat on the steps, a magnifying glass in hand. Scanning slowly, he studied the text on the page of an oversized book.

"Who writes this small, anyway?" Crane remarked with a caved brow, his study growing lethargic.

Barnes replied, not lifting his head from the page, "According to Pop it's called 'fine print'—meant for less important words, I gather."

Crane howled several restless sighs, seemingly with intent to annoy.

"Think of it as a puzzle," Barnes added, still engaged in his own assigned reading.

"According to Pop, all print is fine print," Crane huffed. As his head drooped, the book fell to the floor, and the glass with it. "We should really open a window in here," Crane said, peering over at Barnes.

"No," Barnes quickly rebutted. "Why?"

"It's too quiet in here; besides, the air is kinda thick." Crane sniffed.

"I like the quiet," Barnes bluntly stated, Crane's activities growing more irksome.

"Well, I don't," Crane retorted, placing his book down on the pile. He rose and began stepping through the maze of books across the library over to Barnes's reclining figure. With Crane rooted beside him, Barnes's attention finally broke from his book.

With visible agitation in the twisting threads of his cheek, Barnes looked up at Crane, inquiring about the persistence of his lingering. "Can I help you?"

"Yeah, move. You're in my way; I'm trying to get to the window."

"I told you to keep it closed," Barnes restated with a rising scowl.

"I want it open!"

"And I want you to be quiet." Barnes knotted his flailing arms. "Guess we don't always get what we want."

Crane marched forward, knocking down Barnes's legs, pressing through to the window. He ripped up on the sash lift with little recourse as the frame remained sealed, summer-swollen shut to the sill. The old wood bowed as he tugged, panes rattled, though still no crack in the seal.

"You're going to break the—" Barnes's scoff was cut short as, with a snap, Crane fell back, the pewter sash lift in his glove. "—handle . . ." Barnes shook his head, looking down on Crane, having returned to his seat. The younger brother simply shrugged, tossing the broken handle with a clattering bounce across the floor.

"Well, guess we're going to have to get the Carpenter," Crane chuckled.

"I'm fairly certain we're capable of attaching a handle to a frame," Barnes said, taking notice of Crane stubbornly going back to pull up on the window again. "Or, at least, I am," Barnes sullied. Crane pressed against the glass, digging the tips of his fingers at the sealed sash. After several aggravated pulls, the seal was severed.

"Ha-ha—I got it!" Crane rejoiced. As the frame lifted, a gust of air rushed in, lifting a layer of dust off the pages, wafting visible clouds into the air.

"Thanks for that," Barnes muttered, brushing the dust from his arms. As if on cue the sounds of the farm rolled in with the warm summer breeze. The beating of the timber, the clank of the nails, the whispers of the wives, all whisked by. Crane smiled as he spun back into the library, tripping over Barnes's stack of books. The stack tumbled over, falling out of sequence.

"And they say *I'm* the clumsy one," Barnes snickered.

"Are you done?" Crane asked, looking at Barnes as he leaned over the pile.

Barnes nodded, silently pleased with Crane's follies, the product of the kind of rivalry only brothers usually share. Crane ruffled through the books, returning them to order for a few moments, then piling them discretely after losing interest in the titles. Reaching the bottom of the stack revealed a large folio-sized book bound with turquoise cloth and fringed in silver trim. Crane lifted the book with a curious glove, cradling it in his arms. He drifted across the room, eventually falling into a schoolchild's cross-legged pose on the floor. Opening the anchor embossed cover, he peeled to a random page covered in calligraphy.

"Hey, Barnes."

"What?" Barnes shrugged, losing his place once again. He dropped his book on the floor in defeat.

"Come look at this," Crane summoned. Barnes sat beside Crane. The brothers scanned the pages with an eager curiosity they so rarely shared. Crane turned the thick, ink-soaked page, the light illuminating off copper foils in the manuscript. The parchment was covered from corner to corner with a map labeled THE OLD VIRGINIA COAST. Miniature ships, far out of scale, floated freely around a string of islands. In the center, a gold star teetered on the corner of a small landmass, marked THE ORIGINAL COLONY.

"There—right there—that's Roanoke." Barnes pointed to the island with the gold star crown. "It was one of the first human colonies. They lived free, agrarian, simple. The humans' humble beginnings." He reckoned, "Not too different than ours, really . . . ya might say."

"I'd say. We are one of the first colonies."

"Yeah, Crane—except theirs disappeared." Barnes looked up for a moment and read Crane's reaction before returning to the page. "I read this once before." This fact further engrossed Crane into the book. Barnes sat back, drawing his distance, in proximity and perspective.

"What do you think happened to all those people?" Crane asked, audibly eager.

"Died off," Barnes plainly responded, rising to his feet. Crane shook his head, leaning in closer as he read on. Barnes lifted several of the books from his pile, shuffling them in his hands as he read off each title in an attempt to return to his labors; by doing so, he removed himself from Crane's web of distractions.

"They think they went CRO!" Crane rallied. "CRO—like us: 'Crows."

"I don't think that meant to them what you think it means." Barnes shook his head, paging through his books. Crane's returned silence drew Barnes's attention back to his brother. Dropping the books to his chair, Barnes returned to the floor next to Crane.

"Look here!" Crane pointed to a series of paragraphs with correlating illustrations on the page. The illustrations, photographs of ink chicken scratching, had several explorers, armor-plated, swords at their sides, surrounding a tree with carvings in it. Centered in the carvings, a single word appeared to draw their eyes hypnotically. "It says everyone vanished. No sign of any of 'em, neither of war, nor distress, plague or famine—just gone." The brothers leaned in, shoulders matched. Barnes turned the page to another flourished map. Crane explained, "Only the carved message in the tree remained." Crane sat back, marking the end of Barnes's lesson. "To them 'CRO' meant 'Return' as in return back to earth, to nature, to the soil." Crane looked up at the ceiling, picturing the events in his mind. A grin creased in the corner of his cheek as he reveled. "To begin again."

Barnes read Crane's joy, causing his sullying return to the text. "'Return' is all well and good, Crane, but you missed the part where they all raised blades and slaughtered one another."

"What?!" Crane's folded smirk grew to a bewildered scowl in Barnes's direction. "No, it says—"

"It's right here; you didn't turn the page," Barnes retorted, with no scarcity of hubris. Crane's scowl faded as he lifted the book onto his lap, reading the referred paragraphs. Barnes rose, shifting back across the room. "They were humans, Crane. Don't you think you're romanticizing the whole thing?"

"No, I—" Crane defended.

"Humans," Barnes said, cutting Crane off. "If they didn't die off from some natural thing or starve, they most likely killed each other—swords in hand."

"Maybe they broke away, forged off in their separate ways, just moved on, other islands, other colonies." Crane said as he looked up to Barnes who, in waning interest, failed to respond, having returned to his book. "I see weight in that—even just the idea of it—starting over, ya know? I mean, if you had the chance to start all over, would you?"

Crane waited for Barnes to respond, admitting he wasn't actually reading. After a few moments, Barnes rested the ink of his book against his flanneled chest.

"I hold no particular fondness for the idea the way you do." Barnes looked over at Crane, taking care with his response. "But I could see it, if ya had to start over. The humans, they likely had to."

"I bet Roanoke is one beautiful place, a kind of 'paradise by the sea,'" Crane said, reciting a line of text.

"I'm sure it is, Crane," Barnes said, with the sincerest of sarcasm to his voice as he lifted his book, sinking into Barlow's chair.

Attention occasionally drifted. Crane curled onto a perch atop the steps, still locked to the page. "Sometimes I think you only read the books you aren't assigned," Barnes quipped.

Crane ignored Barnes as he felt the words, his lexicon growing with each line. The last word, hanging on the corner of the page, resonated with him as it pooled in the thickest splatter of black ink.

CROATOAN

CHAPTER VIII: Artifacts

The walk down Main Street didn't feel quite the same. The street was quiet at midday when Barnes strolled to the schoolhouse. With the fence construction fully underway, and the expansion of the textile house, much of the once-bustling laborers and kind words of the street had moved out of the village. Even for those few whose shops remained open, work was to be done, and there was little time for a simple "good day." Barnes passed by the two-story bungalow of Malthus the Mason. His family, the largest in the village, had grown exponentially in the previous season, now counting in at over thirteen Scarecrows—more hands for the labors of the Mason. Though many saw this expansion as a break in the equality of their shared labors, Barnes thought little on the matter as he moved on toward the schoolhouse.

Quill's voice fell unheard as her dismissed students filed by. No pupil took the time to ask any last-minute questions as Barnes stood in the back, as he always had before, collecting the books. Quill flustered gaze matched that of Barnes's as she sighed and began cleaning the chalkboard. As Barnes started his task Attucks approached him, taking a seat on the nearest desk. Silently, Attucks ran his glove across the sheen of his prized pilot's jacket as he rested his boot on the opposing desk. To Barnes's surprise, Quill said nothing.

"Can I ask you somethin'?" Attucks inquired with an unusual tick of urgency.

Barnes first looked up at Quill who shook her head before making a silent exit. Barnes then turned to Attucks. "Sure."

After stalling with several crass words, Attucks finally presented his question. "Did you always want to be the Reader's apprentice?" Attucks began assisting with gathering the books, taking hold of a few from desks within his reach.

Barnes cocked his head, thinking for a moment, as he rested the stack on the adjacent desk. "I guess so. I never really thought of myself as being anything else."

"Guess that makes sense." The two 'Crows stood, in pensive proximity. "Here," Attucks said, reaching out and taking half of the load. "I'll help you carry 'em to the library."

Surprised, Barnes nodded, lifting his half. The two Scarecrows started down Main Street. The shadows of several Flying Crows crossed over the empty path. Reaching the edge of town, Barnes broke the silence. "Just out of curiosity, Attucks, why do you ask?"

"Been thinking . . ."

"Yeah?" Barnes said. "What about?"

"Well, since my father's a runner, I don't got something set, like you. And, well—I've been thinking of all the things I could do, ya know?" Barnes offered him an understanding nod, encouraging Attucks to continue. "Came down to what I was good for—figured I must be best at *something.*" They reached the hill overlooking the farmhouse. This landmark matched Barnes's realization at the inevitable conclusion of the conversation, a revelation he dreaded. "So figured I'd best be a soldier." Attucks looked at Barnes, reading into the slump of his posture.

Several yards from the northwest corner of the farmhouse, in what was once the home's backyard, stood the remains of a playground, a mangled mesh with rusty crossing bars, rotted horizontal beams forming platforms, and slides of different heights. The structure's paint-chipped and peeled surface of ornate purple and gaudy yellow had greyed and soured, having received little care or use since the times of its human inhabitance. Barnes's restraint was brief, lasting barely until their arrival at the yard. Dropping his books on one of the slides, Barnes abruptly turned toward Attucks.

"And this seems like a good idea because . . . ?"

"See—I knew that's what you'd say!" Attucks shouted, dropping his portion of the books.

"If you knew that's what I'd say, why'd ya ask?"

"Hopin' you might be different."

Barnes paused, holding back the words he knew would push Attucks away. He took a seat on the wooden platform. "Did you talk to Quill about this?"

"Why do you think the 'Crow's got that scowl? She already thinks she lost another student to Pettick."

Barnes shrugged. "Can't say for sure that she didn't."

"It's not a loss," Attucks said.

"How's it not?"

"Being in Pettick's army ain't somethin' every 'Crow gets to do. You're serving under one of the founding Scarecrows. You're a part of somethin'."

With his jaw clenched Barnes thought for a moment, trying to stop the impending argument and the resolute words he wouldn't be able to take back. Attucks waited for a response, impatiently oscillating the chain of the swing between them.

"You're also no longer a free 'Crow. You can't interact with us; you couldn't talk to me like this. Doesn't that mean something?"

Attucks heaved, attempting to contain his anger. Barnes moved across the yard, hoping that distancing himself from the conversation would cause it to take a different path.

"I didn't have a path set for me; I don't have my life already written. If I were so lucky—"

"And you think I do?" Barnes swung around the swing set, unbridled aggression drawing him in Attucks direction. The speed of both voices escalated, leaving little room for thought between words.

"You walk the same path every day, an obedient hound. You say 'yes, sir,' and you make no move, speak no desire to walk a different path." Attucks's shout stuttered. "Besides, your father wouldn't have a job, were it not for my father, out in that dangerous world, bringing you those worthless books, riskin' his life for the old fool and his hounds tucked safely in their cave."

"At least my father is here!" Barnes shouted, only realizing the harshness of his words in the aftermath of the echo.

Barlow watched from the window of the library as the two young 'Crows continued their discourse. Several minutes after Attucks stormed off, Barnes stepped through the door of the library, the entire stack of books in his arms. The room was quiet as Barnes began shelving the books. Barlow remained by his study, trying to gather wisdom, or words, to share with his son. Sighs of frustration trembled from Barnes, veiling Barlow's own failed attempt to speak.

"You cannot choose the path for others to walk, only your own," Barlow lectured, looking up from his book.

Barnes held the weight of one of the last books, running his thumb along the binding. "Yes, sir." Barnes shifted aimlessly around the room. His thoughts malleable in his hands though void of form. Looking up from his gloves, he noted Crane's absence. "Where's Crane?"

"The basement," Barlow said.

"Pop?"

"I know what I said," Barlow huffed, the breath of elder woes, "but he is my son."

* * *

Lines of scratched brick surrounded the well of books like the rays of light from a child's drawing of the sun. This drawing, never completed, no matter how much Crane wished it would end. He added another ray of fire to the drawing, lifted his shovel, dragged across the dark chamber, and emptied the load of books into the stove. The pages of Keats, Marlowe, Steinbeck, Hugo, and Elliot cried out to Crane as they fluttered like birds inside the burning cage, longing for a freedom Crane had only known from the touch and smell of the ink on their feathers. These cries shrouded the faint noise of Crane's own sorrows. Whimpers and snarls heightened, till a sudden realization froze Crane in his path. His cries were not lone.

Crane cocked his head toward the direction from which the whimpers were emanating. Dropping a pile of books in front of the stove, Crane turned to the door of the fruit cellar. The large padlock sealing its latch rattled. Crane stepped closer and the quiet pattering of his shoes was answered by a rustle of noise from beyond the door.

"Hello?" A voice sounded from beyond the door, startling Crane. "Is someone out there?" The voice was low with deep swallows from the throat, giving the otherwise young voice a weathered tone. "Can you let me out?" the voice asked sympathetically. Crane choked for a moment, finding within himself a tender voice to carry his words.

"No, see, I can't." Crane stuttered for a less obligatory answer: "I—I don't have a key." He sat down on the two steps in front of the door. The voice was silent, save the whimpers. "Wh-why are you down here?"

The voice cleared its throat. "I was changing the tire on my Chevy when these things jumped me, said they'd cut my belly open if

I fought back." The voice exhaled. "They bound me good, drug me back here—whatever hell this is—"

"You have an automobile?!" Crane interjected.

"Yes . . ." the voice replied with disinterest and confusion.

"That's amazing!" Crane reveled, not bothering to disguise the rising clarity in his eagerness. "I have—well, it's not *mine*, but a friend of mine has one."

"What kind?" the voice asked.

"I don't know, it has a bed in the back, rounded wheel wells, and a large front engine barrel."

"So it's—it's a pickup," the voice rhetorically stated.

"Yeah, and it was made by a human named Ford."

"So it's a Ford pickup truck."

"Yeah, that's it," Crane said with an excitement the voice failed to share.

"Good for yer friend." The voice receded, moving back from the door, returning with aggravation and urgency in tone. "Listen, you seem to got a brain; you wanna tell yer friends to let me the fuck outta here? I promise not to tell no one. I don't give a shit what yer doin' out here—nobody does. Just please—"

Crane sat back, piecing together the facts he gathered from his new friend. "You're not from around here?"

"Me? No."

"Wait, what colony are you from?" Crane asked.

"Colony, like the thirteen? Or you talkin' states?" The voice's incertitude grew, evident in the swaying tones of its words and the disintegration of its sentences. "What'd you mean?"

Crane simplified his questions. "Where are you from?"

"Philadelphia."

"I think I've heard of that before. Where is that?"

"Pennsylvania? I—uhhh—I—Uhh . . ." The voice cracked to a lower register, slowing with more deliberate clarity. "Listen I don't got time to spit about this. I'm a good guy; I don't belong here. Just do me one and let me out. Please."

Crane could hear the sense of urgency in the voice's words, the scared quiver in the undertone of its breathing. "I guess I can talk to someone." Crane thought for a second of those he could talk to, having now made a promise he felt unqualified to make.

"Thanks," the voice said, exhausted with relief.

Crane's regrets receded, sensing the comfort his words offered. As silence persisted, marking a close to their conversation, Crane jumped up, starting for the door.

"Wait!" the voice echoed.

Crane spun back to the fruit cellar. A hand appeared from the vent. Visible hairs of the forearm rose from static. Crane jumped back, realizing what the hand belonged to. He studied the hand, which reached out in a way Crane had never seen. It seemed gentle, friendly, even welcoming. Crane trembled as he got his first real look at a human hand up close. The skin was dry, cracked, but still smooth. Previous notions believed to be true, of scaly skin and sharp nails, fell away. Gashes lined the knuckle where grease-lined wrinkles and human sap dried and crusted. There was a freckled uniformity to its scarring. The hand unfolded as the palm turned skyward.

"I'm Jamie."

Crane looked down at his gloves, animating the extent of their motion. Fear's attempts to paralyze failed as curiosity overcame him. Reaching out, the fingers of his glove met the skin of the human. Static transferred, the current flowing through his threads. Crane tried to restrain the nervous tremors in his fingertips as the human's fingers wrapped, cradling his hand. The wrist shook. Crane recognized the ceremony of this gesture, falling into its shaking motion. After several seconds, the hand released the glove, and the arm coiled back into the darkness. A grin cornered Crane's cheek as he read the palms of his gloves. After several moments passed, he leapt to his feet, starting to the stairs.

Jamie asked, "You'll be back, right?" There was fear in his voice, an impulsive affectation incurred by the returning loneliness. Crane shuffled to a halt, a cloud of dust gathering about his feet.

"Yeah." Crane lifted his rucksack from atop the stack of logs, pawing for his journal, which he quickly drew.

"Please get help," the worn voice pleaded once more.

Crane grew taut for a moment, realizing the necessary secrecy their interactions would require. Feeling helpless, feeling dumb, he stood still, as if tied to a pike in the center of the room. "Jamie?"

"Yeah?"

"I wanna help—" Crane needlessly gestured with his hands and then, realizing the futility of this, relieved his gloves.

A sigh prefaced Jamie's words. "I'm sensin' a big 'if' here." A shallow chuckle, the epilogue.

"No one else can know we spoke, okay?" Crane urged, shifting back to the door, awaiting an answer.

"How will I know when it's you?" Jamie asked.

Crane looked around the room, searching for signal, simple yet remarkable. He caught sight of the well of books, the stove and its leaking spout of grey smoke. "By the smell of the stove and the sound of my voice."

"Right. Hey, you got a name?"

"Crane."

"Good to meet ya, Crane."

"You also, Jamie."

A human name. Crane now knew a human name. He raced up the stairs, peeled off down the hall, and leapt over the threshold of the front door. Midday sun bathed over the grey and blue folds of his flannel, washing away the cold of the cellar. Downwind of the house he dashed even faster, escape keeping the confusion at bay. Yet steadily a sense, a feeling, spread from his belly, engulfing him quickly. The knowledge he had just gained made him feel isolated from the rest of his common Scarecrows.

Outside the garage, Crane slid to a halt. He kicked gravel in rhythm with his heaving sunken chest. For the first time he felt unsure whether this was the right place to go; if his knowledge and its burden were a fair weight to share. Crane ran on, westward, feet off the ground, fear in chase, without a place to hide.

* * *

Threads spun, spinning, weaving, needles pierced, catching, tangling, work flowing, fast, yet not as fast as necessitated by Pettick's recent quota. Demands were being shouldered by Wade the Tailor, who marched along the rows of the tables, prospector of the threading gloves. The chamber was filled with a heavy, waxy air; singed threads and such momentum, hands could not keep pace with their toil.

"This drudgery is unconscionable," Gwyn remarked.

"What did you just say?" Jasper huffed as he shot a befuddled glance across the table.

"Un-con-scio-na-ble," Gwyn pronounced out the syllables, acting as if it were a colloquial article of her lexicon.

"And what does that mean?" Mare asked.

"I don't even think that be a word," Jasper added.

"She spends all her time with the Reader boy. I assure you, it's a word," Mare said, looking over at her daughter who briefly looked up from her labors only to offer a guilty smirk.

Wade hobbled forward, now only several chairs down the line. The laborers intensified in their work with his passing. A needle fumbled from a 'Crow's thumbs. Wade laid out his tailor tape, wrapping it across the 'Crow's back, snapping in recoil. She took the hit, picked up the needle, and continued her labor with even greater haste.

"Waste of grain," Gwyn muttered.

Wade's weight teetered on his heel. Spinning around, he shot toward Gwyn. With a fast glove, Wade clenched a tuffet of Gwyn's hair, ripping her head back. "What did you say, you rancid little—"

"I called you a waste of grain, jackass," Gwyn stoked.

Wade ripped Gwyn out of her chair and dragged her several feet across the wood planked gallery. Clamoring for footing, her boots scattered, rubbing roughly against the hand-planed planks. Her gloves tore at his sleeve. The laborers' attention broke from their work to look at the unfolding altercation. Wade smacked the back of his glove across Gwyn's face, sending her to the floor. Mare jumped between Wade and her daughter as Wade drew back his hand once more. Before his recoiled glove could gain inertia, Wade collapsed to the floor. Jasper stood over his unconscious body, an iron in her glove.

Pettick arrived several minutes later to quell the hysteria. "So what you are telling me is you couldn't handle a couple of women! That a salty batch of quim got the best of you, huh?" Pettick chastised Wade, his shouts echoing in the hall, music to the ears of the remaining few still holding true to their labors. "I pray you are never on the front lines with an army raging your way, thirsting for your blood. I know a deserter when I see one, and you certainly fit the bill."

Wade's chin quivered as he took every insult to heart. Gwyn refrained from giggling, though several squeaks passed from her, much to Mare's disapproval. Pettick gave a commanding look in Gwyn's direction, leaving her cold and unsettled. Shaking his head, he flashed a brief crooked grin, spun around, and exited the building.

Barnes crossed the meeting ground and started up the path toward the house. Looking west he caught sight of Attucks by the well. Having matched gazes, he stopped his stride, since the obligation to make amends seemed unavoidable. Barnes turned toward the sun and took several casual steps toward Attucks. With a furrowed brow, he stared at his friend through a cloud of gnats thriving in the waves of heat above a puddle of brackish water.

"Guessin' apologies are in order?" Barnes swatted the air to little effect.

"Just be thankful I didn't sock ya." Attucks offered a cocky grin, as if to further denote the pleasure in his brawn. He peeled away his leather jacket, tossing it beside a neatly folded bundle of clothes wrapped in twine on the lid of the well.

"Pleasant," Barnes scoffed.

"Would you expect anything less?"

"From you?" Barnes couldn't help his widening grin. "No. I think that'll suffice."

"Good." Attucks unbuttoned his white-and-navy pinstriped short sleeve, peeling it away and tossing it beside the jacket.

"What are you doing?" Barnes asked.

"I've got a uniform now—Pettick's orders." Attucks slid his belt around, revealing the sheath of a knife on his hip. "Wanna see somethin'? Look what Gunner the Quartermaster just gave me." He abruptly drew his weapon, brandishing the tarnished silver blade. Barnes stood by with little interest in Attucks's new toy. "Sharp enough to skin a human from their flesh!" Attucks grinned, running the thumb of his glove along the blade. Sensing Barnes's disinterest, he returned to his task, retrieving the bundle and swiftly splicing the twine.

"So, no more jacket?" Barnes sighed, pocketing his gloves.

"Afraid not." Attucks shrugged, returning the blade to his hip, void of the sentimentality Barnes seemed keen for.

"It'll be hard, picturing you without it." Barnes said.

"Well then—here!" With one arm through his shirt, Attucks tossed the jacket to Barnes. Barnes cradled the jacket, running his hands over the seams, along the zipper, up to the patches which varied from cloth symbols of eagles to embroidered stars and stripes.

Barnes presented the jacket back to Attucks. "I can't take this."

"You have to," Attucks said, standing in his ranked patched and numbered green cloth shirt. His hair fell to his brow.

"Oh, and why is that?"

Raking a comb through his hair, Attucks argued, "'Cause wouldn't you rather wear it, than see it on some new Scarecrow comin' down the line?"

Barnes remained silent. Nodding, he ran his glove through the sleeve, throwing the leather hide onto his shoulders.

Attucks chuckled. "I thought so." Throwing his arms around Barnes, Attucks shook his friend with an endearing hold. Barnes broke from Attucks's lock as the two stumbled down the path.

"You know, humans had a word for other humans that acted like you," Barnes quipped, burying his gloves in his pockets.

"Yeah, what's that?"

"Asshole."

Attucks chuckled, giving Barnes's arm a loving slug, knuckle to patch. "And what's it mean?"

Barnes shook his head along the curve of his crooked grin. "Not a damn clue."

And, on his way back to the farmhouse from the textie barn, Pettick stopped in mid-stride. At his feet, a young female 'Crow of only a few seasons, toddler-size, with long dirty-blond hair and corduroy overalls, sat playing in the center of the path. Having not seen such a simple sight occurring in a long time, or having just not taken the time to notice, Pettick considered the beauty of such a thing. The girl had three small figures, twine and fabric scraps, tied and stuffed into miniature Scarecrows. A scene was unfolding between two of the figures in a house, the imaginary structure realized in a square of gathered sticks. Pettick was taken aback by this unfolding scene—the awe-inspiring glimpse of a creation creating. Pettick sat with the child, planting himself in the middle of the crowded path and crossing his legs like a schoolboy. Without hesitation, consideration, or judgment, the girl handed him two of the figures and picked up the third to play with. Pettick inspected the figures in his gloves. The figure in his left hand had a felt vest and a blue-rag handkerchief, much like himself. The figure in his right hand was larger, wearing a small Stetson, clearly made in the image of Mawkin.

With a tender smile, Pettick sat the figure of himself within the house walked Mawkin's figurine into the scene, greeting the figure in the girl's hand. He animated the articulation of the figure's limbs, waving to the girl. After seating the figure in her hand, the girl took hold of Pettick's figure. The young girl began to mimic Pettick's actual movements with his figure, his seated position, his criss-crossed legs, and his playing with the girl. Pettick observed this with a tilt of his head and a curiosity to her actions, the act of puppetry and manipulation, the imitation and replication of life as it unfolded.

Several Scarecrows began to gather at a distance, observing their leader at play with a small child in the middle of the path. Chatter rose. Mawkin shifted through the crowd for a glimpse at what the 'Crows were taking notice of. Pettick and the girl were laughing, though his wistful exhausts seemed stricken with a slight grief. Mawkin looked at the judging gazes of the loitering Scarecrows. These gazes disgusted and saddened Mawkin. With hesitance, Mawkin approached Pettick and the girl.

"Pettick, sir, what are you doing?" Mawkin asked. Pettick did not respond and continued playing and laughing his sad laugh. Mawkin looked at his gloves. Laying hands on him, Mawkin lifted Pettick to his feet. The crowd remained. Mawkin turned to address them. "Do you not have labors to attend to?" The Scarecrows did not sway. "Go on, get outta here, before I make ya!" After a few lingering moments the Scarecrows dispersed.

Malthus the Mason came by, lifting his child into his arms and backing away from Pettick and Mawkin. Without acknowledging Malthus, Pettick started down the path.

"My apologies, I assure you," Malthus said, sounding perturbed.

"It's fine." Mawkin nodded. Malthus left. Mawkin, still standing in the center in the path, cocked his head, peering down at Pettick who was wandering to the house in a drunken stagger.

Pettick slid his hand along the edge of the wooden dining table, causing his sleeve to ruffle as it collected the many years of dust. Mawkin passed the doorway, doubling back to see Pettick's hunched figure alone in the dimly lit room. The large 'Crow shifted, centered in the door frame, watching his superior for a pensive moment.

"Pettick?"

"Mawkin," Pettick wryly retorted.

"What are you doing in here?" Mawkin looked about the dining room as he entered. It was a place he had seldom been before. He began encompassing the table, reading each individual element from chair rail to floorboard as he scanned at a slow pace.

"Do you know what this room is?" Pettick asked.

"What?"

"Do you know what this room was for—what humans used it for?" Pettick asked.

"No," Mawkin replied.

"Huh," Pettick huffed. Mawkin continued to study the room, as Pettick lectured from his seat. "So you never thought about or wondered why this room was here?"

"I did not say I never thought about it, I simply didn't feel the need to ask—till now," Mawkin said.

"Then ask—"

"Ask you?"

"Yes." Pettick shrugged, annoyed by the lagging pace of their conversation.

"Why is it here?" Mawkin feigned interest for a moment, though his true and intrepid curiosity came through. Pettick sifted through the artificiality and genuineness of Mawkin's curiosity, cocking his head as he looked Mawkin in the face, further engaging their discourse.

"Humans, they would sit here every night and consume together."

"Is that all?" Mawkin asked.

"All of what?"

"Is that all that happened here?"

"No." A grin cut clean across Pettick's face.

"No?" Mawkin paused, reading into Pettick's words, though not enough to warrant prying on the topic. "So why are you here?"

"I always found human ritual fascinating," Pettick mused.

"Oh, is that so?"

"Your use of sarcasm truly is improving." Pettick smiled, finding a kind of solace in Mawkin's growth.

Mawkin passed behind Pettick, taking post by the door. "Thanks."

"'And together we fed, for family is made at the dinner table'," Pettick quoted an unknown text with restraint to his words.

"What?"

"Nothing." Pettick muttered.

Respecting Pettick's solitude, Mawkin retreated to the hall, passing through the doorway up the stairs. Alone, Pettick slid his hand forward on the table, running the fingers of his glove along a narrow gash in the table, which pierced the stain, exposing the untreated wood.

"Not all that happened." Pettick confessed quietly to himself. Shaking off his anger with a chuckle, he rocked back in his chair.

* * *

Pitch, formerly the Carpenter, now fulfilled his duties without the denim overalls that once made him. He rolled up the sleeves of his uniform. The green shirt, faded and stained, gave less of a professional impression, but marked his loyalties to Pettick's army. Tightening the straps of his harness, he made the ascent up the metal rungs of the wooden tower. The tower, a single utility pole that once ran power to the farmhouse, now dangled wires for transmitting messages from the speakers Pitch was installing. Pitch reached the top of the tower, the warm air running through his threads. He looked out over the farm where he caught a glimpse of a pair of young 'Crows, Crane and Barnes, playing a game of catch a few yards down the hill.

Crane gripped the laces on the ball, rubbing his fingers along the seams where the layers of skin met. Crane reached back, launched the ball along the crops, causing the object to vanish in the late day sun before landing in Barnes's mitt. The laces of the mitt stretched with the impact of the ball.

"Nice!" Barnes said, returning the ball with a matching arc. "Where's Pop? Said he'd be here by now." Barnes peered up at the hill, lifting the edge of his cap.

"He hasn't exactly been around much recently," Crane added.

"You don't have much faith, brother—"

"Faith, in him? No." Crane launched the ball with a heavy curve. "You gonna let it go?" Crane bitterly remarked, kicking the clay at his feet for a better stance.

Barnes examined the ball, sneering. "Maybe if both of you tried—I don't know—not being assholes," he said, returning the ball to Crane.

Moving into its trajectory, Crane made the catch. He paced, burying the ball into his mitt. "Ass-Hole, glad to see all that reading is improving your vocabulary," Crane quipped, turning back to Barnes. "It's between Barlow and me; just stay out of it!" After ensuring Barnes made the catch Crane broke off again, looking up at Pitch as he bolted the speaker into place.

"There, that's the problem—'Barlow.' Since when are you on a first-name basis?" Barnes broke his stance, gesturing further with the conversation. "You don't respect him. 'Sir' ain't a hard word to say."

"I said stay out of it!" Crane shouted, frustrated with Barnes's continued prying. "Sorry we can't all be such obedient dogs."

"What do you know about dogs?" Barnes said as he whipped a fastball at Crane, nearly pelting him in the arm. The ball smacked into his mitt, causing a resonating *crack*, a satisfactory sound to Barnes.

"I do read," Crane said, getting back into stance.

"Hopefully better than you throw," Barnes muttered.

Crane tossed a fly ball in Barnes's direction. The speakers cracked to life, blasting a piercing cry over the farm, sending Barnes jumping. The ball flew past him, vanishing into the crops. "Dammit, Crane!"

"What? You jumped!" Crane shouted in jest, chuckling as he watched Barnes begin searching. "Wimp," he muttered to himself, pushing up on the bridge of his cap to get a clearer view of the speakers.

"All right, Kindle, we're ready!" Pitch shouted as he clamped the insulation around the speaker wire, waving down to Crane before descending the pole.

Peering back to the fields, Crane watched Barnes's tall brushed silhouette continue searching through the crops, backlit by the draining blood-orange sun. Static crackled over the speakers, drawing Crane's attention again. Pitch followed the insulated line a couple dozen yards to the meeting ground, stopping in front of the stage where a box sat, the place of the line's termination. There Kindle stood organizing a series of metal boxes and plastic cases on the edge of the stage. His gaze then shifted to a book, its pages weighted open on the deck. He stood before the box, plugging the cable into a turntable.

"You sure this magic box of yours is gonna work, Tinker?" Pitch stuttered, dropping his toolbag onto the stage, curiously intruding on Kindle's workspace.

"I hope so," Kindle huffed, looking at Pitch with an expression of whimsy. Pitch shared his fellow craftsman's faith, patting Kindle on the back as he made room for the Tinker to work. Kindle brushed the straws of his beard, glancing once more at a diagram on the page. Resting the silver microphone next to the box, he pulled a 45 rpm record from his toolkit. Blowing the dust from its face he read the inscription on the label, *Glenn Miller's Hits*, before aligning it on the turntable. He turned a knob on the front of the box. Lifting the arm, the record began to rotate. "Here goes nothing." He exhaled, resting the needle on the edge of the record. The needle floated to center in a rhythmic bounce. The speakers cracked, clearing their throat from years of silence, before the rolling needle's vibrations faded in.

Barnes spread the crops as he pressed into the clearing. "Found it!" he shouted, holding the ball above his head.

With a charming boom, the music rolled in, sending the swinging melody of "Stardust" in crashing waves over the farm. Every Scarecrow raised his head toward the speaker. Pitch leaned toward Kindle, throwing a rocking arm around him.

"It works! What a hoot!"

Kindle smiled with an air of confidence.

"Pettick will be pleased!" Pitch shouted to ensure his voice was heard. "Now even the eldest 'Crow will hear his voice!"

Kindle nodded.

Barnes approached Crane, planting himself next to him, his younger kin focused only on the speakers. "You read the same books I do," Barnes thought aloud. "Is it just me, or are we getting more—"

"More what? Human?" Crane snapped.

"Yeah," Barnes sighed, thinking for a moment before adding: "Haven't started killing each other yet . . ." Barnes shrugged as he looked over at Crane, who stood entranced by the invisible waves emanating from the speakers. Barnes shoved Crane with his gloves, setting off his balance and breaking his trance. A moment of playfulness returned, fading away as quickly as it came.

"What ya thinking about?" Barnes asked.

Crane dropped the ball into Barnes's glove as he passed. "Thinkin' this may be the last quiet day in the colony." He began stripping his mitt as he walked up the hill in the direction of the farmhouse.

Barnes stared at the ball. "Right . . ." he looked back up at the speakers once more before following Crane up the path, stripping his own mitt from his glove as he went.

The saxophone bridge carried with it a muffled trumpet that whaled with melancholy as melodic cries of lost loves howled in the thin summer air. The needle slid to the next track, "The White Cliffs of Dover." The sound carried to the farmhouse, tapping the glass.

Pettick looked out his window, where, like a painting captures, there was a picturesque view of dusk. He leaned over, sliding the latch above the sash, and pulled open the window just enough so that the warm air carried the crisp sound of the record through the parlor. He shifted over to his chair. Reclining, he set his legs on the desk. A smile crossed his face. His head bobbed lightly in tempo with the tune. Pettick gently said, "I think that's all for today." He looked across the desk at Barlow, who was planted at the typewriter. Barlow nodded, sifting the papers into their stack, sealing the ream in the box. "If you hurry, you may still make that game of toss with your boys."

Barlow sighed, placing the lid on the typewriter. "No, I'm afraid that time has already passed." He shook his head, pensively stowing the manuscript in his case.

"You didn't even look at your watch?" Pettick inquired, lazily gesturing to his breast and wrist.

"Oh, I don't have one." Barlow gave a gentle smile. "That sense comes from before my minutes were counted."

Pettick stood up, taken aback. "Ahhh, I see . . ." He stopped bobbing his head and moved around the desk to see Barlow out.

"I do remember that time," Barlow ached, shuffling to the door.

"Oh, what time was that?" Pettick inquired, running his hand along the hairs of loose thread on his chin.

"The time before I needed a watch." Barlow said.

Pettick sighed. "Don't we all." He gave his weight to the desk as the door sealed, leaving him alone in the parlor, the music flooding in, filling the bath of sound around a thought-ridden Scarecrow. "What a funny thing."

* * *

"Oh, you should have seen it, Crane, I turned around and gave him this look, you know the look, like I wasn't his Scarecrow and he didn't own any part of me. And I looked at him hard," Gwyn regaled, accentuating her words with a fantastic bite of pride.

"And then you socked him?" Crane excitedly interrupted.

"Well, no—I told him what a waist of grain he was."

"Okay . . . so . . . then you socked him?"

"No, there was no socking, Crane," Gwyn said reasonably as she stood with a backdrop of stars, playing out the incident to Crane who reclined in the field of grass below.

"Then how did he end up unconscious? He's been walking around with that swollen head all week. The whole village has been talking about how 'Gwyn the Cobbler's Daughter gave mean old Wade the Tailor a piece of her mind.'"

"I did! I told him to buzz off, if you'll let me finish the story—"

"Sorry, go on."

"No." Gwyn crossed her arms and legs in refusal and dropped to the grass.

"Why?" Crane asked.

"Because, you'll just be disappointed by the ending."

"What makes you think that?" Crane asked as he reached for Gwyn, unsuccessfully.

"Because what happened was Jasper knocked him out with an iron, that's all." Gwyn read the hidden disappointment she had predicted on Crane's face. "There's far less romance in rebellion than you're ripe to believe," Gwyn reckoned. With a puff of air she blew the feathers from her brow. "I need to get outta that place, do something, else—anything else! More."

"More? Like what?

Gwyn cocked her head, shooting Crane a daring accusatory glare. "You think you're the only one with bigger plans, Crane?"

Crane respectfully shut up.

"Well, if you must know, I've been thinking about botany. Plants, you know, like the sunflower I gave you. I grew that myself in a little trough behind our shop."

"You did?" Crane asked, attempting to veil his surprise.

"Yeah," Gwyn replied, smiling proudly.

"I thought you picked it from the wild patch. You know, the one out by the orchard."

"Nope. But that is where I got my seeds. Plucked 'em from the patch last autumn before they got too cold. Kept them dry and warm, hidden in this tobacco tin, wrapped in some old linen in the cupboard behind my sewing kit. I'd hold them in my glove every day, felt them scatter in the fabric, to make sure they were still all there, still dry and tender. Then I'd tuck them away till the next day came, when I would draw my school supplies or needles from the drawer once more." Crane was able to read every which way Gwyn felt about the words she was sharing. "I even took them to the textile house with me once, kept them in my cardigan pocket against my bosom. Got to thinking they could be lost or get too cold or wet. I was terrified they'd been ruined, but had no way of knowing for certain. So I swore never to do it again." Gwyn smiled at the thought. She surprised herself, choking on her words and the thought of confessing such a thing. "Crane, I never thought it would grow. I planted them, and never thought they'd actually bud, nor turn into anything really—especially not that. When the first bud broke the soil, I cried. I couldn't contain my excitement. I just wanted to tell everyone."

"But you didn't?"

Gwyn smiled, almost embarrassed by the confession. "No. No, I didn't tell a soul."

"Huh," Crane exhaled.

"Huh?" Gwyn inquired.

"Yeah," Crane paused in thought, reflecting on what he was actually thinking. "I just didn't know that about you. Guess everyone's got their secrets, right?

"Right," Gwyn reasoned, thinking further on the matter as she fell into the grass aside Crane. "So what is yours?"

"Mine?" Crane asked.

"Your secret," Gwyn restated, continuing, "and don't you dare try and tell me that you ain't got one."

Their flat backs rested on a bed of grass beneath the stars. Crane's palm pressed to Gwyn's, both hands in a tangled waltz. Focus shifted from gloves to sky and back again.

"It's not so much a secret . . ." Crane thought aloud, navigating his way toward a response.

"What are you searching for, then, anyway?" Gwyn negotiated for an answer she greatly desired to possess, an inquiry instigated by Crane's persisting silence.

"What do you mean?" Crane purported.

"It's just lately, when I do see you, you're lost in your mind, like you're searching for somethin'. I just wanna know—" Dancing fingers parted, gloves fell to the grass. "—what you're searching for."

"I don't even know anymore," Crane exhaled, aware of the uncertainty in his reply. Crane raised his chest, rolling his elbows into the grass; his words resonated in their alcove of brush. Gwyn twisted to Crane for a moment and then went back to her pod, like a separate branch of the same flora.

"I mean, tell me I'm being crazy, Crane, but there's something you're keeping from me." Gwyn said.

Crane sat up and drew his knees against his chest, resting the weight of his head on them. Resisting the urge to reach for one another or retreat to looking at the stars, the Scarecrows remained tied in tightly wound coils.

"Truth be told," Crane reckoned, "I'm not even certain I know the answer."

"Then how will you even know if you find it?"

"Maybe then this feeling will stop."

"What feeling?"

"That this—all this—we're meant for better," Crane confessed. "There was a point in time when I thought I could never keep secrets from you—I was eager to tell you my every thought, every dream, every desire, no matter the perversity or admonishment in its clause. Now I'm not so sure."

"So there is something. Something unraveling your straws?"

Night gathered in phlox patches along the horizon.

Crane nodded silently, his hair and arms concealing his face.

"Crane, when you're ready to tell me, I'll be here to listen. Okay?" Gwyn's words, tender and deliberate, settled to the soil. Crane pursed his upper lip, blowing the hair from his brow. Unfolding his arms, he reached for Gwyn, who remained in a ball as Crane wrapped his arms around her, pulling her in. In their silence, nature's nocturnal chorus rose. Gwyn was pensive, though Crane did not ask what was on her mind. "Meant for better?" Gwyn thought aloud.

"Yeah," Crane sighed.

"Is that a real feeling or a wish?" Gwyn asked.

"Both, I guess," Crane said, taking to heart the meaning of the words. "It's just that when you call it a wish, it feels further from being true."

With fading interest in the topic, their words fell to artifact. Crane wrapped his arms tightly around Gwyn. Playful banter ensued, carefree exchanges, true to their youth. The tangled bodies fell back to their bed, careless of place, only shifting stars marking their time.

CHAPTER IX: Telltales

I held the knife tautly in my glove as its sharpened edge dug several inches into the dried rust-orange clay of the road. Pulling out the blade, I stood, the knees of my jeans stained with clay. I raised the blade above my head. I remember so vividly the echoes of the screams. The surrounding pikes, now empty, stood as a backdrop to our rally as I turned and we began our march up the hill. The sky above of red and orange surrounded the farmhouse. Several lights were in the window as it neared dark. The grass was tall around the house; it acted as our camouflage, though I could sense old man Tucker knew I was—knew WE were coming for him. So we grabbed the weapons of our kind, pitchforks, knives, shovels, reapers, and other pointed instruments, for our twisted fun. We lit torches, though they risked damage to the flesh of our kind. We had every intention of burning the house down.

Surrounding the house, the flares of the torches flashed against the paneled wood as the last of the sun left its own red glow. I stood in front of the porch just outside the front door along our border several feet from the house. I do not remember the moment, but rather the feeling, stepping forward from the line.

"Tucker!" I yelled, but only his silence followed. I looked at my kin for a moment. That was when a most triumphant caw *was heard, and we rallied with it. The front door opened. Tucker's eldest nephew stepped out. I rose to meet him on the porch. I reasoned for a moment, but after our failed discourse he let out an awful torturous cry. With a swift slash of my blade, we drew first blood. His body fell to the planks, the sap from his neck flowed, a sweet nectar, down the warped valleys of the grain, pooling at my feet before draining between the cracks.*

The sounds and figures blurred in that moment as we rushed the house. The doors shattered open, boots clattered up the stairs. That was when the screams were most real. Tucker screamed the loudest; that fact was of little surprise to me. I stood in the upstairs hall. I closed the door behind me, locking it. Ahead of me was the old man, dragged by one of my largest companions. His knees ran raw against the wood floor. His eyes looked up into my face, where his face reflected. But the shadows must have left me in disguise, for he didn't recognize me then.

In the dining room, that is where I followed them to. Tucker was laid out on the table. His nightwear was a heavy flannel to protect him from the cold. We quickly removed his top, revealing the pale exposed flesh. His raw knees bled similarly to the calluses on his hands. I entered from my perch in the doorway. The moon shined through the window, reflecting off the finish of the table. He asked what kind of animals we were. We quickly gagged him. He had countless chances to speak, and he never took them—for any good words, anyway.

I leaned forward into the light, my face now visible to him. I needed him to see who and what I was—who we were. His face confirmed to me that he knew. I raised my blade. His eyes shined. And I nailed him to the table. He shook for but a moment before those eyes glazed over. And in that moment, things had changed—changed forever here.

I looked out at the moon. The violence of the house died out. The bodies were lifted, carried down the hill to the fields. That is where they were placed, roped, nailed and lashed, strung up to the pikes, where the Scarecrows hung no more.

In the distance, drums sounded.

"I can hear the drums," Pettick said. "Can you?"

The drums sounded in a beat of triumph as Pettick fell, supine with fingers laced atop his chest, into the creaking chair. Recollection of memory faded. Barlow sat back from the typewriter, scanning the wet ink on the page. Before the ink could fully dry, Barlow lifted the page from the typeset and added it to the heaping ream of the manuscript.

The drum line of four stoic Scarecrows in revolutionary costumed battle garb marched down the path towards the meeting ground. Led by Quill the Teacher, her long red hair tied back; her flute sung a heroic melody that could be heard as far as the farmhouse up the hill. The meeting ground was bustling with excitement as the celebration of the Revolution of the Scarecrows was underway. The sun was high in the midday sky, providing one of the truly beautiful days of summer. The band played triumphant melodies, hymns of victories past. Fiddles and banjos, trumpets and zithers all slammed and spun, with stomping heavy beats. The platform shook with the vibrations, sending the vermin that burrowed and slumbered beneath out into the world. A fox scurried into the crowd, its red tail becoming the focus of much enjoyment as the creature hopped away. A large rat followed, and the terrified creature moved in circles before running up the leg of a Scarecrow, burrowing inside his threads.

"It's inside me! Ahhhhh!" the small 'Crow screamed out, followed by a shrieking laugh. The 'Crow danced around, drawing the attention of the surrounding Scarecrows, who, taking audience, laughed at his expense.

Barnes circled around the bunch of Scarecrows, watching the small 'Crow dance like a fool. Breaking off from the circle, he paced the meeting grounds, searching for his kin. By the well he spotted Gwyn and Crane playfully dancing. "Crane!" Barnes yelled as they danced by.

"What?" Crane responded, taking not a straw of attention away from his partner.

"Crane, come here!"

"I'm a little busy." Crane smiled, spinning his partner, rolling her out and pulling her back into his arms as if there were a ripcord between them.

"Have you seen Pop?" Barnes continued, brandishing his still mild frustration.

"What?"

"Have you seen Pop?"

"Nah, but I'm sure he's around."

"Yeah, so am I," Barnes discontentedly muttered, shifting away from the lovers. Running his glove along the rough of his neck, he headed back into the crowd.

The sounds of the celebration carried in near perfect clarity up the hill to the farmhouse. Barlow stood at the window of Pettick's parlor, looking down at the festivities.

"Watching will simply make it worse." Pettick's voice carried from his reclined position at the opposite corner of the parlor.

"I know," Barlow replied.

"Then get back to your typewriter," Pettick sneered, "before I chain ya to it."

Barlow sighed and returned to his seat, placing a new paper in the typeset. "I don't see why we have to work today of all days," Barlow grumbled.

"We are behind schedule; besides, I'm feeling inspired." Pettick chuckled, resting his feet on the desk.

"Fantastic," Barlow scoffed. Shifting his gloves to the keys, he typed the page number on the corner of the page, then set return to the next line on the manuscript.

He typed the date, hesitation in his hands as he silently concealed his quandary. He hit return and started on the next sentence.

* * *

The locomotive pulsing of the horses' gallop was the only true measure of time. An influx of soldiers on horseback through the narrow paths of the forest gave little room for Attucks's mind to wander, lessening the symptoms of his nerves. The team of riders, invaders in the night, reached their destination, a rustic Victorian ranch house, overlooking its corn fields. The door shattered open. By the *click—snap—ting* sounds of Attucks's bolt-action rifle reloading, the humans were disarmed, herded, and immobilized.

Dropping from a swing around the porch post, Pettick strolled around the house, following Mawkin's seemingly wayward tracks. Rounding to the back of the house, Mawkin sat, half-veiled in darkness, huddled atop the reel of a pale blue harvesting combine. Pettick took notice of the dubiety on Mawkin's face, and continued his stroll to the field ahead where a small patch of buckwheat had been planted. Pettick extended his arm to touch the stalk of wheat; the hairs ran soft tickles of intimacy to his glove as he cradled the string of chaffed grains.

"Fascinating flora, truly the Jewel of Babylon." The *crack* of a shotgun round sounded. Pettick continued, unfazed. "And we are the product of this harvest."

"Fascinating," Mawkin quipped with the utmost of sarcasm on his tongue.

"Ah, now who is jaded, my friend? One day, dear Mawkin, you will learn to again appreciate such marvels."

A scream resonated from inside the house, followed by the scrapes of a scuffle.

"I'm certain I will. What I can't understand, though, is this," Mawkin said, gesturing to the house.

"What *about* this?" Pettick asked. A gunshot followed, a small shallow *pop* from a pistol.

"You preach of peace. But—"

pop-pop-pop

"Mawkin, if you preach of peace, the devil will still come knocking. If you preach of violence, all they will know is that. Scarecrows want to feel safe. So we offer them that safety, that peace of mind, the pleasure of ignorance."

click

"You still didn't answer me." Mawkin said.

"How so?"

BANG!

"Why are you knocking at their door?"

click-click

Pettick smiled, a terminal grin. "We all have our debts."

A shout sounded, accompanied by shallow screaming which abruptly, brutally, cut out.

Silence.

"Oh, well, that is, uhm, very helpful," Mawkin sarcastically scoffed, hopping down off the combine, annoyed by Pettick's perennial indirection. He took several paces past Pettick, planting himself just beyond the patch of wheat. At his feet was a small garden of basil, tomatoes, peppers, the homemaker's culinary patch. Pettick thought for a moment, choosing careful words before he returned to Mawkin's side.

"Why are we here Pettick?" Mawkin said, interrupting Pettick before he could let out his carefully curated words. "The humans have never attacked us. Not once." Mawkin puzzled, continuing, "And I am comfortable with the lie, because I can make sense of it. Yet we incite such violence by knocking—"

"You see those woods?" Pettick asked.

Folding his arms, Mawkin glanced down at Pettick and nodded his head, though clearly annoyed by the conjecture.

Pettick continued, "Our farm is but a hand's count of miles through those woods. A road could be built between our farm and this one, a completely uncharted passage."

"The humans have built no such road. How are they a threat?"

"You are not following me here, Mawkin," Pettick sighed, his words direct, ideas acute. "We are reaching a certain plateau in population. Our tract does not supplement growth. We will simply remain stagnant, like a stunted calf, until a dust bowl or famine comes, from which we will die off. This patch here," Pettick opened his palms, gesturing to the buckwheat at his feet, "is testing for rotation. Shows us that the soil is ready for wheat. For grain. Straw. Scarecrows. Come next season, we could have a satellite colony set up here."

BANG!

"And a full field of this harvest." Pettick grew impassioned with the prospects of his words. "Survival is merely a margin of profit and loss."

"Isn't everything?" Mawkin huffed.

click-click

Mawkin turned back to the house, and both 'Crows stood in a noteworthy silence, staring onward in opposite directions, existing in that space between silences. The 'Crows started back to the front of the house. Mawkin broke the silence. "There is one thing more I gotta ask."

"And that is?"

"Why no masks?"

Pettick pulled down his neckerchief from his chin, fully exposing his straw face.

"To humans, the presence of a loaded gun in a Scarecrow's hand is imposing enough." Pettick spoke with a slight crooked curl to his cheek, a sentiment Mawkin shared.

A shout echoed, a strangled rueful caw, from a Scarecrow who burst through the front door. Mawkin and Pettick hastened their strides, rounding to the front of the house to see Attucks on horseback, launching into a gallop, disappearing into the woods with Veidt shouting after him.

"What's your problem, weed-head!" Veidt shouted.

"What happened?" Mawkin inquired of his 'Crows.

Several 'Crows poured out of the front door.

"Somebody wanna tell us what the hell is going on?" Thalo asked as he and Paquin joined the circle, darting occasional glances at the nearby woods.

"Veidt, what the hell is going on?" Pettick asked as he stared down Veidt, who was stuttering, spitting more woodchips than words.

"He—uh—he," Veidt began. Pettick nodded, pulling out the words with his glove as he crossed his arms. "Attucks took off—"

Turning an extricating shoulder to Veidt, Pettick asked impatiently, "Thalo, wanna tell me what happened in there?"

"We were loadin' the prisoners and the kid just lost it on the big fella, started hittin' him—real efficiently, I might add. But then, rather suddenly, he stopped movin'. He stood there for a few moments, like a dumb mule, then started throwing things around and darted out the door." Thalo paused, looking around, then discreetly up at Pettick and continued, "Sir, he kept asking why the humans weren't fighting back."

"Shit!" Mawkin shouted, breaking from the group, Pettick at his heel.

"What?" Pettick inquired, leaning closer to Mawkin. "What is it, Mawkin?" Pettick offered an ineffectively admonishing glance.

"That's the kid. The one I found sneaking into the silo barn a while back—that's him. He knows what were doing with the humans. And now he knows where they come from."

"Fuck," Pettick added, a strange article. "Go get him; we'll sort this out back at the house."

Pettick rallied the company, ordering the 'Crows homeward, without prisoners. Mawkin took off ahead of the rest of the group, catching up with Attucks who was driving his horse hard, winding aimlessly, recklessly through the pines.

"Hey, kid, slow up!" Mawkin ordered. Mawkin kept close watch on Attucks who rode with abandon, sporadically weaving through the trees. His vision grew too focused on Attucks. The crack came suddenly and painfully to Mawkin, a branch knocking him off his horse.

Attucks arrived at a winding road which ran through the woods, dividing the forest with but a few feet of clearing. Distracted by the clear star-freckled sky and the weight of being alone, Attucks collapsed onto the paved ground while his horse, unrestrained, continued on. As a wave of rage gave way to silent dislocation, the Scarecrow let out a mournful howl. The piercing cries echoed through the open air. Attucks winced, facing down the road where two orbs of light crested the hill, fast approaching. His body remained frozen, his gaze locked on the lights that grew at a fierce rate, a predator on approach. The mysterious animal's growl sent tremors along the cracked and scraped pebbles of the pavement.

Mawkin leapt from the forest, pushing Attucks into the brush. The large burning eyes of the orbs cut sideways; the steel beast, a Chevy Impala, clipped Mawkin, knocking him to the gravel. The car jolted to a hault. Its engine idled, but no one stirred from the cab. After several moments, the tires screamed, and the car continued into the night, vanishing over the hill. Mawkin rose to his feet, the straw of his leg snapped as he made his way toward Attucks.

Pettick reached the road, with several riders by his side, halting at the edge of the clearing where he dismounted and ran to Mawkin. "Mawkin, stop!" Pettick screamed. Mawkin's fists beat heavily into an unresponsive Attucks. The young 'Crow remained limp as each blow rose and fell. Pettick ordered louder. Veidt, Thalo, and Paquin stood by the horses, staring in disbelief. Without yielding, Makwin continued pounding his fist. Dashing forward, Pettick took hold of Mawkin's arms. The pressure and strength came as a surprise to Mawkin, who fell back as Pettick released his pull. As Mawkin rose to his feet, Pettick ordered with a venomous glare, "Don't make me have to do that ever again."

Mawkin nodded in understanding, shuffling across the gravel road and lifting Attucks.

Pettick turned to his company, ordering, "Let us hurry, before whatever did this comes back!"

The 'Crows mounted. Pettick held back, watching Mawkin and Attucks mount; Mawkin gave a remissive glare before slapping the reins and riding into the forest. Alone, the road was silent, save the fading sounds of marching hooves. Pettick swung his horse, neighing, as its iron shoes clattered atop the gravel. Beneath the heavy inhale and exhale of the horse's belly, several scars of black rubber ran along the road. Pettick smacked the reins, rising off the saddle, driving the stallion on in a relentless gallop into the black halls of the forest.

* * *

Crane nodded, signaling the dazed guard. As he opened the door, slight tremors rushed through his hand, akin to the sensations he felt before an interaction with Gwyn. It was an excitement Crane certainly had never before felt when going to shovel books. The flat of the shovel sparked along the newly drawn ray of sun as Crane lifted the stack and dropped it into the glowing mouth of the stove. Crane looked back toward the fruit cellar where the hand appeared from the vent. Crane set down the shovel, meeting his glove with the hand.

"Crane, is that you?" Jamie asked.

"The one and only," Crane replied with an inflection most gentle.

"I'm so happy it's you."

"So am I." Crane pulled out his journal and a pencil out of his rucksack, taking a cross-legged seat on the steps.

"You got anything to eat on you? I'm starving."

"What can you consume?"

"At this point, anything."

"I'll see what I can find," Crane said.

"The other one that talks to me—he's an asshole, sayin' I'm never gettin' out. He won't let me leave, but he won't tell me what the hell I did, neither."

"Sounds like you're talking about Pettick."

"Name sounds about right, heard him talkin' to another fella outside the door last time, used a similar name."

"He's our leader," Crane stated, enthusiasm fading.

"I was afraid of that." Jamie's sigh could be heard through the door. "Guess the whole 'helping me outta here' thing ain't goin' so well?"

Crane remained silent.

"I know that answer," Jamie stated.

Whimpers dripped from the vent. Crane felt helpless, as though he were behind the barrier of the door. He thought of what he could possibly say to bring comfort to a human, only concluding what a Scarecrow might. "What's Philadelphia like?" Crane urged, drawing Jamie back from his sorrows. "Jamie, what is Philadelphia like?"

"It's a shithole. Makes sense, it is where this whole Godforsaken country started."

"So you left?"

"Yeah. Funny thing, though. Right now, I kinda miss it."

"I thought you said it was an s-h-i-t-h-o-l-e?" Crane pieced together the ideas as best he could. "Doesn't sound pleasant."

"Just 'cause a place is full of trash don't mean you can't love it, even miss it. I'm sure you get awfully restless 'round here. Sometimes think this place is hell."

"No, I love it here; it's home."

"Well, Crane, sounds like you're content. A little bit of a romantic, too, I suppose. What is her name?"

"Gwyn." Crane's smile faded to curiosity. "How'd you know?"

"Fella is content in a place like this; must be a hell of a piece."

Crane had trouble deciphering certain words Jamie used. He wrote them down on the top right corner of the journal page.

"If you're saying what I think you're saying, then, yes, she is. But don't get wrong thoughts about me, sometimes I do think of getting out of here, seeing what else is out there."

"Truth comes out!" A sharp laugh flowed from the vent in a tone Crane hadn't yet heard from Jamie. "You get me outta here, Crane, and you are more than welcome to follow me 'round. I'll take ya to all the places worth seein' in this world."

"Like where?" Crane asked, a growing enthusiasm trickling through his words.

"Well, I was on my way to California when they jumped me. We could stop in Pittsburgh, then Chicago, Detroit, make our way to the coast." Crane eagerly scribbled misspelled variations of the cities in his journal with his pencil.

"I've read about some of these places before. Never been. You drive to all these places?"

"No, not all of 'em, sometimes I hitch a ride, catching out. There are some coal barges headin' up and down the Allegheny and Ohio you can stow away on—"

"Sounds dangerous."

"Not really, most fellas just enjoy the company. Freight trains gettin' more and more difficult to hop on. The trainmen hired some union trash to keep 'em clear. But if yer smart, you know when to ditch."

"That's exciting!"

"For a small-town farm kid like you, I'm sure it is."

The floorboards bowed above Crane, raining dust onto his face. He quickly shook off the gray coat, leaving a whispered: "No."

The door at the top of the steps cracked, opening the gates for several voices which echoed around the room. Crane jumped back from the fruit cellar, throwing his journal into his rucksack, dropping his pencil on the floor. "I never talked to you," Crane whispered as he scurried towards the stove, scraping the shovel heavily into the brick as he heaved a stack of books into the fire. Mawkin and Pettick appeared behind him.

"Shouldn't be down here alone," Pettick said to Crane, who turned to acknowledge him. "From now on you have the guard come down here with you, understood?"

"Yes, sir." Crane nodded, dropping his shovel.

"Good. Now, back up to the library."

Crane nodded with a jittery rise and fall to his chin. He picked up his rucksack and scurried up the stairs. Pettick waited to move till the door closed at the top of the stairs. Crossing to the fruit cellar door, he turned, holding both palms upward. Mawkin handed him a key in one hand, and a rounded glass bulb in the other.

"Wait out here, make sure the Reader's boy doesn't come back."

"You certain you'll be safe?" Mawkin asked.

"Don't patronize me, Mawkin, I can handle myself."

Pettick reached behind him, handing Mawkin the .45-caliber M-1911 Colt he kept in the small of his back. He then turned around, unlocked the door, entered the darkness where Jamie's figure sat, a barely visible grey against black. Pettick reached into the air, screwing the bulb into a socket that squealed with each turn till the bulb began to glow, effuse a sodium yellow, lighting the tiny room. The walls were brick and the floor was dirt. The only decor in the room was a shelf set against the wall that once held the fruit jars, and a wooden stool at Pettick's feet. Pettick looked down at Jamie, who shot back a look of fear and confusion, not knowing what to make of the mask on his captor's face. Mawkin closed the door and turned back to the stove. He suddenly stopped, leaned over, and picked up a pencil from the top step. A pulse of curiosity struck his brow.

Jamie leaned against the back wall. His brow winced from the light, his hands snug inside the pockets of his leather jacket. Dirt from the floor covered the side of Jamie's body where he had slept. It ran in patches through his curly black hair, and was smeared on his white t-shirt and on both knees of his jeans.

Pettick stared forward, pushing his glasses further up his face as he moved the sheath of the knife around his belt, brandishing it on his hip. “We have an understanding?”

“Perfectly, boss.” Jamie nodded, rising, putting his weight against the wall.

“Good,” Pettick said, flashing an artificial grin. “I would really like to talk to you. If you don’t mind, I’m going to keep a record of our meetings.”

“Not like I got a choice,” Jamie quipped.

“This is true.” Pettick spoke quickly as he took a seat on the only stool in the room. “Please sit.” Pettick gestured to the area of the cell across from him.

“I’m good; besides, you got the only stool, friend.”

“The floor has suited you well, so far.” Pettick cocked his head.

Weary of the proximity, Jamie lowered himself to the ground across from Pettick, the move pleasing his captor.

“I want to first start off by apologizing for the way our last meeting ended. I do not want it to have to be that way every time we speak.”

“Let me outta here, and it won’t be an issue.”

“I’m afraid that is not an option. Cooperate, and we may discuss it at a later date. So, James—”

“It’s Jamie.”

“Right. Jamie. Tell me about your life.”

“Why?”

“Call it curiosity,” Pettick shifted on the stool, crossing his legs. “We don’t hear much about the outside world here, especially from the coast.”

“I saw those fences you got up out there, you should wonder why.”

“Yes, those do have their disadvantages, but they serve a purpose.”

“Ah, and that’d be?”

“Keeping this colony safe.”

“I see. Ain’t got nothing to do with keeping anyone from gettin’ out, neither?”

"You are an observant one, Jamie." Pettick gestured with his pen, a professor finding pride in his pupil.

Jamie looked up at Pettick, flustered by the questionnaire, though keen never to miss an opportunity. He inquired, "So, what is it, then? What're you all doin' out here? You Communists?" Jamie looked for a response. Finding none, he jumped to his next thought. "Nazis?"

Pettick laughed, genuinely amused by Jamie's remarks.

"Worse, you're from our own government, aren't ya?" Jamie eagerly speculated. "One of Eisenhower's little experiments?"

"Eisenhower is president?" Pettick inquired.

"Yeah, has been for a few years now. You freaks sure don't hear much 'round here, do ya?"

"Good choice; military background will serve him well." Pettick eagerly scribed, lifting his pen, gesturing in accordance with his thoughts. "Now we are getting somewhere!"

"That's it! You are spies, aren't ya? Lookin' to get some secrets? Well, sorry, pal. You picked the wrong fella—I don't know shit!"

Pettick swallowed his laughter. Pulling a handkerchief from his pocket, he unbuttoned his glasses from his face, and began rubbing their lenses. Jamie tried not to stare, enamorured and disturbed at the exposed black pits of Pettick's sockets—wells of true darkeness. Pettick returned the glasses, fastening them to his face, then looked back to Jamie, all the while still containing the laugh beneath his crooked smile.

"That's enough, you can stop. We are none of those things. Though, I will tell you," Pettick's voice lifted, a scientist presenting the statement of his hypothesis, "you are a part of a great experiment." Pettick closed his journal, remarking, "We are just a colony of beings, a new species, choosing to exist differently in this world."

Jamie's thoughts darted around the room. "You aren't queers, are ya?"

"No." Pettick chuckled, though he was clearly growing agitated. He rose from his seat and approached Jamie. "I'm here trying to learn more about the world beyond these walls; that is all I am asking of you."

"Right," Jamie responded, looking up at Pettick. "You got a smoke, Pettick?"

"Ah, you are a smart one—picked up my name." Pettick walked in a circle back toward the door. "Tell you what I'll do: I bring you some food and a cigarette, you repay my generosity with some answers to some questions. Do we have a deal?"

Jamie glanced at the floor before returning his gaze toward Pettick, his mind evaluating the situation. "Deal."

"I'll be back in a couple of minutes."

"All right."

Pettick reached for the lamp, unscrewed the bulb, and the light immediately died. Under cover of darkness, Jamie slid his hand down into his boot, retrieving a black handle. As Pettick's silhouette reached the door, Jamie lunged forward, knocking him to the ground. After throwing open the door, Jamie pressed a button on the handle and a knife blade flipped open. Mawkin spun to the door as Jamie leapt from the dark room, lunging the three-inch blade into the center of Mawkin's belly. Mawkin took almost no pain from the knife, feigning little as Jamie looked up at Mawkin, and a terrifying realization read across Jamie's face. Mawkin swung his arm, the trunk of it knocking Jamie several feet, where his body collided with the brick wall and crashed to the ground. The pain of the collision and the weight of his failures challenged his attempts to rise, returning his body to the floor. From the darkness of the fruit cellar Pettick appeared, a scowl branded across his face. Jamie held his chest as the air from his cough blew clouds of dust on the floor in front of him. Mawkin reached down, grabbed Jamie's throat, and thrust him against the wall. Mawkin's grip tightened, raising Jamie further up the wall, his feet dangling beneath him. Gasping for air, Jamie stared at the knife, still lodged in Mawkin's belly. Mawkin turned to Pettick, waiting for his order.

"Let him go," Pettick ordered.

Jamie fell to the floor, his hands quickly grasping his neck as he continued to cough and gasp for air. A small bead of blood dripped from his mouth. Pettick tilted his head, ensuring that Jamie was watching as he gripped the handle of the knife, pulling it from Mawkin's torso. Several strands of straw tore away, gathering on the blade and falling to the floor. The shock and terror grew wide on

Jamie's face as Pettick turned the blade toward him, pressing his body against the wall.

"Jamie," Pettick said, grabbing Jamie's face, clamping on his jaw. "James, fool me once, shame on you." Pettick lowered the blade to the crotch of Jamie's jeans, pressing the point of the blade into his zipper. "Fool me twice—well, there will not be a third time." Pettick released Jamie, pocketing the knife and starting for the door. Mawkin witnessed the shifting rage as he went; the joy Pettick felt from his power over Jamie.

"James was your father's name, wasn't it?" Pettick asked, passively.

Jamie looked at Pettick who took only pause in his stride to look back to Jamie for his silent answer, before disappearing up the stairs.

Mawkin laid his glove on Jamie's shoulder, ripping him along by the skin of his leather jacket. With little fight left in him, Jamie surrendered to the darkness. Pettick's words were paralyzing, imprisoning him even before the door could reseal the darkness around him. Mawkin clasped the lock, resting his glove against his torso, applying slight pressure to his wound. Realizing it was useless, he released his glove and shifted across the basement, stumbling upon the well of books. Alone, Mawkin scanned the room from the stove to the stack of books, still piled shin high. He leaned down, lifting a blue paperback novel crooked between his fingers. Mawkin paged through the book, wan parchment smeared true black ink letters.

Crane traced the paths of the threads on Gwyn's hand like roads and rivers on a map, endlessly weaving across seemingly chartered routes, concordantly lacking or desiring a destination. The two lay blissfully along a narrow shade of pines in the sun-washed field.

"Do you ever wonder where they start?"

"What?" Gwyn asked, baffled with Crane's seemingly rehearsed inquiry.

"Where the first thread was tied, where the end of it lies in you?"

"Do you ever *not* think?" Gwyn asked, rolling onto her side. Leaning over Crane, her hair dangled around his face.

Crane shuddered for a moment, fighting the urge to take her in his arms.

"What do you mean?" He raised his glove, running a fair strand of her feather-hair through his fingers.

"Like, have you ever tried not asking why, and just accepting, whatever it is, for what it is: unknown."

"No, not really," Crane replied.

"Didn't think so."

"Besides, where's the fun in that?" Crane defended.

"I'm just saying, there are some things better left unknown." She tilted her head, curling back the stands of her hair. "You may reach a point where you realize you spent more of your life analyzing it than living it," Gwyn added, half hoping to simply dodge confrontation.

"I disagree," Crane firmly stated.

"Yeah?"

"Yeah."

"That's fine," Gwyn assertively retorted. Giving concise end to their argument, she laid back down onto the bed of yellow grass. After several moments of passing thought, Crane sat up and leaned over Gwyn.

"Oh, now you're apathetic?" Crane read the lines on Gwyn's face as the sun outlined in late-day scorches behind her, thinking of the consequence and strategy of Gwyn's games.

"Yeah," Gwyn said with a widening smile dividing her cheek.

"Fine," Crane said.

"Fine," Gwyn said.

They shared a laugh.

"Can I ask you something?" Crane inquired.

"Does it involve where and what lies at the end of a straw?" Gwyn offered a sarcastic glare.

"Indulge me," Crane said. The two 'Crows turned inward, their faces only inches apart. Crane lifted a blade of long grass, running his fingers along the stem.

"You're not helping your case," Gwyn said, smiling, looking up at the straw in Crane's hand.

"Funny," Crane said, dropping the straw. "Do you ever consider—*would* you ever consider running away?" Crane led his question with an analytical stare, reading every nuance Gwyn's face had to offer, every motion like the preamble of her response.

"From here? What, to another colony?"

"No," Crane's eagerness faded, "like out into the world."

"No," Gwyn quickly replied.

"Why?" Crane insisted.

With a pursed chin, Gwyn turned her head back toward the sky.

Crane's brow grew taut, realizing the words that he had allowed to pass by. Silence persisted. "I'm sorry, you don't need to answer that; I don't need to know."

They lay separately in their silence. A breeze blew through the weeds around them. Gwyn perked up, spotting a patch of color in the brush above, pale blue pedals with yellow disk florets. She was lying on her stomach. Brushing back the weeds, Gwyn drew out the flower, careful not to uproot it from its stem.

"*Aster Cordifolius*," Gwyn determined.

"What?"

"Heartleaf Aster, and it's a flowering," Gwyn smiled, a small smile, successfully identifying the plant.

"Ah . . ." Crane looked at her with great bemusement. This prolonged stare Gwyn felt.

"What?" Gwyn asked.

"I didn't know that," Crane confessed.

"Well, you do now," Gwyn said.

* * *

Mawkin drew his glove to his head, removing his hat, unleashing his locks of golden hair into the saturated sun. He rested his hat on the wood planks of the playground platform. Seasons of Pettick's insults, restrictive clauses, and base thoughts burned in Mawkin's mind. Mawkin drew the blue softcover novel from his pocket. He studied the lines of the skewed globe on the cover. He tried to read out the tilted words, naming each letter he could in the sequence: "B, R, A." Skipping the next two letters, he continued on to the next word. "N,

E." Recognizing the second letter as the end of the first word, he went back to the first word. "B, R, A, V, E." And with the understanding of the first word, his yearning only grew. A smile creased his cheek, then faded. For the functionally illiterate, this, a single word, was a success.

Glancing up from the page, he spotted several young Scarecrows blissfully skipping by, bounding down the path, vanishing beyond the orchard. Mawkin smiled at the sight, this joy less quickly fading. His widened gaze captured the sun's dance just above the orchard, atop the flowered trees. Running his glove through his hair, with a twitch of his muzzle, he returned to his study, until last-light's valiant demise ended the lesson.

Chapter X: *Strange Fruit* Pies for Betting Men

Night's darkness collected on the edge of the farm where a convoy of woodcutters prepared to move out. The cart was loaded with a pile of tools, rope, saws, axes, and chisels, the area lit by lanterns on mantles tied to each corner of the cart. Late season's cool air cut against Pettick as he stood watch over their departure. He returned his journal to his satchel, burying his hands into his field jacket as Mawkin approached.

"You be careful with them lanterns out there," Mawkin ordered. "No rain yet this season. Forest is thirsting for a bath or a burn."

"Yes, sir," the woodcutters unanimously chimed. The lead horseman, a soldier, signaled to the group as they mounted, lumbering into the forest. Mawkin planted himself beside Pettick.

"I am worried," Pettick said, speaking softly, swaying with his thoughts, both spoken and withheld.

"About the rain?" Mawkin asked.

"Yes," Pettick said.

"Me too."

"We need to be careful."

Mawkin weaved new information into the fragments of their current stream of conversation. "The Reader's boy—I caught him speaking with the human down in the basement."

"And did you speak with *him*—Crane?" Pettick asked.

Mawkin was caught off-guard by the lack of attentiveness Pettick took to this news. He thought for a moment before responding. "Yes, I'm assured he will keep silent on the subject; it will not happen again." The success of this lie was in Mawkin's favor, an outcome he did not wager on as he attempted to avoid another Attucks-like incident.

"Good, that is good." Pettick, still seemingly disinterested, focused on the woodcutters' convoy as it filed into the forest.

"Is there something I should know?" Mawkin asked, troubled by Pettick's lethargic tone.

Pettick sneered. "They are uncountable."

"Sorry?" Mawkin asked, confused by Pettick's response.

"There is always 'something' you should know, but you do not." The lights of the convoy began to flicker, as their visibility faded in the dense brush. "It's time we start moving the humans into the new facility. The silo barn is ready."

"In time, perhaps—"

"We are at a crossroad, Mawkin," Pettick reckoned, finding some sentiment of the idea amusing. "We waste in wait, and in this confluence we cannot afford to," Pettick stated, and the Scarecrows started back to the lights of the village. Pettick continued to talk, muttering as if he were alone, though he knew Mawkin could hear these words. "With season's coming pass, deadlines will fade, and debts are paid."

August burned, though night cooled day's wounds. And it was by day, the laborers at the fences were suffering the toil of Old Egypt as the field-workers grew spoiled by the prosperity brought on by their newfound technology.

"What did you say was wrong?" Kindle asked Herb, standing with his toolbag several yards away from one of the large tractors that sat cold in the center of the field. He looked over at Herb, and the scrawny, green-whiskered 'Crow seemed particularly meek, without apparent cause. Pettick appeared, forming the third part of their triangle.

"An obstruction in the front axle is jamming the steering column," Pettick answered assertively for Herb, his attention drawn to several farmhands fooling around next to the slumbering tractor. Pettick shot Herb a glare, in reference to Herb's loitering workers.

Mawkin, atop the tractor, turned to Trinket and Fallstaff, two of the 'Crows fooling around, and ordered them: "Make yourselves useful! Grab a wheelbarrow from Gunner the Quartermaster and fill it with hoes and shovels. You can work with your hands like the good old days." The two harvesters snickered insults as they moved to the opposite side of the tractor, replanting their sloth. Mawkin, his brow furrowed, turned back to the steering wheel and removed the key from the tractor. He called Pettick's name and tossed him the keys. After hopping off the tractor, Mawkin leaned over and picked up a shovel from the soil.

Pettick tilted his chin, whispering, "Wait a moment," to Kindle and Herb, directing their attention to Mawkin, who was approaching the two harvesters.

Mawkin swung the shovel, causing it to collide with the back of Trinket's head, knocking him to the dry soil. The triangle shifted, observing the unfolding quarrel. Fallstaff let out a squeal as Mawkin swung the shovel back on its path, uppercutting him. The shovel fell to the soil. Sympathetic swallows of regret inched their way through Kindle's threads as Mawkin's fists made repeated contact with the helpless harvesters like hammers bashing an all too small nail. Herb approached Mawkin, attempting to intervene. The crowd of farmhands scattered from the tractor in trepidation. Mawkin's arms swung wide, knocking Herb to the ground with the recoil of his elbow. Trinket's yelping grew quiet as Mawkin decided he was tired of this discourse, giving one last blow with his boot to the 'Crow's torso, then heaving himself away from the crowd which gathered like an undammed river back around the tractor. Reaching for the few availible tools, the crowd was quick to return to their labors.

Pettick gave diabolical applause as Mawkin approached, passing without fray.

"Brilliant!" Pettick lauded.

"I didn't do it for you," Mawkin said.

Watching Mawkin mend his gloves and disappear up the path, Kindle could not restrain his comment: "You condone such 'encouragement'?"

Pettick responded, devoid of contempt, "Yes, I do."

"I do not see how you can," Kindle dissented.

"There are many things you fail to see, Kindle. That is why you serve a simple purpose here, a service which can be performed silently. Now let us do that service without such obstinance." With a closing nod, Pettick strolled after Mawkin, hands in pockets, the sun on his face.

Kindle lifted his toolbag, the weight of which shackled him to earth as he inched his way to the tractor. Crouching to his knees, he laid his back onto the soil, sliding beneath the belly of the giant. He stuck his glove between the mechanical mesh of the steel ribcage. His hand grasped a black tube covered in a slick residue. This tactile connection sent a frenzy of thought to his mind, ideas sparking as he placed his gaze on the fuel line in the carriage above.

* * *

Sequestered within the floral labyrinth of the orchard, the tack house and its paddock were bustling with young 'Crows bathed by the midday sun. Quill's youngest had been gathered at Shepherd's corral to train her students in riding, saddling, mucking, and duties that fit the life of a Rider. Each student's horse was drawn by an older 'Crow, with lead line in glove. Shepherd and Quill hung on the fence outside the tack room. Barnes lifted his boot from a pile of manure as he approached Shepherd and Quill.

"Horse dung!" Barnes whined.

"I think the humans called it 'shit,'" Quill chuckled.

Barnes grimaced.

"See, still teaching you, seasons after you were her student," Shepherd added, resting his arms to the fence.

"Thanks," Barnes said.

Quill smiled, shading her gaze to block the sun, and Barnes's read on her smile.

The animals slowly returned to a rotation around the coral. Gwyn turned to Crane who was leading the horse behind her. "You let him bite me again and I'll have Moose here kick you in the face." Gwyn turned forward, running her hand through the dark mane of her horse. Crane's smile grew mischievous as he let slack build in the lead line. The horse picked up its pace; its head extended forward to nibble on Gwyn's hair. Crane looked up at the small 'Crow who sat sprightly on the saddle and they shared a mischievous grin.

"Crane!" Shepherd shouted. "If her horse kicks you, I'm not going to stop her."

Gwyn shook her head. Crane sighed, tightening the line.

"You got off easy," Gwyn playfully hissed.

Shepherd smiled, turning back to Barnes and Quill who were still in conversation. Barnes continued, "You know what I wonder sometimes? Why don't they just build adults, why does the Creator even make young ones?"

"I'll tell you why," Quill responded, gesturing to the outside of the coral where Veidt stood watch, picking the weeds that grew on his arm. "That's why," Quill continued, "growing up, or 'childhood' as the humans called it, is necessary."

"It prevents dumb hands from multiplying," Shepherd added.

"Was he made full grown?" Barnes asked, staring at Veidt nibbling on the weeds from his own forearm.

"I believe so," Quill responded.

"Is that why he is that way?" Barnes asked.

"Not the only reason; there are always many reasons." Shepherd watched the yearling merry go round spinning before him. "Many factors: bad seed, too much rotted timber." Peering over to Veidt chewing on the weeds coating his arm, he said, "But I can promise you, it contributed."

"When you take away a being's necessary process of growth, when you stunt that or rush it, it has detrimental effects," Quill wryly stated. Barnes nodded as the trio of 'Crows shifted their gaze from the decrepit officer to the corral, its youth, and all the potential within its boundaries. "Though simple, such a sight." Quill smiled, a sentiment shared by her fellow elders.

Jamie cradled the dented tin cup, gulping down the remaining water that painfully gave moisture to the dried cracks on his lips. He wiped the dirt and sap collecting on his jaw. "More," he said, lifting the cup, the simple act taking much of his strength.

Pettick looked up from his opposing seat at Mawkin. "You heard the boy."

"You sure you want to be left?" Mawkin asked, gesturing to Jamie who sat limply folded on the floor of the cell.

"I think I can handle it. Besides, me and James have an understanding. Isn't that right?"

Jamie remained silent, his exhausted eyes moving in the direction of the conversation. Mawkin shrugged, lifted the cup from Jamie's hand, and exited through the wooden door, securing the metal latch as it shut. A silence followed despairing sighs that crossed through the cell for several minutes, humming like the whistle of the devil's strolling tune.

"I'm going to die here, aren't I?" Jamie sighed.

"Let us be honest with ourselves, James: were you actually living a life? A scratch of purpose? A life with anything meaningful? Tramping selfishly across the country—no family, no job. When was the last time you did anything outside your self-serving existence?"

"Sugarcoat it, why don't ya?"

"There never was thought to your future. Until now."

Jamie spat, giving a disgusted teary smile. "Wish I could say you're wrong."

"That's the problem with you. The humans in your generation just missed the cutoff of your great war by a handful of years, so now you live in the glory with a righteousness on your leather sleeve. One you didn't earn and therefore have no appreciation for."

"I don't want your pity, Pettick. You can go fuck yourself for all I care."

"I'm sympathetic, really." Pettick stretched, straightening his back. "But that's it! That's what I'm talking about. Instead of adding anything—in saying, bringing anything to the conversation—you cast it out. You reject all of it—the good and the bad—brandishing a resentment toward it you're not qualified to posses. Allowing yourself to be defined by your apathy." These words resonated with Jamie, though he refused to show it in word or gesture.

"What can I say? We weren't all lucky enough to have an enemy to shoot at to prove our worth."

Pettick chuckled, with an evident disgust for the sentiment. The door rattled. Mawkin entered through its threshold several seconds later. He handed Jamie the tin cup, then planted himself, crossing his barrel arms, with his back against the door.

"We should be so lucky," Pettick said with a crooked smile bereft of sympathy.

"If you are expecting a confession of some kind, you can forget it." Jamie slurped down the water, creeks forming through the creases on his face, forging routes down to his chin where they fell to the floor.

"In good time, James. In good time." Pettick looked up at Mawkin, noticing Mawkin's attention to the conversation. Rising from his seat, Pettick looked back down to Jamie. "For now, find penitence. One cannot live on the laurels of few good deeds."

The brim of the tin cup fell from Jamie's lips. As Pettick and Mawkin made their exit Jamie's vehement eyes followed them out, eyes that rolled and teared with the snap of the latch, a preamble to his yelping cry. Jamie threw the cup, tin bouncing with a splash of the remaining liquid against the wall.

"FUCK!"

* * *

Barlow removed the completed page from the typewriter, blowing the ink dry with several exhausts of air, then placed it on the stack. "Shall we continue?"

"No, that will be all for today," Pettick responded, shifting from the window and strolling about the parlor. Barlow took no time to pack, placing the unbound papers in a folio and returning the typewriter to its case. Pettick ran his fingers along the spines of books, turning to Barlow. "Tell me, how is that boy of yours, Crane? How is he progressing?"

"He is a good apprentice, a fast learner," Barlow huffed with a paternal smile. "And he has much to learn."

"That is good."

Barlow pivoted in his chair, rotating toward Pettick, crossing his legs beside the desk. Lifting his silver pen, he placed it precisely in the breast pocket of his vest. "Why do you ask?"

"Can a colony leader not take interest in his sheep?"

"A colony of several hundred—"

"I only mention," Pettick's arms fickly crossed and unfolded, "as I see he does not tend to ordinary behavior." Arms unfolded again, palms reputedly to the ceiling in gesture. "Do you not worry?"

"He is my son. Of course I worry—"

"As any father should," Pettick said with an endearing tone, taking a seat on his desk as Barlow headed for the door. "We do tend to get too close, don't we? Too close to see what's wrong. So close, with only best of interest in heart, yet we forget our roles of why we were put there in the first place."

Barlow turned back to Pettick, sharing an understanding that he had yet to find in him. "True. Tomorrow, then, Pettick."

"Tomorrow, Barlow."

The heavy door shut, leaving Pettick alone once again.

Patches of light reflected from the slot, giving a red glow to the waxy skin of the Braeburn apple Crane handed to Jamie. Jamie took only seconds to devour the morsel, and two beads of nectar ran down his taut, smiling chin. Through the crushing chew of the skin and pulp, Jamie's muddled words broke, "Crane . . ."

"Yeah?"

"I don't think you should keep talking to me."

"Why?" A silence followed Crane's question, later broken by the rustle of Jamie sitting up, wiping the dirt from his clothes and the juice from his chin.

"I don't want no one seeing me like this, even you."

"Well then, it's good I can't see you," Crane said.

Small bits of joy penetrated the whimpers coming from the dark side of the door.

"Right," Jamie sighed, with little effort or interest in Crane's levity. "Got anything else to eat?"

"No."

"Damn."

"I had to barter with a harvester just to get that. There aren't many trees on the farm blooming with that fruit this season. Orchard's been dry. Gwyn says they are Biennial—is why. Except for one tree, and I don't like to go around there. Pettick is often lurking there, just pacing—"

"Asshole commie," Jamie interjected with a biting, disgusted tone.

"What?"

"Nothin'. Talkin' bout Pettick." The two shared a moment of silence. "Hey, Crane?"

"Yeah?"

"Why do you keep comin' down here to see me?" Jamie ran his callused hands, feeling how much stubble had grown on his cheeks. "You ain't got no obligations. You know that, right?"

"Because I want to," Crane quickly replied.

"All right. Just makin' sure you ain't doin' me no more favors. Don't like debts, ya know."

"Right."

Silence.

"Hey, Crane?"

"Yeah, Jamie?"

"Why do you want to?"

"What do you mean?"

"I ain't never had a conversation with a man where he wasn't trying to get somethin' out of it." Jamie's words and sentences flowed with conviction in tone and substance. "Everyone's got an agenda, Crane."

"Well, I do get a lot out of this."

"Oh." Jamie tried to sound surprised by the candor in Crane's response. "And what's that?"

"I learn about humans and what they're like, and what it's like outside—" Crane cut himself off, realizing the potential revelation of his words and an exposure he sensed and feared was near.

"Crane?" The silence lingered. "Crane?" Silence followed his reprise. "What do you mean you're 'learning about humans'?"

"I—"

"Crane?"

"Yeah?"

Jamie reached his hand through the slot, presenting it to shake. Crane froze, seized by his thoughts. Lifting his right hand before his face, he examined the leather and suede of his glove. He looked once more at Jamie's bare callused palm. Drawing the glove from his threaded hand, he felt the nuances of the texture of his makeup in the contact of his forefingers. He reached forward, fingers wrapping threaded flesh around Jamie's hand. The skin of Jamie's fingers slid along the gentle ridges of the threads, quickly recoiling as if bitten by a snake. Crane fell back to the steps, distress read in the folds of his brow. With moments pass, Jamie's silence broke.

"What are you?"

* * *

The gauge's needle rested against the *E* as Kindle twisted the lever on the pump, tapped the nose, allowing the last several drops to fall to the dirt at his feet, then returned the nozzle to its metal holster. He remained by the pump, under the dead lights of the fill station canopy. He looked out into the night, and in the distance the lights from the village traced the terrain. After closing the lid on the last barrel, he tightened the straps and the eleven barrels whined, clattering together. He closed the wooden tailgate before shuffling around to the cabin. Sliding into the cab of the cattle truck, he rested his weight on the large steering wheel. An exhausted breath materialized into a cloud in the air before him. Kindle turned the engine over, and the idling truck rolled forward.

Mindful to be quiet, he took the long way around, mindful of the necessity to remain unseen, mindful of the need of his actions, mindful of the hope he'd not forgotten, mindful of deliberation in his treason. The dim taillights disappeared up the ridge.

Barnes enjoyed the silence of the library in the evening, since it seemed to be the only time reading could truly be done—alone. The last pages of *The Grapes of Wrath* flew by. Barnes closed the heavy red cloth cover, rising to the bookshelf beside Barlow's desk. The piece slid into its slot, completing the puzzle. Barnes turned to a silent Barlow in the doorway, his stance gently swaying, the typewriter and a manuscript box under his arm.

"You all right?" Barnes asked, sensing the hollow rift, the ghost's hold on Barlow.

Barlow marched forward to his desk, where centered on the tabletop sat the abandoned copy of *Frankenstein*. Barlow was silent as he set the typewriter and manuscript onto the desk beside the novel.

"Sir?" Barnes summoned. The old 'Crow shifted across the room, sinking into his chair, taking his ritual pensive gaze out the window. "Father?" Barnes said as he pulled up a stool, planting himself right before Barlow.

Barlow looked over his son.

Barnes looked to his father. "Pop, tell me what's going on."

Barlow's gaze wandered, drifting around the room.

Barnes rested his glove on Barlow's face, drawing the old 'Crow's focus. "Where have you been? You come in after we've gone to sleep, depart before we wake. Have you even talked to Crane?"

Barlow's pursed chin quivered in a negative response.

"That's what I thought." Barnes swayed in his chair, a visible faith draining from him, a cynic regression Barlow couldn't help but notice.

"Barnes, this is when I would tell you it is not of your concern; that you are not of age to understand." Barlow's gaze shifted about the room. "But that would be wrong. You are no longer a young 'Crow. And now I feel keeping things from you and your brother only widens what fissure there is between us. I am without a mate to lessen the burdens of this weight. And . . . and I don't know how to talk to my son anymore." He paused, running his glove through his beard, taking in the full impact of these truths. "I would like to believe that if I had a mate she would know what to do, what to say to him."

"If I am old enough to understand that, then I am old enough to understand what you and Pettick have been doing locked away in that Parlor all day, am I not?"

"No," Barlow said.

"No?" Barnes asked.

"This," Barlow said, gesturing to the desk where the typewriter slumbered, the manuscript sealed in its box atop it, "baffles even an elder. It is no matter of age."

Barnes rose from his bedside manner, shifting to Barlow's desk. He retrieved the box from atop the Remington case and returned to Barlow's side. Glancing briefly at its contents, he laid the box open on Barlow's lap. "You are as much of a fool as I am, Pop."

"Excuse me?" Barlow asked.

Barnes cocked his head, adjusting the roll of his sleeves. "Your problem, and your solution." Barnes levied the invisible variables in his gloves, "You want to relate to Crane, to connect to him." Barnes waited for Barlow's gestured response. "Answer's in your hands."

Barlow looked down at the manuscript. "I don't want the need of a bargaining chip to speak to my son."

"It's not a bargaining chip, Pop. 'Less you let it be. We both know the measure of history's sway to shaping the present. No one thirsts for that more than Crane. Call it common ground." Barnes offered a solicitous smile, lifting Barlow's glove, resting his staidly felt fingers on the manuscript.

"I'm proud of you," Barlow said. "Both of you. You know that, right?"

"We know, Pop. We know." Barnes rose, throwing his jacket over his shoulders.

"Where in the hell are you runnin' off to?" Barlow asked. "I thought we were doing some—whatcha call it—father/son bonding?" Barlow chuckled, ruffling the threads of his chin.

"Oh, we are, sir, but being the good son is quite the exhausting task. And so, I think I've earned an evening off."

"Right you are." Barlow smiled.

Barnes wrapped the leather aviation jacket around himself, pulling the zipper, after several failed tugs, up to his chin. In the fullness of the jacket, Barnes still looked scrawny. The door sealed. Failing resistance, Barlow paged through the manuscript. Slowly, inevitably, exhaustion took hold, and with it, the solace of sleep.

The sun rose as quickly as it fell, its slingshot swift, over the village where the workers rose from their bungalows and began migrating into the fields. Down winding paths through the orchard, the sun rose up high, bright, mighty, burning down on trees, the orchard, the farmhouse. Pettick sat behind his desk, reading through a large clothbound book he had peeled open. The top right corner of the page read: I Kings 17:1. The door shook with several intrusive knocks, followed by immediate entry.

"Pettick!" Veidt barked, approaching the desk.

"What?" Pettick asked, not moving his attention from the book.

"The tractors are down; can't get 'em to start up," Veidt answered, now piquing Pettick's interest. "Which? One of the fat men or the little one?"

Veidt waited a moment to respond. "All of 'em."

An urgency struck Pettick, launching him from his chair as he grabbed his hat, moving with direction and purpose out of the door.

"Where are we going?" Veidt asked, hastily straggling at Pettick's heel.

"To visit the Tinker."

"Been a while." Kindle's voice echoed down the bay as Crane turned up to the catwalk, a widening smile gashed across his face, seemingly severing his threads.

"What can I say?" Crane said. "Been busy."

"Excuses like that don't keep old 'Crows from gettin' lonely." Kindle started down the steps. "What have you been up to?"

"Oh,you know," Crane said, "lots of reading,"

Kindle turned from the final step and faced Crane. "You really do need to work on this lying thing."

"Why do I need to work on lying?" Crane stuttered.

"'Cause you ain't very good at it. How is Gwyn?"

Crane smiled in response, following behind Kindle in a trot across the bay. A flock of Flying Crows swooped down, arcing back to the ceiling, landing in the rafters above. Kindle stopped walking and looked around the garage.

"Something wrong, Kindle?" Crane asked. Kindle remained trapped in his thoughts, cocking his head to the slightest of sounds. "Kindle?" Crane reached out, touching Kindle's arm.

"No, it's nothing," Kindle said, smiling briefly as he continued his stride toward the end of the bay where a toolkit sat open beside the rear of the last truck. Crane looked up to the rafters, taking notice to the birds.

"I thought you never let those things in here. You said—" Crane rustled his voice, lowering tone and tempo, mimicking Kindle, "'Dumb things think it's fine to make home stacked atop a carburetor!'" Kindle chuckled, squatting down to his toolbox.

"Sounds like somethin' I might have said, though it sure don't sound much like the way I'd say it," Kindle clarified. Crane laughed, pulling up a stool as Kindle began to work. With several feathered grunts the old 'Crow slid beneath the chassis. "Hey, Crane?"

"Yeah?"

"Can you hand me a pipe wrench?"

"Sure thing." Crane looked up from Kindle, moving to the worktable where the pipe wrench would be. The slot on the corkboard was evidently vacant. Crane looked at the table covered in junk, scrap metal, and tools, and began rummaging through the pile. "Hey, Kin?"

"Yeah?"

"I don't see it; it isn't on the table."

"Oh—uh—check in the box behind the winch." Crane strolled across the bay where, in a pile of tools and junk, a red toolbox laid open, empty. Looking up from the box and scanning the bay he took notice to the clutter that had collected around the usually organized shop.

"You find it yet, kid?"

Starting back toward the truck, Crane's sight caught the end of a wrench atop the metal bridge of the tow-truck. "Found it!" Crane placed the wrench in Kindle's hand, which was followed by a minute of clunking and frustrated grunts. "Hey, Kindle?"

"Yeah?"

"Couldn't help but notice, the shop's not as clean as it usually is."

The sounds of work ended with a grunt and an exhausted breath.

"Been busy, kid, haven't had the time I'd like." The work resumed.

"Know the feeling," Crane mumbled. "Done?" he asked when he saw Kindle slide out from beneath the truck.

"For now. You wanna help an Old 'Crow up?" Kindle held out his glove and Crane pulled him to his feet. "Thanks, kid." Kindle moved around the front of the truck, growing increasingly pensive again. "You know, it's not an excuse." Kindle drew his glove along the straws on his chin. "I should not have said that."

"What do you mean?" Crane asked.

"Time. It should never be the reason you don't do the best you can." Kindle looked for understanding in Crane's face. "It's up to you; don't make the same mistakes as 'Crows like me and your father."

Crane nodded.

Kindle smiled as he turned back to the front of the truck. A horse's neigh flared outside. Kindle shot his head to the window. Movement had brown dust stirring on a white and tan canvas sky. Kindle turned to Crane. "Go out the back, and stay low."

"But Kindle—" an unfamiliar feeling grew from Crane's curiosity, a sense of despair.

"Don't question me now, kid, just listen."

"Kindle, what is it?"

"Go! Now!" Kindle commanded. Crane shook his head, darting away. Kindle watched Crane's figure slip between the trucks. Turning, he moved up the front of the bay and peered through a window. Framed by dirt and crystallized refractions of light, Pettick's figure approached, while Mawkin, along with several soldiers, remained behind. Kindle dropped from the window and began shifting around the bay, picking up tools and returning them to their designated resting places. The front and rear man-doors simultaneously opened, then shut. Pettick moved quietly, slowly, his hand shifting along the oil-dusted walls, cutting through the rays of midday light, where his glove made contact with the hood of the Ford pickup.

Crane scurried through the junkyard, climbing onto the hood of a round-nosed Chevy Deluxe, running along its hood and windshield, gripping his rucksack on his back as he leapt off the roof of the car, traversing the fence, and rolled into a run.

Pettick turned at the edge of the Ford's hood. Kindle appeared by the exhaust pipe. "Astonishing," Pettick reveled. "In this town, you are the only one still not locking his door."

"In this town," Kindle sneered, "I am probably the one who most needs to."

"I will not argue with that." Pettick tilted his head to the Ford as he ran his hand down the side, approaching Kindle. "We cannot pretend this day wasn't expected. Some things are, by their very nature, inevitable. Like the rust which will one day collect on this truck." Pettick kept his gaze locked on the automobile as he ran his glove around the bed of the truck.

"Rust is merely a sign of neglect, and there is no such scar on this automobile," Kindle assured Pettick.

"At the moment, yes." Pettick smiled, reaching for the handle of the driver door, where his fingers instinctively clasped, then consciously released their grip. "I never want to see a beautiful creation fall to ruin." Pettick's hand fell from the car.

"I see no such ruin," Kindle said, his gaze locked to Pettick's glasses that refracted light as he peered around the garage.

Pettick broke away from the door, continued his stroll, unattached, rounding the front of the Ford. "This doesn't have to be this way; we were once friends for many seasons. Lest we forget—"

"Something inside me often tells me my memory is not a place I should go to for facts," Kindle said, his brow wincing with his words, "only feelings." Kindle shared the brief, crooked smile he found on Pettick's face. "Though I fear that sentiment has been buried in you for some time, now." A murder of Flying Crows rustled in the rafters above. From this perch they watched. "It offers no surprise that, as an accuser, you cannot look me in the face, Pettick." Kindle stated in a softly ironic tone.

Pettick turned up from the front of the pickup where he stared at a stain surrounding a drain set in the concrete. "It is a shame that this car will rust." Pettick said, finally looking at Kindle, who was still plastered by the exhaust.

"It is a shame," Kindle said.

The Scarecrows remained silent as Pettick looked for one last shred of surrender in Kindle's body language. Finding none, he turned from his gaze and crossed through the rays of visible light. They could hear the sound of a door opening, but it did not shut. A gust pushed a cloud of dry copper soil, skirting Pettick's path as he walked in a steady stride past Mawkin.

"Take him."

Pettick continued on his course as Mawkin, leading his soldiers with several orders, filed into the garage.

***

Remnants of age, old and new, materialized in the mesh of Dutch woodwork mating brick and concrete strongholds inside the underbelly of the renovated silo barn. The rumors were true; the silo barn was being renovated, but for what? Kindle thought, continuing his ritual of near coherence as two of Pettick's Scarecrows drug his limp body down the narrow cellblock, forcing the two pawns to put the maximum amount of effort into their simple task. A single row of industrial bowl lights hung every few yards. The unabated luminance of the light left sharp shadows along the open cells incrementally set down the expanse of the hall. As the hall reached its termination, the view of open cells became one of closed cells, leaving Kindle questioning their vacancy. At the end of the hall, adjoined to the silos, a large steel door gave opening to an incomplete chamber where several pipes punctured the wall. The 'Crows stopped and turned to an open cell where Kindle was to be sequestered. The chamber at the end of the hall remained an affliction of Kindle's mind as the door latched and the lock clasped. Claustrophobia set in for the first few passing hours until, with an inevitable storm, Kindle sensed the something wicked coming his way.

The cell door swung open.

"Good day, Pettick," Kindle said. "What can I do for ya?"

"You know damn well," Pettick replied.

"Refresh my memory, anyway. You said it yourself, us simple 'Crow get foolish in our old age."

Pettick huffed, his impatience rattling him as he entered the darkness. Two soldiers and Veidt filed in behind him.

"Problems in paradise, Pettick?" Kindle scoffed.

"The tractors," Pettick said. "You will fix them."

"Is that so?"

"The fuel, Kindle. Where is it?"

Kindle was silent.

"Get him on his feet," Pettick ordered. Paquin and Thalo ripped Kindle to his feet without altercation.

"This is not a game, Kindle," Pettick said.

"You're right, Pettick, it isn't." Kindle addressed him resolutely. Pettick approached Kindle, reading the threads in his face as Kindle did likewise.

"We will do this your way, then." Pettick backed away from Kindle, beginning his retreat to the door. "Leave him here to rot while we find our leverage." Kindle fell to the floor as the soldiers and Veidt disappeared through the door, leaving Pettick alone with Kindle. The

Tinker rose to a stoic pose, void of penitence. "Last chance to use your nonexistent brain . . ."

"Doesn't take a brain to fool you, Pettick."

Pettick moved outside the door, the shrinking darkness framing around him—from Kindle's perspective—cradled in a sinister compliment to his character.

Harvest is comin' Pettick. Better get a movin', or else they'll have to feed you to the crows!" Kindle felt fleeting satisfaction from Pettick's burning gaze as the door closed, echoing through the cell like the beating of a dying chest.

The *E* on the gauge was etched in the glass, and Pettick's reflection appeared beside it. Gas tanks, which had appeared to be long since empty, had finally matched the expectations of their abandoned fill station. Several feet away, Mawkin and Veidt watched as the arch of Pettick's back shifted, snapping and twisting, with the tension rising through his body.

"Kindle's taken it all, eh? It's cleaned out. Could've hidden it in the forest—that's miles away, though." Mawkin stated, with a sardonic tinge to his words. He took several steps toward Pettick, holding at the shadow line cast by the station's rotting canopy. "What was your plan for when it *did* run out?" Mawkin inquired.

What Mawkin feared and ironically conjectured Pettick's silence reassured.

"So you had no plan?" A sickened smile arose on Mawkin's cheek. "You couldn't have thought it would last forever—"

"When did you grow a mouth?" Pettick snapped, turning back to Veidt and Mawkin. "This is not our end; we have alternatives." Pettick broke from the tanks.

"Alternatives out of practice," Veidt added.

"You too, now?" Pettick mounted his horse.

"What are we going to do?" Mawkin asked, handing Pettick his rifle.

"Give me time to think, to find Tinker's weakness."

With a snap of the reins, the horse and its rider rode off. Veidt and Mawkin matched gazes as they leisurely mounted their horses.

"You think he losin' it?" Veidt asked.

"I think he lost it a long time ago." Gripping the reins, Mawkin turned to Pettick's figure riding in the distance. "Now the strings begin to come undone."

"Maybe," Veidt said.

"Maybe?"

Veidt's marble irises rolled over, peering up at Makwin, his body postured in an uncannily colloquial hinge. "Or Pettick is right; yer thinkin' too much."

Veidt buried his right and only spur into his horse's side, launching it into a gallop. Mawkin remained pensively locked to his gaze, evaluating, analyzing, processing, thinking.

* * *

Winds danced through the clearing, wrapping around the paddock, skipping along the flowered edge of the encompassing orchard, ruffling the leaves in an implicit dialogue with Shepherd. Closing the gate to the corral, Shepherd glanced across the field. A gray-haired burro wandered in the distance, a brushed figure in contrast to the tawny folds of the bines and shoots. He followed the scattered tracks of the burro, intertwined with an intruder's ebbing bootprints.

Continuing along the labyrinth of trails within the pinked trees, he arrived at a crossing, paused, and gave weight to his staff. Within the dirt of the hoof imprint at his feet sat a single kernel of cornmeal. Shepherd leaned down, lifted the morsel, and inhaled its scent. The setting sun peaked through the leaves, casting projections of anamorphic figures in the trees. He followed the burro's tracks out of the west end of the orchard, up the hill approaching the slaughterhouse, disappearing into the shadows of the barn. He rounded the corner to the cattle barn, standing in the daylight of the doorway, having no desire to cross the threshold into the darkness where the adjusting light revealed the Creator lounging, feeding the burro from his hand.

"Come, Benjamin," Shepherd called to the burro who continued to feed.

"He knows not of authority, only hunger," the Creator said.

"No wonder you two get along," Shepherd quipped, bowing.

"This coming from the only other Scarecrow, outside of the loony Tinker on the hill, who refuses to join in this *society*." the Creator remarked with animated emphasis to the drag of his hiss.

"All things considered—"

"All things considered, we should really be friends." Silence followed the Creator's words as he readjusted the straw toupee atop his head, replacing his hat atop it. The moment grew stagnant as did the rise of Shepherd's discomfort. Then the silence broke. "What do you desire from me?" Shepherd impatiently replied, sullying the Creator's enthusiasm.

"Whatever do you mean?" the Creator said, feigning ignorance.

Shepherd gestured down at the cornmeal in the Creator's hand.

"I know not that he hungers so, if you did a better job leading such a creature, maybe less would be lost to wolves."

"We agree on one thing, I'll give you that," Shepherd said. He reached into his long coat, rolling a mason jar, brimming of glowing emerald light, into his glove.

"You and I, we are more alike than you tend to believe, we are both leaders, we are both shepherds who guide helpless beings through the world."

"Aye, you are the Shepherd of the Damned."

"None of you seem to appreciate, or at the very least, respect the parernal nature of my labors. Every last one of you . . ." The Creator counted in the air, his finger landing lastly on Shepherd. Shepherd shrugged. Long curled tendril-like fingers gently landed, stroking the downy grey fibers of the burro's mane. "Think maybe you should let me keep him; he'd be a real contribution to some experiments I have been working on."

"My animals are not toys for your playtime," Shepherd said, tossing the mason jar to the Creator.

The Creator released his grip on the bridle, catching the jar, briefly examining its contents with a slick grin. Shepherd stepped into the darkness, tugging on Benjamin's collar as they both receded into the light.

The Creator remained seated as Shepherd led Benjamin down the hill, away from the barn and its spectre. Reaching the trail into the orchard, Shepherd looked back to the dark rectangle at the top of the hill where the Creator now lingered, leaning in the frame of the doorway, watching.

CHAPTER XI: Wayfarers and Audie Murphy

September. The school bells chimed, rhythmic in an inadvertent melody, its sonorous reminders bounded through cool late summer air, peeling down empty Main Street and flowing aimlessly across the rising fields. The bells rallied visceral memories, a kind of nostalgia which Barnes dutifully ignored as he quickly strode toward the schoolhouse. The wave of young 'Crows passed by, followed by Pettick. He passed silently, the brim of his hat tipped forward to shroud his face from the wind, as well as to avoid any further interactions his presence might yield. Barnes stopped in the open doorway of the schoolhouse while a distraught Quill paced silently in the back of the room.

"Quill?" Barnes remarked.

Quill continued to pace, taking only a brief moment to acknowledge Barnes before shaking her head and exiting through the back door. Barnes followed, weaving through the desks, out onto the back stoop.

"I just saw him, wandering alone." She swallowed the gravel in her voice. "Pettick didn't notice. If he did, sure didn't raise a lick of care." Quill spoke softly, peering out into the fields. Barnes stepped down off the stoop, moving beside her, scanning over the field for a glimpse at the subject of her distress.

"What is it, Quill?" A small patch of clouds gathered above the colony, painting the field in shades of grey. Barnes peered into the distance where a figure appeared, wandering the edge of the forest. "Attucks." Barnes started into the crops, turning back to Quill, who shook her head and retreated into the schoolhouse. Barnes trudged through the stalks of corn, then into the thorny briar patches and yellow wild grass. The washed-out landscape forged an uncanny background as Attucks's figure edged closer to the dark catacombic forest beyond the colony's boundaries. "Attucks!" Barnes shouted. The figure swayed with the waves of the grass, a wraith that hardly resembled Attucks. Barnes again called to his friend, his voice carried by the currents. Barnes stopped, and the two 'Crows stood only feet from the reaching hands of the forest. "Attucks?"

Attucks continued wandering past, like the victim of a heavy trance. Barnes cut ahead of his path. Only with the touch of Barnes's glove to his ashen threads did Attucks acknowledge him, his eyes giving a blank tragic stare, his chin quivering.

"Attucks, what is it?" Barnes voice trembled. "Speak to me."

"Arent you curious?" Attucks whispered.

"What?"

With a shudder, Attucks let loose a simple sentence: "Things ain't right here—it ain't right." Attucks shook his head. "Pettick ain't right."

Barnes let go of his friend, who continued on, withering into the forest. He ran his hands over the skin of his coat, feeling the threads of the patches and rough of the hide, before burying his gloves in the pockets. A cool breeze cut along the blades of grass, and with it, dust.

Pettick peered into the sky where a flock of Flying Crows made a collective dive, drifting back into the air in perfect formation. A piece of the larger black mass fell off from the flock, a crow with a dumb wing, abandoned by the rest of its murder. Pettick observed this. The Flying Crow flew just overhead, clipping the gable before plowing into the fields behind the house. Pettick strolled into the field, his gloves buried in his pockets. He stood over the fallen Flying Crow. The bird was still alive as it struggled for air in its crushed shell of a body. Its chest cavity drastically, frantically inflated and deflated like a balloon that Pettick could simply pop with a pin.

Barlow sat rocking back and forth in the chair. It was several hours into the afternoon, and he was alone in Pettick's parlor. The desk before him was scattered with books, many of which Barlow had read, and a few he had not. He leaned forward with a twitching muzzle, mulling over the pile. Falling back into his chair, he considered the tardiness of Pettick and the silence of the room. And then temptation struck him, the sirens of curiosity, along with the ease of his trespass, which he found hard to resist. He remained seated before the desk as the sun continued its journey past the window.

"Shit," Barlow proclaimed after gnawing at the prospect for several minutes frozen in his chair. He rose to his feet, darting glances back at the unguarded door to the hall. He stepped around Pettick's desk, the fingers of his gloves running along the beveled edge of the wood. He thought to himself how he might have made Crane proud in this moment, if ever he were to speak of it, which he most certainly wouldn't. He slid open the drawer, which, to his surprise, Pettick had left unlatched, the lock being nowhere in sight.

And there it sat, square in the drawer. He lifted Pettick's Journal in his unbridled fingertips. Setting it on the desk before him, he pondered once again. Pulling up Pettick's chair, Barlow sat behind the desk and opened the journal. The thick pages in the front of the book stuck together as if adhered by a thin coating of wax, requiring Barlow to peel apart the parchment to read the text he had arbitrarily selected.

How much the art of handwriting, Barlow thought, *is lost due to the mechanization of the typewriter.* This idea lingered briefly in his mind as he could feel the frenzy of the scribe from the slant of the script, the weight of impressions, and the expression of the loops of the vowels. Each entry was dated. The first entry he read was nearly twelve years old—in human years, that was. He was uncertain how the measure of time would be associated with Scarecrow years. After one final quick glance at the door, he began to read:

October 12, 1944

Planes flew over. The high-level bombers left contrails, drawn like children's crayon scribbles in the sky. A Stuka screamed as it cut just overhead. We watched it clip an old mill and crash into the fallow fields ahead. The explosion was magnificent fireworks, and we wanted to cheer, yet all fell silent—until our boy who took him down passed over; then it was the Fourth of July. We marched further down the road and chatter rose as we neared the field where the plane was downed. Jennings had the bright idea that we should check it out, and despite my protest, we did just that. Diverging from the path, we pushed into the barren field. Approaching the wreckage with caution, I inched ahead to see just what everyone was so choked up about. The man, the pilot, hung half out of the cockpit. His body lingered there, smashed through the glass bubble. We debated whether or not to put a bullet in his head, but it mattered little as his wounds bested him within the first minute or so of our rubbernecking. It was the first time I saw a man die up close. Another plane screamed overhead, and our chins rose to the sky, where, with trailing lines of white Crayola, a fleet of high-level bombers banked east.

Barlow found only more questions and great confusion from this entry. So he flipped farther on in the book, to a page which didn't need to be peeled, as it had been dog eared and certainly referenced by Pettick many times. The hall was still, so he continued reading:

February 28, 1945

The rain pattered against the roof. Heavy drops tinging in a steepened ping—tap—ping draw, one which felt like a finger tapping my forehead over and over and over.

"I find them fascinating," Mr. Joseph said, posted by the window, musing about a skirmish between a would-be escapee and a guard. I could hear only the shouting and the eventual siren that would have awakened me, if ever I slept. It was sick the way he watched, like it was a fucking play. I fucking hate it. His figure, as it stood, did not sway.

"What's the score?" I asked.

"Two-zero, the Roma," he said, offering the statistics, turning back from the window as the freezing rain tapped against the pane. In the dim light, the blonde streak appeared to glow within his jet-black hair. His hands were folded, contorted to a downward point. "You're having nightmares, are you not?"

I sat up, rubbing my eyes. "Only when I'm awake," I joked. Though the humor was lost in translation, I fear he appreciated the sentiment. He shifted to his study across from my cot, switching on the light to take notes.

"American ball games, they offer much more sport. Better balance of odds. I'm certain. Are you well this evening, John? I am assured you are comfortable. Trouble sleeping?"

"Well, you very well know I hear the screams from the floorboards."

"I'm sure you do. Have you enough food?" Mr. Joseph asked.

I nodded. He kept asking questions I was in no mood to answer. My feet touched the floor. It was very cold; that was all I could think of.

"I am told the tenacious Americans have made it to the Fatherland." He told me this, though I did not take anything he said with weight, as the last thing I needed was for him to instill in me a false sense of hope. The last thing I need is the belief that I will make it out of here. As I catch myself whispering that, Joseph watches, scribbling his fine notes with his perfect silver pen. There was a sounding gunshot. Joseph stood, shifting back to the window. "And the Germans take the game." There was no victory in his words, rather he just seemed disappointed it was over.

"Poor bastard," I lamented.

"That's what I like about you, John. It is actually why I chose you."

"What's that?" I asked.

"A man who looks at the world with feeling and emotion. I respect empathy, John—that's the word—I respect your *empathy, even though I do not share such affections. I tend too greatly to reason.*

"Empathy—right," I stuttered. I thought and realized that refusing to talk would not do me any good. I needed to wield my words, for they were the only weapon I had. So I told him a story. "When I was a young boy, I had a friend who lived on a farm. He was an unassuming child who kept to himself. But he would—on multiple occasions, mind you—capture and collect the bugs he found in the barn and the toolshed, holding them captive in mason jars on the shelf. Spiders and scorpions, mostly. They were his treasures. And whenever he had all three, he would put a brown recluse, a black widow, and a scorpion in a jar together and have them fight, to see who would win. Several times he did this. And every time the brown recluse would spin a web to the top. And it would wait at the lid, wait and watch, as the scorpion and the widow fought it out, and one of the two won. It was more often the scorpion, or so he said. The scorpion couldn't spin a web. Eventually it went to sleep at the bottom of the jar. And the brown recluse would wind down and sting the victor while it slept. It would scurry back to the lid, and wait, wait as the poison took hold and the spider or scorpion would squirm and die. And there it is—every time, like clockwork. I'm still unsure what made the brown recluse always win. Perhaps its cunning, its ferocity, or simply it being just a more intelligent being—for a bug."

Joseph nodded, tilting his head as he looked at me. "That is a fascinating story, John. But you didn't ask yourself the right question."

I said nothing, not asking for input, nor having any desire to hear his voice. He likes hearing his own voice far more than I do. So he waited for me to ask. And so eventually I yielded, "What? What question should I have asked?"

"Why did you put the spiders in the jar?"

Barlow could hear stirring down the hall. Before closing the book, he flipped it open again to the same page, noticing a small scribble at the bottom; a small confession was avowed in ink at the bottom of the page, as if its own paragraph, or simply an idea:

Why are we so afraid of each other?

Barlow sealed the Journal, returning it carefully to the same orientation, centered in the drawer. He sat behind the typewriter, resting his palms on the ridge below the keys. Pettick entered and threw his coat on the hook.

"Good day, Barlow."

"Good day, Pettick."

"Where shall we start today?" Pettick asked.

Barlow did not immediately respond.

Pettick shifted behind his desk, glancing over to the Reader as he unbuttoned and rolled up his sleeves. "Well?"

"Where are you from?" Barlow asked.

"Excuse me?"

"I think that since we are writing a book about this colony—our history—we should write where we come from. The great question of any being is: where do we come from? And for that, I'm asking a founding Scarecrow, where do you come from?"

Pettick thought for a moment before confessing. "East."

"A colony east?"

"That's right." Pettick nodded, unclasping the drawer and retrieving the Journal. He dropped it on the desk, watching Barlow's face follow the object as it landed. Barlow felt himself stare and shifted back to the typewriter at the study. Pettick fell into his chair, reclining his boots with a clank onto the desk.

"Why don't I adapt directly from your text?" Barlow asked rationally. "You already have a written account. I could translate or at the very least have the opportunity to read your firsthand account. Our shared history, in your words—"

"Barlow, no."

"Why?"

"It is my personal account, an account I cannot share. I've exposed myself and shared before, and I will never be subjected to such a perusal again." Pettick let out an exhausted sigh and glanced up to Barlow, followed by another confession. "Writing that book saved my life."

"Is that why we're doing this? You think this book will somehow save this place?"

"I can only hope." Pettick pondered, passing the moments measured by his heavy breaths and dodging glances. "You can doubt my motives all you want, Barlow; many do. But never doubt my devotion."

"There is no doubt in that," Barlow asserted.

"Good."

The session was productive, yet Barlow couldn't shake the memory of the words—words he had read yet did not understand. It felt as if he were reading one of the novels in the library, challenged by an author who knew very well he was outwitting his reader, or perhaps an author merely misleading his audience. Though Barlow still believed this to be a personal account, he was unsure of whose account it was. As Barlow closed the door to the parlor, he found himself whispering a reiteration of the same thought, the same phrase, a confession verbatim.

"Why are we so afraid of each other?"

* * *

Crane raced down the wooden planks, descending into the basement with an excitement seldom expressed when approaching dungeons. The corner appeared to be longer as Crane's shoes slid around the bend, raising ash as he cut back to the fruit cellar door.

"Jamie, it's me, Crane."

Silence.

"Jamie?" Crane took his seat on the steps, crossing his legs tightly to his chest. The entire room steadily shifted as Crane sat in persistent silence, alone. After several passing minutes, Crane rose to his feet, turning back to the furnace. As he turned the corner, Crane's foot pressed into the brick and sealed his stride. Mawkin stood in equal stillness beside the chute.

"Do you have something to tell me?" Mawkin asked Crane who was unable to respond with any semblance of calm.

"I—uh . . ." Crane stuttered, finding no words leading him to a simple exit. "I just was down here shoveling books." Mawkin tilted his head from the unlit stove to the floor beside him where beneath the chute only scrapes in the floor remained.

"Right. Is that the story you're sticking with?" Mawkin asked.

Crane's gazed from Mawkin to the empty book well where Mawkin had glanced and then back to Mawkin. The credibility of his excuse was feather-thin.

"It's the only one I got," Crane said, shrugging.

Mawkin ran the tips of his fingers along the fur above his lip as he paced in an arc around Crane.

"Well, go on, get out of here."

Bewildered, Crane turned to Mawkin with a concave brow and raised cheek. "You're not going to—"

"I'm going to change my mind if you don't get out of here. Now."

Crane disappeared quickly up the staircase. Mawkin remained for several minutes after Crane was long gone, thinking. Brushing the fur on his chin, he broke from his pensiveness and circled around the room before disappearing up the stairs, sealing the basement door gently behind him.

The door into the garage eased open, and Crane quietly passed through it.

"Kindle!" Crane's voice echoed in fading resonance across the bay. "Kindle?" Crane walked along the path of the bay from one end to the other, cutting between the trucks, before slowly moving up the stairs to the catwalk.

Crane's hand gripped the knob of the door that sealed Kindle's office, fearing the silence which made the action debilitating. The imagined 'Magician's Chamber' that Crane had long believed real vanished as he passed over the threshold of Kindle's dwelling. The blemished reality: a quickly fashioned cot sat beyond a series of wooden and metal toolboxes in varying sizes and conditions in masses resembling that of the library. Beside the bed lay a stack of books, volumes Crane had brought to Kindle over the seasons, atop which a feather sat collecting dust. There was a second cot folded in the corner of the room also collecting dust. The room was dry, with a vacancy which Crane could sense had existed for days. Crane fled the garage without a word, just a vivid imagination creating the scenarios of Jamie and Kindle's whereabouts that he could not help but believe to be true.

* * *

Darkness, immeasurable darkness, surrounded Kindle for what could have been years. Persistent silence and persistent noise, an analogous din, all sounded the same. Until, in one single moment, the silence broke and the darkness receded, and a figure appeared in the doorway. The contour of the figure, majestic in shadowed white, remained a silhouette as it fell into the room, the limp body bouncing hard against the concrete, darkness following with it. Kindle approached the body, drawing his glove through the thick damp black, reaching out in as gently and friendly a fashion as possible. He felt breath inhaled and exhausted with the rising and lowering of the chest where Kindle placed his glove. The figure remained unconscious as Kindle retreated back to the corner of the cell, uncertain how to deal with no longer being alone, locked in a human cage with one of the specimens.

Several hours passed, or so it seemed, before the screaming began. "Huuuuhhh-help—ahhh—hel—" Pressing against the wall, Kindle slid further away from the human, uncertain of the lucidity of his cellmate. "Help! Hel—" At first, he tried to ignore the human's cries, not knowing what to make of them. But minutes passed with continuing whimpers and screams, cries he knew only to be pain and fear. Kindle ran all the scenarios through his head, inching closer to the human, cautious to its movements. With a nervous glove, he lifted the human's arm, dropping it to the floor in response to the human's sudden movement. Observing the emaciation and weakness in its body, he made contact with the human once again, sliding the human's shoulders onto his lap. Cradling his arms under its back, Kindle could feel the healing scars, the swollen bruises scattered in plots on the body. The human was still asleep, yet Kindle shared in his nightmares. Amid the fever of the dreams the terrified hands of the human wrapped around Kindle, clenching his coat. Kindle remained a silent guardian as nightmares surrendered to dreams, and then lucidity in turn. As the human slowly awoke Kindle retreated to the corner of the cell. Hours passed, or so it seemed.

"You always talk in your sleep?" Kindle asked, his low voice magnified by the refracting concrete chamber. The human rose, painfully, searching for the origin of the voice, tracking it to the corner of the room.

"Do you things even sleep?" the human asked, coughing through his words.

"The earth does, why would we not?"

"Right—" the human sarcastically spat, refraining anger. Kindle waited cautiously for his new cellmate to react to his situation. "You got a name, friend?"

"Kindle."

"The Tinker?" the human asked, exhausted.

"Yes. How'd ya know?"

Any anxiety the human had felt faded as he found the opposing wall to Kindle, pressing his leather jacket against the concrete and sliding to the floor. "Crane spoke a lot about you."

"You're a friend of Crane?" Kindle asked, bewildered.

"You could certainly say that."

"He's a good kid." There was much to question regarding this fact, but with Crane's recent absence it made sense to Kindle. "You got a name?"

"The name's Jamie," Jamie said, pausing with a huff. "I take it, you and me being locked in here together, yer not the most favored by Pettick."

"I certainly would not call him a friend." Kindle rose to the doorway, pressing his face against the steel. "Which brings us to the question of why you were put in here." Kindle backed away from the door, returning to his corner, idly swaying. "What are you up to, Pettick?"

As his eyes adjusted to the darkness Jamie scanned Kindle over, only seeing amorphous shapes at first, but slowly details etched in the folds of Kindle's jacket and the threads of his bearded face. "Why is that?" Jamie asked.

"Why is what?"

"Why do you think he's up to something?"

"Because," Kindle said, twisting back to Jamie, "there are twenty empty cells on this block, and he put you in this one."

"And why would he do that?" Jamie asked.

Kindle lifted his large gloves and ran them down his face, muffling his response. "I don't know." The two sat in silence, searching for words. "Least now I can measure the time." Kindle spoke with a somber relief he truly felt. "Can't remember the last time I had a conversation that didn't resolve in idle threats."

"You're assuming I'm gonna be friendly," Jamie grew groundlessly defensive. "Wouldn't count on that just yet, pal; last one of you things to lay gloves on me, I stuck a springer into its belly."

"Oh, and how far did that get ya?" Kindle asked.

"Funny," Jamie scoffed, giving some semblance of containment to his anger. "It's not that I don't trust ya or nothin', just odds aren't in your favor. Of your kind I met, the better half have tried to kill me."

"Better half?" Kindle looked puzzled.

"It's a figure of speech."

"Ah. Right," Kindle reasoned, pretending to understand. "I'm just saying we both want the same thing."

"Oh, and what is that?" The grease folds gathered in Jamie's shirt, his hand slid up his abdomen, holding the tender ridges of his gashed, emaciated ribs.

Kindle saw the scars he had felt before. "To get outta here."

"That's not all I want." Jamie lowered his shirt, flapping tight his jacket in a territorial way. "I want Pettick where he belongs, strung to a fucking pike."

"I ain't stoppin' ya there. We may even be of use to one another."

"How's that?"

"You and I. Pettick may not realize he gave me something to fight with." A grin cut through Kindle's beard. "You and me, we got a whole lot to learn from each other."

"Lotta good that'll do—"

"Trust me, kid. In a place like this, knowledge goes a long way."

"Oh, and how well has that worked out for you thus far?" Jamie quipped, gesturing at the interior of their cell.

Kindle huffed, peering back to Jamie, a judging grimace on his brow. "You ever count the scars on your fists?"

"No," Jamie replied, shaking his head.

Kindle ran the edge of his finger along the knuckle of his glove. "Well, I have."

The sun ran its final course as Pettick planted himself on the edge of the ridge. The vast ball of fire in the distance fought valiantly, dashing in streaks of bleeding fire along the horizon, then fell away. Pettick gazed at the dying lines in the distant sky, seeing only his disquieted thoughts that blurred all surrounding realities. The Flying Crow's caw sounded. A peripheral movement caught Pettick's attention. Atop the water tower a figure sank, occasionally peaking over the brim of the barrel. Pettick took several steps toward the tower, looking up at the face of the Reader's son who reflected his most queer and curious gaze. Galloping hooves, clattering into the dry earth, sounded. Pettick spun around to see his third in command driving toward him, leading a second steed.

"Pettick! Pettick!" Veidt shouted as he approached. "I think you should see this!" The 'Crow halted his horses, taking no time to dismount.

"What is it?" Pettick asked.

The following words were too quiet for Crane to decipher, though their significance must have been great since it drew Pettick away. The young 'Crow remained still as the two figures mounted, launching the horses into a hurried canter down the sloping ridge. Crane turned to the horizon, exhausting a relieved breath at the situation's outcome. In the coming minutes, night triumphed.

"Stand down! Lower your weapons, for Crow's sake!" Mawkin rallied his infantry, curtailing the lead of the reins, rounding his horse at the edge of the main gate. The spotlight swung over his frame as it scanned the ground, halting forty yards from the fence, a quarter of the way between the gate and the road. In the light three figures rose—framed silhouettes, iconographic and contoured with piercing white—approaching in a seasoned stride. Speculative voices muttered from the surrounding 'Crows. Mawkin dismounted and peered through the grid of wire. He lifted his glove to the fur on his lip and ran his finger along the threads as his lip shaped into an upward crescent. The spotlight followed the figures' approach, causing their details of their appearances to materialize, transforming a nearly unanimous fear in the atmosphere into one of curiosity.

The strangers moved in a triangular formation, led by a tall stoic 'Crow of commanding presence who very nearly towered above Mawkin. His face wore a beard, roughly a foot in length, which came to a point in the center of his chest. To his right, limping with visible spite, was a smaller broad-shouldered 'Crow who had a face of scarred spirals and carved war paint. To his left was a 'Crow layered in fabrics of varying origins, lavish colors, and freckly jeweled. She was of medium height, but her long tar-stained blond hair gave a sense of verticality to her stature. As the strangers reached the gate, the leader was clearly sizing up Mawkin.

"It is good to see you, brother," the leader said, a worn sagacity in his tone.

"And also you, Constantine," Mawkin returned with a smile. The two shared a gaze that Mawkin broke only to relay orders to his soldiers. "Open the gates!"

The large beams of the gate cracked and roared as the single center trunk, pierced by light, severed in two. Retreating his horse, Mawkin made a quick scan of the colony as the figures entered the opening that quickly sealed behind them. Constantine presented Mawkin his hand. Mawkin looked down at his own glove, and began wiping the dirt and soot onto his jacket before accepting it. After shaking Constantine's hand, he did the same with his fellow travelers, Zara and Acre.

"We have much to talk about," Constantine stated.

"Yes, we do," Mawkin replied, nodding.

Constantine scanned the visible perimeter of the colony. observing the technology scattered about, before returning his attention to Mawkin. "Hasn't nearly aged enough, has it?"

"Lest we forget—" Mawkin replied ironically.

Mawkin's response ignited a bulging laugh from within Constantine's chest, which spread to his fellow elders.

"Clever, now!" Constantine said jovially.

The words coming from two approaching pale silhouettes cut into the conversation with a persistent voice, "Welcome, friends, welcome!" The crescent on Mawkin's face began to fall, forming a mirrored image of itself. Pettick and Veidt came into the light. Veidt held back as Pettick joined the proximity of the conversation, welcoming the Scarecrows with open arms, along with other politically coy and overplayed gestures. "Constantine, Acre, Zara, it has been too long."

"It has, Pettick." It was clear Constantine took little to no interest in pleasantries, and offered Pettick only the barest minimum of due respect, "Some major additions, I see," he said, feigning marvel and wonder as he turned to observe the massive towers of the fence.

"Yes!" Pettick looked briefly to the height of the behemoth project before bringing his attention back to his guests. He expanded his arms in a gesture of grand reception. "Come, come to the house; we have much to discuss!" Acre and Zara exchanged a glance before meeting Constantine's eyes. He nodded to them before turning back to Pettick. "Shall we?" Pettick urged, presenting a smile. The company started toward the house. Before they were halfway there, Pettick slowed his stride and fell back. Turning to Mawkin, he held his hand inches before Mawkin's chest.

"Mawkin, secure the perimeter. Ensure our good friends were not followed."

"It's fine, I assure you," Mawkin said, recoiling.

Now the palm of Pettick's hand pressed firmly against Mawkin's abdomen. An Imperative.

"Do not make me put you in your place before our guests." Pettick cut a concealed grin as he continued on, while a hindered Mawkin remained. The Crusaders continued their steady stride up the hill; the frame of the house rose ahead.

"Since when are Scarecrows residing in this bastion? I recall a time when we swore this house would become a pile of ash," Zara remarked.

"Yet you insisted we keep such relics," Acre interjected, glaring at Pettick. "As if we ourselves weren't reminders enough."

"I am not one for mirrors, Acre," Pettick scoffed.

The 'Crows continued into the house, their prolonged silence a reminder of their long separation. Once sequestered in the house, the 'Crows dispersed to separate plots around the parlor. Constantine sat at the chair before Pettick's desk. "You remained well versed in literature and language without my presence," Pettick observed.

"Quite. But it appears I cannot say the same about those in your presence. That Mawkin of yours, is he still functionally illiterate? He seems to show great improvement colloquially, though."

"He can understand what is needed of him."

"Ah, I'll take that as a yes, then." Constantine cocked his head. "I know your definition of a blunt object."

Taking his post at the window, Pettick ignored Constantine's conjecture. "It has been—"

"Years, yes," Acre added, biting his words.

"And your travels?" Pettick asked as he drifted toward his chair. "A fruitful crusade, I hope." He began spinning a thread between the thumb and the first finger of his glove as he matched the gazes of the Crusaders, pushing to speak, but finding no words.

"Something wrong, Pettick?" Zara knowingly asked.

"No—no," Pettick stuttered for words.

"It's fine," Constantine interjected. "You do not need to search for small talk; we'll get to the point. Zara?"

Zara approached the desk. From her satchel she pulled out a package. The package, a book cocooned in a waxy butcher paper sleeve, had several swatches of worn rags bound with twine, and landed with a loud thud onto the desk, propelling a layer of dust into the air as it did. Pettick held himself to his position with visible angst.

"Well, go ahead," Acre absolved.

Pettick uncoiled, pulling apart the rags and revealing a book he found most sacred. The black cloth cover was inset with faded red letters in a font so elegantly curled it nearly appeared to be foreign, displaying the title *Grimm Tales.*

"Your prize," Zara stated.

"It'd better be," Acre added. "We had to trek nearly halfway around the human world to get it."

Pettick scanned the cover, A grin cut his cheek, the lamp's light reflecting atop the words on his glasses.

"There is more." Constantine said.

Pettick lifted the manuscript as Acre moved closer to the table with his satchel. He opened it and turned it upside down. A pile of books, magazines, and newspapers cascaded out of it in a flood, trickling over the sides of the desk, causing Pettick to snicker. Acre threw the empty bag to the floor and retreated to a seat in the corner of the room. Pettick laid the copy of *Grimm Tales* delicately atop the pile, and, with a keen tremble, reverted his attention back to his guests.

"So tell me . . . tell me about your journey."

The sun rose the next morning, yet nearly six hours passed before there was any movement from within the parlor. Pettick stepped onto the porch, running his right hand down his face. He stretched toward the ceiling, his slender form contracting with several searing snaps.

"Long night . . ." Mawkin said, rocking back and forth in the chair—Pettick's chair.

"Suppose it was."

"And our Crusaders?"

"Resting in the parlor," Pettick yawned. "We will find them proper quarters tonight."

"And our plan for the day?" Mawkin asked.

"We will call a meeting, a grand presentation of the Crusaders' unprecedented return to our colony," Pettick plainly stated, too exhausted for any semblance of enthusiasm and worn of the hackneyed prospect of making any grand gesture—platitudes.

"There will be many questions," Mawkin said. "I can assure you of that."

"And there will be a multitude of answers." There was a mocking tongue detected in Pettick's words as he rested his gloves on his hips, looking out on the flaxen wash of morning's light over the farm. The perfect late summer breeze passed by; its mild cool tinge brought a smile to Pettick. He rolled up the sleeves of his flannel, exposing his straw forearms.

"I have questions too, you know," Mawkin added.

"I'm sure you do."

Pettick stepped off the porch and continued down the hill. Mawkin watched, a huff in his muzzle as he steadily rocked in his chair.

* * *

Gwyn dashed through the reeds lining the ridge, her feet barely pressing to the soil as she approached the water tower. She called to Crane as she began her ascent. There was no response. As she reached the top she saw Crane's figure sink behind the opposite edge. She pulled herself onto the barrel, remaining fixed on Crane's gargoyle pose for several passing breezes. She spoke his name but got no reply. She reached out to him, a tender kindness to her fingertips. Crane barely responded to Gwyn's touch. She tried not to be hurt by this. Gwyn was growing jaded by Crane's recurring dislocation and his childish refusal to address or share the cause to his sorrow. This pushed the fervency of her words. "Crane, talk to me."

"He's gone," Crane said.

"Who?" She moved beside him, not knowing the subject of Crane's sorrow, or how to react to its persistence.

"Kindle—he's gone." Crane turned away. "I went to his garage. He hasn't been there for days—weeks, maybe."

Gwyn leaned against him, resting her head on his shoulder; she laid this way for several moments before raising her chin to his shoulder, staring intently at him.

"I'm sure he's all right," Gwyn said. Sullen and pensive, Crane moved back to the cave of his mind, whittling the nothingness in his hands. Gwyn held the rough of his neck. "I want to tell you something."

Crane looked into Gywn's eyes. "What is it?"

"Do you remember the Crusaders, the story of the Harvest Scarecrow?" Crane's gaze remained transfixed on the horizon while Gwyn continued. "Scarecrows made of the purest straw and autumn leaves. Constantine, the first Crusader was constructed of these autumn leaves, weaved with the waxy skin." Gwyn could sense she was failing in distracting Crane from his woes, pushing further her emphasis on the wonder in her tale. "Constantine, the Crusaders—

along with Pettick—were the founders of this colony. The Harvest 'Crow's return is considered great luck or so we've been told."

"Yeah, Scarecrows who departed from our colony before we were made," Crane said, growing visibly vexed. "I remember the stories from when we were in school, Gwyn. They were just that—stories. And we're not kids anymore; we can't always believe what we were told."

"Well, they're here," Gwyn said.

"What? Who?"

"The Crusaders. They returned last night," Gwyn said. Crane perked up, his shifting energy grew predictably spry. Gwyn smiled.

"What?! Why didn't you tell me?"

Gwyn furrowed her brow, uncoiling a crooked smile. "Hey, you were the one up here sulking." Crane rolled back, swinging down to the ladder. As he descended the ladder he looked up at Gwyn who smiled down on him, the instigator of his ardor. "Hey, Crane?"

"Yeah?"

"Whatever you find down there, just remember—"

"I know. We aren't kids anymore."

***

Rumors spread like disease. Little could contain the hearsay; and with the culling of facts, the tales even less resembled truth. The crowd rallied with their fragments of legends, reviving a missing energy back to the village, an excitement in the air Pettick reveled in.

Mawkin leaned toward Pettick. "What, you're not going to put a sheet over them?"

Pettick scoffed and started for the stage in order to escape Makwin's hearty laugh. The crowd was thick, garrulously urged by curiosity. Gwyn and Crane pressed forward, sifting their way through the web of families and workers. Pettick took his station center stage.

"Friends, I welcome you. Now, whether you know it or not, this is a very important day for our past, for our present, and for our future. Yes, a major turning point, for we have witnessed much in our time here. But this return . . . this return is unheard of. Their journey was long—their great crusade lasting many seasons, full of danger, crossing paths with humans, which they overcame for the good of their colony—for *our* colony. They overcame. And we are forever indebted to them for that. *I* am forevermore indebted to them for that. So now I present to you these brave knights, the three that faced all adversity to reach their grail." Pettick raised his hand high, swinging in drawn crescent that terminated at his side, palm, skyward. "These Crusaders—let them rise!"

From beside the well the Crusaders marched toward the stage. A gasp blanketed the crowd. The march seemed to last longer because of the silence. Each collision of chain, leather, pendant, each pull of thread, could be heard from their bodies.

"A smattering of our flock may remember them: Constantine, Zara, Acre."

The Crusaders stood on the stage in a humble row, with Acre and Zara gently nudging Constantine forward.

Near the front of the crowd Barlow stepped beside Barnes. "The Crusaders?" Barnes skepticly asked his father.

"Yes," Barlow said.

"Why have you never mentioned them?" Barnes asked.

"I barely remember them."

"You barely remember—then, when did they leave?"

Barlow, entranced and confused by the visitors, and his own increasingly tenuious grasp on time, remained silent as Barnes continued his questions.

Acre leaned over to Constantine, whispering, "Should we say something?"

"What is there to say—"

"What *can* we say?" Zara added.

Constantine took a step forward. He glanced at Pettick, then peered out over the audience, their faces unrecognizable, their needs great. "Peace upon you all," Constantine said as if blessing the crowd.

Pettick turned toward the Crusaders and gestured for them to leave the stage. They made a final acknowledgment to the audience before heading back to the house. The presentation smiles faded with distance.

"*Peace upon you*," Acre grandly mocked. "What the fuck, Constantine? And I thought *I* might say something dumb."

"For a 'Crow so verbose," Zara said, rustling in her garb as she looked back at Pettick, "he sure don't ever *say* anything."

Pettick continued to address his Scarecrows. "I leave you with these words as these indigenous 'Crows remain a beacon of hope, a triumph for our colony: keep on fighting. You may return to your labors." Pettick, moving off the stage, came down the steps to where Mawkin stood. "Mawkin, ensure that the crowd remains back; we shouldn't have them interact with the Crusaders just yet." Mawkin remained behind as Pettick started after the Crusaders.

Crane and Gwyn breached the front of the crowd as the mass began to dissipate, flocking toward the village. Crane shot toward the side of the stage, where Mawkin stood before him. "Excuse me," Crane said, attempting to pass. Mawkin remained in Crane's path.

"Father," Barnes said, pointing to a dispute ahead of them.

Mawkin swung. Crane's body collided with the soil. Barlow broke from his trance, his paternal instincts shifting into gear.

"Crane!"

Barnes darted forward, catching Gwyn's fist as she prepared to thrust it towards Mawkin. Barnes wrapped his arms around her, pulling her back as she struggled forward.

"Mawkin!" Barlow marched forward, following the large 'Crow as he turned toward the house. "Mawkin!"

Mawkin looked back, matching Barlow's glare. "They can't. Pettick said no one talks to the Crusaders. Not yet."

"Why, Mawkin? Why?" Barlow stated.

Mawkin turned away and continued up the hill in a persistent stride.

Barlow returned to Crane, lowering his hand to his son, who rejected the gesture. Crane leapt up, preparing to lunge up the hill, but Barlow took hold of his son in the recoil.

"Let go of me!" Crane shouted.

"Let it go, son," Barlow said, composed in word and body.

"No!"

Barlow's grasp tightened as he held on to his son with all of his strength. "Let it go."

"Get off!"

Barlow broke his stance, dragging Crane to the ground. "I said let it go! That's an order!" Barlow shouted. Crane jerked his arms away while Barlow renewed his hold, pressing his weight onto his son. Several sympathizers stood watching in the distance.

"Can I let go of you now?" Barnes asked Gwyn, both 'Crows continuing to stare at the quarreling of their kin unfolding before them.

Gwyn replied, "I'm not stupid enough to mess with this."

Barnes released his hold on Gwyn as Critch and Mare approached.

"Should we intervene?" Mare and Critch inquired, gesturing towards Crane and Barlow's quarrel.

"No," Barnes and Gwyn chimed.

A cloud of dirt rose several feet in the air. The two struggled for several moments, ineffectively overcoming similar attempts to overpower the other till Crane's energy faded. Barlow continued his hold.

"Son, please let it go."

"You don't get it" You never question—never!"

"I do, Crane. I do—every day—but for now you will have to let it go."

"You never—"

"Yes, I do!" Barlow looked at his son with a clear disposition. Calm slowly collected the labor of their breathing.

"And how will we—"

"We will figure it out, but not this way," Barlow pleaded with a cadence to his voice that showed a patience only acquired with age. As he released his grip, the two 'Crows slowly rose to their feet. "Barnes, take your brother to the bungalow."

"Sir?" Barnes questioned with a bewildered brow to his father.

"What?" Crane scoffed.

"I am not asking." The old 'Crow gave purposeful looks to both of his sons before the argument could continue.

"Yes, sir," Barnes replied. Crane remained silent.

Barlow turned to Critch. "Will you ensure that my boys get home safely?"

Critch nodded. "Of course."

"Father?" Barnes asked. Barlow started up the hill to the house. Barnes turned to Crane, reaching for his brother. Crane ducked away, shoving off with a stumble, heading north in the opposite direction of Barlow.

The stairwell was dark and quiet, save the small bits of noise resonating from the separate dwellings above, and the milky sabers of white light from the hallway window which cut through the air, making visible storms of dust as figures passed through. Mawkin briskly scaled the wood ledges, peering casually at the empty hall. Pettick appeared above him making tight quarters for the two of them to have a conversation. Pettick stared down at Mawkin as if waiting for him to act.

"I want you out checking the perimeter," Pettick swiftly ordered.

Mawkin's shoulder dropped as if to move down the stairs in submission. Pettick lingered, a stench now seemed to culminate, salivate in a pungent acridity, in the close quarters. Mawkin stood plastered in place. Then, with a decision easily read below the brim of his hat and the mat of blond fibers of his hair, he recoiled back up the steps.

"Not yet."

Pettick leaned forward, his hands resting on the railings. "Could we not postpone this deliberation?"

"No," Mawkin said. "It—it will be discussed here—now."

Pettick's fingers curled in a dance around the rail. Leaning back, the light hit his nearly silhouetted frame, causing the two round lenses of his glasses to glow.

Mawkin continued: "You must explain why you, with much de . . ." he paused to concentrate, "*de-lib-er-a-tion* have persisted to—"

"Mawkin," Pettick interjected, now sounding markedly cross, "you were always a good second—loyal, obedient—but when did you grow a mouth? What is this questioning?"

"You're keeping them locked up; you're keeping them from us. Why?"

"There is more to this world than you know," Pettick lectured. "Don't you forget that."

"But these secrets—" Mawkin said.

"You know the truth," Pettick interjected.

"What truth is that?"

"You know."

"I know what? That—"

"That they are all much happier not knowing—at least, not everything." The glare vanished from the glasses as Pettick's face receded. "As are you." Silence remained for several uninspired moments. "We will discuss this. We will meet, all of us, in the coming days. If you value the little leverage you have, then appreciate that." Pettick remained only long enough to glimpse surrender on Mawkin's face, before retreating to the parlor. Mawkin turned with the seal of the door as Barlow appeared at the steps below him.

"Shit," Mawkin muttered to himself and began drifting down the steps.

"We need to talk," Barlow insisted.

"Look, I'm sorry I hit yer kid—"

"It's not that," Barlow said. He could see the confused blank expression on Mawkin's face as he continued, "We have not seen eye to eye very often, but as for this . . ." Barlow urged with a learned resilience. "I know we must."

"Right . . ." Mawkin said. He began moving down the stairs past Barlow "I feel quite certain I have no idea what you're talking about."

"I think you do," Barlow said.

Mawkin remained still for only a moment. A thought stirred within him, then broke away. He descended the remaining stairs, leaving Barlow alone with his reckoning. Barlow whirled his head and continued climbing the stairs and inched his way down the hall at the top. The sounds and beats he heard turned into words and sentences as he approached the parlor. Words steadily dripped then flowed, leaking beneath the door:

"You want us to believe that you—"

"You may believe whatever you wish."

"Pettick, there is no fool in this room; we know what you—"

"Tell me, Pettick, how many of them know—know the humans aren't the monsters you made them out to be? They aren't all Tucker, Pettick—" A rustling movement traced by the doorway, causing Barlow to back off and then slowly inch closer again. "—we must tell them."

"You have been gone for a long time—" Pettick's voice sounded as if it were trying to find solid ground on sand.

"That was *your* doing, Pettick. You sent us off on—what?—no crusade, it was a scavenger hunt! Why? Did you figure that with us gone, you could lead without reproach?"

Constantine's voice overwhelmed the rest. "Time has barely marked this place; it is *you* I fear time has scarred."

Barlow abruptly moved away from the door, traveling swiftly along the hall. Veidt rose into sight, ascending the grand stairwell. Barlow managed to cross over to the servants' stairs on the opposite end to avoid being seen. A moment later he found himself running from the house at a speed at which he never before knew he was capable. At the meeting ground ahead of him he heard the sound of playful banter. As he got closer he could see children utilizing the few fleeting minutes remaining to them before the sun would fall and the moon would signal curfew. Barlow held his glove to his chest. He stumbled, looking over his shoulder as he fell onto the meeting ground. Soon it was silent. The sun had set, and the children had all gone home.

CHAPTER XII: Steelbriars

Dusk, the fleeting golden-amber minutes when the land glints of treasure. The Lamplighter shifted along the row of bungalows on Main Street, opening the glass chambers atop each lamppost, and methodically, mechanically lighting the lamps. At the same time Main Street was also host to a small procession. The Crusaders were marching along with Veidt in the lead, grunting and grinding his teeth on a bit of straw as he walked, and a pair of guards closing at the rear.

"Can we slow down a bit?" Zara covertly asked her fellow Crusaders. "I think he can hear us, and I can still smell him."

"What can I say? They don't make 'em like they used to," Acre added, heckling.

"That's enough," Constantine said, with a briefly concealed smile. The trio continued to follow Veidt at a slower pace. The Crusaders noticed small patches of 'Crows gathering to stare curiously at them as they passed by, causing them to feel a sense of alienness within themselves. Zara glanced at one of the bungalows and saw the residing 'Crow within, looking high-strung, staring right back at her through the barrier of the screen door.

"What are they staring at? It's like they're scared of us, but they know who we are—"

"No, I don't think they do," Constantine softly stated as he himself stared through the screen of Hardwick's hut. The skittish 'Crow immediately disappeared into his bungalow. "What *else* has Pettick not been telling them?" The number of spectators diminished as they continued past the town square crossroad where several Flying Crows were perched on the signpost.

Veidt tilted his head, glaring back at the Crusaders as he pulled the strap of his rifle further up his crooked shoulder. "Try to keep up," he grumbled and swaggered.

"Quite an increase of numbers in just a handful of seasons," Zara remarked. In addition to the population growth, she couldn't help but notice the way the soil in the road changed with each phase of expansion.

"Yes, but—I wonder if—" Acre began, staring at the two story bungalow of Malthus the Mason.

Constantine held a finger to his lips, looking behind him at the two guards who continued to trail in a disinterested attitude similar to that of Veidt. The company reached the end of Main Street where Veidt ascended the stoop of the schoolhouse, and pulled open the heavy wooden door.

"Your quarters," Veidt said, gesturing as though he were welcoming royalty.

"Gratitude," Acre said with a strong tinge of sarcasm in his voice.

Veidt held out his hand, palm up, as the Crusaders silently passed. "Skin-lovers," he muttered to himself. He lingered in the doorway and turned toward the trio of guests as they explored their new surroundings. Changing his tone, he said, "And our leader did require me to remind you not to leave your quarters unescorted."

Constantine turned to Veidt, both 'Crows fading in perception with the expanding dark. "A request?" Constantine inquired.

Veidt offered a tacit smile.

"Ah, *orders*!" Acre said.

Veidt passed between the two guards as he shifted off the stoop. "Keep watch," he told them. As he began the walk back up Main Street, his marble eyes rolled, wild, within their sockets.

Constantine leaned out the doorway, scanning the street. He reached for the brass handle, then sealed the door. He slowly turned back to his comrades whose expressions bore an understandable weight of concern.

"Years out in the world, and we need protection *here*?" Acre inquired, pulling up a chair.

Constantine remained silent.

"The disposition of a pedant 'Crow," Zara sighed, in reference to Pettick.

With a perturbed concave in his brow, Constantine said to Zara, gesturing to the commoners outside: "I fear those words mean nothing to them. We will share the truth with them just as Pettick and I agreed . . . in due time."

* * *

The scattered flock wandered in the small patches of remaining green beneath the Perfect Tree. Shepherd looked out over the sable valley. A cool wind crossed his shoulder where he rested his crook. He thought for a moment, lowering his crook; the dangling jars chimed a simple dry melody. He gazed into the last jar, only lit by a single firefly whose glow gave a final burst—its microcosmic supernova—before it shimmered, exeunt, black.

"Good evening, autumn," Shepherd announced over the valley as a breeze brushed his whiskers. The Scarecrow wandered to the edge of the forest where a group of gathered lights in the distance formed into a convoy of woodcutters. As he approached, a short, stout Woodcutter offered a smile that only widened his stature. He waved to Shepherd, greeting him several feet from the loaded cart.

"Evening, Shepherd," the Woodcutter said. "What can I do for you?"

"Could I entreat you for a handful of candles, if you can afford to spare them?"

"Certainly." The Woodcutter moved to the front of the cart. He opened a small cigar box and presented a handful of candlesticks to Shepherd.

"A thousand thanks," Shepherd said.

The Woodcutter nodded to Shepherd, following the cart as it began its march into the thick of the forest. With the light of the final candlewick, Shepherd continued his stride by the edge of the woods. His herd followed.

A breeze broke several blighted leaves, which lost their grip and fell from their home, each tree no longer a sapling but rather an aging quiddity on the last phase of its epic yearling journey. In the distance, the neigh from one of Shepherd's animals sparked a scattering of the animals. They leapt fearfully around the Perfect Tree.

Shepherd froze when he saw a figure, a shadow, a blank black canvas of imagination outlined in darkness, dart across the field like a hungry wolf in chase, sinking into the forest. The presence of the figure remained in Shepherd's mind long after its disappearance from sight. Shepherd used his crook to scan the edge of the woods as he retreated to the Perfect Tree, where he met his flock. A burro stumbled toward Shepherd, burying its head affectionately in his cloak. "I know, I know—" Shepherd spoke with a soft resilience as he ran his spindly fingers through the burro's mane. "Let us make our way home now."

Shepherd lifted his crook, waving it high above his gray brow, then lowered it as the animals gathered behind his stride.

* * *

"Crane?" Barlow shouted in the direction of the stars, a cadence to his inquiry. He stood at the base of the water tower, wading in near silence, excepting the sounds of the bugs and birds. Encompassing the tower, he tried to see the top. Unsuccessful, he moved to the massive supports, pressing his hands against the wood and cocking his head up the crossbeams, following up to the ladder which began at the tank. "Shit," Barlow huffed. The old 'Crow crinkled his brow as he reached for the first post, hoisting himself skyward, all the while calling Crane's name.

An exhausted Barlow reached the plateau of the tank and, with a final heave, his body lay flat, staring at the stars. He rolled over, sighing as he realized the vacancy of the tower. The Scarecrow edged to the end of the barrel, and gently, carefully swung his legs over the side. The 'Crow's legs locked in their dangle. Barlow watched as a breeze washed over the ridge, moving in a tide through the valley. Barlow remained entranced by the small lights of Shepherd's crook as they hovered along the hill before the village. He sat back, thinking on the quiet; from a distance it was all so peaceful, muting the conflict, the anger, the questions, and the fear. "I get it now, Crane," Barlow said, his head bowed to the constellations. Barlow's legs began to swing as they dangled. Running his hand along the lid of the barrel, he felt an edge within the grain of the plank. The Reader looked down at two carved words, a pact, sealed in the grain of the wood:

CRANE
AND
GWYN

Barlow smiled, feeling the tension in his strands release. He turned his gaze back toward the sky. An unseen Flying Crow violently cawed. He tilted his head back down to the lights of the village, and over to the woods as several unusual flares of red pulsed. The illumination rapidly expanded a glowing orange in the outlying forest.

The heavy imprint of Mawkin's boot formed a canyon in the earth as the large 'Crow dismounted several feet from the main gate. His serving Scarecrows made acknowledgments to their commanding officer as they held their posts, going through the motions to ensure their tasks were again complete. Mawkin looked up the tower where Paquin peered down from his watch.

"Can I help you, Mawkin?" Paquin inquired, leaning over the railing.

"Just securing the perimeter."

"Isn't that a little . . . well . . . busywork for you?" Pacquin said, with a tinge of jest.

"Special guests—you can never be too careful," Mawkin tactfully responded. "Now get back to work."

The 'Crows shared a laugh as Mawkin continued along the fence, wrapping his jacket around him. The horses neighed; a Flying Crow cawed.

"Mawkin!" Paquin shouted.

"I said back to work."

"No—look!"

Mawkin turned up to the 'Crow, following the lookouts' gazes out across the farm where, down by the village, a column of glowing orange smoke rose into the night sky. "No—" Mawkin uttered to himself, transfixed in disbelief before starting back to his horse. "Remain at your posts! Remain at your posts!" Mawkin pointed to two of his 'Crows on the ground nearby. "You two, come with me." The three mounted and immediately drove hard in a heavy gallop towards the village. Along the path one of the 'Crows broke off towards the house upon Mawkin's order.

Main Street glowed with orange- and yellow-tinged flashes, causing flickers of light to dance down the road, which was now scattered with Scarecrows. The crowd parted as Mawkin galloped through. At the end of the street Mawkin dismounted, the contour of his frame glowing, becoming a moving silhouette in the high rising flames of the burning schoolhouse ahead. Mawkin stopped as though standing before a material fear, the heat of the fire adding to the weight that filled his body. The frame of the structure remained intact as several of Pettick's soldiers arrived on horseback, pails of water in hand. Mawkin grabbed one of the 'Crows attempting to extinguish the flame.

"Keep everyone back, protect the perimeter, don't let it spread."

"And the building, sir? The Crusaders—"

A gust fed the inferno.

"It's too late." Mawkin sighed. With his coat flapping in the wind, he whipped around and started back for his horse. Mounting, Mawkin rose as the pressure of the heat let off a wail, screams that turned to cracks which, followed by a large flare of fire, marked the collapse of the structure. The schoolhouse crumbled. Fluttering sparks rose. Mawkin looked back to the crowd. "Get back to your homes! Lock your doors!" The crowd slowly began to disperse.

Veidt and Thalo approached on horseback.

"What's going on?" Veidt asked, looking up at the yellow sparks rising into the black.

"Can't you see?" Mawkin reasoned.

Veidt and Thalo remained silent.

"Where's Pettick?" Mawkin asked.

"I don't know," Veidt responded, while Thalo silently shook his head in awe at the expanding blaze.

"Where did you just come from?"

"The house," Thalo replied.

"Stay here, keep watch. Contain this." Mawkin smacked the reins hard, and the horse's hooves crashed in small eruptions, leaving imprints along the dirt path.

Mawkin swung over the saddle, dismounting at the front porch. Upon entering, he scanned the empty parlor before rushing up the stairs and continuing down the hall to Pettick's quarters. After beating his heavy fist against the large oak door and hearing no sound from within the dwelling, he gripped the doorknob—something he himself had never before touched—and turned it. The door swung open to reveal an empty bedroom. Mawkin entered at a slow pace, stopping before the bed where the cotton covers were perfectly formed and tucked into the frame. The chamber was dark and the air was stale. Pettick's sparse effects sat in perfect order on the bureau. Pictures lined the wall, vestiges of a human past frozen in time. As Mawkin leaned in closer, he was able to observe the deliberate disfigurement of the faces each picture contained. Before him a faded photo of the Tucker family, the eyes of each face having been punctured through. Every visible picture of a human had the subjects' eyes removed. Mawkin scanned the frames. Some were blank, the images having been torn out completely; the small frays of paper in the corners being the only evidence the photo ever existed. As he turned away from the wall, shifting back toward the foot of the bed, he stumbled over a wooden chest on the floor. A garish silver padlock sealed its lid shut. He pondered what effects, either cherished or spurned, might be locked away inside it. Mawkin sat on the bed. On the nightstand beside the headboard stood a framed picture. This image, uncanny in its normality, had remained otherwise unscathed. The image was of a young woman, eyes staring back, her smile wide, hair curled and flowing, by all accounts observably happy in the framed moment. Mawkin ran his thumb over the glass, collecting no dust.

The floorboards creaked out in the hallway. Mawkin stood up, returning the picture to the nightstand, and moved toward the doorway where shifting light revealed movement at the far end of the hall. Closing the door behind him, he stepped quietly back into the corridor, heading around the corner to the entrance of the parlor. Mawkin froze in the doorway, observing Pettick, who stood like a statue placed in dramatic pose, looking out the window over the orange glow of the village. Mawkin remained quiet as he scanned the room. Pettick's body shifted as he grew aware of Mawkin's presence. Mawkin looked down at the desk where several tubes lay scattered. These were road flares, capped and unused, though Mawkin knew nothing of their function. Pettick turned back to Mawkin, glaring at him through his glasses.

"As I said: war," Pettick proclaimed, heavyhearted, placing his jacket atop his desk, concealing the tubes.

"Right," Mawkin said, halfheartedly assured.

Thalo appeared in the doorway, shaking and out of breath. "Come quick!"

"I thought I told you to keep to the village—" Mawkin said.

"There was screaming and a glow from the woods; the woodcutter convoy has been attacked."

Mawkin and Pettick turned to face each other, their expressions sharing the look of mutual disillusionment.

A knee-high lake of smoke lingered above the charred ground of the remains of the convoy, the only early-morning mist as the dry night gave itself to dryer days. Mawkin stood over the charred remains of one of his Scarecrows. The twisted strings of the hand, singed at the edges, were wrapped tightly around a dust-coated rifle. Gently, respectfully, Mawkin's gloves unpeeled the fingers from the stock and trigger guard. He lifted the rifle, with strength renting at the clip, eventually sliding it open to reveal a full magazine. He returned the rifle to the ash, thinking. Mawkin bent down and ran his glove through the ashes, where he discovered a concealed round tube coated in black soot. This he quickly pocketed as he rose to a distraught Pettick entering the clearing, who silently but openly rallied in the remains, shuddering: "This is why."

"This is what?" Mawkin mustered, disinterested in an explanation as he circled the site. At the center of the remains of the cart, four wooden pick points rested where spokes jutted violently skyward. Beyond sat the remnants of a half-burned torso of straw, the lower half disintegrating into the surrounding soil. "Grey?" Mawkin stated, turning back to Pettick who was perched atop a stump on the edge of the clearing. "What was Grey doing out here?" Mawkin lifted the singed remains of Grey's suspenders by the clip.

"The birds if I know," Pettick replied.

Mawkin mounted his horse and gazed down at Pettick—ash-filled furls coming from the horse's canter as he rode off.

"Scatter the remains. Return to the farm," Pettick ordered, marching through the smoke, careless to the ashes he stirred. Mounting his own horse, he pursued after Mawkin, the rays of sunlight from the forest canopy cutting across his torso.

* * *

The contents of the shelf shifted forward, gathering at the handle where Mawkin's grip released, the shelf falling out of its slot, scattering the contents onto the floor. There was no lock on the hasp which typically sealed the top drawer of Pettick's desk. This came as a surprise to Mawkin. His glove shuffled through the pile of books, papers of crumpled forgotten reminders, and a journal so loyal it was thought never to have left its scribe. Mawkin continued to hunt around the parlor, pulling the charred tube from the inner breast pocket of his long coat, studying the object, then returning it next to his chest.

The gallop of Pettick's horse resonated across the farm, timing Mawkin who began to hurry with the blistering siren. Mawkin shifted to the window where he could see in the distance Pettick breach the hill. The large 'Crow shifted back into the room, restating order to the shelf, and turning back to the door. In a frozen moment, Mawkin turned back to Pettick's study, and pulled open the shelf once more.

Pettick reached the doorway of the parlor, expecting confrontation, but found the room empty. Sealing the door, he moved to the bookshelf and pulled out a red book with the title *The Day of the Locust* etched along the spine. Opening the book revealed a hollow center cut into the pages within, which left only frangments of text along the surrounding edge.

Mawkin exited Pettick's bedroom, placing the most valuable contents from the drawer in his jacket as he continued silently down the servant stairs in the back of the house, cutting down the long hall where he could hear footsteps on the stairs. Mawkin cut across the hall and into the unguarded basement, silently closing the large oak door behind him. The footsteps continued down the hall.

Mawkin quietly descended the staircase. He rounded the corner, watching the beams bow and tremor beneath the footsteps above. As he tilted his chin down from the rafters a 'Crow appeared, frozen and silent by the stove.

"Crane?" Mawkin asked.

"I'm sorry, there was n—"

Mawkin moved to Crane, wrapping his arms around the young 'Crow, muffling his words with his glove, causing Crane's fear to escalate to a tremble. The wafts of raining dust passed over the Scarecrows, continuing towards the porch.

"Shh—quiet! I'm not going to hurt you," Mawkin said, his own muffled words an even greater confusion to Crane. "Now, I'm going to let go of you—stay quiet, stay calm." Mawkin released his grip on Crane. "All right?" Crane nodded, a bewildered roll to his brow. The two 'Crows raised their heads toward the beams above. The silence only lasted a moment before several geysers of dust erupted along the beam running to the edge of the stairs. Mawkin looked down at his chest, pulling Pettick's Journal from his coat.

"What is that?" Crane asked, denying recognition. Mawkin recoiled his hand for a moment, then reached out, handing the Journal to Crane.

"Listen, I don't know if I can trust your master, but I know I can no longer trust mine." Mawkin spoke with urgency, lowering down to Crane's height. "I know you are looking for answers, and I'm sure you will find them here."

Crane read the sincerity in Mawkin's voice, both 'Crows glancing at their leather-bound secret.

"Just, whatever you do, don't let him find you with it."

Voices gathered at the top of the stairs. Mawkin scanned the room, turning to the concrete steps leading to the outer cellar door. He placed his gloves on the large wooden post that sealed the door. Grunting, he thrust the timber over enough so the right-hand door could swing open.

"Run. Don't look back. I'll find you again."

Crane looked at Mawkin's face once more, still in disbelief as he lunged out the door. The seal of the door and return of the timber brace echoed as the door at the top of the stairs opened, followed by a stampede of footsteps.

Pettick, alone, appeared around the corner. "There you are, Mawkin." Pettick glanced around the room. "What are you doing down here?"

"Wanted to question the prisoner, to ensure he hadn't broken loose, to see if he knew anything."

"Ah, I see, quick thinking." Pettick turned back to the stairs, pausing, "Only James is no longer down here, remember?"

"Now—yes," Mawkin stuttered. "I had forgotten."

"Right. Well, good . . . good thinking. We shall go question him together, then."

"Right," Mawkin huffed, hesitantly following Pettick up the stairs.

Mawkin and Pettick filed shoulder to shoulder down the narrow hall of the silo barn. The hall's massive construction work was still in full swing, though its skeleton crew worked the daylight hours during these final stages. Still rhythmic, the *clank-tap-tap-ratcheting* of their labors echoed through the shaft. Mawkin's chin rose toward the rafters above. What was normally perceived as a low-hung ceiling of darkness at night, without any worklights, now contained several scattered workers, tasked in their labors, scaling the infusion of metal and timber beams up, high, to the vaulted pitches of the roof. The guard opened the door to Jamie's cell, escorting Mawkin inside. Pettick stood outside the door, his attention down the hall where, unfazed by Pettick's security, the Creator strolled in, casually managing to lay a hand on every surface down the hall. Inadvertently, his glove collected samples of the residue on each surface, from rusted oil on the bars to woodchips in sawdust.

"Can I help you?" Pettick resentfully hollered.

"Ahh, Pettick!" The Creator smiled, a feigned gesture, as he approached. "No, I helped myself."

"I can see that," Pettick observed as the Creator continued past, clearly intent on making it to the end of the hall. Pettick reluctantly followed in the direction of vault door at end of the hall. The Creator stopped before reaching this door, taking interest in an adjacent cell. A lock of golden strawberry hair fell through the bars. The Creator held out his glove, stroking the strands between the crook of his slender fingertips.

"I quite like your menagerie," the Creator marveled.

"As you can see, they truly require subjugation," Pettick listlessly stated, making eye contact with the woman, whose green eyes and strawberry hair quickly retreated from the bars.

Mawkin glanced behind him as the door to the cell sealed without Pettick following in. Mawkin scanned the space, his gaze resting on Jamie, a coiled heap of black hair, bruised flesh, leather and denim, asleep on the floor. Jamie remained still, a convincing act, having made a profession of pretending to be asleep in a previous life. Mawkin rested his glove on Jamie's shoulder, though the human failed to stir. "I am sorry," Mawkin said, resting on the floor next to Jamie. The room felt stale, damp and cold, an anomaly in the severity of drought. He lifted his chin to Kindle, who was huddled in the corner. Kindle stared right back. Mawkin buried his whiskers in his gloves. He could hear the voices down the hall, echoing.

The Creator pushed through the metal door at the end of the hall, moving into a dimly lit chamber containing several worktables, the space vaguely resembling the textile barn. Each table of heavy lumber held a chain point, a drop-forged dock ring, anchored in the center. The chamber, a thoroughfare into the silos, was otherwise open to the vaulted shell of the barn in which it was constructed. Every sound was magnified by its own echo. After behaving like a child in a museum, the Creator followed several of Pettick's soldiers turned laborers currently tasked to repairing the damaged silo. On the opposite side of the chamber were two doors, each one centered at the base of a pair of towering cylinders. Sunlight peaked through the first open door. After briefly considering his options of door #1 or #2, the Creator entered door #1. Standing in the south tower, a one-hundred-ten-foot grain silo, was humbling. It felt as if standing atop the primer of a hollow bullet, chambered in the barrel. Pettick was in the place of the penitent; looking skyward, one could touch milky spears of lights as they ricocheted within the chamber of the metal cathedral. A small pile of straw at no more than six feet tall was stacked in the center before them. To the right, a scaffold rose to the dome ceiling where the roof had taken scars from the whirling wind, prized from his framework, peeled back like a can lid, exposing the sun.

"And this?" the Creator asked. "This is your vault? Your reserve?"

Pettick nodded. "All that is left."

"When there is but a straw left," the Creator chuckled as he leapt into the pile of straw, playfully tossing a heap into the air which rained down around him as it fell. "You should really keep a better lock on this place."

"We're running out of locks . . ." Pettick muttered as he stood by unamused.

"Join me," the Creator jested.

"I have not much fondness for such tomfoolery."

"Really . . . You seem to enjoy fooling me a lot, or so I perceive."

"You don't get out enough," Pettick scoffed.

"So tell me," the Creator said as he puckered and bloated his cheeks, "what it is you're really doing here?"

"Isn't it obvious?" Pettick mumbled, looking away.

"Oh, quite—you're replacing me with them," the Creator clarified, pointing out the door. "Those humans—you plan to put them to work—make more of us," he rationalized, "faster, but with less care to their hands. It's quite brilliant, actually, but with one major flaw . . ."

"And that is?"

"Will to work," the Creator resolved.

"Survival has a tendency to motivate. Not withstanding, a loaded gun will do the same."

"In theory . . ." the Creator quibbled.

"I have witnessed its practice." Pettick disdained this particular conjecture, accosting his detractor. "Rest assured; its execution renders impressive results."

The Creator stepped higher up on the pile, looking down at Pettick, though still losing ground. "But they will lack precision, care. See?" The Creator gestured to one of the workers. The 'Crow turned to Pettick, searching for his command before stepping into the center of the silo. The Creator ripped the nervous Scarecrow to him without care to the 'Crow's articulation of motion, nor his will to move in such directions. Pressing down on the 'Crow's head, he exposed the nape of his neck, presenting it to Pettick who nodded in order to sooner end this demonstration.

"This type of herringbone stitch is not the work of the careless. No, it takes quite a lot of practice to reach this level—" Pettick nodded, stepping carefully out of the pile of straw.

"Your craft, arcane as it may be, like any trade, can be taught," Pettick added. The Creator extricated his hands from the worker, shoving him away with the shooing gesture of his gloves.

"And entrusted to the hands of the enemy?" the Creator inquired, watching Pettick's shift toward the exit, knowing full well he was getting under the prophet's skin.

"You didn't wonder when you refused to take an apprentice that your practice would not have a legacy."

Mawkin entered the silo.

"What is he doing here?" Mawkin inquired, grimacing in the Creator's direction.

"He was just leaving," Pettick assured Mawkin.

"Well, I'll find my way out, then," the Creator hopped down, brushing the residual straw from his cloak. "Don't want to overstay my welcome."

"What's he on about?" Mawkin inquired as they watched the Creator stagger from his stoop in the hay, down the long hall with still exploring hands.

"A play for power—that is all. We all fear losing our place in this world," Pettick huffed, dropping his head to the straw at his shuffling feet. "Petty Rook."

Exhausted from the day's unraveling, Pettick removed his field jacket. The pale dun fibers, once a pungent green, had faded to a rusty brown. He opened the drawer in his desk from which he pulled a manuscript, the very one the Crusaders had brought him, and began to read. He continued searching the drawer for his journal as he moved to his armchair, pulling open the drawer on the side table into which he ran his hand along blindly. After several seconds of searching, Pettick's confusion rose quickly as he noticed the absence of the journal. He shuffled back to his desk and ripped the drawer out of its slot.

"No . . ."

***

Crane huddled atop the water tower as a gust of cool air cut across the brim of the barrel. The valley was quiet. No Scarecrows could be heard or seen. The wind whistled as it pushed its way through the otherwise motionless valley, setting the stage for the leaves' dance. Crane scanned the valley to the hills and the wall of pines. He slid his hand into his rucksack, receding with Pettick's Journal clasped in his trembling fingers. The journal was leather-bound, made of a thick red hide, sealed by the strapped anchor of a brass ball stitched to the front flap. On the bridge of this flap, the initials *J.L.* could be felt, but were otherwise invisible, having been worn away by time and abuse. Crane opened the flap, where the script was bound. The title page contained several areas where words had been scribbled over and rewritten, the depth of the imprint telling of the desperation of the words' erasure. Above these violent scratches a new title was written in ink and read:

THE LIFE AND TIMES OF PETTICK

Crane hung his head skyward, then to the valley, then back to the journal as he turned the page.

CHAPTER XIII: Flint

Reluctantly, Mawkin entered the parlor.

"Sit," Pettick said, offering the chair opposite the desk to Mawkin as he entered the room.

"I'm fine," Mawkin quickly declined.

"Why not?"

"I'd rather stand."

"What if it were an order?" Pettick inquired with the sincerest of weight in his question.

"I'd still prefer standing," Mawkin astutely recoiled.

"But would you sit?"

"Is it an order?"

Pettick chuckled, "It certainly has evolved."

"What's that?"

"Forget it," Pettick exhaled, as if imitating the huff of the Tinker. "I need you to move our good friend James to the Creator's tonight."

"Why?"

"It's time we cash in on our leverage; see what he may have learned from his time with the Tinker," Pettick said.

"I'm not sure this one will simply break," Mawkin said.

"I know Kindle. He's the type to grow an indecent empathy. If we properly motivate Jamie, Kindle will tell us where the fuel is. Worry not, Mawkin, in time you'll see."

"Right—" Mawkin bit his words as he turned to the door.

"Oh, Also—I want you to be there," Pettick added.

Mawkin refused Pettick the satisfaction of a response as he silently disappeared through the doorway, running his hand along the matted golden fibers of his head, and placing his hat atop.

* * *

"How about you, Kindle?" Jamie inquired, picking at his wounds. "What freedoms do you long for?"

"Well, I—I miss the sounds right now—smell of the shop, the oil," Kindle inhaled, jollying, "the roar as you turn over the engine—the sense of it all."

Jamie rested his head against the wall. "That makes two of us. We ever get outta here, first thing I'm doin' is taking ya to a race."

"Race?"

"Yeah—like an automotive race," Jamie gestured holding an invisible steering wheel, fascinated by Kindle's ignorance of the topic. "Stripped down, suped-up Chevys and Roadsters they got tearing down the sand at the shore in Jersey, or in circuits on these tracks. Rum Runners and Swindlers, thrill seekin' kinda folk, good company, long as they're kept at blade's length."

"And what do you do?" Kindle inquired, his curiosity rising, "watch them go by?"

"Yeah."

Kindle grew skeptical, restating, "Going around, on a . . . uh . . . uh—track?"

Jamie nodded, encouraging Kindle as he continued piecing together his sparse human knowledge to gain understanding. Little did Jamie know, Kindle's ignorance was false.

"Yeah—" Jamie pushed, still sensing Kindle's confusion.

"And they watch for what? What for—for pleasure?"

"Yeah, pleasure," Jamie stated.

Through his beard, Kindle let out a low guttural chuckle. "You humans are so strange."

Jamie quipped, with his own aching laugh, "Right back at'cha, boss."

"Can't say I understand, not being behind the wheel." Kindle raised his arms, mockingly gripping the invisible steering wheel, ideas Jamie had thought fell to misunderstanding. "Not helming the clutch," Kindle shook his head as he reached his right glove down, gesturing shifting the clutch and gear stick. "Don't see much pleasure in that," Kindle stated, and Jamie nodded, finding understanding in the fact and the feeling. Kindle sputtered his whiskers as he continued in his race, huffing and spouting the sounds of the speedway. Laughing at the sight, Jamie mimed taking hold of the steering wheel of his own car, giving chase. Kindle pressed the gas, gaining speed, down shifting into a lean as he peeled around a corner, tumbling into a collision. Feigning to his side, Kindle's arms dropped, the roadster vanishing from around him. Jamie spun out, tumbling flat, releasing the chassis around him in the chatter of their jest—whimsy vanished.

"Man, it all makes me think of bein' a kid." His laugh triggered a painful cough. Jamie spat brown sludge, without the dip. "What's yer line, Kindle?"

"Huh?" Kindle arched forward. Bewildered and exhausted, he fell back to his seat against the wall. In the dim light Jamie read the confusion, brushing away the dirt from his jeans as his chest sunk, pressing him back to the wall.

"What's your job? What you do for a livin'? Tinkers do lots of things; you got a specialty?"

"I'm the Mechanic, by trade." With a clever grin, Kindle looked across the cell to find understanding in Jamie's face. "But, I tinker as any Scarecrow with the tools and curiosity may."

In the darkness, a white-toothed grin cut through the dirt and grease. "I have just decided," Jamie declared.

"Oh? What might that be?"

"Me and you, Kindle, we are gonna be friends." Heaving chests settled in the following immeasurable moments of silence. And with silence's inevitable close, Jamie smiled. "Shit, that made me feel like—like I was a kid again. Even for that moment. Thank you."

"I'm happy for it," Kindle offered, in the soft-spoken warmth of his venerable ways.

"When I was a kid, few years north of the depression, though coulda fooled me, coulda fooled lotta people. Well, we didn't have much. Stole a lot to make it by. Least, that's what we always told ourselves. Summer in Philly was rough, crime always up 'cause of the heat and all. So some summers I'd head south—family sent me—had this farm outside of Richmond we used to work." Jamie visualized the scene, the memory of night skies mating the rolling fields of tobacco and bean sprouts materializing before him. "In the fields outside the city, nights were habitable. Didn't swelter, bloat, n' bust holding the heat like the blacktop and brick. There, the nights were cool. But in June, that's when the air was just right, and the fireflies would come to mate." Jamie reached out his hand, stroking the tips of his fingers as if touching a tactile image, a reel playing out the scene, manifesting just above him. "The fireflies would coat the fields in their glow." He licked his swollen lip, clearing his throat. "And us kids would run to catch them—try an' contain 'em in jars and pop bottles—wantin' nothin' more than to take hold of their glow. To posses their emerald and golden sparks. To hold their magic." Jamie cradled one of the sparks in his palm, drawing it from the reel above, bringing memories' glow as a light to the dark shrouding his face.

"Magic," Kindle smiled, though hardly seen in the darkness of his beard, he knew the sentiment was shared.

"Yeah—yeah it was," Jamie continued. "It was the little things then." Kindle exhaled, sharing pleasure in the simple joy memories bring. Jamie choked a slack-jawed laugh, "God, I fucking hate farms."

Affable laughter faded as footsteps approached outside the door, drawing an abrupt silence within the cell. The metal door clanked and growled as it swung open, increasing the amount of light. Jamie looked away, his eyes temporarily blinded, only catching a glimpse of a large Scarecrow marching through the doorway. Through Kindle's subsequent pleads Jamie was able to discern the identity of the large 'Crow as Mawkin. Mawkin lifted Jamie to his feet, dragging him out of the cell into the blurry shifting shapes of the hall. Kindle's voice faded. Jamie flailed his dangling legs into a walk as the rubber of his boots dragged against the concrete. Mawkin ripped him along, the tip of the Scarecrow's firearm pressed into his side. With Mawkin's jarring grip on his neck, Jamie winced down and away, the hazy distorted world growing in its clarity with each passing orb of lamplight. Several yards further down the hall Jamie noticed, through his blurred vision, the doors shifting on his right. He squinted, peering through the light, focusing on each passing cell.

As bars and chains came into focus, faces materialized in the dark spaces between them. Tangled hair shrouded the scarred faces, eyes clearly shined beneath these shadowed veils, marble-white crescents encapsulating dark hues of blue, green, hazel, and brown. For the first time Jamie knew for certain he wasn't alone in his plight. Gasping for air, Jamie stumbled, losing his footing, yet not missing a step as Mawkin ripped him away from reaching hands. Scarred, shaking, gashed skin, hands of flesh pressed through the bars. In the terminating darkness at the end of the hall, Mawkin threw Jamie into the caged thoroughfare, unbolting the chamber's metal seal, releasing him into the night. The grip swiftly returned as a boot's drag rallied clouds of dirt down the path. The open air outside the barn gripped Jamie in an autumnal cold, giving certainty to the measure of Jamie's length of incarceration. Summer's height had come, in all its blister and sweat, and gone.

* * *

The switch of the power was flicked with the long crawl of the Creator's fingers, harkening with a clanking hiss as sharp rays of white-light shone throughout the abattoir. The fixtures' fluorescent tubes flickered before settling with the ambience of a sharp metallic hum. Jamie could only make out the shifting figures, blurred by the newly installed lights that revealed the violent surroundings once left to shadows. As his eyes adjusted, the figures grew in detail and the circumstance he found himself in grew more terrifying. The Scarecrow Mawkin released Jamie to, Thalo, dutifully stripped the weak human of his jacket, peeling skin from skin. The Creator strapped Jamie's arms to the metal table as several other figures filed into the room. Jamie pulled at the stained leather restraints. The metal table was depressed, with a two-inch ridge on every side. In the small of his back Jamie could feel a round risen ridge, the ridge of a drain. He knew what kind of table this was, and what it was used for. Exhausted and immobilized, he took hold of his breathing, trying to remain calm, trying to think straight, to remain right and whole.

Pettick appeared in sinister bliss at the foot of the table. "Good evening, James," Pettick greeted. Jamie spat and several drips of saliva infused with blood seeped into Pettick's threads. Pettick scowled, crossing his face with his jacket sleeve. "Now what did you do that for?"

"So you'll remember me. Some stains just don't wash out." Jamie Condemned, blood spotted spittle on his chin.

Pettick chuckled, moving around the table, leaning inches away from Jamie's face.

Jamie could smell the rot in Pettick's breath and the stink of his moldy cloak.

"Remain calm, Jamie," Pettick derided, adjusting the bridge of his glasses further up his face. "You are a part of a great experiment."

Jamie stared with a furled rage. His body froze as Pettick smiled and, turning to Veidt, ordered, "Bring him in." Pettick watched Jamie's stare widen as the Creator appeared from behind the table and set down a wooden pail. The water in the pail formed a sea that crashed in waves, breaching the brim, falling, collecting in rivulets along the floor.

"It is my understanding that some lesser 'Crows have a soft spot for humans, ignorant to the inherent monsters your species create." The rivers converged, falling through the crusted black- and red-stained perforations of the drain.

"You're one to talk," Jamie scoffed.

"Oh, wonderful, another one with a predilection for sarcasm. Here, let me try something, James—" Pettick began to move around the table like a predator circling its prey, damming the rivers. "You are going to be just fine; you are not going to die tonight—oh no—not at all. Instead you will die a peaceful and dignified death a very long time from now." Pettick coiled like a snake around the table, eventually placing his face next to Jamie's. "How am I doing, James?"

"Terrible," Jamie stated with a crooked smile akin to Pettick's.

The doors swung open with a fierce scream, like that of a hawk. Veidt and Paquin appeared, dragging a limp and beaten Kindle behind them. Pettick said, in strange jest, "See? This is fun! I'm having fun, you're having fun!" Pettick moved away from the table and leaned down to Kindle. "How are you, Kindle? Having fun?" Kindle bit down on his whiskers. Pettick examined the torn patches of straw projecting from Kindle's cheek and brow, though Kindle's chin remained taut. "Nothing?" Pettick meddled with mockingly congenial welts to the shoulder, followed by an even more discomforting embrace. "Come on, old boy!"

The Creator appeared next to Jamie, pushing a metal cart carrying two large tractor batteries and a pile of cables. Kindle looked beyond Pettick, where Jamie matched his gaze. Pettick watched the interaction, swaying his fingers back and forth, tracing the imaginary line of their gaze. As the connection of wills that was their gaze cut away with Kindle's lowered head, Pettick's crossing hands began a giddy clap, jumping back to capture a frame of the room, then closing his arms in, clasping his gloves.

"Fun!" Pettick's rapture echoed through the otherwise silent hall. Remembering one last variable, Pettick looked around the room, and then over to the door. After several seconds he turned back to the Creator who stood impatiently next to Jamie, a cable clamp in each hand.

"Let us begin," the Creator insisted.

Pettick nodded.

Jamie's eyes rolled down to the Creator's polymeric gloves that placed the red handled clamp on the welded ridge of the table. The Creator dipped his glove into the pail, wringing a wet rag that he ran over Jamie's head. A twisted grin etched like ink seeping across the Creator's face. Jamie clenched his hands to the side of the table, pulling his wrists on the leather straps that snared his flesh. The Creator turned to the cart, squeezing the opposite red clamp, which he lowered onto the corroded post of the battery.

The current made contact with the post running into the table. Jamie's torso bounced violently, convulsing atop the metal conductor. His legs kicked violently, though the convulsions were silent. As the Creator released the clamp, the shrieks rose.

"God Fuu-uhh—Fuck!"

"I'm sorry, did he say something?" Pettick chuckled.

"I'll fucking kill you; I swear to Christ!" Jamie screamed. "Fuck you—you fuck!"

Kindle rolled his head, trying to look away, only to find himself staring at Jamie's scarred leather jacket lying before him in a puddle on the floor.

"Again!" Pettick ordered.

The Creator connected the clamp, the current bounced through the air and several sparks burned against the Creator's coat. Jamie's body shot forward as he rose onto the treads of his boots. The convulsions stopped.

"What's wrong?" Pettick inquiringly shot to the Creator.

"I don't know, it worked on the mule till smoke came out its ears."

Kindle looked up at Pettick, letting out a huff of contempt. Veidt returned the sentiment, drawing his fist and throwing a heavy blow to Kindle's face. Jamie's chest heaved for air.

"Veidt, grab his feet," Pettick ordered.

"Nooo—" Jamie screamed.

Veidt tugged on Jamie's left boot. As he reached for the other Jamie kicked Veidt in the face, knocking the Scarecrow to the floor. Jamie's body landed on the metal table, shaking violently. The convulsions continued in a forced oxygenless silence. Mawkin appeared in the doorway, the flares of the sparks igniting the tension in his body that increased as he scanned the room. He took his stance next to Pettick.

"Ah, Mawkin, so glad you could make it; I wanted you to see this," Pettick acknowledged, without missing a glimpse.

The Creator removed the clamp. Screaming broke the silence, harmonized by the violent whimpers of Kindle.

Jamie gasped for air as flares of smoke flowed from the burning patches of cotton and the flesh of his shoulder blades. Jamie's eyes reached Kindle, but Kindle hated this gaze, understanding that Jamie's pleading was not for forgiveness or reprieve, but rather for a silence Kindle was nearly losing.

"Don't you do it—Doaah—" Jamie's words broke through his grinding teeth as the Creator once again brought contact with the current. Mawkin's head turned down to Pettick who let his twisted smile run up to him, waging for a moment before returning to the show.

"Why torture him? Why not ask the question first?" Mawkin asked with a calm melancholy tone.

Pettick craned his head to Mawkin. "Why restate questions, when you can get the answers? Besides, there is a lesson here."

Mawkin saw the glare of the fire in Pettick's glasses, the gleam of madness in his bliss. Pettick took no time to read Mawkin's reaction before turning back to Kindle. The tension of Mawkin's jaw began to sever the patches that had grown invisible in his face.

"This is why you never forget the smell of burning flesh," Mawkin whispered.

Pettick, unremoved from his splendor, gave no response that Mawkin could see. Mawkin remained pensively transfixed as Pettick lowered himself down to Kindle, waiting for the old Tinker to break.

"The fuel?"

"You sick—"

"The fuel, Kindle?"

"In the junkyard under the hoods! I'll give ya the plate numbers—stop—just stop!" Kindle spoke with a tone devoid of solace, turning his head to avoid giving Pettick the satisfaction of reading his face.

"Much obliged." Pettick rose, turning to the Creator. "We're done here."

"Are you sure?" the Creator spoke with an unsatisfied scowl. "Wouldn't require much more time."

"No, let him live . . . for now." Pettick then ordered Mawkin, without looking at the 'Crow. "Clean him up, then get him back to the cell."

"And Kindle?" Veidt asked.

"Bring him to the house, and put him in the fruit cellar. I want to keep a close eye on him."

A sheet of smoke settled atop Jamie's body. As the Creator unstrapped him, his body crumbled to the floor. Pettick turned once more to Mawkin, before disappearing through the swinging doors. Veidt and the other soldiers followed while dragging Kindle, who kept his gaze locked on Jamie as they pulled him away.

"Skinlovers." The Creator said to Mawkin as he wheeled his sadistic toy cart passed, out the pylon doors, appurtenances squeeking and clattering as he went.

Mawkin stood alone, the last Scarecrow in the room. He knelt down, took ahold of Jamie, and lifted him to his feet. Jamie coughed, gasping for air, barely holding his own weight. Jamie's feet dragged as he inched to the door. Mawkin stopped, picking up the leather jacket with his threaded fists; he silently lifted his hand, looked into Jamie's swollen eyes, and handed him his jacket.

* * *

Looks darted through the crowd, filled with guilt and suspicion. Gwyn's hands trembled. Critch took notice of this and, as a worried father, took his daughter's hand. His steady gloves were calming for Gwyn, a paternal shelter, safe. Pettick's words spilled with less than precise measure, slurred and impudent, as he looked down on the crowd.

"This behavior will not be tolerated, I assure you that. So I ask now, only once, that if the journal is returned, and those responsible step forward, they will not be harmed."

Silence lingered over the crowd, a culpable silence—as Pettick read it.

"Should I need implore repentance!? I can only extend this offer here, now, for after—" Pettick's stare rocked downward, his voice a metallic echo through the speakers as he drew the microphone from his face "—there will be consequences."

Critch could feel Gwyn's hand start to tremble again. A flock of Flying Crows flew over, catching Pettick's attention. The shadows cut through the faces of the crowd. Pettick considered many words over the following moments of silence, wanly giving a final resonating word: "Please." Pettick turned silently from the crowd, exiting the stage. Stepping down off the last step, Pettick started directly for the house.

Mawkin, watching every movement, was silent, rueful.

"I'd better not find out you had anything to do with this," Pettick said to Mawkin in passing.

Veidt followed Pettick up the hill, hopping at his heel. "Pettick, wait! Is there anything you want us to do about it?"

"We wait this out; let the accusations begin."

Veidt fell back as Pettick continued to the house. With Pettick at a distance, a wildfire of discourse spread through the crowd.

"I don't understand. Why?" Gwyn said, looking innocently up at her father.

"Neither do I," Critch responded. "Neither do I." Gwyn and Critch split off from the bustling gossip of the crowd and started down the path back to the village, their gloves still tightly clasped, their arms swinging with their stride. Critch glanced down at his daughter, reading the worry on her face. "Something I should know?"

"No." Gwyn's hair fell around her face as she shook her head. "Why?"

The caring father did not sway his gaze from his daughter. "What's eating at you? You're my daughter; I know when something is wrong." Worse to the worry in Critch's chest, Gwyn did not respond for several minutes.

Gwyn's silence broke with her head tilting up to her father. "I wish you could pick me up, carry me home. I miss that."

"So do I, Gwyn." Critch smiled, tightening his grip as their arms swung and they strolled down the path.

Pettick crossed slowly down the stairs before cutting right into the dining room. The room remained unchanged over the past several months, since Pettick had last entered its hallowed walls. The chairs where he and Mawkin had sat now displayed two layers of dust in different levels of encroachment. Pettick ran the finger of his glove along the top of the table, drawing in the dust, which accumulated on his fingertip. Stagnant residue draped along the finely beveled edges of the cabinet. Pettick opened the framed glass door which did not concede to its purpose without reluctance. Glasses were lined in separate rows based on size, and had remained that way, an artifact of the last human's touch. Pettick scanned the glasses, twiddling his fingers as he turned around, searching the room for a tray. The silver-lined handles of the tray still shined through patina as Pettick ripped it from beneath a row of candlesticks, moving back to the cabinet, and stacking as many glasses as would fit atop the tray.

In the kitchen Pettick turned the knob on the sink. The spigot sputtered until, like a broken dam, the calcium seal bloated, then burst, and tarnished water flowed freely, gradually purifying from rank brown sludge to clear unalloyed fluid over the course of its flow. Pettick filled each glass to its brim before carefully carrying them on the tray from the counter to the stairs. After Pettick reached the top he began placing glasses sporadically and strategically around his quarters and then in the parlor. The glasses of water plotted the bookshelves, the windowsill, the desk, the study. Pettick placed the final glass, then sat behind his desk. The parlor was quiet and he was alone. Hours passed with the clock's tick-tock, yet never did the rook stir from its perch.

* * *

May 7, 1947

Tucker asked me to make him a scarecrow, for the fields were rampant with crows, our "black-beaked devils" as he refers to them. So I gathered my materials—a bale of hay, an old broomstick, some of Tucker's son's worn flannel, trousers, and boots (big boots). I bound its legs with twine and, stuffing it full, saw its legs burst with the frayed hairs of straw. Tucker's son was a conscripted sailor, so I had his knit sweater. I stuffed it full of the straw as well till the chest bulged. I set my friend upon a fence post pike amid the seeded till-lines abutting the creek. It was garish and base, but I figured it'd do. "Mawkin!" I declared his namesake, and smiled at my new friend, who did not return such a gesture back to me. Instead, its head fell limp, which made it look quite sad—pathetic even. I sympathize with my new friend.

Crane closed the journal and hastily stuffed it, along with several loose handwritten pages, into his rucksack and pulled out another book as Gwyn scaled the beams of the water tower. Breaching the top, she crawled across the barrel to where Crane sat reading.

"Hey!" Crane feigned surprise.

"Hey." Gwyn lifted Crane's arm, burrowing herself into his side and wrapping his arm around her. "What's that?"

"A book."

"A book?" Gwyn shot him a look, calling Crane out on the vague simplicity of his response. "What book?"

"*Twenty Thousand Leagues Under the Sea*," Crane abruptly replied.

"Oh, what's it about?"

Crane flipped through the pages of illustrated text, rolling the binding between his gloves. "Humans and monsters," he said, handing it to Gwyn.

"Is it any good?" She thumbed through it, stopping on a page that pictured several men fighting off a giant squid. The tentacles of the squid were constricting one mariner, who, wielding a hatchet, was fighting valiantly for his survival. Gwyn closed the book, handing it back to him.

"Real good." Crane bobbed his head.

"That *all* you been reading?" Gwyn asked. She watched the arching of his back and felt the strain and release of his threads.

"Well—no," Crane said.

"What else have you been reading?" Gwyn shook Crane's arm. "What else, Crane?"

Crane broke his stare from the sky down to Gwyn, their faces only inches apart.

"Just—books about monsters," Crane said.

Gwyn nodded silently, waiting. "All right," Gwyn quietly sighed.

Crane returned his stare to the valley; To Gwyn, Crane's solipsism grew, a tired game.

"There was a town meeting this morning," Gwyn said. "You missed it."

Crane was silent, still, and getting good practice at hiding the truth—he was scared.

"Someone stole Pettick's Journal."

"Don't figure he just lost it?"

"Don't figure," Gwyn said. A lone cloud passed in front of the sun, leaving the colony in a gray-wash for several minutes. "He's pretty adamant about getting it back. He's not going to take kindly to whoever took it."

"Right." Crane's head dropped. Gwyn ran her fingers along the plaid lines on Crane's flannel arm.

"You didn't, did you?" Gwyn inquired.

"No," Crane quickly replied.

The two remained silent as cool-edged winds cut across the field.

* * *

Water came from an overturned glass, seeping through the cracks of the floorboard, dripping into the fruit cellar. Kindle used these drips to count the passing time, calculating the span between drips, and using that increment to measure the passing hours. The sun was the only other way to gauge the passage of time, as the light moved through the visible cracks late in the day. Kindle appreciated the light. Though minute, it was better than the complete darkness of his previous cage. The footsteps that crossed the cellar door left a map that Kindle could trace as a large Scarecrow circled above, pacing for several minutes before moving to the cellar door, where it began its descent. The figure then stood for several moments outside the door, and a heavy exhaust of air could be heard before the door unlatched. Light spread as Mawkin appeared in the doorway.

"Makwin, what do you want?"

"I need to know what this is."

"What?"

"What is this? Tell me what it is." Mawkin shot forward, handing the tube to Kindle, who examined it. Kindle's gloves ran along the tube pressing against the ends where a black powdered resin clung to the tips of his fingers.

"It's a flare—a chemical candlestick, essentially. It ignites fires—rather dangerous with this drought we got here." Mawkin's face fell to his feet, an occurrence the 'Crow did little to conceal. "Mawkin, where did you find this?" Mawkin took back the flare. "Where did you find it?" Mawkin turned his back to Kindle, leaving himself unguarded. "It was in his parlor, wasn't it?"

Mawkin's silence sounded louder than many 'Crows' screams.

Kindle swayed as Mawkin started for the door.

"Let me come with you," Kindle pleaded. "I can help you."

Mawkin turned his back, opening the cell door.

"He won't take kindly to traitors, you know, Mawkin. Mawkin?"

Mawkin slammed the door.

"Mawkin!" The echoes of the contact resonated for several moments. His footsteps moved quickly, driven and heavy, even still, they dissipated, eventually trailing off.

* * *

Seemingly out of place at the edge of the crops stood a table with two chairs, in which sat Pettick and Herb, the Head of Agriculture—strategists in nature's battlefield.

"We have to wait," Herb stated.

"What do you mean, wait?" Pettick leaned back in his chair.

"We cannot harvest now; most of it will wither as soon as it leaves the soil. We should keep it in the ground for longer and—"

"And hope that a good rain comes?!" Pettick voraciously interjected.

"Yes." Herb nodded, folding his gloves, resting his forearms on the table.

"I do not lend much to hope." Pettick abruptly stood and turned toward the field, distancing himself from the table.

"I know you don't," Herb muttered, expecting a more composed response.

"What?"

"Nothin'."

Pettick stared into the field. He raised his pointer and middle fingers to his lip, inhaling as if pulling a drag on a non-existent cigarette. After several moments, he grew aware of his fingers' tick and dropped his glove to his side. He continued to stare into the field, willing a different outcome, though it remained unchanged.

* * *

Mawkin advanced down the narrow cellblock in the silo barn. Upon reaching a cell halfway down the hall, he abruptly halted and turned to face it. Sliding the metal slot in the door, he peered into the peephole then down the hall where a guard, Dirk, one of Pettick's most eagerly loyal 'Crows, stood watch. Mawkin looked down at the padlock. The lock was silver-coated and garishly ornate, sticking out against the door of forged sheet metal. Mawkin dug his glove into his pocket, retrieving a ring of two dozen various keys. Thumbing through the selection, he found the matching brass key. The sound of shifting metal echoed down the narrow shaft as he unlocked the door. Dirk took notice, stirring from his post. He began heading towards Mawkin.

"Mawkin, where are you taking this prisoner?"

"Are you questioning me?" Mawkin stated with the full resonance of his deep register, slowing the gaurd's advance.

Dirk stuttered, receding for a moment before gaining disillusions of courage.

"I didn't get approval from Pettick on this. I'll have to ask you to—" The stutter worsened. "Pettick specifically told—" Mawkin's elbow collided with the 'Crow's face, causing his body to silently collapse to the floor. Taking no pleasure in the result of this interaction, Mawkin opened the cell door. In the corner, Jamie lay in a heap, coughing.

"Come on, let's go," Mawkin ordered.

"Do I have a choice?" Jamie wheezed, rising to his feet with the support of the wall against his shoulder.

Mawkin cautiously approached Jamie, curious as to why the human kept his hands concealed. Pulling Jamie into the light, Mawkin noticed that Jamie's hands had been tightly bound, and now were turning a dark purple and black. Makwin pushed Jamie out the door. Jamie leaned against the wall, his head resting against the door of the opposing cell. Looking back he caught his first blurred glimpse of the guard on the floor. Mawkin came back to the guard's body, dragged him into the cell, and sealed the door.

"Is that how you treat all your company?" Jamie snickered, blood dripping from his slack jaw atop encrusted layers of old spittle.

"Shut it." Mawkin grabbed Jamie's jacket as he hastily pulled him down the hall like a wayward mutt.

Crane appeared small beneath the cool starry night. He felt small, too, wrapping the blue denim jacket around him he had recently acquired from Kindle's loft. It was an artifact he recognized from his reading. He examined the embroidery contained within a patch on the chest. The red-and-white patch read the name CHANEY in an oil-stained red thread. The passing wind turned the pages of the journal sitting on his lap. Crane continued to read, rapt, and yet scared of the sympathies and hatred he garnered with the words he read.

The ink on the page, sloppy and erratic, left scarred indentations on the opposite pages of the journal. He felt the scars with the tips of his fingers.

October 29, 1947

I was standing on the ridge overlooking the world—my world—when I turned, and there she was, strawberry locks blown sideways, wingtip heels sinking among the weeds, looking at me with those sad green eyes which glinted and swelled, glazing over as she stared. I've never felt so dissected before, this gaze, a silent diatribe. In her silence she asked of my actions. How I could be the man I was—and what was I becoming. She was scared; I did not want that for her—I never wished that for her.

"John, what are you doing?" she asked.

"Look what I built for you. Do you like it—our kingdom of straw?" I spoke with excitement overlooking the ridge at the dozens of scarecrows I had made.

She backed away from me.

And then she screamed.

There were words on these pages, but they had been blotched out in thick layers consisting of thousands of lines of lead and ink. Crane continued to the next legible words.

I grew aware of my feet and the place where I stood. At the crossroads, the path that bisected the fields of the farm, was an old beech tree, its branches—arms with a thousand elbows—jutting and swooping a hundred different ways. The leaves were of autumn's hues, but not just gold or red, but orange and purple, all on a single branch. Peering ahead, I had to, at first, question what my eyes saw, as they so often lie. A man stood there, lounging in the shadowy eaves of the aged beech tree. He was a tall cypher of a fellow, and the shadows cast over any memorable part of what I could perceive. He lit a cigarette, causing smoke to emanate from his palm like the magician he could very well be. I did not sway from this place, as if caught in the crosshairs of a hunter and afraid to move. Yet he raised his chin to me. I fell to my knees, and the crows landed on the road before me, two blackbirds, with the blackest eyes. They mocked and slanted, rooks which bartered with cunning precision. I struck a deal. An exchange, worth ten years—and a chance for the world. A world made straight, righteous, clean. The porous sand, this rust clay of the road, sifted through my fingers. Looking up at the tree, where the man stood no more, they pecked my eyes, and then I could see everything.

The air was waxy, thick, and the scent of the salt down my face smelled of the sea. I was not alone. There was a resounding snap. They dropped from the pikes, the scarecrows through the fields, breaking the binding of their posts. There were screams and caws, a flocking rally of freaks. My friends.

* * *

Barlow sat on the edge of the stage, the manuscript *A History of Scarecrow* resting on his lap. The meeting ground was empty at midnight. An old world surrounded him, and this he felt; it seemed calm, but Barlow sensed the coming chaos in the winds. He fanned through the pages he had typed, running his fingers along certain segments as if trying to blot out the ink. Tilting his head from the pages, he glanced at the brush between the meeting ground and the toolshed. Standing on his aching feet, he began walking toward the brush, the stack of papers in hand. Barlow pulled back the brush revealing thickets of weeds and thorns which had gathered to form a brier atop the stone well. It had been sealed with a set of wooden planks, which had long since rotted. The boards screamed a low resonating wail as the old 'Crow pressed against them, sliding the lid off the edge of the orifice.

In the exposed gash, damp air met the dry stagnant air in a waltz, before dissipating in a pungent rot that was sweet and slightly resembled petrichor. Barlow glared down at this empty wound. He clenched the papers, raising them just high enough to breach the gap. His dry gloves tore into the paper. A gentle wind blew silently. Barlow released his grip and the manuscript descended into the well, parting into hundreds of black-and-white raindrops as the pages fell.

Jamie continued to stumble and drag his feet as Mawkin wrenched him further along the orchard's western edge. Jamie looked down at the path which he had failed to notice was now covered with tall stalks of ferns and wild grass. Jamie looked up. Before him were the long beams of the incomplete fence just barely standing out from the brush of the surrounding south forest.

"Where are we goin'?" Jamie asked.

Mawkin remained silent.

"Where we goin'?" Jamie slowly repeated, the vowels of his speech thin from the gathering hysteria collecting in his throat.

Mawkin stopped, releasing his grip on Jamie. Jamie barely remained standing as he fell to one knee, then rose back to his feet.

"Naah, man," Jamie pleaded, knowing that this was where he was to meet his end. "You can't do this—you can't, please—please."

Mawkin tilted his gaze away from his prisoner, settling for a moment on the sky.

"Please!" Jamie's plea grew guttural.

Mawkin unsheathed his knife. The blade shined in the moonlight. Jamie remained standing, his gaze locked on the dark voids beneath Mawkin's brow. Mawkin approached Jamie, holding the knife at his side. He grabbed Jamie's arm, throwing him forward.

"Not like this—" Jamie cried silently skyward.

Mawkin ran the blade parallel to Jamie's arm, quickly slashing upward, severing the rope that bound him. Jamie stepped forward, both Scarecrow and Man exhausting a heavy breath similar in their mark of relief. They matched glances. All was resolute. Mawkin's face read void of tension, a face Jamie never saw before.

"Go," Mawkin nearly whispered.

Jamie continued staring. "Why?"

Mawkin was silent. Jamie read the answer on the 'Crow's face as it grew tense, collecting shadows. "There's a gap, 'bout quarter mile up, head south, stay near the creek—settlement not too far off."

Jamie silently nodded before pressing into the night. Looking back briefly, he could still see Mawkin's figure lingering at the edge of the orchard.

Barnes closed his book as he swayed with the stalks of grain down the path. The air was thick, as was the silence. He could sense something in the surrounding patch, cause to his trembling "crawl down the spine" sense of being watched.

"Hello?" His voice dropped.

Silence.

A breeze passed over the stalks of grain, sending a wave of moonlight shimmering over the tuft. Barnes looked back down at his book, which the moon embossed with the title *The Strange Case of Dr. Jekyll and Mr. Hyde.* A stick snapped in the grass ahead, stealing Barnes's attention. Barnes slowly stepped back, starting up the path. The stalks beside him shifted, sending an overwrought Barnes (and several Flying Crows) up into the night. Barnes picked up his book from the path, brushing the dirt off, shrugging his shoulders, thankful for the lack of witnesses to his embarrassment. His head cocked, shaking off the jitters. As he turned, a hand grabbed his arm with force, sending him skyward again. The hand belonged to Barlow.

"Come with me," Barlow ordered hastily.

"What's wrong?"

"We need to find Mawkin."

The two Scarecrows trudged quickly up the path.

Pettick approached the door to the parlor. Lowering his hand to the knob, he noticed light bleeding from under the door. He sighed, knowing what awaited him, then turned the knob and entered the room. The door shut. Pettick turned to the coatrack standing in the corner behind the door. Removing his field jacket, he hung it on the hook and the diluted yellow waves of light further aged the jacket from its former green. Pettick remained by the door.

"Mawkin," Pettick somberly uttered, still fixated on his jacket, wiping dirt from a warn patch on the sleeve.

Mawkin hung, silently posted by the window. Pettick's post. "Pettick." His head rose to the small piece of night framed in the window. Pettick scanned the room, shifting to the bookshelf.

"Was I expecting you?" Pettick asked.

"For long now," Mawkin softly replied, his heavy gaze still locked out to the stars, continuing, "you were." Pettick nodded. The Scarecrows stood in silence, both drowning in their thoughts. "You once told me this was paradise; that we were truly blessed."

"Yes, I recall—"

"Do you believe that? Did you *ever* believe that?" Mawkin stated with greater skepticism than inquiry.

"I suppose."

Mawkin tilted his gaze toward Pettick. "For a 'Crow so cast in black and white, that answer was rather gray."

"Suppose it is," Pettick said.

"Why did you need us to hate them as much as you do?" Mawkin asked. "The humans, I mean."

Pettick was silent.

Mawkin shook his head. Pettick continued to set his gaze on every other place in the room. Mawkin turned back to look at the lights of the village in the distance. "Did you ever think this would work?"

"What?" Pettick asked.

"This—all of this," Mawkin said.

"Is it not?" Pettick said. Mawkin turned his shoulder back, looking at Pettick who quickly looked away.

"There is no need for lies. I had hoped you'd leave that part of you, then and now." Mawkin turned back to the window. Pettick ran his fingers along the books, stopping at a red bound gold-trimmed book that he slid from its place. Mawkin peered into the window changing his gaze to the reflection of Pettick behind him. "It never could have worked." Pettick placed the book on the edge of the shelf.

"When did we stop seeing eye to eye?" Pettick recoiled.

"Did we ever?" Mawkin rhetorically stated.

"I'd like to believe we did once."

"I have no fondness for illusions."

"Neither do I."

"Some would disagree," Mawkin said, gesturing out the window. "Or is that it, you have forgotten it is an illusion; you, most of all."

"For a 'Crow so ignorant, you speak of things you don't understand with such an earnest eye." Pettick curiously bobbed his head, thinking on the reading Mawkin had been doing. "Commendable."

"I don't lie. I see it for what it is—should I not?"

"Do not—"

"Do not what?" Mawkin uttered. "Stand between you and your desires?"

"My wants are nothing." Pettick said.

"Your wants are everything!" Mawkin broke his low register.

Pettick cut away from Mawkin, recoiling. "And you know nothing of them."

"Then tell me—be honest," Mawkin beseeched. "What could it be you want?"

"Honest? Is the truth not inherent in my answers?"

Mawkin paused, staring at Pettick.

Pettick flashed a rebutting smile. "Sarcasm." Pettick said as he began a slow stroll around the perimeter of the room. "Honestly, Mawkin . . ."

"Yes, honestly."

"I wished," Pettick said, before correcting himself, "I *wish* for friendship—for kinship."

Mawkin exhausted his chest, gasping for words that unexpectedly fled. "Aren't they?" Mawkin gestured toward the village.

Pettick turned back to Mawkin, looking directly to him, without any false smirks or didactic personas. "Were you not?"

Mawkin stepped back, registering the sincerity in Pettick's utterance. "Not what I know of friendship," the large 'Crow said, swaying in thought. "But then, you call them friends."

"Out there on that platform I address my people," Pettick responded with opened palms lifted skyward.

"You order followers, who follow a shepherd out of hunger and fear—fear you place upon them. You burned own. You burned your own kind."

"And they follow in numbers," Pettick scoffed with a crooked frown, peeling his hands inward to a clasp.

"Then you've got it all," Mawkin sorrowfully reveled. "Everything you wished for."

"What have you been reading?" Pettick thought aloud as he turned to look out to the window where Mawkin's reflection stood beside him. Mawkin lifted his hat from his head, releasing his tarnished golden hair onto his brow. He ran the brim of his hat through the fingers of his gloves, looking down to this hat as he placed it in the ceremonious precision of a hunter, atop Pettick's desk. Mawkin's reflection vanished from the window. Pettick sighed away from his lone reflection.

"Why, Mawkin—why are you the one who has to?" The two 'Crows grew closer in their discourse.

"Because of you—because whatever good was in you is long gone. You said to Jamie, one can not live in past good," Mawkin resolved. Pettick nodded, then he raised his head to match Mawkin's gaze.

"I am sorry, old friend," Pettick uttered, his words seeming to linger.

"Aye, friend, so am I."

Pettick shifted, a flare falling down his sleeve and into his hand, he swiftly lunged forward, pressing into Mawkin.

Mawkin shuttered as he grew limp for a moment. An object fell from his left hand, a knife. He then grabbed Pettick. He looked down at Pettick's hand within him, then back up to see the fire in Pettick's framed glasses. The blank stare those pits gave back was both heartless and heartfelt.

"This is why you never forget the smell of burning flesh," Pettick said as his hand twisted, then quickly recoiled. As Pettick stepped away the flare began to glow within Mawkin. The fire spread quickly. Reaching out, Mawkin's glove clenched, tearing at Pettick's neck. Pettick prized away, the patch of threads severing, exposing flesh beneath the layers of veiling straw. Mawkin's gaze remained on Pettick's black pitted eyes, eyes of anger and pity framed with straw and glass, masked by flares of blue and yellow refractions. The flames silently engulfed Mawkin's body.

ACT III: THE AUTUMN

CHAPTER XIV: Eulogies

An autumnal gust cut steel cold, slashing saturate red and yellow leaves from the trees and sending them perilously to the ground. Crane shot from the meeting grounds, his feet barely touching the dirt as he dashed through the hazel stalks of the field, though even with voices fading, the words chased. "Mawkin is dead!" The crowd's gasps filed in close pursuit. "A human attacker—a human who broke free and made an attempt on my life. And Mawkin, our dear valiant Mawkin, perished saving me. I narrowly escaped, and I did not come out unscathed." Pettick peeled back the wrapping from his neck, revealing a patch of torn straw, earning a respectable reaction of disgust and dismay from his audience. "I only regret that I was unable to stop him, I wasn't strong enough and he is out there, friends, he is out there, and I have no doubt in my conscious mind that he does intend to return to finish the job."

The crowd's whispers rose.

"So now I tell you this in hopes that I will be joined, that you will join me, by my side. Our militia is small, but I know in your hearts, in my heart, our numbers may grow. I have feared these words, but I will use them for I now feel it necessary to declare it." Pettick shuddered. "We are at war."

The crowd exploded with cries of outrage, of human vilification. Barlow remained at the meeting ground as the final 'Crows scattered to the village. Neither son in sight, he found himself alone, frozen in the center of the grounds like a scarecrow.

Crane huddled small on the water tower. He unfurled his arms reaching down into the rucksack, and retrieving Pettick's Journal, which he held tightly in his grasp—the perilous object he couldn't allow himself to let go. He opened the binding, using the string marker to flip near the end of the book, and continued to read.

Gwyn could see Crane's unresponsive figure outlined at the top of the water tower. She pressed through the grass, wrapping herself in her cardigan as she reached the open plain of the ridge where the wind whirled and chimed, and screamed, and died, only to do it all again.

Gwyn ascended the tower and sat beside Crane, who remained an impalpable monument overlooking the farm.

"You ran off so quickly," Gwyn said softly. "I couldn't follow."

"That was the point," Crane said.

"Was it?" Gwyn sighed. "Running? From me?" Crane remained silent. Gwyn looked hard at Crane's silhouette. "What is it? What is eating away at you?"

Crane remained silent.

"Crane, tell me the truth."

"The truth—" Crane huffed—the huff of his father—turning away. "What do you want from me, Gwyn?"

"To be around me—I want you to be with me." Gwyn's tone grew less gentle, almost paternal, rigid in flux and tone. "Stop hiding up here like a child!" Gwyn looked for a reaction in Crane's face. "I don't live to yearn for your validation or your happiness, Crane. I can't be the only thing that grounds you. I'm here for you, but that has to go both ways. You have to at least try and find the good in us, even with all that has happened."

"I don't hide from you," Crane dismissed.

"Yes, you do."

"You know where I am."

"No, I don't. Your body is here but you're somewhere else, somewhere in the stars, and why should I have to find you?"

"'Cause I'm trying to keep you safe," Crane said.

"Safe? Safe from what?"

"Me."

"What's so dangerous about you that I don't already know?" A realization washed over Gwyn, all doubt ebbing with it. "You have it, don't you?"

Crane looked away, then shifted slowly, pulling his hand around to reveal the journal. Gwyn looked down at the book, then up at Crane's face where she locked steadily on his cheek, in the same place where her hand laid heavy and remained for several moments.

"It's all right—all right." Gwyn said.

"But I lied to you," Crane sighed.

"I know," Gwyn responded with a firm and earnest face, concealing the anger and the hurt, knowing the expression of it would be of no use.

"I lied to you—that's not all right." Crane said.

Crane swayed away again. Gwyn immediately pulled Crane into her as he broke down, steadily crumbling.

"We'll be all right—we'll be all right." Gwyn cradled Crane as he burrowed into her. A cold wind blew over the ridge.

Gwyn gripped the leather skin of the journal, taking the weight of its binding. "We need to find a place to keep this; he can't find us with it." Crane nodded, perceptively reading into the weight of Gwyn's use of the word *us*.

Gwyn slid her glove across the ridges of their carved initials. Pulling open the one-foot diameter lid on the top of the barrel of the tower, Gwyn and Crane peered down into the stagnant black water which gave no reflection. Spanning the structure, a beam rose from the still, black sheet. She leaned into the hole, resting the journal delicately centered on the ledge. Gwyn looked up at Crane's nodding approval before sealing the barrel.

The light entered through the slot, an object falling through, chased by the returning blackness. Kindle moved to the object, picking it up and rolling it in his hand; there was a hollow bounce to its weight. It was a long tube. The door broke open, offering a blinding ray of milky light, which bathed over Kindle, before a figure appeared, blocking the light from reaching him.

"Mawkin?"

"What's left is dust," the figure replied. Kindle felt helpless beneath the dark figure looming above. The light surrounding the figure gathered, drawing lines and shapes in shadows, revealing Pettick.

"Your presence is never good news, is it Pettick?"

Pettick's initial reply was another terminal grin. Kindle shifted further into the cell as Pettick entered the room. "You leave me little choice. When you act like a rabid dog, I must treat you like one."

"Oh, is that it?"

"Precisely it," Pettick said as he took a seat on the stool across from Kindle.

"Tell me something, Pettick, when did we all become the enemy to you?"

Pettick found amusement in Kindle's postulation. "You have me all wrong, Kindle—I am not your enemy."

"Well, from where I'm sitting, one can't help but question."

"Yes, now as for you," Pettick concurrently assured, "you are a hostile." He adjusted his position on the stool. "As a traitor of your kind, and a reputable one at that, you must be treated as such."

"I'm not one of your simpletons; don't talk to me as one."

Pettick smirked. "Fine, then." He knelt to the floor and lifted the tube into his glove. "Few could have known what this is, and it was no mystery our friend Mawkin wasn't the brightest of the bushel—"

"Your point?" Kindle interrupted.

"He came to you looking for answers. And the worst part—"

"The worst part?" Kindle inquired, entertaining Pettick's need for such conjecture.

"You were right." If ever a more decrepit grin were flashed, Pettick used his well-trained smirk. "I'll let you keep this, as a little reminder." Pettick tossed the used flare casing to Kindle, but it lay unattended in his lap. "I have another up in my desk drawer, and I'm saving it for you."

The smirk slithered away as Pettick rose, turned back to the door, and swiftly disappeared into the searing light which faded behind him, leaving Kindle alone in the gloom of his cell.

"Fuck," Kindle muttered with a slurred drawl, disconcertingly burying his hands in his gloves.

* * *

With the fading minutes of the sun's intensity, a yellow luster danced across the grass, lining the fields. Shepherd's flock gathered, grazing on the scant traces of remaining green beneath the Perfect Tree. A stranger, one of recent memory, approached.

"Well, if it isn't good, handsome Shepherd guarding his handsome flock," Jasper bundled her floral brushed shawl, being sure to expose the finely sewn gold buttons adorned at the fabric's ends. Shepherd expanded his widest grin.

"How are you—truly?" Jasper asked.

"Oh, I am well. And yourself?"

"Well, to be frank and honest, I'm feelin' . . . tired."

"We are no fresh harvest these days," Shepherd said.

"Speak for yourself!" Jasper laughed with a joy that faded in a cadence of shallow breaths. Her hold on the bulging threads of her chest firmed.

"Are you sure you are all right?" Shepherd extended a glove to Jasper, offering to hold her hand. "I would be more than happy to help you home; my flock tend not to wander by day," he said, sharing the balance of his crook.

"Oh no—no, I can make this walk myself, thank you kindly." Jasper shuffled in the direction of the village, repaying Shepherd's kindness with a smile before starting down the hill.

"It is a beautiful day," Shepherd said, basking in the light.

Jasper stopped and turned toward the sun, joining in Shepherd's view. "Truly." A smile crossed her face. "Most whittle the weather down to only small talk. But you are always genuine with its happenings. I like that about you, Shepherd."

"Always, Jasper," Shepherd said, bowing his head, concealing the heavy grip he took on his staff. "I'm so glad I had a chance to see you."

"I as well," Jasper said, giving Shepherd a last look before turning toward the village.

Jasper could hear Shepherd's voice as it traveled toward her, carried by the warm waves. "Farewell, Jasper." Offering a comforting smile, he remained, sentinel to his flock. In time, Jasper's figure vanished into the wan sheen of the reeds. "Farewell."

* * *

Word of Jasper's passing broke at dawn the following morning. Gwyn sat at her worktable, staring at the empty seat. The station across from her was as immaculately clean as it always was by this time of day. Gwyn refrained from moving from this place of mourning for several minutes past the dismissal bell before Mare arrived to retrieve her.

"Come, dear, or we'll be late."

"What's the rush? If she's anywhere, she's here. Last one out—right?" Sullen, Gwyn's words were soft and void of any reproach.

"Right." Mare's glove clenched the gathering folds of Gwyn's cardigan.

"Not going to be the same without her, ya know . . ."

"Yeah, I know."

The majority of the village congregated downwind of the Perfect Tree in the winding patch of brittle wildflowers—common dandelions, sharp hepatica and purple dead-nettle. The phlox garden was scattered with several artifacts of its human past, marked by headstones dating back to the time of "this land's great revolution" or "emancipation," dependent on its proclaimer. Gwyn heard little of the wisdoms sowed over the departed, more trite coercions to reason, to understanding "the cycle of life and all its fortitude." Gwyn's palm glided down her blouse, from her bosom to the wrapped layers of her wool skirt, running the fingers of her glove along the stitching of her leather belt, a product of Jasper's generosity and ardor, a true eulogy. Her glove dropped to her side, falling into that of another 'Crow's. She looked beside her. Crane held her hand tightly, cradling it, his fingers wrapped around hers. She felt the warmth of his presence.

A fluttering *thwap-thwap-thwap-thwap* sounded from above, along with the caw of a distant bird. The arc of the collectively risen chins directed to the western sky, where a shiny bird with a carcass of metal spliced the heavens, hovering, suspended in defiance of gravity. Pettick brought his glove over his glasses, peering up at this spec, a dual-prop plane, a blemish in the cloudless blue of his sky.

Barlow stepped beside Barnes, both catching an acknowledging glance at one another's presence before Barnes looked back at the sky. Barlow watched as Gwyn and Crane, hand in hand, strolled down the hill. Barnes took notice of his father's longing.

"Come on, Pop." Barnes led his father off.

Pettick stepped into Barlow's path. "We have work to do, Reader."

"Not today, we don't." Barlow wrapped his arm around his son. "My boy and I are going to spend some quality time together." He gestured at the surrounding garden. "Surely you can understand."

"Fair, but soon." Pettick cocked his head, bowing out of Barlow's way.

"Yes, soon." Barlow nodded.

Up the hill, Shepherd watched from a distance, though it would not be recorded that he had attended.

Crane and Gwyn wandered aimlessly from the garden, further down the path, to the bend of the creek just downstream of the bridge. Gwyn moved ahead as Crane glanced back up the hill to see the remains of the lost being scattered and taken by the winds. Gwyn stood atop a rock beside the creek. To Crane, Gwyn's figure shimmered against the horizon like a lighthouse to a sailor longing for shore—an idea, a feeling Crane had only read about but was now palpable to him. He pulled her beside him. She stood resilient in her distance.

"I didn't expect you to come," Gwyn said with a slight veneer grin cornering her cheek, trying to hide how truly relieved and surprised she was to see him, though still visibly distraught.

"You didn't?" Crane exhaled, not knowing what to say to Gwyn's persisting dislocation.

"No."

"Strange—I never really left." Crane laughed, but Gwyn did not share in the sentiment. Crane stumbled for comforting words.

"You're sweet, Crane," Gwyn passively stated.

"I know."

"And humble," she added, the slightest smile on her cheek.

"Yeah, that too."

Gwyn's sorrows faded. "I gotta ask you something."

"What is it?" Crane asked, seeing that the question weighed heavy on Gwyn, giving her pause, in a moment of hesitance. "I'm no tin man; I know what I think and I know what I feel."

"Yeah, that's well and good, Crane, but we are not kids anymore; we eventually have to take responsibility for the things we feel," Gwyn asserted, seriousness in her heart. "Do you love me?"

"I love you," Crane replied without hesitation.

***

Barlow sat, a statue of a scarecrow in thought, before Pettick's desk in the parlor. The space was still. The typewriter remained as it had, on the desk across the room, though no papers sat beside it or within it's typeset. Pettick's desk was cluttered with the usual stacks of books. The room was as it always was save the Reader in his seat who remained in thought for what might have been hours. Voices could be heard from the stairs and then became clear as they came to the hall. Pettick entered, stopping at the door.

"Wait here," Pettick ordered to the 'Crows behind him who turned and retreated down the hall. Pettick entered the room, closing the door behind him. "What is it now, Barlow?" Pettick remained by the door, scanning the room before returning to Barlow.

"I'm done. I'm through, Pettick," Barlow said.

"Excuse me?" Pettick asked.

"You heard me."

Pettick's chest sunk slightly as he looked around the room again, stopping at the typewriter. Pettick stepped forward toward the typewriter then cut across the room around the desk where he looked at Barlow, then down at the desk, opening the drawer before him. The fibers in Pettick drew taut as he pressed the fingers of his glove against the wooden bottom of the drawer.

"Where is it?" Pettick asked.

"Where it will never be read," Barlow said.

Pettick pressed his hands to his face, then tugged his chair, taking a seat, placing the weight of his arms on the desk. Pettick chuckled. "I can just write it myself, so there is no merit in your rebellion."

Barlow remained still. Pettick's false grin dimmed from his face.

"Then it will be a product of your hand—your words, not mine," Barlow said.

Pettick dropped his left hand, pushing himself back from the desk. The two remained this way for a moment before Pettick stood from his seat, shaking his head.

"Why, old 'Crow? Why? What makes you so mad? Mad that you would refuse this? Mad that you would refuse me?"

"We both know why."

"If I do, then do us a favor and remind me, save us the trouble and tell me why you won't do this?"

Barlow let out a breath, cocking his head slightly to match gazes with Pettick before letting out a simple sentence: "One less lie in the world."

Pettick continued to heave heavy breaths, trying to hold still, his anger swaying him. Barlow remained stoic in his stare, matching Pettick's. Pettick shot around the desk in a rage, landing beside Barlow, slamming his heavy hands onto the surface of the desk. "This will be your great undoing!" Pettick shouted.

"I think not," Barlow stated, unmoved.

Pettick, speechless, breathed heavily as he hunched over the desk. He stepped back, standing as tall as he could make his body stand. "Then we are done here." Pettick stormed out of the parlor, swinging the door wide as he flew into the hall. "Take him, put him in with Kindle."

Pettick's orders rang from the hall as Barlow remained still in his seat, staring at the char-black scars of the floor where Mawkin had burned. The door fell shut.

The wind blew over the roof of the bungalow, causing the small structure to moan with each shifting draft. Main Street was dark; not much light washed in as Barnes stared at the door, waiting for his kin. Barnes pulled his leather jacket tighter around his legs, which were pressed hard against his chest. The door swung open suddenly, a draft following with it.

"Pop?" A figure appeared, hanging in the dark of the door for a moment before stepping into the room. "Crane!"

"Shit! Barnes, you scared me," Crane said.

"I thought you were Barlow."

"No, just me." Crane fell in a heap onto his cot, his belongings settled around him. "Wait, where is the old 'Crow?"

"He's not here," Barnes said.

"He's not here?" Crane asked.

"That is what I just said," Barnes reiterated with clear annoyance.

"Where is he?" Crane asked.

"Don't know. Been late more and more often, not that you've been around to notice."

"Yeah, but never this late." The two sons sat on the edges of their respective cots.

"I'm worried."

"Why?"

"'Cause Pop's missing," Barnes said.

"Lotta of 'Crows been missing around here lately," Crane said, peering out the window at the framed piece of night. "But he's not missing—he's just late."

"Pop's not late, he's never late. He's not late," Barnes said, knowing himself that this wasn't true.

"Well, he's not here now," Crane said.

"No, he's not."

The boys looked at Barlow's empty cot before matching gazes at the door that bounced off its frame from the gusting wind.

Pettick strolled down the path of Main Street, marveling at its intricate simplicity. As he made his way past the closing shops, a group of young Scarecrows crossed his path, running playfully, sending the rust-orange dust of the road into the air. Watching the blissful innocence of their play, he continued on, unfazed. An unseen Flying Crow cawed a screaming sound. Pettick froze in his tracks, planted in the center of the crossroads, the town square of Main Street. A flock of Flying Crows scattered above as one Flying Crow broke off, fluttering down, landing on a branch of the beech tree that marked the roads crossing. Pettick stared, haunted by this, looking above at this Flying Crow. The Flying Crow cawed again, peering down at Pettick, cawing once more before hopping along the branch, spreading its wings, and flying away. Pettick watched the bird as it vanished in the distance. His gaze then cut down to the dust at his feet as he pondered for a moment.

"Ten years . . ." Pettick privately recalled.

The sounds of the playful young Scarecrows became audible once more as Pettick broke from his disassociative gaze, looking both ways down the road before continuing his stride.

The table had been set again at the edge of the crops, a field of tawny dry stalks of grain. The Creator rocked back and forth in his chair, staring at Herb, the Head of Agriculture, whose focus was planted in dutiful study on his books. A dried cornstalk sat on the table next to Herb's ledger. The Creator wrapped his fingers around the stalk, examining the husk where Herb measured the plant's level of dehydration in varying tick marks up the stalk leading to the severed strings where the reaper ushered harvest.

"Counting, I see," the Creator remarked.

"Aye, counting," Herb responded.

"Hmmm . . ." The Creator returned the stalk to the table.

"What?" Herb asked.

"Oh, nothin'," the Creator said.

Annoyed, Herb continued counting as the Creator rocked his creaking chair. Veidt stood by the table, anxiously pacing.

Frustrated, Herb grunted, slamming his fists against the table. "Would it burn you two to be still for a moment?"

The Creator rocked forward so that the back legs of his chair lifted from the soil.

"Well, with centuries of stillness upon our backs, it just might," the Creator chuckled.

Pettick approached. "Arguing already, are we?"

"No, just fooling about," the Creator said, kicking Herb's chair.

"I don't think this any time for foolery," Pettick lectured.

"No, it is not," Herb said with all seriousness, catching the attention of all the 'Crows. His head rose, looking up to Pettick.

"Our situation has not improved?" Pettick asked.

"No, it has not," Herb stated.

The Creator grounded all four legs of his chair onto the hard soil. Pettick leaned forward, placing both hands on the table.

"What must we do?" Pettick sighed, gripping the edges of the table.

"Well—uhm—well," Herb stuttered, hesitatingly shuffling his papers.

"Words," Pettick urged.

"Well, it is worse than we feared. We have only barely enough crop for the Flying Crow. That will not fill any quota of grain for reproduction, and hardly the corn for feeding the livestock. We will be forced to use all the corn for livestock, and still have to slaughter half the lot.

"God damn it!" Pettick shouted, turning several paces away from the table.

"I'm sorry. What, sir?" Herb inquired.

"Nothing." Pettick said.

The Creator stood up, swiftly walking around the table, darting towards Pettick who was gradually staggering farther up the hill. "Pettick!" the Creator entreated.

"Not now."

"I cannot have a season devoid of work; it will not fit our—"

"Not now!" Pettick shouted, cutting toward the crop as the Creator stood by. Pettick reached the edge of the crop running his hand along the dried hairs of grain. "I prayed it twenty-four," Pettick quietly confessed. The group stared at Pettick impatiently. Pettick felt these hard gazes, lifting his chin to the sky. "We must make good on our deal with Flying Crow."

"But we must reproduce!" the Creator said willfully. "We mustn't cut short on our expansion of 'Crows; our village needs it—we need it." The Creator snapped his fingers, cocking his head as he approached Pettick.

"We have a deal, and I do not take lightly to such a weighty clause," Pettick said.

"But our people, our armies?" the Creator persisted.

"We must," Pettick stated, passing around the Creator and starting back to the table.

"What about one," the Creator proposed, "just one?"

"A child?" Pettick said. "No, the weight is not worth the work."

"What about a soldier worth its weight, large, strong, made of only the best straw, timber infused?" Leveraging his argument with the most swaying results, the Creator branded: "The perfect soldier."

Pettick stopped, turning back to the Creator. The two matched gazes. "The best," Pettick nodded.

"The best," the Creator agreed.

Pettick turned back to Veidt, ordering, "Go with him. Make sure he gets what he needs. We move forward from here. Flying Crow help us. Crow forgive us."

Veidt and the Creator started down the path. Herb's button nose fell to the table where he made a mark in his leger, the ink seeping into the threads of the page.

"Are you not pleased?" Pettick asked.

"Does it matter what I think?" Herb responded.

"No, it does not."

"I figured as much." The Scarecrow stood up, turned his back to Pettick, and started up the path.

Pettick returned to the table and took his seat. He pondered, leaning back in his chair, lifting the front legs from the soil. He whistled a tune, reminiscent of a forgotten melody.

One by one Barnes's guests filed into the dim flaxen glow of the library; Quill the Teacher, Critch the Cobbler, Herb the Head of Agriculture, Shepherd the Herdsman, and Malthus the Mason were all in attendance.

"Where is your brother?" Critch asked, vigorously rubbing the polish from his gloves with a rag tied to his trousers before shaking Barnes's hand as he entered through the door.

"I asked him to be here, but . . ." Barnes said. "I don't know, he's been dodging everyone lately, even Gwyn."

"Yeah," Critch said, bringing his gloves to his hips. "Yeah, I know."

Barnes guided Critch toward the circle of stools and chairs compassing the lamp in the center of the library. The mounds of books had been pushed back, creating a ceremonial and physical boundary for the circle. Barnes then joined the circle, addressing his guests with the cause for their assembly.

"I know my father has expressed, with most of you, his concern over the direction in which our little society is headed, and the impeding frailty of our leader."

"Yes," Malthus interjected, "but it was Barlow who approached us, not his boy."

"I know, but my father is missing," Barnes sighed. "I assure you, even if he were not, this meeting would still be happening but with him in attendance."

Quill broke her silence. "He's not the only one; no one has heard from Kindle for weeks, and Grey hasn't been seen, either."

"Lotta 'Crows been going missin' around here, of late," Critch added.

A silence proceeded, with darting gazes and sorrowfully pensive exhalations. The brief meeting passed with little noteworthy tasks that did little more than reinstate previously held fears shared by its attendees.

"Thanks for doing this, Barnes," Shepherd said, resting a glove on Barnes's shoulder before ducking out the door. "We will find your father, do not worry."

Barnes realized that he had never seen Shepherd indoors before, and found the sight queer, though his words and touch were comforting. Malthus turned to Barnes, giving a parting nod as he made his own way out the door.

"Malthus," Barnes said, suspending Malthus's exit, "I asked you here because it is no secret that your family, being the largest in our little colony, has some sway. I do hope that you will keep this hush, whether you agree with our faction's assembly or not."

"Secret's safe with me, kid," Malthus said reassuringly in the deepest gravel of his voice.

"Thank you. Please think on it." Barnes extended his hand. Malthus looked down at his glove, understanding the respect involved with shaking Barnes's hand, a respect Barnes had earned.

"I will, kid," Malthus said.

Quill looked up to Barnes and, taking a stance beside him, wrapped her arms around his waist, a gesture he returned by resting his glove on her opposite shoulder.

"Your father will be proud," Quill spoke softly, though her venerable words resonated with Barnes.

He nodded, offering her a goofily strung smile.

"Every rebellion has to start somewhere, and you've got something here, Barnes, in these 'Crows. All you need is expansion."

"I don't need a revolution; I just need to find my father," Barnes said.

Quill's smile narrowly softened. "Then you underestimate what you have done here tonight."

* * *

The door to the library swung open. Pettick stood transfixed in the doorway. He scanned the room, which was silent and still. The sun washed in with precise beams of light. To Pettick, this light froze the dusty room like a picture that had yellowed and faded. Pettick swiftly moved through the paths of books, scanning each stack quickly as he passed it, blindly searching for the *A History of Scarecrow* manuscript. His chest exhausted a large breath, recoiling and holding back the next breath before exhaling even heavier. He reached the center of the room. Being surrounded by the piles of books reminded him of all the great books, friends he once knew. But that notion swiftly passed. With a steadier, persisting exhale, Pettick planted his feet in the center of the library and looked up at all the shelves. The moments between exhales grew smaller. Pettick crooked his head. A great exhale followed, along with a frantic break in his stance. Pettick overturned the piles of books, throwing jackets and pages into the air. He went to Barlow's desk and began sifting through the stacks, with no profit to his search. He gripped the lid of the desk and flipped it over.

"No—no—no—no—no!" Pettick trudged through the piles of books, overturning the stacks in a wave, birthing a solid sea of letters, pages, ink imaginations, and memories. Pettick tore at the books; pages ascended to the ceiling before raining back down like the feathers of a bird. "You'll burn for this. You'll burn for this." His chest heaved, a cadence to his words, as he reconciled defeat, collapsing to the floor.

In the vacant lot west of the schoolhouse sat a American beech tree, its eastern half blackened from the fire. And with autumn's breeze, black leaves fell to earth from this tree. These black leaves formed ink-like blots in the traces of autumn's truest hues. Quill sat atop the charred remains of a wood-topped metal frame desk, adrift in a sea of cinder. Barnes drifted through the rubble, as if on the way to his daily book pickup at the schoolhouse. The site had seen neither disturbance nor salvage since its burning. Lifting the lid to the desk Quill was touched by joy, unrelenting to current happenings. She retrieved a burnt spinning top from the desk, an article of contraband Quill often found the pupil of this particular desk stowing. Quill set it to a spin on the opposing table. Barnes took a seat on the adjacent chair. The top whirled before him, its path etched in pin-sized ash recesses along the desk.

"We'll rebuild. You know that, right?" Barnes assured Quill, though these words appeared to mean little to her.

"One could only hope." Quill tightened her cardigan.

The top tumbled. Catching it in his glove, Barnes set it into a whirl once more. The wind made efforts to topple it, but to no avail. Barnes watched how the cold affected Quill. Pulling off his jacket, he threw it around her. She took it with a smile, kneading its excess in her gloves. She tugged the cuffs of the sleeves over her palms, clamping her fingers down to cover her wrists. The jacket was far too large for her small figure. Barnes laughed at this, a contagious affliction. Quill fell for his chaste affections, resting her head on his shoulder. Barnes had not seen Quill so docile, so ready to take any advice, nor her desperation for it. Barnes started to whistle a familiar tune. Steadily, like with most popular melodies, the tune grew familiar and Quill joined in.

The top teetered to the edge of the desk, where, as in past classes, it would fall.

* * *

The sole of Crane's foot pressed onto the floorboard, locking into place as he swung wide the door of the library. "Pop?" he called out to an empty room, hearing only silence respond. "Barlow?" he called instead. The silence persisted. Stepping into the library, he heard the door fall shut behind him. Before him the library had been torn to shambles—pages strewn from their bindings, stories now made incomplete and at a loss for their endings, happy or tragic. He stepped over a pile of books onto another, where the pages pooled like a rug over the floor. He paused. Kneeling on the floor, Crane scattered several books where, below a layer of cloth covers, he recognized a familiar title he had regrettably parted with. He drew his copy of *Frankenstein* from the pile, unfolding its pages like a hymnal in his gloves.

Crane sat tightly curled up on the window seat of the observatory. The collapsed gold telescope leaned against the wall. *Frankenstein* sat on the sill. The small potted sunflower, the brightest color in the ashen-washed room, was atop the stack of books beside him. Crane opened Pettick's Journal, and paged past an undated entry reading:

"It's quite a task, removing one's eyes, but once you do, then—and only then—can you truly see . . ."

Crane quickly, deliberately, flipped past this entry, routing toward the end of the bound pages, nearing the blank space where both he and the author had stopped. Before the final page were the remains of several torn sheets whose edges held true to the glue of the binding. On the page opposite, a small entry at the top confessed:

I tried my hand at poetry once, but I wasn't much good at it. So, as such, I tore out the pages and discarded them into the wastebasket—what fiction could save me now?

These entries also were undated. Crane continued on, thumbing back to dated entries on previous pages, to when the scribe held weight toward the merits of time. Shifting his body forward and crossing his legs, Crane turned the page to a particular entry he felt a need to read once more; the yellow of the flower outlined the words.

September 30, 1947

I wonder how many life decisions have been made behind the steering wheel of a car. I've pondered that my whole fucking life. It's the perfect time for decisions; the steering wheel is in your hands, and all you have to do is spin. Chaney was talking, but I wasn't much listening. How could she do this to me—how could he*—was all I was thinking. What kind of monster is he? Blake McCallister, the apish fool.*

When I started to listen to Chaney he was going on about the nature of people and things, as he so often does, spinning the steering wheel fast to slide us off the roadway and into the fill station. We were back at the farm.

Chaney said, "You can't force people to feel a certain way, nor should you bear the weight of trying to change someone's mind. A mind like Tucker's is far less malleable than most. Age has sealed his mind in ways you cannot sway. It has encased his beliefs in concrete. He is the way he is. Nothing short of another great war will change that."

Chaney threw me a set of keys; they were silver and brass. An emblem was engraved on the largest key. We were in the garage, sitting in the cab, having just backed the Ford into its bay. The engine was still humming when he tossed me the keys. He followed the gesture with a huff.

"What are these for?"

"For you. She's yers. Just take good care of her, will ya?" He slid off the bucket seat. I followed suit through the passenger door, and leaned on the hood.

"What—you're giving me the Ford?"

"Yes, that's precisely what I'm gettin' at. Don't get all sentimental; save us both the embarrassment." He muttered some shit like that, I wasn't paying much attention—I was too busy wrapping my head around what he was really getting at.

"Chaney, I can't accept this," I responded, still transfixed on the silver key.

"Yes. Yes, you can. You can, and you fucking will," Chaney said. "There is a condition."

There's always a fucking catch.

"Yeah? And what is that?" I asked. There's always a motive—always.

"You leave." The driver's-side door was still ajar. He rocked back and forth as he hung through the window. I watched him for a moment, attempting to gather my words.

"What?"

"You heard me, John. You need to get in that rig and get the hell out of here, move on to better things—better places than this. No good will come of you sticking around here, kid. If there is one thing I know—one thing I'm sure of—it's that."

"Chaney—"

"Just get in, drive off, and don't come back."

We were both quiet. I read every line on his face, telling me he was being sincere.

"Tomorrow."

"Assurances."

"Sir, tomorrow," I told him. I lied. I moved to walk out the bay door of the garage. I turned to him with some curios thought, a gestating question, begging to be asked. "So you used to work for General Motors, right?"

"Yeah, why?"

"But you drive this truck. It is the only thing in the world you own, and it's a fucking Ford."

"Spite," Chaney replied.

I nodded. He smiled, one of the saddest smiles; it was short and sweet, and creased the grease on his face.

October 4, 1947

It smells like raw hamburger left out in the sun, rancid mixed with some sweet scent I wish were more prevalent. The blood is pooling, collecting in a madly perfect river, winding like the Colorado or the Rhine, winding down, down. I watch as it flows down the concrete, binding with the motor oil. It's been a while since I've seen this much blood. German—German-like amounts of this red sap. Chaney died the other night. He tried to hang himself from the rafters by hopping off the catwalk, but the rope snapped, along with his neck, and his unconscious body bounced off the hood, hitting the floor with such force his head cracked wide open. The blood pooled, running a consistent current into the drain under the chassis. And here I am, alone, left to clean it all up. Alone. I went up to our quarters and searched around for his cologne, which I generously doused into a rag to plug my nose. The sun had that perfect glisten over his head like a halo till clouds just rolled in and masked the ironically angelic rays. I now smell the old Chaney I once knew. Not the rotting one staining the concrete floor before me. Damn. I should have bought better rope.

The door to the library swung open, but Crane took no notice of it. Barnes scanned the wreckage of the library. Speechless and uncertain of the cause, he considered for a moment that perhaps Pettick had caught word of their assembly. The pages of the books took up nearly all of Crane's line of sight. He continued to the next entry:

October 11, 1947

The other day I came upon the field where the scarecrow stood and I was quite pissed to find it had made friends with the black-beaked devils. They were all over the crop, scattered in patches, pecking the meal of a crop ripe for harvest. Several were perched on the scarecrow itself, spread along his arms and atop his head, as if they hadn't a care in the world. We hadn't yet buried Chaney and his soured corpse was rather rank. I stood over him, with clippers in hand, pondering. He had those beautiful golden locks. He was a beautiful man in that way. The parts of him that worked, worked wonders. So removing this from him was a hard thing. I cut around the mushed parts. Taking only what I needed, I fashioned a wig and strung the hairpiece to the head of the scarecrow. Because why let a good tuft go to waste?

I then re-crafted the face, with a finer more acute backstitch, adding detail to the complexion, ribbing to the brow, muzzle, and mouth. Splicing the yarn X's, I gave him a mouth and articulation for the jaw. I wanted to create the illusion that my new friend could speak. Speak to me. What do you reckon he might say?

Once done, I returned him to that same patch. The rooks did not stir to his side again. They feared my handsome straw man. And so starve they will, starve when they see the kingdom of straw I will make of my friends.

"Crane, are you okay?" the figure asked.

Crane shook, slamming the book shut, quickly concealing it behind his back. Barnes stepped back, disturbed by his brother's anxious dislocation.

"Yeah, I'm fine. I'm just fine," Crane lied.

"Are you sure? Crane?" Barnes reached out to his brother. Crane stared forward, his body in the library, his head in the stars, or some terrifyingly macabre place. "Crane?"

"Yeah?" Crane responded. His stare was still locked on the plant, the yellow luster pedals which sat before him. "Nothing—it's nothing."

"Really—"

"Yeah, I—I gotta go." Crane leapt up, shoving the journal, and *Frankenstein* in his rucksack, and making a pass around Barnes.

"Wait—wait! Where are you going?" Barnes asked.

"Gotta go—gotta talk to someone," Crane said.

"Okay," Barnes muttered, "don't be too verbose or anythin'."

Throwing the strap over his shoulder, Crane looked back at Barnes, then hurried down the stairs, cutting to the door, unmindful of the wreckage.

Barnes followed, his words firm in chase, "Did you know Pop was writing a book?"

Crane stopped just before the door, turning back to Barnes as he came down the steps, planting himself at the bottom of the stairs. The brothers stared at one another from opposite sides of the room.

"What?" Crane asked.

"I said," Barnes swayed, "did you know Pop was writing a book? It's the history—*our* history. He's writing it. Did you know that?

Crane's head dropped. "No . . . no I didn't."

"Yeah, well, he is." Barnes's chin quivered but he held taut. "I just thought, before you give up on him, you should know that—that it's something you should know."

"Well I—I," Crane stuttered.

"Yeah, I know, you gotta go," Barnes said to Crane as they both stood for a long silent moment, absolved by a fleeting nod.

Crane ran out of the library, slamming the door behind him, the last pile of books falling over in his wake. Barnes's feet were still planted in place, though his body swayed.

"Everyone is always going somewhere but me," Barnes reckoned to himself in the silence.

* * *

Crane walked through the desiccated bluff of dying grass. Reeds snapped liked twigs under the weight of his soles. The field, now barren of green, left little resemblance to the place he had slumbered with Gwyn a short few months ago. The field of brush sat as a cemetery, with the wired statues of leafless stalks memorializing times not so hard. Crane trudged up the hill to the largest monument. The Perfect Tree creaked and whimpered in the wind as its arms cut cracks in the graying sky. The trunk appeared to sink into the pile of dead leaves with Crane's ascending march.

Shepherd stood silently before the Tree as Crane took post beside him. The two Scarecrows swayed, looking out toward the winds cutting across the plain. "This was once a beautiful place," Shepherd said.

"It was," Crane agreed as he looked up to Shepherd before returning his gaze to the field. "Where is your herd?"

"No point in bringing them here—no feed. All they would do is wander, and I would wonder . . . wonder where it all went . . . where it all went . . ."

"Then why do you come here?" Crane asked.

"Someone has to," Shepherd said.

"Someone has to what, stare at the wasteland all day?"

"Someone has to wonder."

Crane turned to Shepherd, who fought for several seconds before releasing his watch on the farm, turning his head to Crane. The two unshackled Scarecrows shared a mutual understanding as the wind curled between them. Crane reached into his pocket, retrieving a small set of papers topped with a folded letter displaying Shepherd's name sealed in graphite on the cream-toned parchment. The letter moved to Shepherd's hand where it shook in his trembling grasp.

"Right," Shepherd said, looking up from the piece of paper.

"You'll know when," Crane said, burying his hand in his jacket pockets. The two took a last gaze at the valley before Crane started back down the hill. Shepherd remained silent, the letter still shaking. Crane froze once more several feet downhill, turning up to Shepherd. "You're right—this was a beautiful place. As long as we don't forget that . . ."

"Crane," Shepherd called after him.

"Yes?"

"Do you know . . . what kind . . ." Shepherd stumbled over the meaning of his words, "what—what this kind of tree is called, if I were to tell of it?"

"No, do you?" Crane said, glancing with a sweet longing up at the Perfect Tree.

"No."

"Gwyn would know." Crane smiled, then continued down the hill.

Shepherd silently nodded, putting weight on his staff as Crane's body disappeared into the fold of the grey sky and the pale brown earth. Alone, Shepherd's silence broke as he reckoned.

"Oh, what a world."

CHAPTER XV: Wormwood

It was in October's fleeting hours that Main Street was busier than it had been in weeks, perhaps months; the shop owners packed away the goods of their shops and sealed tight their belongings to their bungalows as if preparing for an approaching storm. Critch sat at the workbench in the front of his bungalow, the sole of a shoe in hand. Mare came from out of the bungalow.

"Put that away," Mare demanded. "You can fix it tomorrow."

"I'm almost done, I promise," Critch said, continuing his work.

"Same words, different day," Mare rebuked.

"I know."

"Not yet, but you will," Mare lovingly threatened, gesturing toward the sky. Critch looked at his wife, then up at the kinetic sky. He handed his wife the shoe. She took hold of it, placed it in the basket in her arms, then retreated back into the bungalow. Crane approached and Critch stood at his stool wiping his hand with a rag.

"Critch!" Crane shouted, crossing the road.

"Crane, to what do I owe the pleasure?"

"Have you seen Gwyn?"

"Not since this morning. Why, is there something wrong?"

"No—no, could you just tell her to come find me?"

"Sure, where—the library?"

"No, just tell her; she'll know where to find me."

"All right, then," Critch skeptically agreed.

Crane moved to walk away, then turned back to face Critch. "And could you also do me another favor?"

"Sure, what is it?"

"Take care of her—like you always have—ya know," Crane rambled. "I know you will."

"Sure." The veil over Critch's skeptic face fell to worry. "But she has you for that."

"Yeah," Crane grew remarkably docile. "Yeah, she does."

"Crane, what's wrong?" Critch inquired, resting a glove on Crane's sunken shoulder.

"Everything is going to be fine," Crane said assuredly. "Everything is going to be just fine."

Crane turned away, rushing back up the road. Critch leaned against the post of his front porch, returning the tied rag to his back pocket as he watched Crane run, disappearing further down the crowded street.

"Critch, what's wrong?" Mare asked, standing in the doorway.

"Crane. There's something, wrong with Crane."

"Has he found himself in trouble again?"

"I don't know," Critch pondered.

Pettick stripped off the laces of his boot. As he held the hide in his right hand, he reached down with his left to the table beside his rocking chair where a tin of Kiwi shoepolish sat. Rubbing a rag in the tar-black polish, he scooped up a precise clump and applied a layer to the scarred toe of the boot. The tanned blemishes disappeared with each lather he applied. He completed the first boot with a sense of accomplishment, setting it on the porch beside his chair, moving on to the next with as equal vigor as the first. Veidt approached.

"Pettick!"

"Not now, Veidt."

"Sir—"

Pettick cut Veidt off. "I said not now; can you not see I am busy?"

"I think you need to see this." Veidt tried to catch his breath, making a terrible wheezing sound.

Pettick continued polishing his boot, his focus not leaving his task as he spoke. "A task is not completed until it is finished, Veidt. Like with this boot, if a blemish is left unprotected, the entire hide is compromised and what good is a single boot?"

"There are humans across the road!"

"What?" Pettick broke from his task.

"Humans with an automobile—three of 'em on the hill—east, across the road!"

"You saw them yourself?" Pettick inquired.

"I did," Veidt exhaled. "Worse off—"

"Yes?"

"I think they had the boy with them."

"What boy?" Pettick asked, leaning forward in his chair, his round glasses shot to Veidt.

"The one we locked in the cellar; the one who burnt Mawkin."

Pettick dropped the rag and the tin. The tin bounced and spun like a top before resting on the planks of the porch. Pettick lifted the rag from an already stained floorboard, quickly wiping the layer of excess polish from his boot. "You saw this?"

"I swear it," Veidt said with notable focus and sincerity.

Pettick stood up, lacing his boots, the toe still showing blemishes through the thin coat of polish. Pettick tightly wrapped the knots in his laces, grabbed his jacket, and hurried off the porch's edge and down the path with Veidt.

Gwyn's small figure dashed through the vast field of greyed-out grass. Clouds gathered in the distance echoing a sound of thunder and giving birth to a gust of wind that danced along the blades. The water tower rose in the grass before her, Crane's figure atop it. As she scaled the beams and breached the top, Crane was sitting at the opposite edge of the barrel, his rucksack beside him. She crawled across the barrel and planted herself next to him, the rucksack between them.

"Clouds," Gwyn thought aloud.

"Any other time we'd look at that sky with fear. But any thought of rain is a comfort," Crane said.

"You don't fear it?"

"No, do you?"

"I guess not, maybe, I don't know how to feel. I'm just—"

"You're just what?" Crane asked.

"Scared."

"So am I."

"But not of that," Gwyn lamented. "Rather for what's on the ground." Gwyn concealed a whimper.

Crane comforted Gwyn as she did likewise. A bolt of lightning cracked the sky into shards of grey glass; the bolt extended out as if reaching towards the farm. Crane unfolded his hands, curled one into his vest pocket, pulling out several torn pages—letters to Gwyn—which now had been folded. He held them in his hands for a moment, then passed them to Gwyn.

"Keep these," he said. He then pulled out a novel, atop which sat his own journal. "And these, please, make sure they get to my father," Crane said, handing over the books. Finally, he pulled another letter from his rucksack, handing it to Gwyn. "And this—please give this to him—soon." Gwyn looked at the letter, which had *BARNES* inked at the corner of the envelope.

"But Crane—what's going on?"

"Please do this for me," Crane pleaded.

Gwyn sighed away from Crane's tender reaching hand. Then, willing herself stoic, her pursed chin nodded. "Okay."

Crane peeled back the flap of his rucksack, unveiling the yellow petals of the sunflower to the surrounding grey world. Gwyn lifted her glove, cradling a petal, gently running the fragile strand along the crook between her fingertips. She smiled as she did this.

* * *

"That's where you saw them?" Pettick asked with a firm bite to his question, peering through the crossed wires of the fence. The hill across the road was empty.

"Yes, right by those rocks there," Veidt replied. Pettick lowered his small golden telescope, collapsing it and placing it into his jacket pocket.

"Whoever they were, they're gone now," Thalo said from several feet down the fence.

Pettick scanned up the massive wooden mast beside him, at the trunk that acted as a leg for one of the two lookout towers. He continued to raise his gaze to the sky, where clouds gathered above. A Flying Crow flew westward.

"The boy could be a great danger," Veidt hissed.

"Worry not, only a few 'Crows ever interacted with him."

"But Mawkin?" Veidt asked.

Pettick looked toward Veidt after his words, chasing a thought, a memory recalled, turning back toward the farm, pensive and silent.

"Wait . . . the boy—the Reader's boy."

"Sorry?"

"He talked to the Reader's boy—"

"I'm confused."

"Call a meeting."

"What?" Veidt asked, baffled.

"Call a meeting," Pettick eagerly reiterated.

"But the offering—Flying Crow will be here soon."

"Then we haven't much time, have we?" Pettick hurried to his horse, taking the reins from Thalo.

"Yes, but—"

"No time to waste, Veidt," Pettick said as he mounted his horse, looking down on Veidt and Thalo, then out to the road and its adjacent hill. Ripping up on the reins, the horse let out a piercing neigh as front hooves rolled skyward before launching into a gallop—the whole act, an iconographic sight.

"It feels like ten years we've been down in this pit," Kindle said, tracing the small amount of light which leaked into the cell as it crystallized in small specs of sand within the black dirt.

"You old 'Crow, couldn't tell time if your arm had a clock in it," Barlow jeered as Kindle collected a clump of the dirt in his glove, watching the specs refract as he ran them through the light.

"I can tell time," Kindle said, sifting the sand with a smile.

"Oh, and how long have we been down here?"

Some time passed before Kindle responded. "Actually?"

"Actually."

"Approximately?" Kindle asked.

"Approximately," Barlow agreed.

"Approximately . . ." Kindle rationalized. "I don't know, some time . . ."

"How long do you suppose we have been on this farm?" Barlow asked.

"Oh, that is an easy one."

"Oh, is it?"

"I would say . . ." Kindle pondered for several lasting moments, unable to answer.

"*What* would you say?" Barlow impatiently interjected.

"Long."

"Long? Long isn't a number, Tinker," Barlow lectured. "How many days, how many seasons? How often have the leaves changed and the seed been sown and taken by the Flying Crow since you were made here?"

"I couldn't tell you." Kindle paused, taken aback by his own response.

"Neither can I," Barlow said, his voice fading. "Sometimes I feel like I was made old, like I never had what the boys had."

"Ya know," Kindle said, puzzled, "sometimes I feel the same. And I reckon we were."

"We weren't always this old, though, were we? We were young once," Barlow said, with a faint glint of assurance.

"We were—we were younger."

"But I was never as young as Crane. I was never that carefree, that wild hearted. I was never—"

"Now you're talking regret, not years," Kindle reasoned.

"Are they not the same?" Barlow contrived.

"I think not," Kindle said.

"Suppose not, I guess . . ."

"Suppose not."

The two 'Crows remained in their place of solitude, unable to read one another's will as they sat still in the dark. The seal of the door broke, its large mass swinging gently open, the hinges crying under the overbearing weight. Pettick's figure hung in the framed light of the door rubbing the glass of his spectacles with a handkerchief. He sighed as he took a seat on the stool on one side of the cell, while Barlow and Kindle remained equally attached to the other. Examining the sheen, he gave each lens another polish, resting them to the bridge if his nose when he finished.

"Well, aren't you a haggard bushel. I will only ask this once: where is the book?" Pettick said, pocketing the handkerchief.

Barlow remained silent, running the rough callousness of his glove through his fingertips.

"I sometimes feel I live amongst a colony of children. All of you must think yourselves clever, throwing some wrench in the works, as if by hiding my toys you will start a revolution. How petty your efforts . . ."

Barlow and Kindle waited in their silent anguish, till Pettick grew tired of this game and stood, brushing off his flannel before stepping toward the door.

"Maybe a lesser 'Crow can be urged to speak."

Barlow offered a disarming glance, thinking Pettick was insinuating on the location of *The History of Scarecrow* manuscript, he rebutted, "It drowned. Good luck if any ink survived."

The door swung wide, Pettick's figure reappeared, a lingering shadow in the full light of the doorway.

"Like father like son." Pettick said, pausing to read Barlow's face—the face, where all truths are told. This did not elicit the same reaction Pettick expected.

Barlow was puzzled.

"Or did you not know? I know you to be stubborn, but never apprehensive. Or you were never quite this obvious." Pettick pecked at Barlow's unkept wounds. "Funny—you know what we have in common—you, me, Tinker, the boy? Curiosity. We are all curious beings. It binds us. It is our mutual folly."

Crane? Barlow thought, the picture growing ever clearer.

"Guess I'll have to find someplace for the boy, too—"

Pettick spun in the doorway as he continued, either to further scorn or to ensure the Reader his threats were not idle. "Though we are running out of cells . . ."

Barlow lunged forward, making his attack as Pettick turned his back. Pettick whipped around, a flare, unlit, in his grip.

"No!" Kindle shouted. Leaping forward, he knocked Barlow off of his charge, slamming him against the wall. Wrapping his arms around Barlow, Kindle drew a safe proximity between them and Pettick.

"First smart thing you've done, Tinker," Pettick said, minding his footing as he backed out of the cell. Pettick vanished with the slam of the oak, yet the stench of his presence lingered. Kindle held Barlow, who shook, his chest heaving where he pressed his glove, crumbling to the floor.

"My son—my son, what have I done?"

* * *

Pettick stood overlooking the ridge, his gloves buried in the pockets of his jacket. Veidt grunted, fumbling as he climbed up the beams of the water tower. He reached the top, digging his pointed fingers into the wood of the barrel to pull himself up. He spun around, unsure of where the lid was, finding it beneath Crane's carving. Veidt looked at the words, unable to decipher their meaning. The winds were heavy, pounding Pettick's jacket. He stood unfastened, face into the wind. Veidt rose atop the barrel.

"It's here!" He held up the journal high so Pettick could see it. As Pettick approached the tower, Veidt dropped the journal into his hands. He clutched the journal, unclasping the leather skin, thumbing through the pages. On the climb down, Veidt lost his grip on the beam, falling face-first into the grass. Pettick continued reacquainting himself with his journal, paying no attention to Veidt's fumbling. He scanned the pages, looking for any signs of Crane's passing.

"What secrets did you tell?" Pettick whispered to himself.

The piercing whistle of the loudspeakers switching on could be heard echoing across the fields, reaching as far as the Perfect Tree and the garage, the village and the orchard. The small speckles of static and chatter which the transducer picked up, nuances of sounds in a voice which otherwise would remain unheard, amplified across the colony. These sounds rose as Pettick pressed the microphone to his pursed lip. Barnes ran with heavy feet, pressing into the crowd that gathered at the meeting ground. He could see their unresponsive faces as he passed, every 'Crow transfixed in their own separate hysteria. He looked up over the 'Crows, extending his long neck, searching for

Crane. The brim of the 'Crows' hats bobbed and swayed. The motion of the crowd, an undulating drape, blurred in Barnes's view. The colony held an aura Barnes hadn't yet felt, a chaos he hadn't been a part of but was now surrounded by. The voice of the leader resonated, distorting in its waves as Barnes heard it.

"It is almost Zero Hour, the time of our yearly penance—the time in which we reflect and repent with the fruits of our labors and give back to the Flying Crow, which has so graciously given us life. To reflect on the hardships, which we have faced and overcome, and the greatness—the staying power of our kind. It has been a season of hardships, my friends; there is no point in denying such troubles, and we face a long winter ahead for our little colony. We must stop and reflect on our joys, our kind, our life, and what we value in it." Pettick spoke with an uncanny bite to his words, in a manner both acrimonious and inspired. His gaze matched the members of his audience, no single gaze lasted long. "We are a special kind of fewer numbers than we tend to acknowledge. That is why—" Pettick stuttered, sighing as he lowered his head, then seeing the faces of confusion and fear before him, continuing with contempt. "That is why, when we lay a bad seed—when a bad seed walks among us, it is an ever more putrid thing." Pettick looked into the crowd, through the many to the individual, judging each for their slights. "We have reached a roadblock—a crossroad. And now—fuck—now I'm done talking. Veidt, bring them out!"

Over the hill commotion could be heard. A 'Crow on horseback rose with a rifle barrel pitched skyward, the stock against his hip. The barrel exploded, with a slight gusting smoke, the stock recoiled against the 'Crow's hip and a sounding echo hit the bewildered crowd. The Scarecrow horseman rounded his horse, halting at the top of the hill.

"What the hell?" Barnes said, glancing up the hill at the horsemen for a moment; then, refocusing his efforts to the crowd, he turned back, cutting against the grain. Searching for Crane, he pressed through the shoulders of the crowd. All the 'Crows were facing him, but all were looking past, beyond, to the hill. "Crane!" Barnes called, his desperation growing. "Gwyn!"

"Barnes!" Gwyn yelled, catching his attention as they moved toward one another, the only Scarecrows whose sight was not locked on the horseman on the hill. The two pushed through the crowd, meeting finally as a second round went off. Barnes looked over Gwyn, pulling her to him.

"Are you all right?"

"Yeah."

"Where is Crane?" Barnes looked around, then back up the hill at the horseman.

"Barnes," Gwyn uttered, her words lingering.

"Where is Crane?" Barnes locked back on Gwyn, tightening his grip on her arms. Gwyn looked up at Barnes, gently swinging Crane's rucksack around her hip. The bag hung partially open with the head of the flower exposed. The two shared a glance, which froze the surrounding commotion as the crowd screamed, shifting with the third sounding shot. On the path beside the horseman a line of several humans marched, bound to one another like a chain gang. Two 'Crows escorted them on either side, both armed. The line of four humans marched slowly down the path to the stage. The horseman followed.

The crowd continued with its hysterical rambling, with shouts of hatred and vilification toward the humans growing steadibly more audible. Barnes sighed, staring at Gwyn. She gently nodded her quivering chin. With Pettick's presenting hands, commotion rose again. Barnes and Gwyn looked up to the stage where the humans had been led. The horseman dismounted, his straw face was covered with tarnished gold-framed aviator sunglasses, a bandana over his mouth and chin, and his brow concealed by the shadow of a large-brimmed hat. Veidt led the line's march on stage. With the swing of his rifle, the stock collided with the human's ankles, bringing each to their knees.

"Oh no," Barnes whispered at the proceedings playing out before him. His words caught Gwyn's attention, and she looked up at him, then down at the bag, her gloves clenched to the strap. The horseman rose from behind the stage, taking stance behind the row, his tall slender body hanging over the humans.

Pettick looked up at the horseman, noticing the resemblance between the bandanas and goggles on their faces. He scanned over the beaten emaciated row of humans, then turned to the crowd. His movements were precise, exacting, deliberate.

"Isn't it pathetic whenever a creature—a dignified creature—begs? If it weren't so savage, it would have my sympathies. Yet there is someone out there, one of you, one of our own who has grown just such an indecent sympathy. I fear this is the same individual who stole my journal, the history of our people." Pettick paused to hear the outcry in response, a rehearsed theatricality to the segment of his speech. "So here is when I ask for this sympathizer to step forth before harm is brought to anyone else, savage or not."

Members of the crowd grew silently aware of those around them, untrusting fixtures, scanning; as did Pettick from his place on stage.

Barnes's chin dropped from the stage to Gwyn. He grabbed her hand. "Come with me."

She gripped his glove, following him further forward, into the thick of the crowd. The static from the tower grew audible as the crowd grew more accusatory with each passing moment. With Pettick's nod, the horseman opened his coat, and swiftly unsheathed a large hunting knife with a sharp untarnished blade. The horseman moved down the row to the first human, an old man with scars on his knees and knuckles. It was the father whom Pettick had murderously deprived of a son. The horseman whisked the knife through the air, halting it just under the man's jaw, pressing it firmly against the flesh of his throat. Standing apart from the other prisoners, the man remained silent.

"The Journal," Pettick's voice said, coming from the loudspeaker.

The man's silence broke as he gently whispered, words only Pettick and the horseman could hear. The horseman's hands spread, spidering out around the man's chin, forcing it shut. Pettick looked back at the man, leaning down to hear him.

"What? What did you say?" Pettick quietly entreated, muffling the microphone against his chest. The horseman removed his hand, allowing the old man to speak.

The old man coughed, choking on his words for a moment, then began to speak with clear dignity. "It's you—I know it now, it is you—" The man again coughed.

Pettick leaned in closer.

"I knew nothing good came of you. When you came to town, death followed. And she never would—"

Pettick swung his fist across the man's jaw, causing him to fall over. "Silence, you mumbling fool!" Pettick raged while members of the crowd cheered him on.

The old man's cheek was rubbed raw against the wood planks, dripping blood onto the stage. The horseman grabbed him, pulling him back to his knees.

Pettick turned to the crowd, his appearance and posture disheveled. "Well, what is it going to be?" Pettick yelled, spreading his arms out, looking into the crowd. The old man continued coughing, letting out several more words. Pettick took notice, though the majority of his attention remained with the crowd.

"John," the old man said, "she was afraid—"

Pettick scanned the crowed briefly, shouting, "Fine!" He dropped the silver microphone onto the planks with a blaring crash. Pettick turned to the old man, swiftly grabbing the knife and pushing the horseman back. He drew the blade up, cutting it down across the man's throat, then recoiled, driving it into the man's chest. The body fell back, the blade with it. Pettick's chest heaved, his back still to his silent audience. He looked up at the horseman, who nodded. Standing still for a moment, he raised his gloves, trying to wipe the blood that stained the threads on his face. The blood sank deeper into the threads. He slowly turned to the faces in the crowd, still frozen from the shock. He cocked his head.

"Must we do this again?" Pettick asked.

The crowd remained still, silent.

Pettick shook his head. "Ah, the pandemic of silence—okay." Reaching into his jacket he pulled out an U.S. Army issue M1911 handgun, released the safety, and moved toward the next prisoner, a woman, with tears in her young eyes. He raised the weapon, pressing the barrel against her temple, his action within full sight of the audience. He cocked the hammer. "Again—the journal!" Pettick yelled. "No?"

"No!" came a lone response rose from the otherwise silent crowd.

Barnes and Gwyn remained frozen where they stood.

Pettick raised his head to see Crane standing front and center. The surrounding Scarecrows swiftly moved away from him, as if he was a harbinger of a newly discovered plague, leaving a space, a void, in the crowd with Crane, the subversive dissenter, at the center. Pettick lowered the weapon to his side, gently releasing the hammer. He looked down at the young Reader.

"You have my book, boy?" Pettick inquired.

"Yes," Crane firmly replied.

"And you wish to spare these human lives?"

Crane remained silent for a moment, looking around, then back up, his gaze locked on Pettick's face.

"Yes, I do."

Pettick drew a crooked smile, speaking directly to Crane. "Good, I needed them to hear that."

"No!" Crane shouted, stepping forward.

The weapon rose, Pettick firing without taking his gaze from Crane. The body fell to the stage. The blood pooled, seeping through the expansion joints between the planks. The crowd parted. As Crane moved toward the platform, Paquin and Thalo flanked him; grabbing his arms, violently dragging him onto the stage. Pettick checked the number of remaining rounds in the magazine while he paced.

"Crane!" Barnes yelled, stepping forward briefly, but freezing as Pettick stared him down. Barnes looked over to Crane who returned a different glare with similar effect. Gwyn held Barnes's arm. He in turn pulled her close, keeping tight hold of her. For Gwyn, time both seemed to rush by as it also blurred to a painful halt. Thalo forced Crane to his knees beside the remaining humans, a pernicious shameful kind of subservient penitence.

"Stupid boy, you're as foolish as your father." Pettick bit his words. Crane remained silent in his resolve, glaring at Pettick with a steady chin.

"I burned the fucking thing," Crane said scornfully with a crooked smile matching Pettick's.

"No—no you didn't." Pettick chuckled. "Actually, quite the opposite." Pettick opened his jacket only enough for Crane to see, revealing the inner pocket where the journal was concealed.

Crane sighed, defeated.

"Wait a moment; we aren't nearly finished," Pettick said as he closed his cloak, turning back to the scattered crowd. "Go to your homes, ensure they are secure, everyone must be in the textile house within the hour. It is time! Now go!"

The horseman mounted his horse, watching Pettick as he stepped off the platform, dragging Crane after him. The horseman dug his boots into his horse's sides, causing it to neigh loudly as he rode off toward the silos. The crowd scattered quickly in different directions toward the village.

"Right," Crane quarreled. "Send your spectators away before you kill one of your own."

"Not exactly," Pettick calmly replied. "You'd be shocked at how quickly a species will reject one of its own. And, oh my, what a villain I have made of you."

"So you don't plan to kill me?"

"No—I promise you, you are as good as dead—fodder for the crows." The crowd thinned around them. "Take him to the ridge," Pettick ordered Veidt and the soldiers.

Dust rose from all the movement, surrounding Pettick and the soldiers who crossed through the remaining crowd.

Gwyn looked up at Barnes, stepping away from him. She turned to Crane as the crowd between them dissipated and cleared. Dropping Crane's rucksack, she charged toward Pettick and Crane.

"Crane!"

Gwyn collided her shoulder with Thalo, knocking him over. Veidt grabbed her arm, throwing her back; but she caught her balance, and prepared to lunge at Pettick.

"Gwyn, no!" Crane yelled as he was dragged off by Paquin.

Barnes grabbed her and held her back, tightening his grip, while pressing her to his chest. She yelled and wept. Pettick looked at Gwyn, shaking his head, shifting up to Barnes.

"Only smart one in the bunch. Do yourself a favor, boy, don't go growing a brain," Pettick said to Barnes as he passed.

Barnes wrapped his arms around Gwyn. She buried her face in his flannel chest. Critch, Mare, and Quill gathered several paces behind them. They were all that remained as the crowd cleared and the dust settled.

* * *

Thalo and Paquin tightened the ropes around Crane's wrists, straws peeking through his shirt from the tension.

"Tighter now, we wouldn't want him getting free," Pettick ordered his officers as he overlooked his farm from the ridge. "When monsters roam free, we only live in fear." Pettick loosely shook his head. "What a world we have here, eh? Our little world." He turned, looking up at Crane with a queer gaze. The young 'Crow's arms spread, slung around the horizontal member, his body hanging on a vertical pike. "What a useless place to be."

"The world?" Crane quipped.

Pettick chuckled, starting toward Crane. "The world—oh no—no. The pike. Is there ever such a pitiful sight?"

"We both know there is."

"I suppose we do now, don't we?" Pettick sighed. Pitch and Thalo approached with chains in hand. Pettick signaled to them. Thalo threw Pettick something heavy as they moved toward Crane, wrapping the chains around him. Pettick fiddled with the metal object in his hands as he moved in gentle stride behind the pike. "It's a shame, really." Pettick's misplaced smile grew, but vanished as he rounded the pike, stopping in front of Crane. "We two—we could have had a real conversation."

"Suppose so," Crane said, his body remaining limp as he raised his head, resting it against the vertical member of the pike, taking care not to look at Pettick or the farm before him.

"You can look away all you want, it won't change the reality you have brought upon yourself." Pettick spoke with a bite, giving more weight to the words than their initial meaning. "Look at me, Crane—this is real."

"No," Crane dissented.

"No?"

"I read every page—we both know it's not," Crane exhaled, stoking Pettick. "Our kingdom of straw. Is it everything you wished for, John?" The two 'Crows looked directly at one another, a savage pleasure to their discourse.

Pettick stepped away, words failing to immediately gather.

"Well, aren't you a handsome Rook?" Pettick bustled about, thinking. "I did expect a bit more fear from you, Crane, but it is quite telling of your character that I see none of it." Pettick paced. "Though, truth be told, I know it's still there. And if you dare quote another line, I will tear you apart." Pettick looked back to read Crane's reaction. Both smiled. A grimace returned to both faces as Pettick looked away.

Pitch crossed the chains at Crane's chest. Crane watched as he did. He turned back to Pettick, who motioned them away. The two Scarecrows lifted their weapons and took their posts several yards east.

Crane rolled his shoulders, feeling the weight of the chains. "Fuck!" Crane muttered to himself, pulling at his restraints.

Pettick chuckled. "How colloquial—another word I never taught. Your usage was correct, though."

"I do read," Crane said.

"I have seen your library, just as you have seen mine."

"You may have the largest library in the human world—doesn't mean a single book has been read."

"Clever fodder."

The clouds in the distance cracked, flashing in an arc across the sky, catching the attention of both 'Crows.

"Sir, I think we should be going," Thalo shouted as a rumble followed. Pettick took a step toward Crane, taking the lock in his hand and clasping it to the chains crossing on Crane's chest.

"This was all for her, wasn't it?" Crane asked. A sound of thunder bellowed.

Pettick stopped, looked up at Crane, and replied with a lovelorn exhausted sigh—an honest reply from a habitual liar. Pettick spun around, presenting the key to Crane. Then, as he spun back, he swung his arm and whipped it forward, throwing the key.

Crane watched, though he did not wish to see it. The key, thrusting into the sky, vanished in the textured horizon.

Starting for the path, Pettick stopped beside the pike once more, looking at Crane. "What were you so afraid of?"

Crane looked down at Pettick, giving the simple reply: "Apathy."

Pettick understood this. With a shrugging nod, he walked away, his officers at his heel, following the path eastward through the grass.

Crane's head fell forward as the threads of his body released tension. He hung there, completely still, alone, for several minutes, letting his choices sink in. Crane broke, jerking his arms violently, pulling at the ropes. Exhausted, he hung limp again. A stillness came over the farm he had not felt before. "Shit." He raised his head, looking out over the ridge, catching the last rays of light, which vanished as the clouds sealed. A whistling was carried on the wind. The rocks shifted on the edge of the ridge. Barnes rose from the ridge, followed by Gwyn.

"Barnes!" Crane spoke with urgency as the two dashed towards him, staying low. "Get out of here!" Crane yelled as Gwyn embraced him. "It's no use."

Barnes followed the ropes to the chain that wrapped around Crane's body. Thunder barreled through the colony, calling their attention to the western sky. The high-pitched whistle resonated, rising steadily in intensity. Crane was first to notice the small black dot that expanded on the horizon. The blackness spread like a virus in all directions, rising higher into the sky and wider along the horizon.

"What in Flying Crow is that?" Gwyn asked.

Barnes whipped around, wrapping violently at the ropes. Gwyn looked up at Crane, throwing her arms around him.

"Barnes!" Crane shouted, looking directly at him. "Barnes!"

"No!"

"You get her out of here!" Crane shouted.

"Crane, I—"

"You promised," Crane absolved.

Barnes froze, looking over at Crane. "You keep her safe," Crane said with as much dignity and clarity as he could. Barnes nodded, releasing his hold on the ropes. "Get out of here—now." The whistling rose to a hollow scream that pierced the air. Barnes stepped away, moving next to Gwyn.

"Gwyn, we gotta go." Gwyn looked up at Crane, resting her chin on his abdomen. Crane looked back at her, giving her a smile.

"That night, with the fireflies," Gwyn said, smiling back.

Crane nodded.

Barnes ran to the water tower, a length of rope in his hand. He wrapped the hemp around the wooden beam, tightening the knot with harsh pulls on the threads. Leading to the ridge's edge, he dropped it down the cliff, watching the line unravel with its descent. He ran back to the Pike, taking Gwyn's hand.

"Gwyn, Come on!"

"Barnes!" Crane shouted.

Barnes turned back up to Crane. "Yeah?"

"Roanoke."

Barnes nodded, pulling Gwyn along the line. She looked back up at Crane, not taking her sight off him. They slid to the edge, Barnes gripping both hands on the rope. He looked back at Gwyn. "Get on my back!" Barnes shouted. Gwyn nodded, throwing her arms around him, locking her gloves together. Barnes backed over to the edge. "Hold on." Barnes jumped. They swung out over the ledge, his feet hitting the rocks with a thud, breaking his footholds away.

Crane raised his head, looking out over the ridge at the absolute blackness which now engulfed the sky, devoring the horizon. Crane knew what this was: Flying Crow had arrived, and was here to feed.

"Hurry," Crane whispered.

After Pettick dismounted outside the textile house, his horse leapt off in fright. He looked up as the absolute blackness shifted, revealing smaller shapes swarming within itself.

"My God." He looked around at the soldiers still outside, and ordered them with waving gestures of his arms. "Get inside—now!"

Barnes and Gwyn had nearly reached the bottom of the cliff.

"Let go—drop!" Barnes shouted.

Gwyn dropped the last fifteen feet, and Barnes followed. He looked ahead at the darkness, pulling Gwyn up. The skirt of darkness cast several miles in width; its shadow met the edge of the farm. The wildlife in the surrounding forest scattered.

Gwyn trailed Barnes as they dashed into the crops, westward toward the village.

"Barnes, we're not going to make it to the village." Barnes skidded to a halt, watching as the shadow encompassed the village. She turned to her right. "Come on, follow me." Gwyn led Barnes. They cut sideways through the crop lines. The swarm touched down, like a tornado mating the soil, uprooting the crops, churning up detritus where it landed. The shadow cast over Barnes and Gwyn, blocking the last breath of the sun. "Barnes!"

"I know!"

Cutting through the cropland blindly, earth dropped out from under them, sending both 'Crows tumbling down the embankment, splashing into the creek. Gwyn leapt up first, helping Barnes to his feet. Trudging up the creek, the swarm of blackbirds broke out around them, its roaring sounded unbearably close.

"Barnes!"

"Don't look up! Just run!" Barnes shouted, tightening his grip on Gwyn's hand as they trudged through the creek, around the curve to where the river ran straight. The wooden bridge traversed the water several yards downstream. With the depth rising only to Barnes's knees, he shot forward. They ducked as they reached the bridge. Bracing the truss, Barnes pushed Gwyn up the embankment. Feathers violently swirled around them. Their screams seemed silent compared to the raging swarm crashing down.

Crane watched as the turgid swarm washed over the village, stretching east over the gulch, laying hand to the bridge where he'd lost sight of Barnes and Gwyn. The swarm reached the Perfect Tree, diverging within a yard's reach from its canopy, a pleasant sight for Crane. The mass of the darkness was overwhelming, causing Crane to tremble with the primal fear of the swarm's fluidity, the corporeal animation of its flow. Its influx, so unnatural, made its rape of the land ever more terrifying. Crane's logic fell away with the reach of the swarm, leaving only emotion. Crane gripped the pike. Claws, feathers, razor-edged beaks, darkness flashed by, whirling around him. A shaft formed with the pike at its center. Directly above was the only light, a sharp-edged patch of unscathed sky that seemed to shift. Moments of its rays washed Crane's brow. A silence buffered the swarm's roar, followed by an illusory stillness, like that felt with a veiling translucence in the interim of an awakened dream. With clarity came a sense of exposure for Crane, and the sense of air unbinding the intertwining makeup of his flesh.

A single *caw* screamed down the shaft. A flock of black feathers fell upon Crane, masking his figure, which still hung to the pike. And with passing moments, the binding makeup of Crane came undone. The black-feathered figure of the Scarecrow lifted from the pike and dissolved back into the swarm. The light gradually peeked through holes in the walls of the swarm, giving shape to the individual birds, their violent flapping wings, and their razor-sharp talons. The swarm receded, trailing toward the horizon.

The farm was quiet. The fields of grain were now empty rows of reaped earth. Stalks of corn and wild ferns still filled in patches of the plain. The towering pines swayed. In the village, the signs on the bungalows swung to and fro. The tractors remained statues, the red, yellow, and green sheen of their coats unscathed. The meeting ground remained as it was before, save the cluster of Scarecrows which regularly occupied the clearing. A steady breeze brushed the ridge. The lashings hung tied to the empty pike. The chains danced, chattering a tune as they gently swung, the bolt still clasped.

CHAPTER XVI: Hellhounds

Pettick slipped out of the man-door on the side of the textile barn, followed by Veidt and two of his militia. For a moment they all cautiously stood in the shade of the overhanging eave. Pettick then stepped forward into the exposure of harsh daylight towards the spectral clearing of the meeting ground. By the well, the vacant becket still shook from the receding cloud. Pettick looked up at the western sky, spinning around to regard all of it, forms and voids. The gray sky was clear of all birds, all life. Pettick continued beyond the barn to the edge of the field, where he stood reaching toward a single remaining stalk of grain, its rachis still cradling a full ear of wheat. As the glove held the grain, the plant cracked and withered, cultivating a small cloud of fibers of dust caught in the wind. Peering out over the field, former rows of stalks were now an empty expanse of dried dirt and weeds. Several yards down the reaped rows, the cornstalks had been left in their planted scattered patches, but no wheat stalks remained.

Veidt and Thalo approached Pettick.

"We did it!" Thalo exclaimed.

"Yes, we did—we did," Pettick said, with only a sigh of relief. His fellow Scarecrows marked their reprieve with handshakes and cordial embraces. The silence of the farm lasted for a moment, then Pettick heard the sounds, slight tings of metal colliding with metal, engines exhausting their loads, machines making their presence known.

"Pettick, I think you should come and look at this!" Pitch's voice echoed from the other side of the barn.

The Scarecrows remained still as Pettick turned, his stride quickening as he crossed to the other side of the barn, its vertical panels blurred past, opening like a curtain to the sight of the hill across from the farm where several dozen tents stood. Green military vehicles, trucks, jeeps, and wheeled guns scattered and crawled through them. Pettick's feet rallied dirt in an abrupt halt. He stood frozen for several moments scanning the hill. Humans—in all their fable and legend—had arrived.

"How I count the years . . ." a dislocated Pettick whispered.

Veidt and the soldiers approached, stopping several paces behind Pettick, transfixed by the revelation of the sight before them. A variant of wonder, awe, panic, and fear could be read on their faces. Veidt slowly approached Pettick.

"What should we do?" Veidt asked, marble eyes spinning.

Pettick remained silent.

"Pettick—Pettick, what would you have us do?"

A wind blew, bringing with it the sounds of the distant hill across the road, nearly a quarter mile away, in a louder ambience.

"Keep them in the barn; they'll be safe. Bring the fathers, rally the militia, gas the trucks, saddle the horses; we meet at the grounds here in an hour," Pettick ordered, spinning about and darting south toward the house.

"Yes, sir!" Veidt yelled over the rising fury in the wind, his words chasing after Pettick. "Where are you going, sir?"

"To get our soldier."

* * *

The receding swarm reflected off the lenses of Cooper's binoculars. Lowering them revealed a soldier, a human, with reddish-brown hair and red stubble on his chin. He was staring across the road at Tucker's Farm. He pulled a cigarette from a pack of Lucky Strikes protruding from his left breast pocket—the pocket just over the heart, where all lucky and token things are kept. Placing it between his lips and turning his back to the wind, he flicked his metal lighter several times until it was lit. He took in a long drag from the cigarette as he paced the gravel road. Several feet away, three men stood before a Jeep, while a man with more stripes on his shoulder surveyed the farm.

"Cooper. Eyes." The man with more stripes ordered.

Cooper handed the captain his binoculars, strolling over to the two privates, Bryant and Woodley, who stood by a young man out of uniform, a kid of maybe twenty-two, Jamie.

"Mr. Walsh, can you explain that?" Captain Raleigh said, speaking through the binoculars, the long fibers of his white mustache rubbing against the lenses as he dropped them to his chest.

"No—no I cannot," Jamie responded, awestruck.

"Looked like Mother Nature was mighty furious to me," Bryant quipped. "Good old-fashioned tornado."

"You're from Brooklyn, the fuck you know about tornadoes?" Woodley wryly detracted. Bryant exhausted his barreled chest, unkind words hung on his tongue.

"Enough," Cooper hushed his men, putting Bryant at heel.

"Cooper!" Raleigh ordered.

"Yes, sir?"

"Can you explain it?" Captain Raleigh half-rhetorically asked.

Cooper lowered the cigarette from his mouth exhaling a large cloud of smoke into the dry air. He stared out over the farm, unresponsive. Raleigh lowered his binoculars looking at Cooper, at once expectant and indifferent.

"I don't know sir, maybe Bryant's right, just a tornado or somethin'." Cooper's shoulders fell slightly from their stance of perfect-attention. "Or—"

"Or?" Raleigh urged.

"Or maybe the kid isn't so full of shit," Cooper said.

"Right . . ." Raleigh, ever the skeptic, spat his tobacco. "Have Perry buzz Detrick; get Heinrich out here," Raleigh ordered. "Something strange is going on outside Odessa."

Cooper dropped his cigarette and quickly mashed it into the ground before more than a few embers could escape into the wind. The captain matched eyes with him as he passed by.

"Strip it next time, before you start a fucking fire," Raleigh ordered, shoving the binoculars against Cooper's chest.

Captain Raleigh slid into the passenger seat of the Jeep. Woody and Bryant, his driver and escort, respectively, filed in after. The engine started, rumbled into gear, and the vehicle drove them away. Cooper and Jamie stood alone in the middle of the road, silent in the cadence of the fleeing engine. Cooper looked out over the farm before him, dropping the binoculars to his legs where they hung from their strap.

Several crows, birds as black as silhouettes, cawed as they flew over. Cooper and Jamie matched disconcerting gazes. The flock continued west, over the farm.

"What a strange place, hidden from the world," Jamie said.

"Wasn't always this way. Scouting maps show this used to be a major road. Route 61 used to run right through here, north to Centralia. Guessing they moved the highway a couple years back, killed the farm and the town." Cooper shook his head, kicking the gravel in the road. "I hope you are full of shit, kid."

Dirt gathered beneath their boots, entraining pebbles, clumping, forming micro-avalanches that spread and tumbled as they fell into the creek below. Gwyn and Barnes slid down the embankment under the bridge, cautious of their movement. They stepped in the creek bed, looking up at the clear sky, remaining under the cover of the bridge. Barnes stepped out, checking the entire sky that glowed a bright sequin grey, broken by several harsh rays of pure exposed ether. The splashing of Barnes's movement seemed magnified in the silence surrounding them.

"It's clear. Come on," Barnes said as he turned, starting down the creek toward the village. Gwyn stood still. The water caught the bottom of her skirt, rippling it gently with the current. Barnes stopped. Turning back, he noticed that Gwyn was not beside him. "Gwyn, we have to go," Barnes said gently.

"Shouldn't we—we just check? Gwyn said, her feet buried in the creek, body swaying in the non-existent breeze.

"He told us not to look back—now we gotta . . ." Barnes paused, correcting the affliction of his nerves. "We have to go." Unsure of what else to say, Barnes swayed, holding in his breath.

Gwyn shook her head.

"Gwyn—Gwyn, I know, but we promised—we promised, okay?" Gwyn looked down at the creek as the ripples of water made waves in her dress. Her eyes followed the creek bed down to the village, then up to Barnes and his proffered glove that extended to her.

"Okay." Gwyn nodded, wading to Barnes. He took her hand. They started down the creek toward the village, making little disturbance in the current as they went.

Pettick dismounted from his horse and his soles met the ground, leaving deep impressions in the dry earth of the hill before the Cattle Barn. Handing off the lead of the reins to his newly appointed officer, Dirk, he started for the door, pausing several feet away at the beckoning of a sounding *caw*. The bird's scream diverted his attention from the impending hysteria, the impeding human presence, and the desire to meet his soldier. He spun around, taking several paces westward, gazing over the greater half of the farm. The blending hues of the still frame picture in his view acquired much of their pigments from the sky, whose clouds gathered in a thickness so solid, only one contrasting shape could be seen, a blade of light, piercing the otherwise perfect surface, cutting into the village below.

A stillness came over Pettick, a memory recalled with such clarity, it made itself present. Mawkin's figure stood next to him, arms crossed, overlooking the farm just as he.

"Beautiful place we got here, isn't it?" Mawkin said, Pettick looking up to him briefly as he did.

"Yes, it is, Mawkin—how keen a thing to notice." Pettick cleared his throat as he spoke, placing a glove on Mawkin's shoulder for a brief moment. The exchange grew strange. Pettick's hand receded as both Scarecrows turned to the sun-tinged glossy shimmer over the brimming mid-season crop. "Mawkin?"

"Pettick?" Mawkin cleverly responded with a smile, knowing of his wit. "Yes?"

"If—and I know the weight of this question may be beyond your means, but I am curious of your thought—"

"Must every conversation we have be led by the measure of my ignorance?" Mawkin asked, with a still jovial tone.

"No—no, it does not." Pettick smiled.

"Well—you were saying?"

"Yes, well," Pettick continued, "if—if you could rebuild, reconstruct civilization, the world from rubble, what would you do?

What would you keep from before? What would be left behind? Would you shuck it all away and forge from nothing? Or is there something you would keep constant? What's worth salvaging? What's worth holding on to?"

"And you're asking me what *I* think?" Mawkin clarified.

"Yes," Pettick quickly replied.

Mawkin let out a heavy, pensive exhale. "I don't know—quite a weighty question for a 'Crow so base."

Pettick chuckled, then gave an admiring gasp at Mawkin's venerability. "I think any 'Crow aware enough of its simplicity could make judgment on such a question."

"Well then . . ." Mawkin gathered the words.

"Well, what?"

"Honestly?

"Honesty is always the preference," Pettick encouraged.

Mawkin planted his feet in stance, readying his response, and with a huff, declared, "I don't think anyone should have the power to make such a decision."

"Pettick!" Dirk called.

Mawkin faded back to memory as Pettick turned back to the barn.

"You were but a simple 'Crow." Pettick muttered to himself as he walked away, leaving Mawkin's memory behind, an artifact of seasons past.

After Pettick stepped into the Cattle Barn, his 'Crows began sealing the door behind him. The large bay of the barn looked nothing like it had when Pettick had last set foot there. A series of tables had timber, saws, chisels, and other tools scattered across the bay. A series of chains and ropes hung from pulleys, mounted to the rafters that led into the darkness above. The web of lines ran down to a point, centered in the room, holding up a large table of wooden planks and metal straps; additional straps of leather and chains of metal held the creation in place atop it. The lines shifted into their run, echoing the squeal of the pulleys, the table tilting as they did. The lines swung and snapped under the immense weight, pelting dust clouds that rained onto Pettick like clumps of ash. Pettick stepped into the web, approaching the table as the lines halted in a roaring clunk. The face of the table was nearly vertical before him. He reached out his glove, touching the thatching of the figure's chest, running his fingers along the still timber ribs.

"The Soldier," Pettick whispered to himself.

"Beautiful, isn't it?" The Creator's voice carried from the loft.

"Some might say," Pettick muttered, pressing his index finger against the chest.

The Creator chuckled, leaning over the railing, looking down at Pettick.

"Stop hiding out of reach, and come down here," Pettick ordered.

"I quite like the view from up here," the Creator said with a smile, contorting his head up to look even further down on Pettick.

"I'm sure you do."

The Creator jumped back into the darkness, his sharp laughter carrying on in waves. Pettick stared at the railing for several moments, stern, impatiently awaiting his return. He turned, stepping away from the creation, running his hands along the tools atop the tables with an understanding grasp of most of them. He stopped at a hack saw, lifting it by its tarnished metal teeth, he studied the object with abject distaste, then dropped it as though it had been a creature that had just bitten his curious hand. He immediately returned his arms to their statuesque crossing.

The doors of the abattoir swung open. The Creator passed through them as he slid on his working gloves. He stood, picking a dried brown residue from the gloves that cracked as he ran his fingers across it. Pettick watched him as he eagerly peeled away the layers.

"Why isn't he moving?" Pettick said, an uncanny firmness to his tone that even the Creator had yet to hear. He waited for a response. The two Scarecrows stared at the lifeless creation before them. Pettick cocked his head at the Creator, who returned the gesture. "Why isn't he moving!" Pettick's body trembled with the slur of his words. "Negligent fool, why isn't it moving?" Before the Creator could respond Pettick lunged forward and grabbed the Creator's cloak, ripping at him violently, then tore him down to his level, tongue and heel. "We need him."

"I—I don't know," the Creator stuttered, "there is a—there's a—"

"There is a what?" Pettick jerked forward, causing the Creator to fall to the ground. "Waste of grain." Pettick stood back, regaining some sense of composure.

"I do wonder—" The Creator spoke calmly as he stood, brushing the dirt from his cloak.

"You wonder what?"

"Maybe the spark . . . just ran out?"

"The spark?"

The two Scarecrows hung in an unkind silence, as if tied to the pike once more. The Creator broke through this first, having gathered the momentum of his thoughts.

"Fireflies arrive in summer—bulbs burning bright. But carcasses, smashed or not, autumn eventually beckons, and with it the bulbs fade, burn out and die; eventually the fireflies and their glow are all gone, and their magic along with it."

"There is no magic!" Pettick shouted with a disgusted drawl. "Just the plight of ignorant children." His words echoed in the chamber.

"Ha!" The Creator let out a loud hooting drawn-out cackle, howling, "That's remarkable." Keeling over, the Creator continued to laugh, trying little to regain his composure.

"What—what is?" Pettick glared at the Creator, unamused.

"Hooot—woooo—just—it's just remarkable." After several failed attempts, the Creator stood up straight, controlling the exhausts of his breathing, as Pettick stared him down.

"What is?"

"You of all, don't believe. Now that is funny," the Creator asserted, pointing his slender index finger square in Pettick's face who quickly swatted it away as though it were a nagging fly.

Pettick huffed, paced for several moments, then turned back to the creation on the table. He scanned the large thatching of sticks, jointed with the fibers of straw, all tightly woven, fashioned with precision. Its large chest bulged like the timber of its arms.

Pettick inhaled and exhaled, letting out his words quietly. "Find a way to make it work. I don't care what you have to do or by what means you do such things. Whatever needs you have, they will be met. We agrarians and artisans have an army at our gates, awaiting a war this colony is not armed for. We need our Soldier."

The Creator nodded.

"Now get back to work." Pettick walked towards the door.

The Creator waited for Pettick to gain distance before speaking. "It is quite the shame."

"Excuse me?" Pettick stopped. "What is?"

"Your Soldier—your need for such a figure. Guessin' what it is you really need is Mawkin right about now." The Creator spoke with a bite, knowing he was getting under Pettick's threads.

Pettick turned back to the Creator, a shadow cut across his face as he began speaking with clarity. "You seek my attention—well, here it is. Our loss will be greater if you toy around in trivial pasts. Do your job or the last order I make of this colony will be that of my followers to your doors, where they will rip you apart thread by thread."

The Creator remained unmoved for several moments, holding his ground before beginning to pace.

"What was there in prying into old wounds?" Pettick asked with a theatrical sincerity to his victim.

"Just a thought," the Creator said.

"And that is?"

"What hope, less trivial, does this colony have in such a leader when even the loyalist bitch that was good Mawkin lost faith?"

Pettick gave no motion of anger or validation to his reply. "Back to work," turning back to the door, where he knocked for its opening. The door slid open, and he stepped out. The Creator moved to the center of the barn where he could see Pettick by his horse, framed in the daylight through the doorway.

"It couldn't last forever. Nothing does," the Creator said, only loud enough to ensure Pettick heard him.

The two 'Crows matched gazes as Pettick mounted his horse, signaling to his soldiers to close the doors. The darkness returned around the Creator, the giant doors sealed.

"Watch the barn. He doesn't come out unless the Creature is on his arm—walking."

"Yes, sir," the Scarecrows harmoniously responded, gripping their rifles and moving to their posts. Pettick nodded, yelling as he whipped the reins to the horse's side, galloping into the gray. All in chase, memories of dust.

* * *

With an unbridled gallop, four 'Crows on horseback approached the Tack House, a cloud of dust in their wake. Veidt led the charge, Pitch and two soldiers at his side. The orchard was full, though propagated trees no longer bore fruit. However, neither 'Crow nor mare or stallion took notice of the flowers' absence. They dismounted just short of the gate to the range, keeping sight on the building as they did. Veidt hobbled forward, unholstering his sidearm.

"Round the building, wouldn't be shocked by trouble," Veidt ordered, motioning directions with the barrel of the pistol. The two farthest 'Crows raised their rifles, moving around their respective sides of the paddock. Veidt checked the rounds in his sidearm, returning it to his holster, and drew his rifle from the horse's saddle. Veidt swung open the gate to the pen, stepping into the rutted grounds within, Pitch trailing behind him. The dried muck broke away under the pressure of the 'Crow's boots. As they trudged forward, Veidt loaded his weapon, fumbling with the clip before properly inserting it with a resounding click. Pitch and Veidt stopped halfway down the pen, the path growing arduous with the depth of dried muck.

A whipping crack sounded beyond the large door of the stables. The 'Crows on the perimeter climbed into the pen, weapons drawn, moving in a line beside Veidt.

"Shepherd! We're here for the horses; step out of the barn!" Veidt shouted. His marble eyes oscillated, quickly rolling from wall to wall in their black sockets.

A second whip was heard, causing the infiltrators to pause in their stride. With the sound of the third whip the door to the stables slid open, horns and hooves bursting from its womb. The stampede of cattle and horses flowed into the pen, the influx roaring straight for the Scarecrows. The earth severed at their feet.

Veidt dropped his rifle, overturning the trough beside him with a heaving throw. The surrounding soldiers lowered their weapons, retreating. Veidt jumped onto the trough, narrowly avoiding a pair of horns that barreled past. Pitch shot sideways toward Veidt's makeshift island. Dodging the first bovine's path, Pitch let off a round, followed by a squeal, as he fell under the crushing weight of a bull's hooves. Veidt watched as the stampede caught up with the other 'Crows, trampling them in the same devastating trounce, with little honor in the rout of their slaughter.

Shepherd appeared on horseback, galloping along the perimeter of the pen. He matched gazes with Veidt before darting off, leading the stampede, herding north, through the orchard.

"Traitor!" Veidt shouted, careless of whether his words were heard over the roaring stampede. The remaining heard trickled past, and Veidt stepped down, moving across the muck to his affects. He picked up his smashed grey kepi, attempted to reforge the felt grey brim, and threw it back onto his head. Tightening his stained wool scarf, he lifted the barrel of his rifle, examined the bent shaft, and with a growl, threw it back to the earth.

Barnes and Gwyn slunk low among the remaining crops at the edge of the village, ducking as two Scarecrows on horseback blurred past, barreling toward the meeting ground. The heavy hooves shook the soil, causing tremors. Barnes could feel them as he pressed through the stalks, scanning the corner of town. The air was quiet in daylight's dying minutes.

"All right, stay low and follow close," Barnes ordered. They cut out toward Main Street, hitting the side of the first bungalow with a resounding thud. Moving around the back wall, they cut into the alley between two bungalows. Sliding toward the street, Barnes remained tight against the wall, cautiously lingering at the edge.

"Go," Gwyn said, shoving Barnes onward.

Barnes stumbled forward, then recoiled, swinging back into the alley, pinning Gwyn against the wall. A trailing 'Crow on horseback shot quickly passed. Barnes sighed, sticking his neck out to see the rider chasing to catch up with the other soldiers in the distance.

"What do you see?" Gwyn asked, still pinned between the wall and Barnes's chest.

"Just wait there," Barnes said, pulling his arms from around Gwyn, stepping out into the center of Main Street.

"What are you doing?" Gwyn muffled her shouts.

"Come on," Barnes said.

Gwyn inched forward, meeting Barnes in the center of the street. She looked down the dirt path. All of Main Street was vacant, a prevailing feeling of abandonment in a formerly vibrant place.

"It's empty," Barnes said, knowing he was stating the obvious. A curtain of fallen leaves, mid-dance, whispered passed.

"Where do you think everyone is?"

"Still at the well, or—"

"Or?"

"I don't know," Barnes exhaled, fixing the fold in the roll of his flannel sleeve. "Kinda don't plan on findin' out—let's go get your folks."

Restless, Critch paced by the door of the bungalow. Periodically he would shift to the wall, organizing the shoes on the shelf, methodically pulling pairs out of their various slots, perfecting their form before dusting them off and returning pairs to their slots. He shifted back to the window, hunching over so he could see between the smallest space where the shutters met. He remained there for several moments before returning to the shelf. All was quiet.

"Anyone out there?" Quill asked, shifting her attention from Mare in the adjacent cot.

"No, not yet."

"Offering's been over for an hour—" Mare stated, paternal worry sown in her threads. She held Crane's satchel in her hands, the flower still peaking out of the flap.

"We'll wait—they'll be here." Quill comforted Mare, reaching out her glove to Mare's.

"How are you so patient?" Mare asked Quill.

"Remember, patience is my profession." Quill said, with a reassuring smile tacked on.

The door shook and several knocks followed, bringing the room to attention. Critch swung open the door and Gwyn wrapped her arms around him as she and Barnes entered. Gwyn moved to her mother. Quill stood up and moved over to Critch and Barnes.

"Were ya able to—" Critch inquired.

Barnes shook his head in reply.

"I'm sorry, kid." Critch rested his glove on Barnes's shoulder, a gesture Barnes briefly acknowledged, still in the focus of adrenalin.

Barnes looked around the room at this small faction. Gwyn and Mare took solace on the cots in the back of the room. Critch stood with worry and sorrow on his face, and Quill was by his side, his jacket in her gloves.

"Listen, we have to get outta here—we don't have much time."

Critch reasoned, "Well, how do you suppose we do that? Fence has got most of the place surrounded. And I doubt Pettick is keen on our exit."

"Have you ever been in an automobile?" Barnes said with a small wistful smile briefly cornered in his cheek.

"But what about the rest; they don't know. They know not of what Pettick is, and only a feather of what he is capable of." Quill looked about the room for support in her rally—in her reason.

Barnes's smile faded as he turned back to Quill, addressing with a firmness of his father, "You can stay here and try and sway an ignorant village, or you can come with us. Either way, we are getting out of this colony tonight."

Subdued, Quill looked up at Barnes, handing him his jacket, ensuring he heard her words before she sighed away: "So much for expansion."

CHAPTER XVII: Neo-Colonialist

Captain Raleigh stepped into the communications tent, the cool air moving with him as if in chase. He navigated through the tent with ceremonious presence in his stride. The radio operators continued at their work while the clicking and static of the machines washed over the captain as he idly passed. Raleigh stepped around the bullpen of navigators and scanned their maps in passing. Brushing his whiskers, he took time with the map of the farm, examining photos from a recent aerial survey. A soldier approached Raleigh with a communication slip in his hand. Taking hold of the slip, the captain turned, following the private out of the tent, photos in hand. Peering out over the farm, he passed into the adjacent tent.

With Raleigh standing in the doorway of the tent, the soldiers gave attention to their commanding officer. Raleigh placed a ceremonious cigar in the grit of his teeth, lighting it with the flick of a match, which he abruptly extinguished and pocketed. "Innocent American lives—that is what I care about." Raleigh spoke fervently, fists dramatically slamming down on the table, which was covered from corner to corner with a map of the region. "I don't give a fuck if it's the Reds, the Koreans or the God-damn Nazis! We will treat this enemy with the same caution and hostility as any. There are innocent people on the other side of those borders. And compelling evidence in the scars on the boy's body corroborating that they are a hostile community possessing a great capacity for violence. So until every soul is safely accounted for, we treat this as a hostile enemy. Understood?" The captain looked for compliance in all the faces of his men, shifting his attention back to the map when satisfied. "Good."

Smoke filled the tent, thickening with each soldier's exhaust of air. Adjusting his belt, pulling it higher on his waist, Raleigh spat, chewing on his cigar. "Perry will lead the convoy down old 61, the forest surrounding the western perimeter is only two or three miles deep." Raleigh nodded to Perry, then cocked his head around to Cooper. "Cooper, your company will break off, cutting through the south woods on foot. Now they're an hour or so deeper, but the boy has led us to believe the silos and barn where the prisoners are being held is here, along the southern perimet—"

A voice carried from the corner of the tent: "Ya know this ain't just a stroll in the park. Pettick's not some farmhand; he'll know you all are coming." Attention gradually shifted from Raleigh to Jamie, though Cooper's focus did not sway. "Don't expect no white flag, is all," Jamie continued, stepping through the crowd.

Raleigh dropped his head, the palms of his hands pressed firmly to the table as the air drained out of his nostrils, flaring his whiskers. "As I was saying, breaching the perimeter may be difficult. We move at 2100." The soldiers grunted and cursed after their dismissal, filing out of the only narrow flapped entrance. Raleigh shifted over to Jamie, resting his hand on Jamie's shoulder. Tightening his grip, he said, "Keep your mouth shut. Remember, you're a guest here and your mouth is making you unwelcome." Captain Raleigh stepped out of the tent.

Jamie hung silent, staring through the vacant doorway; Cooper folded the map as he stepped toward him.

"All right kid, you're with me," Cooper said, handing Jamie the folded map. "Remember: keep your chin up and your head down. You follow every order, understood?" Cooper nodded, signaling for Jamie to follow him. Jamie followed at Cooper's heel, wrapping around the tent, he thought carefully about his words, vying for Cooper's attention.

"So how do you plan on killing these things?" Jamie inquired.

Cooper lit the cigarette hanging in his lips. The smoke trailed him as he turned to see the genuine concern in Jamie's eyes. "I'm starting to wonder if we shouldn't have locked you up," Cooper declared, a tinge of sarcasm.

"I put a three-inch springer straight in one once—it just looked at me, smiled, and pulled it out."

"We'll figure something out," Cooper said, torn by rationale.

The soldiers in Cooper's company gathered behind a truck, arming themselves with weapons and supplies. As Cooper and Jamie arrived, Woodley handed Cooper a rifle and several clips. Placing the spare clips on his belt, Cooper inserted the last clip into the rifle.

"Listen, kid, I don't know what to make of your little story—just get us to that lock-up." Cooper nodded, looking for Jamie's understanding. With reluctant eyes, Jamie acknowledged.

"Hey, Sarge, who's the civilian?" a four-eyed Woodley sneered, pressing his glasses further up the bridge of his nose.

"All right, lay off, Woods." Cooper signaled for the attention of his small unit of eight men. "This is Jamie, he'll be our guide," Cooper ordered. "He's a—uh—consultant."

"What's he an expert in, freaks?" Bryant interjected.

A cool wind passed. Jamie dug his hands further into his pockets as he watched Bryant help Jones lift a pack with fuel tanks onto his back. Jones was a tall black man, with broad shoulders and a pronounced chin. He set eyes on Jamie, sensing Jamie's eyes on him. Gradually, the company all looked at Jamie, his jacket, grey T-shirt, plaid button-up, and blue jeans sticking out against the green and brown uniforms surrounding him. Jamie noticed them scanning him, which only intensified his discomfort.

"Hey, kid, how about we get you some better clothes—something that doesn't stick out like a moving target?" Bryant leaned over to Cooper and whispered something in his ear, all the while keeping his eyes on Jamie.

Cooper nodded to whatever Bryant was saying.

"What's wrong with my clothes?" Jamie defensively retorted.

"Nothing—nothing at all." Bryant Wryly spoke, smacking the gum in his mouth as he stepped passed Jamie; his figure, a cypher in the fog of green uniforms and patches of
red, white, and blue.

Pettick stood tall, centered on the platform, a newly crafted army before him, an army of straw, wielding barreled weapons of steel and iron buckshot, of pitchforks forged and reapers sharpened, shovels and knives held high. "What tool cannot be made into a weapon?" Pettick rationed, marveling at the results of such an order. Pettick stepped forward, wielding the microphone in his glove. The metallic din of his voice resonated across the valley. He knew his words would reach the hill. These words he wanted his enemy to hear. He reckoned with his fears on this stage and his words were a testament of these fears realized. “I know you are afraid, I share in your fears. I am afraid, and that is justified.”

Several of Pettick’s soldiers raced by on horseback, blurred silhouettes in the night, backlit by the glow of the meeting ground. Barnes signaled the group to remain down as they lay flat, hidden in a row at the edge of the cornstalks. The corner of the supply shed stood ninety yards ahead of them. A few hundred yards beyond that, the meeting ground bustled with the racket and rally of Pettick’s speech. “These humans have brought war to our door!” Pettick’s voice carried clear into the night.

Barnes signaled to the group: “All right, over to the toolshed. Quickly. Quietly.” Barnes stepped out of the crops, looking out as the group crossed to the toolshed. Gwyn reached the shed first, pressing against the wall as she slid to the corner, where the floodlights met the darkness. The light met the shadow on her face, outlining her silhouette in a sharp white aureole. Quill slid beside her, acutely focused on the events unfolding.

“What have we come to?” Gwyn said softly, looking out on the cheering crowd.

“War,” Quill said.

“I thought us better,” Gwyn stated in her awe.

“It is the greatest folly for a species to think itself above it,” Quill added.

Barnes darted forward, following Critch, the group now gathered in the shadow of the toolshed, Barnes scanned the surrounding area, tasking little care to the events unfolding at the meeting ground. He was planning their escape in his head.

“This is our time.” The levels of the loudspeakers peaked with Pettick’s declaration.

“We gotta move, all right?” Barnes whispered. Gwyn and Mare turned to listen to Barnes, the sounds of the meeting still present behind them. “All right.” Barnes looked down at a cream-colored paper in his hand, then tucked it back into his pocket. “The truck is in Kindle’s garage up the hill. Quill, you lead. Don’t wait for the meeting to be over, our best chance is when the majority of them are still occupied.”

"This is our chance to prove our worth, each and every one of you was made for a reason, to matter, there are no such unkind accidents in our species. We all seek such occasions to rise to. We are put on this earth for a cause, our mere existence, the effect . . ." Pettick's voice sounded, his reasoning catching Barnes attention, having heard or read these words once before.

"Where are you going?" Critch asked Barnes.

"I have to get my father."

"Where is he?"

"The farmhouse." Barnes said, calculating the steps in his head.

"I'm coming with you," Critch said, nodding to Barnes.

"All right. You wait 'til it's clear, then you go," Barnes said to Gwyn. Quill continued looking back and forth, torn between the meeting and Barnes. "Ready? Follow me." Barnes nodded to Critch as they ducked behind the shed, rushing quickly back into the crops.

"This is our home!" Pettick's speech drummed a rallying cry, setting a galvanizing echo, though his final words faded in a dreadful cadence over the barren valley.

"We have to hurry, let's go," Gwyn said, pressing her back flat against the wall, signaling for Mare to start for the crops. Quill turned, looking back at the meeting ground. Gwyn doubled back, shepherding her, with the pull of her glove. "Quill—Quill, come on! We gotta go!" The group rose, moving toward the back of the shed, whisking into the crops.

In the thick of the south woods a wooden fire tower rose with the trees, peaking several meters above the pine canopy. The tower had long since been abandoned, evident from the rotted state of its timber. Jamie and Cooper lay atop the escarpment. The old structure swayed with the currents of wind, howling and moaning as it did.

"See that right there—the barn structure connected to the silos?" Jamie pointed to the dimly lit towers several miles ahead. "That's it—that's where they are being kept."

Cooper peered through his binoculars. "And you're sure?"

"I've been there—so, yeah, pretty damn sure," Jamie stated.

Cooper lowered his binoculars, packing them away as he looked forward at the light of the farm.

"Can't be more than a quarter mile between the forest and the back of the facility."

"Yeah, about right."

Cooper slid back, swinging onto the metal ladder on the side of the tower, Jamie followed, trying his best not to look down.

"Don't look down," Cooper said, taking notice to Jamie's slower pace.

"Kinda hard when that's the direction you're moving."

"The key is the rate of climb," Cooper snickered, in jest.

"At least one of you has sense of humor."

"Can't say we are always in a place to be making jokes."

Jamie's pace increased, closing the gap as they continued down the structure. "How exactly do you plan on getting into the facility?" Jamie gripped the bar tightly. Rust and paint stuck to his hand at each release.

"See what we're up against when we get there."

"I know there's a side entrance opposite the silos we could prolly break in—guessin' that'd be east."

Reaching the ground, Cooper sighed. "Jamie, 'we' aren't doing anything." He looked at Jamie as they stepped down off the ladder.

Bryant approached Cooper, handing him his pack and rifle. "Listen, I'm sorry, Jamie, but my orders were to send you back to the base as soon as we got the location."

A shadow cut across Jamie's brow. "You're going to need me! I know how to get in, how to get through the facility. I can help you."

"Orders, kid. Even if your uniform is leather and denim you should be able to understand that—at the very least, respect it."

"Not exactly." Jamie looked away.

"Well, that's on you." Cooper spun around, haste in his stride, stopping several paces up the clearing. Dropping his shoulder back to Jamie, he said, "I gotta understand, kid, what's your play here, why come back? Why would anyone in their right mind come back?"

Jamie offered a silent reply.

Cooper turned away, starting in steady march in the direction of the farm, "Williams, escort James back to camp."

"Yes, sir," Williams responded to Cooper as he passed.

CHAPTER XVIII: The Menagerie

Thick blackness, akin to that romanticized by poets and theorized by astronomers, surrounded the Textile Barn, giving the structure a glow as the light within bled through every open crevice and seam made un-flush. The rioting Scarecrow militia had all dispersed. The electric had been cut across the essential occupied arteries of the farm. The only exterior light, a single yellow lamp, hung glowing above the front entrance, on the far eastern side. Several yards from the northwest corner of the structure, near the plow-line's edge, a rusted trough sat with three onlookers huddled behind it.

"What are we doing, Quill?" Gwyn asked firmly, gripping the brim of the trough, nervous of Quill's response.

Quill momentarily broke from her strategic thinking. "We're going to the Textile Barn," she responded, a cloud of cool air marked the exhale of her breath.

"I can see that, but why?"

"We have to warn the colony," Quill said, rounding the trough, rushing across the clearing and hitting the wall of the barn with a thud.

"For a 'Crow so wise, this is a really dumb idea," Mare said, glancing despairingly to Gwyn.

"I know." Gwyn nodded, looking at her mother briefly as she rose, rushing to catch up with Quill, their figures silently disappearing in the patch of darkness. Gwyn pressed against the wall of the barn, kneeling next to Quill. Mare followed. "Quill, this wasn't a part of the plan." Gwyn spoke with a motherly tone of patience and fervor. "I really don't think we should do this."

Quill swung around, taking Gwyn's shoulders in her gloves. "Listen, Gwyn, I can't—I can't go without letting them know that they've been lied to." Quill gazed through Gwyn, an intoxicated stare. "Lies I taught them." Quill spun away before Gwyn could respond, sliding further down the wall.

"Shit, Quill!" Gwyn said, in a muffled shout.

"Do you think she has a plan?" Mare whispered, leaning next to Gwyn.

"I seriously doubt it."

Quill rushed around the front of the Barn, peering around the corner. Gwyn and Mare followed behind her. She signaled for them to stop. Quill pressed her glasses to her brow. The large 'Crow guarding the door marched a steady pace under the light, a whistle breaking the monotony of his labors. Gwyn and Mare remained spectators at the corner of the barn.

As the guard turned to the tune of his whistle, Quill darted forward, charging with all her weight, tackling him to the ground, his rifle falling out of reach. Both Scarecrows lay on the ground, each struggling for a higher stance. The guard fought with swings far less sloppy, tearing at Quill who, letting out a heavy cry, pressed her opponent down. Quill embraced a survivalist's ferocity, shooting hands forward, reaching for the rifle. Crawling toward the weapon, Quill's gloves tore at the soil. Rising to his knees, the guard took hold of Quill's ankles, sliding her back to him. She let out a muffled scream as she gripped the barrel of the rifle, swinging the stock around, the butt collided with the guard's temple. Falling back, the 'Crow's body grew limp and silent, knocked unconscious. Quill's chest heaved with the effort of regaining her breath as she stood up, lifting the guard's rifle.

Gwyn and Mare approached with caution. Quill fumbled to get the proper grip on the stock, holding it out as if mimicking a picture, only backwards. Finding her hold on the stock, she looked up at Gwyn and Mare who were staring back at her in obvious disbelief.

"What?" Quill said as she blew a strand of her wiry red hair from her face, reading the shock on her companions' faces.

"Nothing—we're following you," Gwyn and Mare chimed. Quill nodded, moving to the door.

"Though I don't know why," Gwyn hesitantly muttered.

The latch squealed as she lifted it from its bracket and slid open the door, the glowing influx of the light giving fight against the darkness. They moved inside quickly, the light retreating with the closing door. Quill froze with the sealing of the door; Mare and Gwyn following suit.

The Textile Barn was filled wall-to-wall with colonists. The crowd grew silent for a moment, staring at the visitors before nervous chatter returned, echoing the length of the hall. Gwyn looked around the room, the lamps mounted on the wall held a flame encased in ornate glass boxes every few feet. The large worktables where she spent many of her days were pushed to the perimeter of the room. The only other exit she saw, the window, was as high as the rafters on the far back wall and blocked partially by the stacked crates, which sloped down into the crowd. Quill could only see the faces as she exhaled, lowering the rifle to her side, keeping in mind the bayonet at the end of the barrel. The noise rose again as, with a more direct paranoia, the heads in the crowd all snapped in their direction.

Leaning to Quill, Gwyn whispered, "What are you gonna do?" Her chin was nearly resting on the Teacher's shoulder.

"I don't know, I'm making this up as I go."

"I can see that, but you gotta say something—we can't just stand here."

"I know." Quill thought for a moment, stepping forward, head high, she moved toward the front of the barn, pushing through the anxious crowd, their worry, confusion, fear, read plain on the faces and followed her as she passed.

Taking hold of one another, Gwyn and Mare followed Quill, looking down at the shifting path at their feet as they went. Passing Malthus and his family, Quill reached the other end of the crowd, against the wall, at the base of the stack of crates. Spinning around, she laid the rifle on a crate and pulled herself atop one of the sewing tables. Gwyn and Mare took post on the floor by the crates. Quill stood tall atop the sowing table, chest forward, looking out on her audience, a furl to her brow. Reaching her glove into her sweater pocket, she searched for a small envelope with her name scribed. Her head bobbed in realizing the letter and its inscription concealed in the fold were left in Barnes's jacket. She sighed, considering the courage she must now muster. Quill fought the weight upon her, inhaling—then exhaling—chosen words.

"Everyone, please—please listen to my words, they are earnest and true." Hearing the echo of her own voice, Quill bit clearly the end of every syllable, looking into all the faces as she spoke. "Pettick has lied to you. Our known world—this colony we have here—is built on those lies. There is more out there—so much more." She stuttered, seeing the shifting tides in the faces of her audience, evidence of a dividing village. "I know—I know this is hard for some to believe, such ideas are difficult to fathom, let alone you be told they are true, and to be expected to embrace such a reality—such a truth." Her gaze reached to the rafters, then fell back to the floor. "I'm sorry, Pettick. I lied to you—I lied to you." The echo rang. "We don't have to live in those lies any longer! There are many very bad things about to happen, but you don't have to wait in line at the chopping block; you have a choice—"

"Traitor!" Hardwick shouted, stepping only partway out of the crowd. "This 'Crow is a traitor!"

"Let her speak, Hardwick!" Malthus shouted, stepping forward, his family behind him.

"Please, I'm just trying to help you!" Quill pleaded, quickly loosing ground.

"These Scarecrows are skin-lovers!" Hardwick declared. "And you know what Pettick said about traitors—they are bad seed—and bad seeds must be shucked!"

Quill, with body whole in gesture, "We are trying to help you! Please listen to us—"

"Not another lie, Quill!" Hardwick demanded as a wave of vilifying utterances flowed through the crowd.

Quill looked down at Gwyn's face, her gaze longing back in a moment turbulently still. The crowd grew wild in disagreement, forming factions among the village of loyalists and defectors. And so quickly words turned to violence.

Several 'Crows rushed forward to grab Mare and Gwyn. Quill lifted the rifle and, turning to the wall, she thrust the rifle forward, shattering the case of the lamp with the bayonet. Oil dripped down onto the blade, igniting as she ran it across the flame. Quill raised the rifle, its bayonet in flame, swinging it down on the 'Crow holding Gwyn. The blade of the bayonet sliced the 'Crow's arms clean off. The 'Crow fell back screaming, the stubs of his forearms singed. With the amputation complete, the hands released Gwyn, who shook them off in a spasm. Quill jumped down to the floor, swinging the rifle, its blade still burning. The Scarecrow released Mare, jumping back into the crowd to avoid the blade.

"Get behind me!" Quill yelled to Gwyn, who followed her order, helping Mare up as they moved behind Quill. "Get out of here! Now!" she shouted, waving the rifle at the Scarecrows attempting to advance.

"Where are we supposed to go?" Mare screamed.

"Climb!" Quill shouted, swinging the blade as several Scarecrows lunged forward.

Hunched atop the bottom crate, Mare spun back to the crowd, the wrappings of her skirt drawn taut, her attention being called through the shouting. Most prevalent were the sounds of a child crying. Malthus locked gazes with her, his arms lifting his youngest child into her arms. The Scarecrow was small, of toddler size in corduroy overalls, with locks of blonde hair. She took hold of the child. Malthus's face showed relief as he sunk back into the crowd, swept away by tearing arms. The child clung to her as she turned back to Gwyn and began to climb.

Gwyn quickly ascended the crates, pulling Mare up each plateau. As the crowd pushed forward, several 'Crows shifted around Quill, cutting her off from her companions, others broke off, ascending the crates in pursuit of Mare and Gwyn. Gwyn reached the top, pressing gloves to the wooden crate that blocked the window. The heavy container slid and tumbled over, shattering on several pursuing Scarecrows, sending them tumbling back to the floor. Gwyn pressed her glove to the pane of the circular rose window. The screams increased. Gwyn looked down on the chaos. She shifted, pressing Mare and the child against the glass as she pulled up on a board from the crate. The nails wailed, rending themselves free from the grain. Gwyn gripped the board, signaling for Mare to move. Plunging the board forward, the petal shape in the frame shattered, sending shards raining down to ground.

With skirmishes breaking out among the villagers, a 'Crow stumbled forward, the burning blade of the bayonet piercing his chest. The 'Crow fell to the floor. The fire spread through the lining of his threads. Several large Scarecrows rushed Quill, separating her from the rifle. Quill's screams continued as the 'Crows of the village tore her limbs from her body, the fibers scattering over the barn. Her torso didn't fully dismember in the initial pull, rather after several violent tears. And clumps of straw pooled atop the floor boards.

With the child wrapped around her, Mare pulled herself up onto the windowsill, sliding through the frame. Gwyn followed, looking down at the Scarecrows of the village who tore at one another like hungry animals of a menagerie all confined to the same cage.

Gwyn's feet hit the ground outside the textile house. She jumped up, helping her mother along. Mare held the child tight, her face buried in Mare's shoulder. From around the barn two shadows dashed forward, tearing at them. Gwyn pulled her left hand free and swung it around, colliding with her attacker's face.

From the night, a swift galloping sound gave way to a large horse and rider, throwing hooves at the attackers. A hand reached down lifting Gwyn up as the long slender fingers wrapped around her.

"Shepherd!" Gwyn smiled, looking up at him. Shepherd cradled Gwyn in his lap as Mare tightened her grip around his torso.

"All right, hold on!" Shepherd said, pulling the reins of the horse around as the large animal spun and leapt forward into the night. With a heavy gallop, the horse sped down the path towards the ridge. The heavy blows of air from its nose rose like the steam of a locomotive. Gwyn let her head rest against Shepherd's chest, her hair dancing in the wind. Even with the growing distance, Gwyn could still hear screams.

* * *

The radio cracked with static of its incoming transmission. The field operator lifted the receiver, looking out on the scattered incandescence of the farm ahead. More static-washed voices came through. The soldier muffled the receiver against his chest, pressing into the grass. Sounds of static rose then cut out. Rolling over, he stayed low, moving down the row of soldiers to his commanding officer.

"Sgt. Roberts: report," the radio sounded, Raleigh's voice in the reciever. He handed Roberts the receiver.

"Yeah," Roberts whispered, pressing the receiver to his face.

"Roberts, report," the radio sounded louder.

"This is Roberts. Go."

"What's your twenty?"

"At the perimeter, farthest west point of Tucker's Farm, where the crops meet the forest—only twenty yards of clearance here."

"Can you and your men infiltrate the perimeter undetected?"

"I believe so. The perimeter fence is incomplete. Once we reach the stalks, it should be a walk in the park.

"You have the order to press forward."

"Right . . ."

"Do you copy? Your orders are to move east. Take the first hill."

"Understood," Roberts replied. Dropping his head, he handed the receiver back to the operator.

"Over and out."

The dry static faded to the rising din of grasshoppers and crickets.

"Making us the pawns," the field operator commented.

"So it would appear. All right—let's do this quietly, shall we?"

Roberts swung his arm several times, pivoting at the elbow, signaling his men forward. The cornstalks were thick, adding to the cover of the darkness. Light came from a tower on the fence several yards away, but otherwise the only light source was in the clear night sky above. Roberts looked up at the starry sky and followed it down to where it folded into the stalks. Tapping the field operator's shoulder, he rose, starting quietly across the clearing. His men followed suit, cautiously scanning the surrounding brush as they breached the border, disappearing into the crops. Patches of the stalks were as tall as the soldiers. The sound of the dried brush was the only notable evidence of their presence. The crunching slide of the soldiers' boots irritated Roberts, who drew his pistol as he led the men through the crops. The soldiers pressed forward up the hill. The clouds separated, clearing the path of the moon above.

"Are we to hold when we reach the clearing?" the field operator asked, following directly behind Roberts.

"Keep quiet," Roberts responded, leaning back to the radio operator for a moment then continuing to his charge.

"Turn back," a voice carried with the wind, cutting through the crops.

"I told you to keep quiet," Roberts said, turning to the field operator.

"I didn't say anything," the operator replied, adjusting the heavy pack on his back, rattling its metal and plastic components as he did.

"Then who—" The two looked around, but none of their company was in sight, isolated and scattered by the thick of the cornstalks as they were. "God-dammit, where are they?"

"Ahead of us."

"How'd they get ahead of us?"

"No, look ahead of us, up the hill," the field operator said, pointing. Roberts turned, following his companion's hand up the hill. As the hill crested, the edge of the crops swayed. Rising above the crop line, seven pikes rose high, a figure hanging from each, their feet hovering a foot from the top of the stalks.

"What the hell?"

Roberts marched forward and the field operator stumbled, staying at heel. The crops grew heavier and higher as they rose up the gentle slope, cutting between the men's view of the figure which hung, a silhouette in the light of the nearly full moon. Roberts raised his weapon. As they reached the base of the first pike the view of the figure grew clearer. A long slender body hung in tattered garb, the dark of the brim cast a heavy shadow on the emotionless face. The arms of the figure were spread, wrapping around the horizontal beam. In the figure's right hand was a scythe tied tightly to its glove. The two men stood at the base of the pike, looking up at the figure who appeared to be looking down on them.

"Is it a prisoner?" the field operator asked.

The sergeant adjusted his position, looking under the brim of the hat where he could see the emotionless straw face with two dark empty pits staring back at him. Roberts sighed, shaking his head in relief.

"No, just a fucking scarecrow," Roberts said turning back to the forest. "Creepy thing, ain't it?"

"You could say that," the field operator said, looking up into the dark pits, noticing the smile cut into the straw face, "Quite creepy."

"Shit!" Roberts said.

"What is it?" the field operator said, moving slowly away from the pike with a fearful curiosity still drawing him close.

"We've got a problem."

The two soldiers met, looking down the slope where they could see several of their men spread out in different places in the crops. Some of them with lit flashlights moved around.

"Radio those idiots and get them to turn their lights out, I don't give a damn how dark it is. We need to find our way without them." The field operator knelt by the pike, pulling off his pack and picking up the receiver. Roberts glanced cautiously back up at the figure, then started down the row of crops which lined the top of the hill.

"Sergeant!" a voice carried from nearby. Roberts stopped, turning around, and froze to hear the voice again. The crops shook from a harsher wind scattering its own false voices with it. Roberts turned, a shadow appearing from the stalks before him.

"Sarge," Perry said, emerging from the stalks once he was within Robert's sight.

"Perry?"

"There's something in the crops," Perry said.

"What?

"We're not alone out here; I found this in the crops," Perry said, lifting his hand up.

Roberts reached out, taking hold of the object in Perry's hand. The cold metal object was strung in a gossamer of fibers and coated in a sticky residue. He lowered it to his hip, shining a muffled light down onto the object, discerning he was clearing away a clump of bloody hair from the face of a pair of dog tags.

"Jesus Christ." Cutting out the light, Robert's breath grew visible in the cold air. He spun around. "Have you seen our radio?"

"No," Perry said, "I thought he was with you."

Roberts looked up at the first pike. Through the duplicity of the veiling darkness the pike appeared empty. He leapt forward, darting through the crops. The heaving of his chest grew a familiar beat with the rate of the passing stalks. He cut into a clear row, stumbling in several drops to the soil. Gathering clouds veiled the moon, casting darkness once again.

"Roberts!" Perry yelled.

Roberts tripped, falling backward into a narrow furrow ditch. "Perry!" He scanned the surrounding anamorphic shades of black. "Shit," Roberts barked. The wind whipped around him, cutting back and fourth through the stalks which cracked and snapped as if figures were passing through the voids. His mind filled in the visuals of these figures. The cracking rose then returned to silence as the wind died down. Roberts stumbled back to up the hill, pushing into the crops. He glanced behind for movement, then forward, reaching the clearing of the first pike. Up the pike, a figure hung above him. Spinning, his attention averted to the crops, the shades of black twisted and flapped in the violence of gusting wind. Looking down the hill he stepped forward and he could see the individual figures of his men, some with flashlights lit, and the surrounding figures, preying on them. One by one the mystery assailants moved in on his men. Cutting them down. One by one the lights went out. That is when the first screams could be heard. Several shots fired.

"God in heaven—"

A figure rose behind Roberts. Drawing a sharp blade the figure slit it across Robert's neck, cutting his flesh open. Choking for air, Roberts didn't see much of his attacker before it disappeared into the crops. His widened glassy eyes looked up the pike where the body of the radio operator hung, lashed like the scarecrow.

Kindle could hear the ensuing chaos of the farm from the basement of the house, though he could not decipher source or measure of the outlying calamities.

"Barlow, do you hear that?" Kindle stood, moving closer to the door. Barlow neither spoke nor stirred. Kindle rested his hand on Barlow's shoulder. "It's going to be okay; we'll get out there. We'll get your boy before he does. Besides, Crane is a smart kid; he'll outwit Pettick, I have no doubt." Kindle listened to Barlow's heavy breathing, waiting for a response. "Right."

A large thud sounded from above them, followed by the shuffle of footsteps at a quickened pace. The door hinge squealed along with a short discourse. Another thud preceded the sound of a heavy object rolling down the stairs.

"Someone is coming," Kindle whispered.

The footsteps rushed quickly down the stairs, then across the floor of the basement. The metal of the door clanked several times.

The voices outside became audible. The sound of a rifle shot collided with the door. The door swung open. Barnes's tall figure stood in the doorway, lit only by the beams of moonlight from the rectangular shafts through the windows. Barnes stepped forward, Critch stood several paces behind him, a rifle in hand.

"Barnes!" Kindle said, wrapping his arms around the scrawny 'Crow. Barlow stood up, moving to his son.

"Sorry it took so long, Pop. We didn't know . . ."

Barlow hugged his son. Barnes wrapped his arms around his father, moved by the gesture, patting his glove loosely to his father's back. He could not recall the last time they shared an embrace. Barlow released his hold, looking up at his son's face.

"Your brother?" Barlow asked, tightening his grip on Barnes's leather jacket.

Barnes lost much of the feeling in his body. For a moment he was again, by all accounts of appearance, a scarecrow. Willing strength, he regained his grip on his father, shaking his head softly. Barlow shuffled his feet, falling back onto the steps into the cell.

"Pop—Pop!" Barnes knelt down in front of his father. "Don't do this to yourself, Pop!" Barnes looked up at Kindle and Critch, both in a state of disbelief. "I don't know what to tell you. He made his choice."

Barlow looked up at Barnes in disgust of something he had said, or just anger.

"I don't know what to say, sir, but we—we gotta go."

Barlow remained, a statue on the steps, a mourning Barnes knew time did not allow.

"Dammit, Barlow!"

Barlow matched Barnes's gaze, a respect in his son's resolve. He nodded. "Right." With Barnes's help, Barlow stood, stepping out of the cell.

Critch turned, leading them up the stairs, "There is something you need to see."

***

The silence in the south woods broke occasionally with distant screams and sporadic bottle-rocket popping of gunfire. Williams pushed Jamie along as a flashlight drew the direction of their path.

"Missing out on all the action," Jamie remarked as he made recognition of his surroundings.

"I'll live. Now shut up and keep moving, kid."

"Yeah, you will." Jamie swung back his elbow colliding with Williams' face. He turned back, throwing his forearm into the soldier's gut and delivering a blow to the back of the head before Williams' body hit the ground.

"How's that, slack-jaw?" Jamie spat.

Williams remained unconscious as Jamie pulled his pistol, placing it in his waist. He searched the soldier's bag, finding a knife and metal flare gun with several colored bulbs, which he pocketed. The flashlight shined into the woods around him and a creek ran several feet ahead. Lifting up the soldier's rifle he dashed forward, running north along the creek, flashes from the light in his hand colliding with the clouds of exhausting air from his chest.

Outside the farmhouse, the four Scarecrows stumbled to a halt, looking up at the clear purple night, a picturesque canvas sky, and its reflecting flashes of light erupting at the opposite edge of the farm. Barnes stood beside his father watching these bulbs arc through the air, returning in dazzling ribbons to the scarred earth.

"Over there." Critch pointed, halting next to Kindle. The 'Crows turned around. The camp set up on the hill, opposite of the farm, was well lit in the night, glowing with varying intensities of artificial light.

"Humans," Kindle said disconcertingly, though void of malice.

"What do you think they're here for?" Barnes asked.

"What does it look like—" Critch said, motioning to the flashes in the distance.

"I know what they're here for," Kindle said.

"What?"

"To free their kind. We're just standing in their way," Kindle remarked, retreating back to the house.

"What did he just say?" Critch asked.

"Kindle, wait!" Barnes yelled.

Kindle turned back to Barnes, though still sidling around the house. "Barnes, the keys are in the lockbox above my toolbench, save who you can and get out of here!"

"Where are you going?"

"Just go!"

Kindle leapt onto the porch, rushing quickly into the house and up the stairs. The hallway was dark. He dashed down the hall, ignoring the pain of his limping leg, and burst through the door into Pettick's parlor. The parlor was like the chamber of a kaleidoscope. Flashes of light from the glow of the beckoning war dazzled in fractured shapes along the walls, each shard burned bright, then faded as quickly as it's effuse came. Searching the room, Kindle rushed over to the bookshelf and grabbed a small statue depicting a man sitting deep in thought atop a rock. Stepping around the desk, he ripped out each of the drawers, searching their contents, then dropping them to the floor. He finally reached for the top drawer, which he expected to be sealed by a padlock, but attached to its face was an empty hasp. Kindle dropped the statue he was holding, hearing the sound of its large thud as it collided with the floor match the rising noises from outside the house. He slid the drawer open and its contents rolled forward. Kindle lowered his glove, removed a single road flare from the drawer, and placed it in the pocket of his coat. He slid the drawer out farther and noticed a large knife rolling toward him—his knife. He held it up, unsheathing it to reveal the sharp blade, then placed it into his coat, as well.

Traces of moonlight shimmered on the grassy bluff in the cool wind. A few hundred yards ahead a convoy of carts drawn by Pettick drove steadily northwest up the ridge. Shepherd saw this and pulled back on the reins, tacking the horse to a halt.

"Time we walk," Shepherd said.

Gwyn slid off the horse before turning back to help Mare down. Mare handed Gwyn the child. Gwyn knew not how to hold the small Scarecrow, keeping her held out at arms-length until Mare hopped down and took hold of her again. After dismounting, Shepherd stepped around the front of the horse, removed the bit, and unstrapped the leather bridle from its muzzle. He looked at the animal, his tall figure allowing him to look face-to-face with the steed. He ran his glove down its head, then gently along its mane.

"Fast—don't look back," he said as he stepped back, motioning his arm southward. The horse neighed, its ears directed to Shepherd, oscillating between his master and the detected danger ahead. "Go." The horse and the Scarecrows ran in opposite directions through the tapering weeds.

The Creator burst through the slaughterhouse doors, carrying a small wooden crate in his gloves. The crate, which had once contained milk jugs, was still covered on four sides with faded hand-painted embellishments, the idealic red barn and rolling green hills of the McCALLISTER FAMILY'S DAIRY FARM. The lid was sealed with a large metal padlock. The Creator carefully set the crate down on the cart beside the Soldier. Looking up at the Creature, he spoke: "I hope you are ready for the world, my friend." He stepped onto a barrel, rising face-to-face with the Creature. His slender fingers ran along its ribs. He jumped down, strolling back into the darkness of the abattoir, returning with a leather satchel, some tools, and a small pistol. He placed the objects onto the cart, then stepped in front of the milk crate, running his glove along its edges.

He dug into the pockets of his cloak, finding nothing. His memory built to a realization he made audible. He reached at his neck, pulling out a fine chain with a key as its charm. His glove lifted the padlock, clearing soot from its face. With the keyhole now cleared, he inserted the key, unclasping the lock. Giddiness overcame him as he removed the lock. As he lifted the lid to the box, an emerald glow emitted from inside, an immense effuse gleaning, fighting away the surrounding darkness all the way up to the rafters. He reached into the box and produced one of several mason jars that filled the container.

Within each glass chamber dozens of fireflies flickered and spun, emitting their coquettish glow. Opening the jar and removing the lid, his long fingers scraped along the bottom of the interior where several bodies were lying dead, already smashed. He caught several live sparks in his hand, the rest floating upwards to the rafters where hungry birds awaited fresh prey.

He sat the jar down on the cart, stepped back up to the Creature, and gently pressed his palms against the empty eye sockets.

"Wake up," the Creator whispered. As he removed his glove, the glowing fireflies now floated like embers in the black pits. The particles steadily combined, spiraling, forming a larger, brighter spark. He stepped back, nearly falling off the barrel. With a sudden jerk the head of the Creature moved. The chest rose and fell and a burst of air followed. As the different members of the body began to properly animate, the Creator's jaw dropped, marveling at his largest creation yet. The Creature's jaw opened, letting out a powerful roar that resonated within the chamber. Awareness of his surroundings grew as he pressed forward, putting strain on the metal straps.

"Oh here, let me get that—" the Creator said, stepping forward, reaching for the clasp on the straps. The Creature thrust its chest forward, the straps buckled and snapped off, sending the Creator to the floor. Now free, the Creature stepped down from the table, its large boots making impressions in the dry dirt floor. The Creator scrambled to his feet, keeping a cautious distance from his creation. "You are a sight seen, my friend," the Creator said, scanning over his creation. A distant shot could be heard inside the barn, catching the attention of both Creator and Creation alike. "Well, we musn't wait, then . . ."

The Creator moved back to the table, reaching into the milk crate and placing several jars into his satchel. He then placed a roll of tools into the bag, closing it, throwing the strap over his shoulder, then picked up the pistol. He closed the lid of the box, turning back to the Creature, swinging his arms to get its attention.

"Nod if you understand me," the Creator said, looking up at the Creature. The Creature failed to move. The Creator demonstrated the motion. "Move your head up then down if you understand me."

The Creature looked down at its creator, gently nodding twice.

"Good . . . good." The Creator smiled. "I am your father—your creator—your master. Nod if you understand."

The Creation looked to its Creator, opening its mouth, and its voice hummed a locomotive rev, low and bellowing: "Master."

The Creator smiled, nodding. "Good. Now follow me."

Outside the barn, the soldiers standing watch paced in their path, meeting in the front by the big door. A large roar resonated from inside the barn, drawing their attention. Several noises followed, then a silence fell. The Scarecrows held their rifles at the ready. The second guard pressed his face against the door. When the door shook suddenly, the 'Crow jumped back, releasing a single shot, which pierced clean through. A wide gaze spread across his brow as he looked over at Dirk, while a ribbon of smoke emitted from the barrel of his gun.

"Relax," Dirk said.

"I d-don't hear anything n-now," the 'Crow stuttered.

"And that's a bad thing?"

"No."

The guards simultaneously lowered their weapons.

Dirk huffed, "You really need to calm—"

A larger roar resonated, and the 'Crows quickly drew their weapons. Dirk signaled to the second to open the door.

He nervously shook his head in response. "Are you kiddin'?"

"Fine," said Dirk, stepping toward the door. He gripped the handle, looking back to make sure the second guard was covering him. The door shook, splintering, then with a sudden burst, ruptured, sending Dirk into the air, his body landing a few hundred feet down the path. The Creature pressed through the remainder of the door, pine snapping like balsa. The second guard opened fire, a half dozen clicks of the lever-action Winchester emptied, the bullets shedding splinters from the Creature's chest. The Creature looked down on the guard and, with one swift motion, took hold of the Guard in his hands, lifted him above his head, and ripped the small Scarecrow in two. Bits of straw fell across the Creature's face. He tossed the remains into the field.

The Creator stepped out through the gash in the door, taking notice of the destruction. "Ah," he smiled, "Rasputin, you certainly are." He picked up the guard's shotgun from the ground. Looking out over the western half of the farm, several flashes of mortar shells and gunfire ignited in the distance. He tightened the strap on the satchel, lowering the gun in his left hand, and turned back up to his creation that astutely looked to his master for orders. "We'll find a different way then, shall we?"

The Creature, Rasputin, followed his creator into the night.

Shepherd ducked through the man-door into the garage. The light from the bulb hanging in the narrow hall bobbed off his head, shifting the shapes of shadows haunting the walls of the mechanic's bay. Mare and Gwyn followed his tall figure, halting in front of the uncovered Ford pickup, a prized statue, like the largest prehistoric predator in the lobby of its museum.

"Isn't it beautiful?" Gwyn smiled, reaching out with her glove toward silver emblem on the hood.

"What is it?" Mare asked.

"Our way out," Barnes said, entering from the junkyard man-door at the opposite end of the bay. Critch and Barlow filed in behind him. Barnes ran past Gwyn, crossing up the stairs into Kindle's office. Barlow moved over to the truck, laying his hand on the hood next to Gwyn's.

"This is what he was so eager for," Barlow remarked in a disconcerting gander.

"Curiosity is admirable," Gwyn said, looking up at Barlow.

"And foolish," Barlow huffed as he retracted his glove from the baneful object.

"You can't hold that against him."

"I don't."

"You don't understand?"

"No, Gwyn, I do. But that doesn't change a damn thing, does it?" He shuffled around the truck, deliberately escaping Gwyn, planting himself on the passenger side. He opened the door to the truck. The relic shifted with his movements, calling a pleasant discourse back to him. Gwyn cocked her head, looking over to Shepherd who was wandering along the back of the bay. She followed his footsteps in the dust along the shelves to the workbench, observing his movements, a curious stranger in Kindle's museum, a child touching all of the exhibits.

"Shepherd! How did you know where to find us—where to go?" Mare asked.

"Crane told me," Shepherd said in the most benevolent and reserved way, as if it were a secret, though he wasn't whispering.

"What do you mean, 'Crane told you'?"

Shepherd reached into his cloak, retrieving a letter in a worn cream-toned envelope. He presented it to Gwyn. Gwyn held the letter in her hand, unable to—by respect for shepherd or fear of truth—open the envelope which concealed it, continually running her thumb along the foxed edges of the flap.

"He told me to watch over you." Shepherd said.

Gwyn smiled.

Rushing out of Kindle's office, Barnes stopped at the bottom of the stairs, having recognized the letter in Gwyn's hand. He looked down at his jacket and, reaching into his pocket, he pulled what he thought was his letter from Crane on matching parchment, only to find this letter addressed to Quill. "I'll be damned," Barnes said, helping Critch and Mare into the bed of the truck. Looking around the bay, ultimately turning to Gwyn, he then asked, "Where's Quill?"

Gwyn did not respond, looking away as she climbed into the bed of the truck. Barnes drummed his gloves against the wooden rail, coping with the lack of surprise at Quill's absence. Barnes crumbled up the note in his hand and tossed it. Gwyn simply nodded, settling in the bed of the truck beside Shepherd.

"How do we plan on getting out of here?" Critch asked, standing in the bed of the truck.

"All things considered, Pettick's got more important matters than chasing us," Barnes responded, retrieving several small metal gas canisters from various hiding places, which he handed up to Critch.

"But how will we—"

"Shit!"

"What?"

"We need to go," Barnes said, pointing at the beams of light passing over the windows. A dozen of Pettick's soldiers were gathered outside, charged with procuring the vehicles. Barnes slid onto the bench seat. Behind the wheel, he pushed the key into the ignition, remembering the steps as Kindle had taught them to him: "Ignition, first gear, step off the break, relieve the clutch, step on the gas."

Resting his head against the window, Shepherd watched as the chains above swung, pitching waves of dust that pelted down in handfuls. The voices from the cab came to his ear, but he made no motion or mention of this.

"Do you know what you are doing?" Barlow asked, watching his son acting with such certainty.

"Yes, sir." Barnes pressed the clutch as he shifted the vehicle into gear. "Hold on!"

Barnes slammed his foot on the gas, and the truck shot forward and cracked the bay door. Several of Pettick's soldiers dodged the truck as the door erupted, but their recovery took only seconds before they began training rifles, firing shots, piercing the bumper and cab. Gwyn found herself lying flat in the bed of the pickup, staring skyward at the spinning stars. The truck shot around the lot, dodging several 'Crows. The headlights exposed new obstacles for the truck, while dust spiraled in its wake. Narrowly missing the fill station, the truck slid in a circle around Thalo. Dropping his weapon to the ground, Thalo huddled in a ball and shrunk his body as small as he could make it. The truck skidded past, clearing him by mere inches. He rose to his feet, spinning from dizziness, and brushed the dust from his uniform. After regaining his bearings, he spotted the truck slipping out of the lot.

"After them!" Thalo ordered the 'Crows on horseback.

Barnes spun the steering wheel quickly, straightening out and shifting the truck into a higher gear. The engine roared with the bounce of the cab as it sped down the path. Horsemen could be seen giving chase in the rearview mirror. Barnes spun the wheel quickly left and the truck slid sideways before its divergence from the path into the tall stalks of grass. The Horsemen gradually disappeared from view.

The truck breached the top of the hill a moment before arcing down toward the main road. Leaning forward, Barlow and Barnes peered through the windshield. A fire burned ahead where artillery or mortar fire had blown open a gap in a section of the fence—an act of fortuitous destruction. The father and son shared a nervous glance. Shifting into fourth gear, faster than he had ever driven, Barnes gunned it through the gap. Barlow, relieved by the success of this passage, released his grip from the dashboard. The spotlights of the two towers passed by and steadily shrank. The Ford's headlights cut into the night. The speeding truck's rubber tires hit the gravel of the road, causing it to bound like an animal freed from captivity, unbridled in its natural habitat.

The '42 Ford pickup continued south down the highway, the farm seeming to shrink to a single particle, nearly vanishing into the distance. True night drew heavily, having not been felt for so long. Barlow focused on the window as it whistled to him. The sound pierced a tune through the seal, a melody to the howling which rattled the Scarecrow as the wind broke over the cab.

"You can open that, ya know," Barnes said to Barlow, nodding toward the window.

Barlow pressed his glove to the passenger window, trying to pull it down by applying pressure to the pane.

Barnes watched his father struggle for several seconds. "No, Pop—Pop, stop!" Breaking his glove from the wheel, Barnes pointed. "That down there. See that lever?"

Barlow gripped the handle, nodding.

"Turn it." Barnes imitated the circular motion of the lever for Barlow.

Barlow successfully rolled down the window. The wind curled in, whipping through the cab, whirling around the father and son. Barlow's whiskers fluttered in his face. The old 'Crow found the initial sensation jarring, and he glared over at Barnes in reprehension. Barnes chuckled at this discomfort, in jest. As the pressure in the cab settled, Barlow gradually eased his glove out the window. The wind lifted his hand, an invitation to press it further into the current. He found this sensation most pleasant. With a rise and fall, he weaved his hand in the wind. Barlow leaned out the window, peering up at the stars that shined so clearly above.

Gwyn also looked up at the stars. She sat with her legs wrapped around Crane's rucksack, as if the potted flower that rose from it were planted in the folds of her floral skirt.

Critch put his arm around Mare as she held tight the sleeping child. The bed of the truck was exposed to the cool air. The Scarecrows felt it run through their threads and raised their gloves into the whistling wind.

CHAPTER XIX: Tooth

Pettick was crouched with his arms wrapped around his knees. He rocked back and forth on his heels by the edge of the ridge. His jacket was on the ground before him. Within its folds was his journal, weighted open with a handful of pebbles and stones. He was reading.

April 8, 1945

I awoke to the sirens, sitting up only to find Mr. Joseph already seated in his study. His black silhouette remained there for a few moments, staring back at me, before he leaned to his side table to switch on the lamp. There was this feeling, one I can't describe other than, suffice it to say, it was the first time in a long while I recall waking up and not wishing I was still asleep.

"The sirens?" I asked.

"The Americans, I do believe." I still did not believe him, so I merely nodded. But then I heard distant popping, gunfire, too frequent to be another failed escape. He continued, "They'll be here soon with their torches in hand, of that I am certain." I was quiet. I made not a noise. I wanted to stir to the window but I felt tied to that bed, even though it had been a long time since I had been tethered to that frame.

"When you go to the pictures? You do go to the pictures, don't you, Mr. Joseph?" I asked.

"Oh yes, German cinema is quite good. Better than your American propaganda, or so I am assured."

"Well, when you go to the cinema, whom do you root for?"

"Don't patronize me, John."

"No, I am quite curious. Never thought I'd get to ask a savage brute this. Are you on the side of the werewolf or the villagers?"

"First off, I am not a savage; I am a doctor, a German doctor. Secondly, I think that is quite a loaded question."

"Oh, I assure you, it is." I flashed a crooked grin, to which he gave a rebutting nod.

"Not in the way you think, however," Joseph clarified.

"Oh, why is that?"

"Rather puerile, this example. If you insist, however, I will argue. We are not all monsters, John. In fact, there are far fewer true monsters in this world than your Grimm Tales *press upon you. Sometimes, John, sometimes the villain is really a good man in a world that makes him out to be a villain and the evil you speak of is far more banal."*

"Food for the people, aye?" I remarked, conjecture he so evidently ignored.

Joseph chose his words carefully, taking a thorough pause for the first time in our talks, calculating, "You do realize this has nothing to do with what is happening out there . . . This conclave—you and I in a room having a conversation. All this is about two intelligent individuals, with their wits about them, in an old house. Nothing more.

"How can not everything be about that?"

"That is a pittance out there. We have shown—" he stopped, reckoning a funny thing, continuing, "John, wars change lines on a map, it takes great wars to change worlds." There was a blast just outside, the gunfire was drawing nearer. It was about this point in our conversation I lost patience with him.

"How do you still have hope?" I shouted. "How do you? We are at your gates. And they're going to fucking skin you. Skinned alive, can you imagine a worse death?" I mocked.

"Yes. An undignified one," he confessed, so simply.

"Well, aren't you a proper savage?" I uttered, yet noticed no reaction from Joseph, not the slightest wince in his cheek or change in his posture or body language. He remained stoic.

I realized what I most needed to learn of him—from him. And my thoughts slipped through my lips: "But you're not afraid."

"No, I'm not," he assured me.

"You're not afraid."

How he had rid himself of the shackles of fear, I wish I could ask. I cannot reckon such a thing without scaring myself.

"Do you have a wife, John?"

"No." I thought about it a little, confessing, "Just a letter letting me know she'd gone."

"You never wrote of her," Mr. Joseph said.

"Never," I replied.

"You should."

There was a frantic knock on the door—a soldier calling for his superior. "Pettick, sir!" the voice called through the door. Mr. Joseph stood up, in a leisurely stride he shifted to the door, swinging it open and speaking softly.

I heard little of their discourse as it was blocked by the door and sounds of a skirmish outside the window. I spent time ruminating on the name, Pettick. Their conversation was brief; Mr. Joseph sent the soldier off, and sealed the door.

"Are you not running?" I asked Mr. Joseph.

He sat back in his seat.

"But your family?"

"They will be taken care of, I am assured."

I hate to admit it, but I respect him for that. He had my sympathies, to say the least.

"And your name?" I asked him.

"It is a name they fear, not a man." His foot tapped the floorboards. Not with anxiousness, but rather impatience. He leaned forward in his chair and gestured. "May I?" I handed him the journal and he scanned the pages with a nod here and a smirk there. It was the most emotion I had seen in his face, though still calculating.

"Pettick?" I asked.

"Yes, my familial name," Mr. Joseph conceded.

"Why have you not used it?"

"It's rather frightening, don't you think?" He briefly looked up from the book with a terminal grin, almost satisfied by it all as he paged through the months of entries I had filled much of the journal with. "You have done good work, John."

"I can't say the same for you," I said, with a great deal of sarcasm.

Mr. Joseph exhaled a slight chuckle, "No, I have not. I have quite the reputation, John, for what some would refer to as terrible things. I garnered such a reputation, and such responsibility I will take."

There was a scuffle down the hall. Shouting followed by thunderous shots, in sequence. Breaking glass, footsteps, another fray unfolded in the floor boards below. A vomitus howl broke out. All the while we carried on, a whispered conversation under the proliferation of fired shots. I held the journal in my hands as the soldiers filed in, tearing Mr. Joseph from his seat. I was scared. I hugged the leather hide and began to cry. After seeing what he had done in the basement of that house, they brought him out into the camp and hung him. As I was taken out of the house, I caught glimpse of the horrors of his experiments. I stepped out the door, through the mud to a truck. Crossing the yard, I glanced across the camp. By the fence I could see his body hanging from the rafters of the guard tower. And I thought of what he had said only a few minutes earlier: it is a name they fear, not a man.

Pettick sat back, closing the journal and sealing the strap to the brass ball. His glove felt along the skin of the binding. He looked out over the farm, then rose, jacket and journal in hand. Over the speaker, horns went blaring and tumbling, a noise heard by the humans on the hill and those Scarecrows fighting on the front lines. At the meeting grounds, at the base of the loudspeaker, Pitch's trampled body placed the microphone beside the turntable. Twisting the knob, he set the needle to the 45 rpm record. And with his final exhausts, the needle rolled to the first track, Billie Holiday's "Strange Fruit." Pettick felt every rolling tremor, every piano key, of the lonesome ballad writhing in his body as the music encompassed him, though he remained stoic. He peered out over the farm, placing the journal in the inner pocket of his jacket. The needle rolled to the end of the record, where it skipped along, eventually trailing off.

The trucks of the convoy, massive Dodge six-by-sixes, entered from the forest, and took no pause as they plowed through the grass onto the fields, the remaining crops crushed beneath their immense tires. As the trucks continued trundling forward, their tailgates crashed open and soldiers poured out. The large white rays of the floodlights mounted atop their cabs lit the battleground, revealing the movements of the Scarecrows, which had been traveling undetected through the field. The convoy of trucks spread out over the field, pushing the lines forward, offering cover to the soldiers that moved on foot beside the wheels. Order was kept as the trucks drove up the hill slowly; the lines moved only far enough to regain those lost in the first wave. Shots could be heard over the course of several seconds, but were by no means rapid.

Perry approached a truck, a wounded man slung over his shoulder. He came beside the carriage, ordering the men who marched in its cover.

"Take this man—he's hit in the lower abdomen." The soldiers swiftly followed his orders, taking on the burden of the wounded soldier. Perry spat a secretion of blood and tobacco. He stepped up to the driver's door of the truck, where he pulled himself onto the metal step, beating the butt of his pistol against the door. "Hold," Perry ordered. The truck slowly teetered to a stop. Perry swung the metal door out, the driver peering down at him, gaging the merit of his patches as he built the words on his lips, floating with the smoke of his cigarette.

"What is it, Sarge?"

"I need a radio." Perry holstered his sidearm. The driver leaned over, handing Perry the mobile radio. Perry took hold of the brick, lowering it to his side. "Can you get in contact with the other trucks?" Perry asked.

The driver nodded.

"Tell them to hold; we want to fan out, creating a line along the western perimeter, lay in some initial cover fire, clear a path for us to move forward. You copy?"

"Yes, sir."

Perry hopped down from the step, and began marching alongside the truck. There was screaming from the wounded men being brought back from the line, but he was unfazed by this violence.

At the road, old route 61, a soldier was walking down the gravel path. His form and posture were in line with the image of an ideal army soldier, reminiscent of world war propaganda. A line of long-range, modified M-5 artillery guns were stacked down the road outside the farm. The guns were massive, with twelve-foot-long barrels which loomed over him as he paced.

Perry's deep voice crackled through over the radio. The soldier raised it to his ear, pushing back on his helmet, listening intently.

"The convoy has breached the fence, moving east over the first crop line. Thirty-four degrees west, twenty-two degrees north. Until otherwise noted, everything east of the hill is out of the safe zone. Over."

"Thirty-six degrees will light up—over," the soldier replied.

"Open fire."

***

Pettick stood on the ridge, his fortification above the kingdom of straw below, analyzing the movements of the headlights as they broke off from the line. An idea struck urgency in him. Ripping the transmitter from Thalo's gloves, he lifted his radio pack, relaying orders to Paquin at the front.

"The lights! Tell them to aim for the lights!"

"Yes, sir."

"Have them fall back to the valley; make your front line there. Copy?"

"Copy," Paquin replied, signaling the orders to Veidt. Veidt turned his horse, relaying the message down the front, cawing in loud shrieks into the air. The 'Crows spread out in the field and, upon hearing the signal, scurried back down the hill.

Pettick stepped away from his post, moving to the cart where a map of the farm was held down with rocks and lit by a small kerosene lamp. Pettick followed the topography of the cropland, tracing angles of infiltrations with his fingers. Thalo approached with a flashlight, following Pettick's hand as it pointed along the map. Pettick turned back to the ridge, lifting a pair of binoculars from the cart. He peered out into the night, tracing the movement. He turned to look eastward. He stepped several yards south, away from the lights of their command post. He peered through the binoculars again, lifting the radio.

"Tower One, Tower Two, do you have any visual of human movement west of the road?" Pettick paused, impatiently awaiting the reply. "Tower One, this is Command, do you—"

"Command, that is a negative. However, there are several large carts traveling in a row along the road itself. Big ones, sir."

"Carts?" Pettick asked, wary of the words' true meaning.

"Yes, sir—large metal ones," the dubious voice from Tower Two carried over the radio, chased by ungulating layers of static. Pettick lowered his radio, victim to the thoughts crossing his mind. "Sir?" the voice sounded once more.

Pettick crossed back to his regiment over the ridge, when the sound of the initial round came barreling through the colony. He turned skyward, watching the arc of the lead projectile take its course. Pettick stood helpless as the first shot of heavy artillery made contact, displacing a section of his line. The impact shook him, but not nearly as harshly as the shocked faces of the Scarecrows on the ridge who now felt their first true impact of loss, a loss he read on each and every face. Pettick gripped his chest, and the moments grew longer till the seconds became minutes; minutes felt like hours; hours, weeks. The night had just begun.

At the road, the solider motioned his left arm, swinging swiftly down. The giant guns exploded, bulging rounds arced skyward. The recoil shook the chassis of the guns, offsetting their line. The shots continued through the sky, then fell to earth. The rounds hit the rows of the farmland, displacing soil. The barrels ejected large casings. The soldier cocked his head back, tracing the arc of shells, their explosions like fireworks. And he reveled in their glow.

Paquin's voice carried over the radio, inaudibly at first under the sounds of the artillery, straggling rounds making landfall. "Sir, we're taking fire, should we fall back?" Paquin asked.

Pettick lifted the radio, looking heavily into the faces around him. "No! Do not fall back! Brace for impact, then press forward!" Pettick sighed, waiting for a response.

"But sir—"

"Do you copy?" Pettick placed his radio onto the cart, looking up at the faces of the 'Crows around him. "Our best chance is to knock out those lights. Without light, they will be hard-pressed to locate our line," Pettick said, defending himself to no'Crow in particular.

The 'Crows nodded.

Pettick turned and walked back to oversee the battle at the ridge. Thalo followed, carrying the radio with him. The artillery fire continued for several more minutes, illuminating the night sky in saturated glowing hues, giving a chemical tinge to the farm from Pettick's vantage point, and casting the putrid musk of sulfur through night's cool air. "Ten years . . ." Pettick reckoned, wrapping his coat around himself as impacts shook the ground beneath his feet. To his right, a chain rattled, a clasped lock bounded off the timber, hanging from the empty pike.

* * *

The floodlights, mounted along the sides of the silos, lit the area in a heavy white fog, with dark shadows tracing the surrounding shapes. Jamie's silhouette hid under a nearby tractor. He watched the guards pace, tracing their paths. Jamie crawled forward, gradually rising to a run along the edge of the darkness, and saw an armed 'Crow several paces ahead. A sound echoed from Jamie's steps. The predator and the prey froze. The Scarecrow turned, looking directly at Jamie. Jamie remained frozen as the 'Crow stared into the darkness, then continued on his path. As the 'Crow rounded the corner of the barn, Jamie raced into the light, taking cover briefly, ensuring the 'Crow's back was still facing toward him before lunging at the 'Crow, knocking the stocky straw man to the ground. Jamie wrestled with the 'Crow, throwing his right fist with the weight of his body across the 'Crow's face. Hearing the commotion, the second guard rounded the building, drawing his weapon and aiming at Jamie's back, he brought the human into his sight. The finger of his glove edged the trigger, preparing to pull.

Kindle leapt from the darkness, throwing the barrel skyward as the trigger was pulled, letting out a shot that startled Jamie, sending him to the ground. Jamie felt his body, finding no holes. In a stride most assertively casual, Kindle's large figure approached Jamie, rifle in hand.

"You should be more careful." Kindle smiled, standing over Jamie. Jamie sat up, finally seeing his savior's identity.

"I liked my odds," Jamie said, stubbornly unabashed, brushing off the dirt. Kindle offered his hand and Jamie took hold, pulling himself to his feet. "Thanks."

Kindle nodded. "Shall we?"

Jamie gave a childish white-toothed grin before picking up the rifle.

Atop the ridge, a disconcerted Thalo dissented, shouting to Pettick, "They have only trepidation, self-preservation in mind, not glory."

Cocking his head to Thalo, Pettick assured, "The lines will hold!"

Thalo retreated, both Scarecrows' attention diverted to the shrinking distances between the lines.

At the front line, Wade the Tailor stood a nervous heap, small beside a larger Scarecrow, one of Pettick's soldiers. Both 'Crows fell into the front line, their weapons in their hands. Wade took unsteadily to the weight of his rifle, trembling for a grasp.

Veidt, on horseback, trailed along the staggered line, glancing over the field as the formation of the enemy breached, in full charge, over the opposing hill. "Hold steady!" Veidt's orders hissed. As the lines fanned out, rifles and handguns were replaced by pitchforks and reapers, or other implements of twisted fun that Gunner the Quartermaster dispersed with munitions in short supply. Flowering clouds of mortar scattered the no-man's-land between the opposing forces. Artillery fire spliced the line, displacing several 'Crows in a cloud of burning straw. Wade shuttered. Hooves shot skyward, with neighing cries, as Veidt ripped up on the reins, steadying his horse, falling into a gallop down the line, barrel to enemy. "Hold steady!"

Perry's line crested the opposing hill, standard in hand, as a sentient scream marked their charge. Tearing through the patches of stalks into the open clearing of the harvested field, the lines' distance vanished.

The last word heard: "Fire!" displaced particles of soil and night, blood and lead, flesh and straw.

With the lift of the lever, the circuit's arc made contact; and with a sibilate squeal, the fixtures lit up in sequence down the main hall of the silos. The two liberators stared down the long expanse. With a nod, they broke off. Each taking a side, they went to the cell doors and unlatched them. Jamie reached a door sealed by a padlock. He peered down the row at the padlocks which locked the cell doors. He counted a dozen or so locks, noting they were all different shapes and sizes, and of different origins and makers—and keys. It was an amassing of all the locks Pettick could get his hands on, yet still many doors were simply latched, not locked. Jamie pulled the Colt .45 revolver from his back. Stepping away, he fired the bullet into the lock. With the sound of a ricochet, the heavy iron fell to the concrete floor. Jamie swung open the door, extending his hands into the darkness. He pulled the young woman to her feet, helping her make her way out of the cell.

The harsh light met the deep blue of her eyes, which she quickly covered.

"Get all of the doors without locks!" Jamie shouted to Kindle, raising the revolver and shifting to the next locked door.

An old man limped past Jamie, then a young boy followed as a steady influx of more prisoners entered the hall, herding themselves down the narrow corridor. Jamie moved on to the next cell, catching up with Kindle who was further down the row. Jamie opened the next locked cell.

A shot echoed down the hall, colliding with the back of a man next to Jamie. Jamie ducked into the cell as a line of blood splattered the door, then pooled on the concrete. The man convulsed for moment, then his breathing slowly faded, body prone, still, against the concrete floor. The humans rushed, in a panic, pressing further down the corridor as several more fell. Turning his rifle down the hall, Jamie drew sight of the gunman, a small 'Crow at the end of the cellblock. Beads of sweat ran down Jamie's face as he gripped the wooden stock, releasing several shots that ricocheted down the corridor, colliding with the 'Crow. Kindle offered the same cover fire as Jamie dropped his rifle, reloading his revolver. Jamie threw himself, barrel forward, into the hall, releasing several rounds into the small 'Crow who fell back to the wall, then quickly regained balance, pressing his boots firmly to the concrete and raising his weapon. Jamie ducked back into the cell, falling to the concrete as the bullets sparked against the metal door.

"Fucking idiot," Jamie muttered about himself, butting his head against the door. "Sure, shoot the Scarecrow with bullets, 'cause *that'll* work."

Ejected casings bounced off the floor. Kindle peered into the adjacent cell, nodding to Jamie who was reaching into the pockets of his jeans for more rounds, retrieving the remaining three. Kindle glanced beside him, where a large bucket of water had broken open with the trajectory of a stray bullet. Kindle dipped his fist into the bucket as he slid up the door. Spinning his rifle around and aiming the barrel down the hall, he began to release several shots. Blasts of light flashed across his brow as the bulbs on the bowl-light above shattered, releasing their sodium vapors, effuse extinguished. The rifle let out an announcing *click* as the final round spent.

Jamie watched as Kindle dropped the rifle and threw open his coat in one swift motion. As he pulled the tube from his coat, he twisted off the cap, holding it out with his soaking hand. Kindle charged down the corridor. The small 'Crow fired shots at Kindle. Several of these collided with the Mechanic, but did not deter his steady charge. Kindle turned the flare, igniting it as he drew it back. The red sparks flickered in the hall. He swung his arm forward and pressed the burning flare into the 'Crow whose small body shuddered, twitching as it was lifted from the concrete.

Jamie stepped from around the door. The light was dim, several bulbs having been shot out. Staring down the hall, Kindle's stagnant figure hung over the smoking remains of the small Scarecrow. Jamie approached Kindle. They stood, shoulder to shoulder, over the remains. Kindle held up the burned-out flare—Pettick's flare—in his glove. A ribbon of smoke rose from its blackened cap.

"I had to," Kindle said, bowing his head with remorse.

"I know." Jamie assuaged.

The echoes of the gunfire settled in the hallowed hall.

* * *

In a raucous stampede, humans burst open the doors of the silo barn, fanning out, knowing only a sightless impulse for escape. Jamie came outside the barn, following the flow of the crowd around the north side where the farm came into view. In the distance, flashes of gunfire and explosions caught his attention. He slid to a stop, backtracking in the opposite direction of the battle.

"This way! This way!" Jamie shouted, directing the humans away from the fighting in the fields. "The woods—head to the woods!"

Several of the humans, seeking guidance from Jamie, led the group in the direction of the south woods.

Pulling the flare gun from his jacket pocket, Jamie cut sideways in the direction of the farmhouse, the crowd furiously flowing around him. The heel of his boots pressed heavily into the earth as his sprint gained momentum. Mortar rounds landed several meters from the barn, abruptly changing the flow of the fleeing humans. With the violent shift, a man collided with Jamie, sending them both sliding to the ground. Jamie fell forward, the pistol falling from his hand. Several terrified feet trampled over Jamie, who was huddled down, staring forward at the pistol in the dirt several feet away. The crowd began to spread around him as Kindle reached down with his large mitts, lifting Jamie to his feet.

"Thanks, friend—now, come on," Jamie said, exhausted.

After retrieving the pistol Jamie and Kindle ran several paces up the clearing to the large green tractor that sat cold, a statue, atop the hill. "Stay here," Jamie said as he climbed to the top of the tractor, pushing a green-capped cylinder into the nozzle. With his boots on the steering wheel and hood he closed the barrel, raised the pistol high above his head and pulled the trigger. Two balls of flame burst skyward, like bottle rockets, pulsing as they arced back towards earth. Flashes of garish chemical green left a pungent glow over the crowd. Jamie lowered the weapon, his chest heaving as he looked at the beautiful embers, the slightest smile cornered his cheek. Green faded to orange as the firing continued in close proximity, a fire growing in a nearby pit where the mortar made landfall. Jamie crumbled to the hood, gripping the steering wheel. Liberators' gazes returned to earth as adrenaline drained and the crowd thinned around them.

With the last of the humans safely in the forest, the sounds of the battle between the Scarecrows and Raleigh's Army took Kindle's attention, moving him several paces down the path. There, at the edge of a newley formed crater, Kindle stopped in his tracks, burdened by the levity of his surroundings. Contained patches of fire and violence blotched the fields. Jamie ached, coughing with shallow breaths as he climbed down from the tractor.

"Will it stop?" Kindle asked longingly.

Pocketing the flare gun, Jamie dragged himself over next to Kindle, lamenting, "Only one way to be sure."

"How?" Kindle asked.

Jamie offered an exhausted look of reluctance before glancing east, in the direction of the camp. "Come on," he said, nodding back to Kindle. "Follow me." Jamie shook his head as they started eastward down the path, flashes of orange and white lighting their way.

* * *

"Can I get a report that isn't fucking crazy?!" Raleigh spat, his eyes darted to the different points on the map shifting to new places with every incoming transmission from the front. A private approached Raleigh, waiting for a signal before breaking him from his concentration.

"What is it?" Raleigh asked.

"We got sight of Cooper's flare, sir," the private said.

"Have we heard from Cooper?"

"No—nothing—his entire company's been out of range or out of communication for several hours." The soldier paused, hoping Raleigh would speak, but was forced to continue, "Should we hold, sir?"

There was a tin of Red Man Chewing Tobacco on the table before Raleigh, its lid displaying an American Indian in full headdress smoking a pipe. Raleigh reached for the tin, dipped his fingers and drew a dab, a turgid brown wad, which he placed between his gums and lip.

"Sir?"

"No." Raleigh rested his arms against the map. "We move forward till we get verbal confirmation from Cooper." With the soldier's departure, Raleigh whispered to himself, looking over the map before him, reasoning with (or rather *bargaining* with) his demons. "We cannot stop that which has already begun." Raleigh spat out brown residue, spittle which stuck to the white fibers of his lip. There was beeping and clicking and screaming within the din of radio transmissions.

The camp growled, a guttural hostile snarl, as if guarded by a slumbering lion; the rumbling generators, the revving trucks, the bustling tents, and screeching radios all gave life to a burgeoning beast. A standard was planted at the top of the hill, well-lit, brandishing its proudest hues. Kindle and Jamie slunk low as they dashed up the hill, the camp rising above, an imposingly expanding giant. Kindle felt the danger he was running towards, but followed Jamie without reproach. Breaching the hill revealed the depth of the camp. Rows of tents ran along both sides of a dirt path several hundred meters long, a main street to the provisional town. Generators marked every four tents with a large tower of lights atop it. The light, a harsh glaring white, blinded him when Kindle peered into its rays.

"All this machinery; I thought you said they just got here?" Kindle inquired, motioning to the large compound before him.

"They did," Jamie responded, compounding Kindle's awe. The two started down the main street of the camp. At the end of the lane, a tent with towers for radio transmission marked the headquarters. The trespassers moved quietly past the bustling tent, cutting west, back toward the hill overlooking the farm, where several vehicles were parked in a turnaround. They reached the center of the turnaround, a muddy, rutted, tire-worn earth at their feet.

"Stop!" a soldier shouted as multiple barrels appeared from all around.

Several soldiers surrounded Jamie and Kindle, moving from behind the vehicles, rifles drawn, barrels trained. Jamie raised both hands in the air. He looked at the surrounding soldiers, then over at Kindle, who froze, not knowing what to do.

"They won't hurt us, just put your hands up," Jamie assured Kindle.

Kindle, in shock and confusion, followed suit.

Jamie nodded, turning back to his captors. "Please! We need to speak with Captain Raleigh—he needs to speak with us." Jamie stepped forward with his words, amassing more barrels in his direction.

One soldier pulled a flashlight, shining it in Kindle's face. "What the hell is that?" Barrels shifted back to Kindle.

"You—take that mask off!"

"It is not a mask," Kindle reasoned, finding slight amusement in the soldiers' fear, as well as in their fascination and ignorance. "It is not a mask," Kindle repeated, retaining his calm demeanor as he knocked away a reaching hand.

As the barrels closed in, Kindle lowered his right glove, pressing the tip of his index finger into the barrel of the closest rifle, garnering a genuine bewilderment on the soldier's face. The soldiers backed off.

"He must listen to us—" Jamie forestalled, pleading with the soldiers who were merely following orders.

"You brought the enemy into our camp; that does not garner you much trust." The captain's voice carried through the crowd. "Let him through; I *do* want to speak to him." The captain motioned Jamie over. Jamie hesitated, then stepped out of the circle and moved toward Raleigh. Kindle took witness to the harshness of the white spotlights cast upon him, watching Jamie reason with Raleigh at a distance, out of earshot.

"What are your intentions, bringing that thing here?" Raleigh asked with a prejudiced tongue.

"You must call off the assault," Jamie said.

"And why the fuck would I do that?" Raleigh asked.

"The humans have been freed; there is no longer need for—" Jamie halted himself mid-sentence, seeing no use in his words. He could already read this fact clearly on Raleigh's scowl. Jamie sighed, shifting his argument, gathering the words he wished he didn't need to say: "A stranger quarry rarely presents itself." Jamie motioned to Kindle, averting his eyes.

Raleigh brandished a crooked smile, placing a cigar in his teeth. "You hold no bargaining chip here. You know that, right?"

"Please—you are about to destroy a new species—a new kind!" Jamie felt the contrition he warranted in every word, though that mattered not to Raleigh who hovered in uncomfortable proximity, the cigar now lit in his mouth.

"Mr. Walsh, you of all people should understand that a species with such a violent propensity does not have rights here—not in my country," Captain Raleigh recanted in a tone of false sympathy. He exhaled, and a cloud of smoke billowed into Jamie's face as any sympathies, feigned or true, faded from his demeanor. "Besides, if we have *him*, we have no need for another." Collecting smoke lingered, fuming from his nostrils.

"That was not my intent—Christ! Stop this—this operation. Your presence here is no longer necessary," Jamie reasoned with increasing desperation. "End the attack before more die."

"I will decide what necessitates my presence and I choose when we are done here," Raleigh snapped with the diminishing of his patience. He adjusted his belt, took a puff, then leaned to Jamie with a harsh pat on the shoulder. "So, thank you. Thank you for bringing him to me. Your services are no longer required here." Turning his back to Jamie, Raleigh ordered his men while he paced around his specimen, a ribbon of smoke trailing his path, "Detain them both." He motioned to Jamie, "We'll deal with him at daybreak. Have Heinrich examine the . . . the. . ." Holding his pace, Raleigh inspected the Scarecrow, completing his jeering thought: "*It.*" He puffed a smoke ring, gesturing orders with his cigar. "Setup transport to Detrick."

"You asshole!" Jamie yelled, lunging at Raleigh.

Several soldiers intervened, restraining his arms.

"You're doing wrong; this is not how this should go!"

A soldier approached Jamie, burying the butt of his rifle into his stomach. Jamie collapsed. The soldiers led them away from the captain, dragging them back down the path of the Main Street. Walking beside Kindle, Jamie eventually regained his breath and his footing.

"What is 'Detrick'?" Kindle asked, alarmed and confused. He looked to Jamie for some sense of solace or, at the very least, answers. "Did you know they'd do this?"

"I—" Jamie shook his head, nodding in no specific orientation as his disillusioned eyes looked away from Kindle, dropping to his marching feet.

* * *

Two benches ran parallel to each other along the length of the tent. Jamie hovered, pensive, by the guarded doorway. He looked over at a defeated Kindle, who was seated at the opposite end. The Scarecrow looked up for a moment, then returned his gaze to his restrained hands, as he felt the leaden weight of the drop-forged steel on his wrists.

"They don't go away," Jamie sympathized, poorly. "Most people think after a while you get used to wearing them. Never really do."

"I figured not," Kindle reckoned. "It's quite ironic, actually."

"How so?" Jamie asked.

"Now *I'm* the one tied to a bench."

Jamie tried to see the humor in it, and failed. "Listen, I'm sorry. I'm sorry I got you into this."

"Good intentions," Kindle said.

Jamie offered a rueful chuckle. "There's the rub. Lotta bad things come about with good intentions, right?" Jamie reckoned the idea, its truth reminiscent of a past he found some joy in as it broke his hardened disposition. "I spent some time traveling with this road show, this, uh, carnie circus out of Boston. Real classy act, did all the towns along the shore, also ran a circuit through Pennsylvania."

"Pennsylvania?" Kindle said, bewildered, deciphering Jamie's parlance.

"You really don't know what's outside those gates, do you?" Jamie remarked, dumbfounded. "Anyway, I was the 'facilities manager' for the animals, another way of sayin' I was the fucking mucker, worked for this guy, this, uh, trainer named Lenny. We all called him Len, the only guy with real experience. He worked at the zoo in Brooklyn 'til they shut it down and moved all the animals to Central Park—at least, that's what he told us. We all knew he was really fired for the drinkin'. Legend has it he got so drunk he fell in with the gorillas, bottle and all, spent the night on the momma's lap, piss drunk."

Kindle interjected, "It's no wonder you and Crane were friends; both of you know how to drag out a story." He tested the extent of his restraints, the clatter drawing the attention of the guard through the mesh peephole in the door. His experiment quickly stopped soon thereafter.

"Didn't know you were in such a rush; I'll get to the point. So Len—good guy, the only one who really gave a shit about the animals—really cared what happened to them on the road. He treated them like living things, not just the property they were. Anyway, one of tigers we had, beautiful white coat, the bluest eyes, named Tooth; he was the prize. But he had a bit of a temper—mauled a kid once, setting the owner back a pretty penny. So the owner tells Len he struck a deal, he puts the prize down, sends a tiger tooth to the family as proof. Everyone lives happily ever after. Well, except for the tiger, of course. But Len won't do it, instead tells the owner he can't put down the animal. See, he saw the creature, this white tiger, as a magnificent unattainable thing. Both saw Tooth as a prize, just one with greener eyes."

Jamie pulled a Zippo out of his jacket pocket, flicked it on, compulsively shut the lid, and repeated the action as he continued.

"Well, they plot to sell him into another circuit. Len's just gotta get the tooth. So one night—had to've been August, molten hot—while I'm mucking the elephant cages, Len goes in with blue eyes, wrench in hand, doesn't even get out the gun to tranquilize the thing when it leapt on him, and tore his limbs off, before I could even get to the second gun." Jamie pulled a pack of cigarettes from his jacket pocket. Without effort he slid his fingers around one stick, pulled it from the pack, placed it in his lips and lit it in a fluid motion.

"You're quite the story teller, kid."

"Thanks, boss. So you see, the story here—right here is the tragic part—see, the tiger, Tooth, had no idea Len saved his life—no way of knowing, I suppose—and killed the only person who actually gave a shit about him."

"And the tiger?"

Jamie spoke with uncertain rasp: "Shot him." He rubbed out the dirt and grease along the calices in his hand, the crevices catching the stains in wrinkles, giving the hands a look of greater age.

"Owner got his hands dirty?"

The smoke began to fill the tent, collecting around the single hanging light.

"No. I did."

"The blue eyes?"

With conviction, Jamie looked directly at Kindle. "They wouldn't have done it like that. I left him with his dignity intact." His eyes watered, a nerve momentarily exposed. They sat, bound by the silence, taking notice of the sounds of the distant battle fading with their cadence. Kindle laughed at the quaint discourse they shared. Jamie returned the sentiment in a laugh that rose and faded at the same rate.

"I won't be an experiment, Jamie."

"I know."

"We both know what curiosity will drive people to do," Kindle said in shared absolution.

"Yeah—yeah, we do." Jamie stubbed the cigarette into the wooden bench, extinguishing its orange glow. "I woulda offered you a drag, but these things prolly aren't very good for ya."

"Probably not," Kindle laughed.

"Probably not," Jamie chimed, enunciating the full word, and, through a wistful chuckle, wiped his face with his sleeve.

A rather tall soldier entered through the door, ducking his balding head to avoid hitting it against the frame.

"Captain Raleigh wants to see you."

Kindle and Jamie shared a glance as two more soldiers entered, untethering the chain from the bench and escorting Kindle to the door. Jamie followed them.

"Not you," the balding soldier said, blocking Jamie's path.

"Are you fucking kiddin' me?"

"Not in the slightest."

A soldier stepped around from behind private bald-and-tall. The soldier was Private Williams, with a grimace and black eye on his face.

At the realization of Williams' presence, Jamie exclaimed, "Oh good, you found your way outta the woods—"

Williams promptly threw a punch square in Jamie's face. The punch sent Jamie to the ground. With a satisfied smirk, Williams turned, latching the door as he exited.

"Oh, come on!" Jamie shouted, holding his nose. He sat up, dusted the dirt from his jeans, and cuffed the blood from his lip. "Asshole."

He sat for several moments looking around the room. Sliding his hand into his boot he pulled out a handle with a button on it. He pressed the button, releasing the switchblade, its swift action matching his spring to his feet. He watched the door as he moved to the back of the tent. Pulling out the bench, he leaned down and plunged the knife into the canvas. He slowly ran the blade down, splitting the threads.

The soldiers shoved Kindle across the camp.

"What the hell do you think this thing is?" the bald soldier asked Williams.

"Boss says it's a Red. Mask or not, that's all that matters to me," Williams said, lifting his rifle, and knocking the stock against Kindle's head. Kindle stumbled forward but continued his peaceful stride. A Jeep rumbled past, sending a cloud of dust whirling around the escort. Jamie slunk through the shadows of the tents, catching glimpses of Kindle as he followed the group's path down the road. Ducking beside the generator, Jamie looked up and saw a large tower rising up with cold lights. The rumbling machine growled. Jamie peered around the wheel at Kindle, who was reaching the hill beside the camp which overlooked the colony.

The captain stood on the western edge of the hill several yards beyond the vehicle turnaround, looking over the battle in the distance. Raleigh greeted his guest with a judging eye over his visage.

"Good timing," Raleigh noted with smacking gums. Kindle remained silent, not knowing what to say, if anything. The captain lifted his radio, looking out over the farm, licking offending flakes of chew off his lips. "Light it up, gentlemen," he ordered.

In a steady progression, several balls of flame ignited in streams in the distance. Bright infernos spread through the veins of the farm, flowing with great speed.

"What is this?" Kindle asked as he stepped forward, awestruck. The flamethrowers were flanked in a line across the northern edge of the farm. Additional incendiary devices were scattered along the front lines, stalling charges and decimating the enemy. The petrol blaze expanded quickly, forming a giant crescent, cornering the Scarecrows' primary offensive. The flames moved in a corporeal slither, brighter, hotter, an unnatural expansion of light devouring the darkest phantoms of night.

"How capable are you of compassion?" Raleigh inquired, a dispassionate witness to the devastation on Kindle's face. "How capable is your kind?"

"Is yours?" Kindle shouted.

"My men lie dead in that field! That does not reflect well on your kind." The captain looked away from Kindle signaling his men to return. "Take him back to holding; we'll get him a transport to Detrick by 1200."

The soldiers grabbed Kindle's arms, tearing him away from their captain. From the center of the turnaround Kindle glimpsed Jamie on the far side, crouched in the shadow of a truck several paces away. Kindle nodded, throwing his weight forward. Swinging his elbow against the balding soldier's chin, he broke free with his right arm. The captain spun around, ordering his men to intervene as Jamie rose from behind the truck. Williams fell back, and Kindle pushed forward, drawing a clear distance and spreading his coat to expose the feathers of his chest. Jamie trained the flare gun with a swift hand that steadily shook in its prolonged aim.

"Do it," Kindle uttered. "Now!"

At the pull of the trigger, a bright green ball barreled from the nozzle, a comet across the blackness of space, touching down on a feathered planet. The ball ignited into particles of pure white and garish emerald, emitting flames from Kindle's chest. Kindle remained with arms spread as the flames chased through his straws like the crops of the farm. Jamie froze at the sight, still aiming the gun. Kindle drew his hand before his face.

"Fantastic," Kindle reckoned skyward, animating the vanishing members of his fingers. Sparks carried with the wind, flickering like fireflies freed to perform their coquettish dance, rising into the ether of night and beyond. Jamie gasped in the spectacle of this image. A soldier came behind Jamie, knocking the butt of his rifle to his head. The two statues, of man and scarecrow, crumbled. Jamie laid flat on the ground, a barrel to his bleeding head as the last words of the magician rose with the flames.

A black figure cut into Jamie's view; the figure of Captain Raleigh now lingered over him. "Get him up," Raleigh ordered with a bite to his words.

The soldiers behind Jamie forced him to his feet.

"Mr. Walsh, you could have walked out of here—just walked away. Now that's no longer an option." Raleigh spat. "What in the hell was that? What the fuck were you thinking?" Captain Raleigh looked down at Jamie.

Jamie looked directly back into Raleigh's eyes with emphatic reproach.

"I'm thinking you lost your trophy."

CHAPTER XX: Croatoan

The towering gray pines of the forest erected columns toward a matching pale morning sky. Ash from the nearby fires gently fell, fluttering down, landing on the shoulders of the six soldiers who marched around Cooper.

"For a moment I almost thought it had snowed," Bryant said, rifle in his hands and a grimace on his brow.

"Sure is fucking cold enough," Jones said.

"Quiet," Cooper ordered as they continued their march over the varying terrain. The ash fell more heavily in the thicket of the forest nearing the farm.

"How much farther, boss?" Bryant asked, an unlit cigarette hanging from his flapping lip.

"About a mile."

"Ya sure, Sarge?" Woodley questioned as he leaned toward Thompson, stealing the pack of smokes from his breast pocket, muttering, "Shouldn't have sent the kid home—we're fucking lost." He stopped for a moment to light the cigarette in his mouth. Looking up from his lighter, he pointed out, only partly in jest: "Is that the same tree?"

"Hold on, Jones. I wanna clear this shit off," Bryant said, stopping to shake off ash from the nozzle of the flamethrower he held. Jones then felt Bryant's hands begin brushing off the ash that had collected on the tanks strapped to Jones' back. "I'll be surprised if there's still a farm by the time we get there," Bryant said. Jones nodded in agreement, his hands shaking nervously, made worse due to the cold.

Cooper gazed up at the sky above, concerned by the expanding rise of his cinder North Star.

"I think I just saw a fucking snowflake," Bryant quipped. "Yeah, that was definitely a snowflake."

"I said quiet," Cooper ordered, looking at the exhaust of his own breath before him. Cooper stopped at a small clearing and turned to look at his men who were staggering to a halt behind him. "All right, we'll take a rest—" A branch snapped behind Cooper. "Hold," Cooper quietly ordered his men, who froze in their respective positions. Cooper listened closely to the soundscape. Distant firing faded, then slowly died out, after which a silence came and voices carried—voices which rose as they approached, followed by a smash and crunch much like the crashing *thwack* of a felled tree. Cooper looked at his boots where he felt the climbing tremors.

"Move—move—move!" Cooper ordered with quiet haste. The men fanned out, taking ready positions behind the surrounding trees. Bryant and Cooper huddled behind the first tree, their shoulders meeting. Jones flanked left with Thompson and Danforth just behind him at a pair of sibling pines. Cooper looked around his tree to see Woodley and Johnson disappear behind a fallen tree on the opposite side of the clearing. The tremors grew heavier and with steady frequency, building upon the kind of suspenseful rumbling crash that sparked imagination—the inception of monsters.

Two figures appeared in the clearing: the Creator and his creation, Rasputin. Both seemed remarkably strange fauna (or flora, depending on the perspective of the witness).

"Hold your fire," Cooper signaled with the clasp of a hand and an urgent whisper.

"What the hell is that?" Bryant marveled.

Cooper turned away from Bryant, peering around the tree to get a better look at the figures. He raised his rifle, gaining a clear shot at the Creator. Slowly his sights focused beyond the slender Scarecrow. The Creature had its back to Cooper, who awed at the mechanization. With each animation of the individual ligaments, snapping vines drew taut along its spine and cracked like a hatchet to a tree.

"Jesus Christ, kid, you *weren't* full of shit," Cooper whispered to himself in disbelief.

The Creator stopped in place, looking down at his boots as the layer of frozen dirt and ash crumbled beneath him. "Stop, my friend," the Creator said, signaling with his hand.

Rasputin stopped, lifted his shotgun in one hand, and scanned the surrounding trees. With the rising light, the flakes of ash grew heavier, binding gray with pure white flakes of snow that were collecting on the Creature's back.

"For a moment there, I thought we had company. Onward, then," the Creator said, turning to Rasputin.

The woods were cold and silent, save the sounds of the flakes landing, tracks laid, and the lumbering exhausts of the Creature's chest. The Creator wandered about the clearing and peered into the separations of the trees like long halls leading to different rooms and grand corridors of a mansion. He turned back to Rasputin. "Hmm . . . which way?"

Rasputin rocked forward, lunging at the Creator, pressing him to the left of a pair of sister pines. He raised his right fist high. Swinging down, the large timber collided with the tree, shattering into splinters. As the side of the tree exploded, the large fist of Rasputin gripped the barrel of Thompson's rifle, bending the metal shaft. With a heavy swing, Rasputin smashed the stock of the barrel back into Thompson's face then recoiled, the strap catching Thompson's torso, throwing him several yards across the clearing. Rasputin turned and began lumbering toward the agonizied soldier.

The Creator clapped his hands, chuckling. "Very good," he said, and then ducked suddenly as the tree shattered above him from rapid gunfire.

"Fire!" Cooper ordered, unloading several rounds.

The shots rang out from all directions. Casings sprang out of the cartridges, bouncing on the ground and landing in the ash. The bullets collided with Rasputin's chest, splintering pieces of timber, but failed to slow his stride as he charged at Cooper and Bryant, who had taken a stance beyond the cover of their tree. Cooper emptied his rifle's clip, dropped it, and drew his sidearm. Rasputin swung his fist, the back of which collided with Cooper's shoulder, sending him flying. Bryant reloaded and raised his rifle at Rasputin, unloading several rounds into the creature's face. Rasputin looked down at him. Bryant emptied his M1 carbine rifle. With the click of the spent clip, he gripped the sweltering barrel and swung the stock around, bashing its polished beechwood against the Creature's face.

Feigning injury from the impact, Rasputin cocked his head back down to Bryan and flicked the rifle from the soldier's hands. Opening his fist, Rasputin clamped his mitt on Bryant's head. Bryant let out a terrible scream as he was lifted off his feet. A series of shots splintered across Rasputin's arm and back. The Creature took notice of the approaching soldiers. His grip tightened as the thick digits closed down around Bryant's head. The screams abruptly stopped as the body hung limp.

"No!" Cooper shouted, catching Rasputin's attention.

Rasputin lifted Bryant's body, tossing it across the clearing where it collided with Johnson and Danforth, reversing their charge. Cooper grabbed his arm and applied pressure to the open wound. He saw where Bryant's firearm had landed, and immediately rolled towards it. Rasputin turned to Cooper and, raising one of his boots, stomped down, narrowly missing the soldier. Cooper lifted the pistol and fired its final rounds, emptying the chamber. The bullets disoriented the Creature. Cooper jumped to his feet, narrowly ducking below Rasputin's swinging arm.

"Bring the fire!" Cooper ordered, dashing toward the overturned tree where Woodley had taken cover. Rasputin spun around to Cooper, letting out a beastly roar before barreling forward, chasing the human across the clearing.

The Creator watched the chase with enjoyment, taking audience behind the sibling pines. Cooper leapt over the fallen tree and ducked beside Woodley. In a burst, two beams of flame shot across Rasputin's path from opposing sides of the clearing. Jones and Danforth had engaged their flamethrowers. Rasputin halted, showing resistance to the flames.

To the soldiers, this fear was the Creature's first evident act of consciousness—a fear which faded quickly into rage and, turning toward Danforth, the Creature pressed directly into the flame, the spray of the petrol barely slowing his stride. Danforth stood his ground atop the fallen tree. Rasputin's arms and shoulder caught fire, the flames quickly spreading across the thatching of his chest. Reaching forward, Rasputin gripped the nozzle of Danforth's flamethrower. The burning monster lifted Danforth above his head as the man let out a shallow guttural howl. Danforth's body flailed, helpless. Flames spouted back towards Cooper and Woodley who pressed against the fallen tree, a wave of fire falling around them.

The Creature and Danforth were now engulfed in flame. With little effort, Rasputin flung Danforth. The soldier's body, tank and all, shot across the clearing, colliding with a tree. The tank ruptured on his back, exploding with the collision and igniting in a cloud of black smoke that muffled the screams.

Rasputin roared as he attempted to clear away the flames; the fuel, in its adhereing viscosity, was sticking to the straw and timber of his flesh like sap. Cooper and Woodley rose from their position, rifles raised, and opened fire. The Creature turned, pressing toward them. The men fell back to the ground. The burning arms of Rasputin swung blindly above his head. Jones peered through the smoke to see the burning Creature was still in attack.

"Cooper—Woodley, move—move!" Jones shouted.

Cooper and Woodley hit the deck, and began crawling forward along the dirt. Rasputin swung down, narrowly missing Woodley as the soldier made his retreat. Jones raised the flame thrower nozzle and pulled the trigger. A beam of flame shot forward, colliding with the Creature's back. The smoke in the clearing grew even thicker—too thick to see through—as though it were dense fog. Jones released the trigger and lowered the nozzle. The clearing was silent for a moment.

"Oh shit," Jones said to himself peering forward. Through the smoke, a burning Rasputin charged, barreling straight for him. Jones raised his nozzle, releasing a small amount of flame. The Creature continued to charge steadily. Jones lowered his nozzle and turned to run. Rasputin reached forward, clenched the tank on Jones's back, and ripped him off the ground. Jones swung his arms, looking over at the Creature's face which was now only a foot from his own. Its jaw opened, letting out a roar that shot burning fuel onto Jones' forearm. Cooper broke through the smoke and, raising his rifle, emptied several shots that riddled across the Creatures back.

"Jones, drop!" Woodley shouted as he stood atop the fallen tree, seeing the soldier hanging by his pack. Cooper lowered his weapon. Moving around Rasputin, Cooper swung his arms, gaining the monster's attention. It turned to Cooper and let out another great roar. Cooper waved his hands wide, dropping his rifle, drawing the Creature toward him. Jones swung forward with the Creature's lumbering gait, the fire on his jacket spreading with each step, nearing ever closer to the tank on his back. Reaching for his chest, Jones unclipped the harness and fell to the ground, sending a cloud of ash skyward. Cooper dashed forward, grabbing Jones by the jacket as Woodley, standing atop the overturned tree, took aim.

"Now!" Cooper shouted as he and Jones jumped up and ran for the cover in the trees.

The Creature turned toward them, unleashing a roaring scream, spewing salivating flame. Woodley pulled the trigger. The bullet collided with the tank in Rasputin's hand, exploding in a fireball that spread through the entire expanse of the clearing, rising high into the canopy.

Cooper and Jones slid atop the ashes and leaves collecting around the pine and pressed against the timber as the cloud of fire and splinters erupted around them. The ground shook as sections of the burning figure rained to the ground. Cooper and Jones collapsed to the roots, chests heaving.

"You alive?" Cooper exhaled.

"Still breathing," Jones responded.

Cooper rose, pulling a pistol from behind his back and handing it to Jones. The two soldiers raised their weapons as they moved around the tree. Smoke rose towards the sky in columns from the various portions of the Creature's remains, which were now spread throughout the clearing.

"Woods?" Cooper called out.

"Yeah—Yeah, I'm still here," Woodley responded, rising from behind the fallen tree. The surviving soldiers scanned the clearing over as they regained their bearings despite adrenaline's free fall.

Sliding around the tree, the Creator took hold of his rucksack, his subtle movements drawing the soldiers' attention. He smiled, an unassumingly culpable grin, then quickly spun on his heels and darted into the forest with the soldiers in reluctant pursuit. The trees blurred quickly past.

Cooper's chest heaved, exhaling a heavy cloud into the cool air. The soldiers fanned out, keeping steady chase over the rolling, rooted mounds of the forest. The Creator glanced behind him, continuing to flee with greater speed at the sight of the pursuing enemy. Woodley abruptly stopped, raised his rifle, and began searching through the pine columns. After squeezing the trigger, he heard his shot echo through the forest. The bullet pierced the Creator's rucksack, shattering one of the jars it carried. The force's impact sent him tumbling to the ground. The rucksack fell from the back of the slender figure as it continued to crawl, eventually sliding down a ravine into the thick brush. Floating from the bullet hole were what looked like several bright-green embers, which spiraled through the air just above the ground. The soldiers scanned the area. Woodley approached the rucksack attracted by the ribbon of green embers dancing at his feet. Gripping the strap, he picked up the bag and looked inside.

"Sarge! You should see this," Woodley shouted back over his shoulder.

In a nearby ravine the Creator slunk low, concealing himself among the brush as Cooper and Jones passed. With the soldiers' voices fading in the opposite direction, he moved slowly down the ravine, like a wounded arachnid, sinking into the ash.

Cooper approached Woodley, Jones only a few paces behind him. The men all gave a bewildered glance into the bag: green fireflies waltzed among shards of a broken mason jar and a leather-wrapped sewing kit. Two jars remained intact. Cooper lifted one of them in his glove examining the contents with an analytical eye.

"What in the hell is that?" Jones asked, shouldering his rifle and peering down at the jar in Woodley's hands.

"Fireflies, I think?" Woodley replied. "I've never seen them so vibrant before."

"A little late in the season, don't ya reckon?" Jones reasoned.

"I suppose," Woodley pondered with a skeptic's curiosity, pressing his glasses further up the bridge of his nose.

"Any sign of our tall friend?" Cooper asked, glancing around.

"It appears we may have lost him," Woodley replied, rising to his feet. "Fucker's *fast.*" He returned the jar to the satchel and threw the strap over his shoulder. The soldiers gazed cautiously at the surrounding woods that had fallen silent, peaceful once again.

"All right, let's get back to the clearing, check our status, regroup, and get back on pace to the farm," Cooper ordered.

"Shit, Sarge, look," Jones said.

Cooper turned. A few paces away stood a young woman. She appeared to be in her late twenties. Her figure was gaunt; her phlox linen skirt, ragged; and her hair, a collection of long locks of strawberry curls.

Cooper approached her cautiously. "Hey, it's okay," he said. Cooper handed his firearm to Woodley, who was cautiously keeping his rifle slung over his forearm.

The woman was shaking. Her eyes glazed over, showing off the deep green of the irises. She held a book in her hand—black cloth, red letters.

"Jesus Christ," Jones said.

Cooper looked over to Jones, then followed his eyeline to the woods beyond the young woman, where humans, seemingly wandering the forest, appeared amongst the trees. The count, by Jones' eye was several dozen, with this girl, this young woman with strawberry-colored hair, leading their way to safety.

"You think they came from the farm?" Woodley asked.

She looked over to Woodley, asserting a tacit response, then back to Cooper. Cooper pulled off his jacket and draped it over her shoulders. The sleeves, longer than her arms, dangled at her sides. He looked down at the book she had handed him while she pushed her arms through the sleeves.

Tugging on the jacket cuffs, she looked up to Cooper and whispered, "Scarecrow."

* * *

Visibility extended only a few feet in the thick sheet of smoke which covered the farm. Order fell quickly to chaos at what remained of the Scarecrow front lines. And on the human side, fallen soldiers piled in the field, their corpses, now cover for the survivors. The Scarecrows' regiments had pushed forward during the initial assault, having little fear for the barrage of lead. However, mortar and grenade fires displaced their lines, spreading the companies in isolated flocks across the field, and with the fires pluming over the land, the glory of victory was but a memory fondly reckoned in each 'Crow's final moments.

The bayonet of Veidt's rifle pierced the soldier's chest with a jagged blow. The soldier remained pinned, a puppet strung by the blade. Veidt pulled the trigger, the force of the bullet pushing the soldier off the blade, his life fading as he fell. With another successful shot, Veidt dropped his rifle and pulled out his Luger sidearm. He fired rapidly as soldiers appeared from the crops and fell almost immediately as they came into range. Rallying his horse, Veidt ripped up on the reins, sending the horse's front hooves skyward.

Perry, a battered and bloody soldier, appeared from the crops several paces away. Veidt turned and pulled the trigger. The hammer clicked, jamming. Perry drew his Thompson sub-machine gun and opened fire on Veidt. The bullets rattled Veidt, the spray of lead running down to the horse. The white fur spattered red, chunks of which broke away, falling to the soil. A fierce cry came from the horse as it fell with a heavy crash; Veidt tore at the earth, his legs pinned under the horse.

Perry approached, gun at the ready, as he and his regiment pushed forward, catiously advancing toward the horse. As he rounded the beast he could see what remained of Veidt's legs pinned beneath the thoroughbred, their top halves sliced away. The stumps twitched as they sunk into the blood that turned the dry soil to mud.

"What the fuck?" Perry uttered. Caught off-guard, the soldier spun around, searching the crops for Veidt. Several more of Perry's men appeared around him, pushing the humans' line further east.

Nearby, the cattle truck, which once sat majestically in Kindle's collection, burned from mortar attack. The bed had cracked wide open, its rear chassis now pitched skyward, its axle bent like a horseshoe torquing around the burning remains of men of straw. The regiment approached the twisted chassis. Perry signaled his men to surround the truck. Ducking down, he checked under the cabin before moving next to the passenger door. He counted with the soldier on the opposite side of the truck, simultaneously swinging the doors open when they reached *three*. The cab contained only the carcass of a Scarecrow, Paquin, half blown apart in the driver's seat. Perry and the soldier shared a glance, remarking the queer and unnerving sight before them. Throwing his gun over his shoulder, Perry reached into the cab and took hold of the pistol that sat on the bucket seat next to the 'Crow. He brushed off the bits of broken glass from the firearm. The soldier on the driver's side pressed the tip of a nervous index finger against the cheek of the straw corpse, the soft threads bowing like the fatty softened tissue of flesh. Perry shot a judging glance at the soldier as he checked the ammunition, counting the rounds in the magazine, before holstering the weapon.

The soldier on the driver's side of the truck looked up for a moment, only managing to get a glimpse of the Scarecrow before it fell upon him. Veidt leapt from the roof of the cab, blade first into the soldier's face, bringing him to the ground. The surrounding men opened fire on Veidt, who scurried on all fours leaping onto the closest soldier, tearing at his face and burying the blade into his chest. Perry emptied the thompson's magazine on Veidt, to little affect. Veidt opened his jaw, biting at the soldier's neck, then moving onto the next, who fired directly into the 'Crow, emptying the magazine of his gun. The soldier dropped to the ground as Veidt leapt upon him. Grabbing for the grenade on his belt, the pin dropped from the soldier's chest. Veidt continued to tear at the soldier's exposed flesh as the chemicals mixed and the grenade finally burst, sending both human and Scarecrow in pieces around the truck. The explosion left another crater, another scar to the soil, where more bodies fell.

On the far side of the south forest, the dark thick of the trees abruptly ended, just as it did at the edges of the farm's perimeter. Above the canopy of pine, a mountain of smoke rose, growing larger and larger with each passing moment. Through the dark negative space of the pines, a tiny figure appeared, growing as it ran into the grass. The tall figure of the Creator dashed through the reeds, looking back only to ensure he was not being followed.

* * *

The flamethrowers, spitting their incendiary venom, continued to feed the inferno from the perimeter of the farm where water trucks and soldiers, pails and buckets in hand, were fighting to keep the fire contained to the forest's edge. The hungry blaze fought to reach the endless kindling of the forest. A gust of wind arced north. A large lodgepole pine touched the flame, and was immediately engulfed. The burning column cracked, falling onto a jeep as soldiers dodged its crushing bow. The fire spread into the north forest, where the soldiers could do little but watch.

And so burned the kingdom of straw; hell touched down on Tucker's farm in such a way the sight of its rolling hills didn't much resemble the images of its past.

Pettick watched the charring cancer spread with a perfect view to his world's end. The flames swallowed the village, dancing swiftly across the crops and finally reaching the textile house, which burned quickly, trapping those inside. The jars of the Perfect Tree shattered, the flame whirling around the branches, bark peeled adrift into flakes of ash. The immense pressure of the heat suffocated the tree, choking its life.

The inferno breached the ridge, rising swiftly up the grassy escarpment. The flames spiraled up the timber of the water tower, which blackened and buckled. Thalo and several Scarecrows threw pails of water onto the nearby fires that spread and multiplied before a single one could be doused. A wave of flames carried by a gust crested, falling down upon them, catching one of the Scarecrows, engulfing him with the hottest of orange, white, and yellow. The few remaining soldiers fled, scurrying eastward, abandoning their posts.

"You fools," Pettick desperately ordered. "Where are you going? Do not abandon your posts—do not abandon me!"

Pettick watched the burning beast that chased them as they fled, running them down. Flames took hold of their bodies like a serpent, choked the 'Crows, then bit away at their threads. Pettick whipped around, seeing the flames surround him, singing the air. He stumbled to the overturned cart, grabbing his jacket. He looked around as the smoke filled the air. Stumbling to the ground, he crawled up to the tower, the opposite face having already caught fire. Pettick ascended the beams of the tower, the flames chasing him as he did. He gripped each timber with a solid hold, wrapping his arms around the beam. In a gust, the winds cut eastward. The flames reached for Pettick. Gripping the brim of the barrel, he lifted himself up, out of the reach of the fire.

Pettick rose atop the barrel as wind leveled the smoke into the ground, revealing the burning farm behind the curtain of smoke and ash. Pettick trembled at the sight of his burning world. The flames devoured nearly the entire expanse. "No," he said, shuddering. The smoke wrapped upward, like a curtain drawn, veiling his world from him once again. He spun around the barrel, looking down at the consuming flames. He inhaled, hot smoke seeping into his chest and bringing him to his knees. Falling forward, he pressed to the top of the barrel with his hands, his fingers touched the etching. He ran his fingertips gently along the words carved into the wood. He exhausted a chuckle at the ironic nature of this symbol. With the sight of the carving, strength gripped him. He slid his right hand into his jacket pocket, pulling out the leather-bound journal. Lifting the small lid of the barrel, he dipped the journal, water embracing its parchment. The tower shook, squealing as it did. The front timbers burned through and trembled under the weight.

Pettick stood, bracing himself. Reaching back, he threw his weight forward, launching the journal westward over the ridge, the leather body disappearing into the dense smoke of the shapeless horizon. He exhaled, trying his best not to take in more smoke with each subsequent inhale. Fire caught his field jacket, and he quickly shed it. With a great scream, the beams of the trussing buckled and the barrel crumbled westward, the water falling over the ridge, in a tremendous wave that quickly drained, seeping into the dry soil, hardly satisfying its thirst. Pettick fell sideways off the brim. His body bounced as it met the earth, the flames coiled around him as he hit. He stood up, shrieking, squealing. The flames burned through his flannel, melting away his threads, which shed and fused, peeling away in scales. Pettick tore away at the layers of straw, exposing the pale human flesh beneath. The flames took a liking to the flesh, burning away as it had the straw. He continued to grope as the flesh and straw fell to the soil. Breaking to his knees he grasped the chain around his neck, tightly holding its charm. The glasses before his eye sockets cracked and shattered. Hot air singed his lungs. The blaze swallowed as he choked on the flames which garroted his apologetic confessions—confessions of the Scarecrow and the human, of flesh and straw, that with cadence, faded.

* * *

At the intersection of a once distant road, the '42 Ford Pickup rumbled and huffed, rolling to a halt. Barnes shifted the truck into PARK. Behind them, framed center in the side mirror, a shaft of cinder rose miles into the ashen sky. He hung his head back, his body exhausted behind the wheel. The cab was silent, save the faint crackling of shifting particles of metal as the truck cooled.

"What's wrong?" Barlow asked.

"Just need to fill the gas tank," Barnes said.

"You know how?"

"Yes, sir."

Barlow nodded in scorned wonderment at his son's newly acquired skills. Barnes threw open the door, as if escaping the cab. Barlow could read his son's frustration as he threw open the passenger door and slid slowly out, gently closing it. The two doors of the cab sealed simultaneously, though without such intent.

"Need help?" Barlow asked.

"No, Father. Really, I got it."

Barnes stretched his legs, shaking them strangely as he waddled into a walk, moving around the bed of the cab. He took notice of his gait on the gravel pavement, the way his stride ran steadily with greater ease as he walked upon it. Barnes made no effort to look back at the cloud, but rather avoided its sight. Barlow leaned against the well of the truck, mirroring Barnes as the young 'Crow emptied the first canister into the tank. Barlow watched Barnes working diligently, then exhaled his breath, blocking the soft-white mid-morning sunlight with his glove as he gazed at the column of smoke.

The road was quiet, except for the sounds from the flock of birds that danced as they flew by. Shepherd took solace in their presence, listening to their individual stories.

"Must be visible for fifty miles," Critch remarked to Barlow.

Mare dug her elbow into his abdomen, stopping him from speaking further on the matter. They averted their attention to their daughter who huddled next to Shepherd, tucked behind the cab, cradling the sunflower in its pot.

Barlow turned his back toward the farm. With his hand on the wooden rail of the truck bed, he slid slowly up the side of the truck, stopping next to Gwyn. She looked up at him for a brief moment, before returning to the plant, stroking its petals gently between her fingers. The deep pigment-drunk yellow glowed against the pale dust in the air and the backdrop of the old cracking road folding into the smoke cloud in the distance. Barnes brushed the dirt from his gloves as he placed the empty first canister on the road. He looked across the bed at Gwyn and Barlow, finding an understanding in the tenderness of their interaction. Gwyn reached out, with gentle hand, touching Barlow's glove. She took hold, pulling his hand to her, stopping with his fingers around a petal of the flower. She guided his fingers along the curve of the blade. He smiled, solemnly gulping in his breaths.

"Thank you," Barlow sighed, retracting his glove. He presented her a smile before turning back to the cab.

"Wait," Gwyn called to Barlow.

Barlow turned back to the bed. Gwyn reached into the rucksack pulling out two books, several notes bloating their binding. Barlow took hold of them and ran his thumb along the cloth covers. Gwyn read the lines on his face as he turned away, drifting several paces down the road.

Barnes sealed the cap on the tank, placing the canisters into the bed. A gossamer layer of veiling clouds gathered above, only gently masking the strong rays of sunlight.

"Looks like we could have snow," Gwyn said to Shepherd.

"Could be," Shepherd basked. "Can I ask you, Gwyn?"

"Ask me what, Shepherd?"

"What kind of tree she was?"

"I don't know," Gwyn said. "But I'm sure we can find out."

Shepherd nodded.

Gwyn thought on, of a truth she found most reassuring. "Serotinous Pines," Gwyn reveled. "The pines; with fire the pines are seeding."

Shepherd smiled a wide and genuine smile.

Barnes walked around the back of the bed. Sliding up to Gwyn, he reached out with his long slender arms, touching the petal for a moment, nodding to Gwyn. He paused, then looked over to his father who was standing alone several yards down the road. Barlow's feet were planted at the intersection where the gravel road crossed the concrete pavement of a more traveled highway. The old 'Crow rocked back and forth in the direction of the wind, holding the books in both hands in front of him, a newly-discovered artifact. Barnes approached him, laying a hand on his shoulder. "Pop, what is it? You all right?"

"This is all I have left, a library of books. A life. And this is what I have."

Barnes sighed, mistakenly looking back to the sky over the farm for but a moment. He wrapped his arm around his father, waited for the words, but none came to mind.

"Come on, Pop, we need to keep moving."

He helped his father into the cab and gently shut the door. Crossing back around the truck, Barnes ran his glove along the hood, making contact with the silver emblem, which shimmered in the reflecting sun. Barlow lifted the cover of the journal, Crane's Journal, taking notice of an inscription below the title, this one addressed to him. He read its brief message, smiling, adding a whimper to his short-lived laughter. Then he gently shut the cover, sealing it tightly in his hands, holding it to his sinking chest. The driver door winced as Barnes opened it. Sliding in and taking hold of the steering wheel, Barnes exhaled his tension, letting out a huff, akin to his father. Gripping the key, stopping before turning over the engine, he dropped his hands and sat back, embracing the momentary silence.

"Never took much notice of the mountains before," Barnes said, peering through the windshield to the Blue Ridge Mountain Range.

"Neither have I," Barlow confessed.

"Where are we going, Pop?"

Barlow relaxed the tension in the fibers of his flesh. He peered out the window, then looked back at his son. The moment took him, the freedom muddled away the pain of age, of experience, of regret and knowing.

"Believe it or not, son, there is a world out there; and somewhere in that world a new home."

Barnes's gaze darted dramatically in all directions. "Any idea what direction?"

"Just start moving; we'll find it along the way."

Both 'Crows found themselves staring on at the crossroads before them. Barnes gripped the wheel, the fingers of his gloves locked perfectly in the grooves. Turning the engine over and shifting into first gear, he looked at his father and let off the clutch.

"Yes, sir."

The truck rolled forward, pulling on to the road, the distance from the farm growing greater. The rubber of the tires gripped the gravel. Dust trailed in the truck's path, some settling, some floating off with the wind. Barnes shifted into a higher gear and the truck sped up, disappearing further on down the road.

EPILOGUE: THE WINTER

THE TWA CORBIES

Coarse clumps of snow fell from the sky, bringing with it winter's freeze over the charred remains of Tucker's Farm; white flakes masked the black and red as gauze to the scarred hills. Soldiers scattered through the fields, scanning the remains, reclaiming those they had lost. As the humans walked the land, two black-beaked crows sat perched high above watching their movements, waiting to feast on the slain. Jones knelt down and ran his hand along the arm of a body whose remains were spread over several meters. He felt along the base of the neck, gathering ash on his fingertips, stopping where grease had melded with particles of metal. It was here he discovered what appeared to be the remnants of a chain necklace containing dog tags. He lifted them for closer inspection. Rubbing soot from the flat surface with his thumb, he could see the raised letters.

Cooper stood alone atop the bluff beside the twisted black skeleton of the Perfect Tree, its arms clenched skyward. He scanned the farm, surveying the empty wasteland. Cooper heard the sound of Woodley's boots pressing into earth, marking his entrance as he stepped beside him. A harsh gust wrapped around them.

"Guessin' Raleigh ain't too pleased," Woodley remarked, bitter in his sarcasm. Cooper swung his rife over his shoulder. He reached into Woodley's breast pocket and retrieved two cigarettes, while producing a Zippo lighter from his own. He placed one cigarette between his lips and handed the other to Woodley.

"Why is that?" Cooper asked, hunching over to light his cigarette, finding no direction from which to block the wind.

"We ain't gonna learn nothin' about whatever those things were."

"Yeah, suppose so," Cooper said, evidently indifferent on the matter. Finally getting a light, he passed off the Zippo to Woodley.

"There is one thing I don't get, Coop."

"Yeah, what's that?"

Woodley exhaled, the smoke from his mouth seeming endless in the cool air. He looked around once more, pondering, then up at Cooper. "Where are all the bodies?"

Cooper looked around, taking in the emptiness. "Yeah, I know . . ." He pushed his rifle strap further up his shoulder. "Well, we all got our merit badges."

Cooper peered up at the remains of the Perfect Tree where the two crows were perched. Then, as if sensing his watch, the birds cawed, hopped along the branch, and swooped down, one after the other, cutting just above him.

"Cooper!" A voice carried westward, resonating from a soldier who stood on the ridge looking down at Cooper and Woodley. "I think you should see this!"

Cooper and Woodley looked up at the figure, then shifted their views downward and stared at the rockface. Cooper nodded, waving off the soldier. Woodley continued to sullenly stare at the massive rock wall.

"Well, shit," Woodley sighed.

Cooper pushed Woodley along, starting him on his march. "Come on, get moving. Don't worry, we'll go around." The two soldiers began marching down the hill. After a few meters, Cooper stopped mid-stride, where his boot no longer made an impression in the earth. He knelt down and began brushing away the layer of snow and ash with his glove, revealing the hide of a leather-bound book.

"What is it?" Woodley inquired. Cooper failed to respond as he exhumed the book and began smoothing down the damaged and singed portions while examining the cover. "Ollie, what is it?"

"Hold on," Cooper said as he unclasped the cover of the journal, opening it to the first inked page.

On the ridge, the two crows circled above Captain Raleigh who stood with his arms crossed, peering over the farm. The white earth and the grey horizon were soft and without much form. Wrinkles wide, Raleigh brushed the whiskers on his lip, warm hands aching in the cold.

Perry approached the group, which consisted of several soldiers and a photographer loading film into his camera. Behind Perry appeared Dr. Heinrich, a scrawny pale-skinned man with piercing bright-blue eyes, sharp features, and pitch-black hair with uncanny strips of silver-grey which curled within the greased back black. He moved methodically, examining the corpse from afar, steadily inching closer. The photographer stood up, aiming his lens at the scene before him. The image captured was four men, standing around the skeletal remains of a fifth. The snow continued to fall in those idyllic crystal shapes as if outlined from a postcard, drawing a sheet over the corpse, a blanket for its eternal slumber.

"This is the only one without tags," Perry remarked.

"What is he holding?" Heinrich sharply noted, his accent a thick Eastern-European.

"What?"

"His hand—it looks like he's holding something in his hand."

With a nod from Raleigh, Perry reluctantly knelt down, wiping his hands on his jacket before offering his Christian respects; he pulled on the brittle forearm, which snapped due to the force of his grasp. After peeling open the fingers, Perry rose and stepped back into the circle. The men stared, silent and baffled. Cradled in the charred glove, tethered to a broken chain, was an engagement ring made of the titanium outer race of a bearing, its finish unscathed by the consuming fires.

Acknowledgments

Acknowledgments

Oh man, I have a lot of people to thank, ranging from those who let me stay in their homes while I toiled away on this manuscript over the years, to the many coffeehouses I have haunted.

But first of all, I need to bring attention the developmental work and edits of Luke Niebler. This book would not be what it is today and would certainly be far less good without Luke's input—nearly ten years of a fruitful collaboration and creative friendship. The design work of Logan Randolph, involving long creative talks over winters, cigarettes, and fires in Pittsburgh shaped this novel.

Additional editing and proofing by Erin Young and David Keefe. Brandon Quinn Smith for his amazing cover design work. The extensive resources of the Carnegie Library System. Steve Tutunick; Greg Nelson; James Erwin; the Marlton-Bemiss Family; Len Newman, for whom this book is dedicated; E. Carlton Hill; Micah Head; Kim Willen; The Wolfpack; The folks of The South; Peg Finberg; Karen and Sue, the teachers who introduced me to the works of T.S. Elliot and Sam Shepard. And of course, not simply obligatory, my parents, Patrick and Ramona.

About the Author

J.P. Reilly is an author and art director from New Jersey. He holds a BFA in Drama from Carnegie Mellon University and when not writing, works in the film industry, splitting his time between Los Angeles and New York. *The Hollowmen* is his first novel.

Lightning Source UK Ltd.
Milton Keynes UK
UKHW022222290920
370750UK00002B/29/J

9 781735 670669